SINGER'S
SWORD

CHRONICLES OF THE CHOSEN

CASSANDRA BOYSON

KINGDOM HOUSE
PRESS

Published by Kingdom House Press

ISBN: 978-1-7322533-1-5

Cover design by Christian Bentulan

www.CassandraBoyson.com

DEDICATED TO

the music pal in my life,
Steven Boyson

CONTENTS

Chapter One   1

Chapter Two   10

Chapter Three   17

Chapter Four   24

Chapter Five   42

Chapter Six   52

Chapter Seven   69

Chapter Eight   76

Chapter Nine   87

Chapter Ten   96

Chapter Eleven   110

Chapter Twelve   117

Chapter Thirteen   132

Chapter Fourteen   144

Chapter Fifteen   150

Chapter Sixteen   162

Chapter Seventeen   176

Chapter Eighteen   187

Chapter Nineteen   194

Chapter Twenty   215

Chapter Twenty-one   223

Chapter Twenty-two   237

Chapter Twenty-three   242

Chapter Twenty-four   250

Chapter Twenty-five   255

Chapter Twenty-six   260

Chapter Twenty-seven   269

Chapter Twenty-eight   277
Chapter Twenty-nine   287
Chapter Thirty   298
Chapter Thirty-one   307
Chapter Thirty-two   316
Chapter Thirty-three   327
Chapter Thirty-four   334
Chapter Thirty-five   344
Afterword   346

OTHER BOOKS BY CASSANDRA BOYSON

CHRONICLES OF THE CHOSEN:
Prophet's Apprentice

THE SEEKER'S TRILOGY:
Seeker's Call
Seeker's Quest
Seeker's Revolution

1

It was known among all in Castlehaven that Hazel was the daughter of highborn criminals. She had been made to pay for those crimes the whole of her remembered life. Though she'd not been imprisoned, she had been scorned and pressed into a lonely existence. Her parents' misdemeanor? Attempted assassination on the king of all Kierelia… the same man who was her distant cousin.

She could not blame anyone for thinking ill of her.

Funny thing was, the king was one of the few who treated her with some semblance of consideration, though it could not really be called that. Politeness, perhaps. A *kind* of respect, though not that either. After all, could one look upon the offspring of the family members who wished one dead and not see corrupt history? Even so, he'd been the one to appoint his own sister as her guardian. It had been considered a mercy to be raised in the castle and she was often reminded of it. But she had other thoughts. Could it really be called merciful to remain in the one place where *everyone* knew one's sinister history?

It was what made her tremble at the thought of entering The Mirror. But it was her turn. She had reached eighteen years. It was required of every person with noble blood to enter at least once upon their first year of maturity. She had often inquired precisely what took place within but had never received a straight answer. All she knew was, despite its name, there were no mirrors involved whatever. It was just a room. Yet, once within, one was suddenly made vulnerable to a precise picture of who they were—one saw oneself with perfect clarity, for the timeframe one spent within the space, at least. Afterward, memory faded. Yet, the impression gained from the experience remained.

She sat in the corridor outside, waiting her turn. There were two others to go before her that day. One had already entered and exited. He'd emerged with a rebellious smirk and an attitude Hazel could not begin to fathom. She knew this boy and understood he honored neither the profoundest nor holiest of ceremonies. She could not say what he had come to understand, but he meant to reject it with all his might.

She couldn't bear it, couldn't bear waiting and wishing the room's keeper would take a reprieve that she might escape the confrontation without anyone the wiser. She knew she did not have the character that could so determinedly reject whatever was revealed, as the boy had. She'd been unable to reject the pictures others had drawn of her the whole of her life. What if she should find she had inherited her parents' murderous hearts?

Of course, she had no way of knowing what their intentions had been. For all she knew, they had some holy cause. But if ever she inquired, she was looked on with a kind of suspicion that made her feel grimy and in need of a long soak in Castillion Lake. It seemed she was to pretend her parents had never existed even if she couldn't get out from under the reputation they had given her.

The door to The Mirror opened and a white-faced Evelyn stepped out. It was clear the experience had frightened her.

"Evelyn, wait," Hazel called, reaching for the girl's wrist.

Evelyn ripped her arm away and continued on.

It was true Evelyn had never seemed to quite like Hazel, but they had spoken twice with enough agreeableness between them. Hazel could not decide whether the girl's response was personal or simply that she could not bear being asked about the occurrence.

"Lady Hazel," the attendant chastised. "It is your turn."

With head bowed, she took a step and then another. She was the daughter of rebels. She had no friends, nor even close acquaintance. Another step. She kept to herself because that was how those in the castle preferred it. She'd convinced neither her guardian nor anyone else to love her. She was unlovable.

She did not want to go into that room.

It was more than what she feared discovering about herself. It was the whole experience. Something peculiar happened between those four walls—something other-worldly. Or so she'd picked up from whisperings and legends. Once, when she'd been but ten years, she'd passed by to the sound of screaming. She'd been too fearful to remain and discover who'd been within or whether they had come out all right. Now, she dearly wished she had.

She approached the door and the keeper turned the knob.

"Mind your thoughts in there," the woman warned. "He can hear them."

Hazel stepped in and spun around only to have the door shut in her face. She was abandoned. But who would hear her thoughts? This was a detail she'd not gathered before. If she was to be faced with the prospect of the truest picture of herself, she would rather it be alone. And alone, it appeared she was, for there was no one else within.

The room was lit by a single torch above the door. There were no windows, no chairs, no hanging tapestries. There was but a large, ornately designed carpet over the floor. She bent to observe a portion and found a kind of chronicle illustrated along the border.

Firstly, was a woman with a sword birthed from her mouth. A strange winged man stood with hands outstretched, prepared to receive it.

Hazel peered up, wondering when this peculiar occurrence was to begin. It felt strange to wait in the dark, the small light flickering behind her. Her heart pounded with the unknown. But as all was still and there was nothing else to preoccupy her, she was drawn back to the carpet. She paused as she came to a king in danger of a large, fire-breathing beast that looked something between a lizard and a horse with wings. The creature was unexpectedly beautiful, but it would destroy the poor king. The figure directly following was a woman with her mouth open and musical symbols floating out. This one drew her, for she dearly loved music. She bent to touch it.

She was bodily thrown back the moment her fingers stroked the fibers. Wave after wave of an invisible torrent flooded over her. She felt herself falling through the floor but discovered she was only held fast to it. The carpet was beneath her, cradling her powerless body.

What surprised her was that she was not entirely terrified, though frightened she was. But there was more to it. There was something—some*one*—in the gust… and they were not unpleasant. They were fearsome and ferocious but also… kind?

She stole a long breath of the gale and relished it. She had never breathed atmosphere so liberating. It filled her with *life* she had not experienced and brought wholeness never afforded. She'd never felt so powerful, nor had she felt so small. She was insignificant compared to all *this* was. It surged on as she savored it until it became too much—far, far too much. She was going to *burst*. Perhaps that was how one saw oneself so truly: their insides erupted from their outsides and they were laid out in defenseless pieces on the peculiar carpet.

In a sharp breath, the storm ceased. It was torn from her so swiftly, she gasped with emotion at the loss. Shakily, she drew upon her knees and bent over with a guttural sob. She clutched her arms over her stomach as if to hold herself together.

But ever so gently, the breeze whispered around her. It was like meeting a kindred spirit. It liked her and she liked it and it was *glad* she liked it. Perhaps this was unusual. Perhaps this force, this presence, was what had caused the person to scream those years ago. Did others not fare under it so blissfully as she had?

Like gentle hands, the presence pressed her eyes closed. Instantly, she was met with the vision of a shimmering diamond. She soon found herself inside it, peering up through the facets. To her horror, a giant war hammer came dropping toward her. She keeled over in a useless attempt to shield herself as it met the wall of the gemstone in a core-ringing smack. She lifted her head. The stone had not even cracked.

Rather, it began to glow and reveal faces of people she knew within its various surfaces. With clarity, she understood their characters, weaknesses and strengths. Finally, she saw her own reflection. It appeared frightened, as she was certain she did just then. But stamped upon either of her cheeks were the words "resilience" and "discernment."

Were the terms intended to describe her? Yes—it was an understanding placed in the center of her gut like a burning ember. Suddenly, she *could* see these characteristics within herself, though she'd never recognized them before.

Without warning, the diamond was stolen up by a pair of blacksmith's tongs and she watched in horror as she was cast into an inferno. She endured every flicker, not spared a moment's pain. She screamed and worked to awaken herself from the experience when her attention was drawn back to her reflection. Her white gown was replaced by golden armor. She was brave, bold, capable, *beautiful*—everything she would ever wish to be. She admired this girl, this other version of herself. How she wished she *could* be her.

With a jolt, the vision was removed and she could breathe again.

"Hazel... my precious daughter," a voice seared through her with heat fiercer than any flame.

She opened her eyes and found herself in the mirror room again.

"Diamond of my heart," the voice continued.

She searched for its possessor but discovered naught.

"Wh-who speaks to me?"

"I am your father."

"My f-father?" This could not be. Her parents had been banished from the kingdom.

"The creator of all things."

She blinked. Could this be the spirit of her kingdom? She had never paid him much thought. Not many did in her circle. What did one call him again? "...G-great Entity of the eternal realm?"

He *laughed* and she was both confused and embarrassed at once.

"Aye, cherished heart."

She fell to her knees. Was *he* the one who would hear her thoughts? *Why* had no one told her? She might have come prepared, done some research. And why was he speaking to her so, calling her by terms of endearment?

"Does everyone see themselves within a diamond?" she asked before she thought. She felt special having seen herself in such a precious stone. The thought that everyone might experience the same made her jealous.

"The diamond *was* you," he said. "Very few see that particular depiction. As you might have gathered, I am quite proud of it."

"Of it... of *me*, you mean?" she nearly squealed in astonishment.

He laughed again. "Who else? It is not every woman who can withstand the blow of war hammers and shine all the fiercer. Not everyone might survive the fires of life and come out stronger and more perceptive. That has been you up to this point... but it is all about to change."

"You mean I won't be a diamond anymore?"

"You will always be a diamond, Hazel. But should you enter this room again in a year's time, you will not know yourself nor anything around you. Indeed, everything familiar to you is soon to transform."

Transform? Did she *want* change? She sensed it would not be trivial. It sent tremors through her. The notion lay like a weight upon her. Yet, how long had she wished things could be different? How long had she yearned to escape what her life had been thus far?

Unexpectedly, a figure appeared before her. He smiled with the glimmer she'd heard in the laughter, but he looked nothing like what she had pictured. He stood tall with dark hair and lively eyes. The furs he wore were like fire. In his hands, he held a chunk of coal.

She stood to her feet. "What is *that* for?" Despite the shock of the Great Entity's appearance before her, she was struck far more by a queer apprehension of that coal.

"It is pleasant to meet you, as well," he said with mirth. "You may call me H.S., if you like."

She found herself smiling back, despite herself. "I *do* like," she said as if she'd known him the whole of her life. They were very alike somehow, though he was so much easier and freer—everything she wished to be. "You can call me Hazel."

"I already have."

She nearly laughed, so absurd was it to be standing in The Mirror, speaking to Kierelia's god as if he were an old friend. Come hell or high water, he made her so very at ease. But she observed the coal again as he took a step nearer.

"What is that *for?*" she asked again.

His eyes grew solemn as he searched hers. "I need you to transform it into a diamond for me."

She stepped back. "H-how?"

"You must swallow it whole."

"Swallow a hunk of coal? How? *Why?*"

"I must ask you to perform it without question if you don't mind."

She *did* mind... But at the same time, she had an uncanny feeling she'd made a friend of this god who presented himself as at first ferocious, then rather terrifically amiable. She could not bear the thought of letting him down.

"Very well," she breathed with a half-laugh. This was absurd.

His eyes lit with flame. *"Thank you.* Would you just open your mouth, please?"

Looking into his eyes, she found it easy to trust him. She did as he bid. Upon her tongue, he placed it. It tasted of blood. She looked to him and he nodded. With a breath and the closing of her eyes, she managed to get the chunk past her throat. When her eyes opened, he was gone.

How empty she felt. She felt like crying but understood her turn in the room was complete, so she went for the door. With her hand on the knob, she froze. Very few claimed to retain any knowledge gained within The Mirror. She could not bear to forget a single moment, to forget the peculiarly wonderful chum she'd found in this H.S., the god-Entity of her realm.

With the narrowing of her eyes, she turned the knob. As she took her first step to exit, she shouted, *"H.S.!"*

The room's keeper widened her eyes. "What was that?"

"Er... what was what?"

"Why, you just shouted something rather obnoxiously, girl."

Hazel glanced back at the open door, into the dark room. "I..." What *had* happened? She felt a weight had been lifted. She was light as a feather. Something was different. She was altered.

She turned back to the keeper. "What did I say?"

"Er, you said, why, I imagine you said something like 'Achess'... What does it mean?" She appeared interested now.

Hazel shook her head. "I cannot imagine." She worked hard to remember, but all she recalled were flashes of what might have been glass. And she tasted... blood.

2

The castle's passages transitioned daily. There were rumors as to why this occurred. The first was that it was rigged to do so from its very beginning to confuse intruders or any enemies who might overtake the fortress—a defense mechanism. Others claimed it was enchanted by the Great One himself, or by his emissary, the prophet, who was said to have been present from Kierelia's beginnings. Still, others insisted the castle was cursed by the beautiful sorceress, Maera, who was said to have existed nearly as long as the prophet, though the prophet said otherwise.

As it was, the castle most often altered itself habitually, in nearly the same reformation every few days. One had only to live there long enough to learn its tendencies. These variations were never witnessed, of course. One merely awoke, opened a door or rounded a corner to find them.

Hazel could never be certain which explanation she believed, but she *liked* to think the castle was enchanted. The prophet, whom she'd known all her life, liked to believe it as well, though he claimed he had nothing to do with it. But he also claimed he'd not been present at the time of its construction and all knew that was not the case. Indeed, it was recorded he'd had a great deal to do with the birth of the Kierelian kingdom. Many said it might never have been born if not for his involvement. And, whenever he happened to be seen looking upon the fortress, it was clear what pride he took in it. When Hazel pressed him one day, he admitted he thought Kierelia the most tenacious of kingdoms upon the planet Kaern.

This morning, as she turned the doorknob of her bedroom, she paused to recall what the castle held outside this day. The day before, it had been the kitchens—always handy when one was famished. But this meant her favorite day had arrived. She beamed as she opened her door to find another door across the hall. Crossing the short distance of the corridor, she opened it and ascended the spiraling, unadorned staircase. Affectionately, she ran her fingertips along its rail, which shone from years of this caressing.

She recalled the first morning upon which the door had appeared before her bedroom. It had felt like a gift presented by the castle itself. Never before had it materialized there and the fortress was not known to make alterations from its customary agenda. This change had been what had made her ascend those stairs for the first time. As she had yet to discover a sensible reason for the occurrence, she was content to presume it a present from the possibly enchanted and perhaps, as she liked to imagine, slightly conscious structure.

Since then, she'd considered the palace her secret confidant— her only one within its walls when the prophet was not there. When he did call upon her, however, she was always reminded of why people lived in the first place. Not only was he so full of life and inspiration himself, he actually asked after her own affairs, even inquiring her opinion above others. This was a point of contention between Hazel and her guardian. Lady Nora despised the prophet for his flabbergasting ways, but that dislike intensified over the very fact that he chose to put Hazel upon such a pedestal.

Contrarily, the prophet influenced the king to Hazel's benefit. One very dreadful, wonderful day, the prophet had requested her appearance at a council meeting to seek her opinion on a matter of trade relations with the southern tribes (a small domain just south of Kierelia). It seemed their land possessed a certain tree that produced rare lumber that the Kierelians wished to possess. Yet, the tribes refused even monetary reward for it, not wishing to see their own forests decimated.

Her guardian had come to her in a huff that day, vexed that they wished to see her most disappointing ward, who now might put her to dreadful shame. Hazel, too, had feared what the royal council might wish to speak with her about until she discovered it was by the prophet's bidding. Then, she was terrified. She knew he meant her only the best, but she also understood how much interest he took in her—interest she knew bewildered all else. And befuddled they had been… except for King Zephuel.

He had been amused but not mocking. It was in the following moments, she was certain, that his opinion of her had altered. It helped, of course, that though she had responded to the prophet's questioning in but a few sentences, they had proved intelligent ones. "…Could we not contract an agreement for the saplings of these trees to grow ourselves? And in the meantime, might they not accept a trade for some of our great lumber, which they do not in turn possess? Kierelian lumber is one of the sturdiest in the vicinity, is it not?" The room had responded with thoughtful silence. But while the prophet had beamed, the king had studied her with newfound pride in the one who'd been birthed of his two greatest enemies.

At last, she arrived at the landing of the long-abandoned

watchtower. Since order had come to the kingdom long ago, it had been forsaken for storage space. It brimmed with abandoned oddities that she'd organized to establish a cozy home for herself. This was her true home and most private place. No one else recalled its existence, nor were they aware she did. Through the years, her guardian had asked after her absent hours when she could not be found to aid in some task. But Hazel always refused to reveal her secret, no matter how stern the scolding.

With satisfaction, she strode to her small bookshelf. It was small in comparison with the castle library. But for a personal one meant as a secret, she was fairly pleased. It contained some books stolen from the larger library... or rather, *borrowed* for a dreadfully extended period of time. Others had been gifts from the prophet, while a few terribly awful but beautiful volumes had been gifted by her guardian. All who knew Hazel were aware of her weakness for literature, but Lady Nora most often attempted to steer her toward reading that would benefit her goals for the girl's future—an attempt to make a truly compliant lady of her. Hazel kept every one given to her, for were not all books beautiful? And though the ones from Lady Nora may have been given with ulterior motive, they were *gifts*. For a girl with no companions to speak of, that was everything.

Hazel took up the historical work she'd been studying for what felt like ages. Though she acquainted herself with every kind of book under the sun, she preferred fictional tales, great legends of old and tales of other worlds which none knew whether were real or imagined. Still, this volume was a better history than most, telling of the wildlands of the southern tribes where its people were claimed to have possessed uncanny voices in decades past, that had a peculiar influence on the world around them such as growing crops with greater speed and lifting heavy objects. Some could do much more, but as this was spoken of with much skepticism, she couldn't be sure just how factual the volume was.

A growl sounded from the bottom of the staircase: Lady Nora. Heart racing, Hazel tiptoed to the edge of the landing. The thought of her guardian having discovered the place to be hers sent her ears roaring.

"*Why* can't that girl ever be where she is supposed to?!"

Hazel released a sigh. Her guardian was beyond the door and starting down the hall. The tower remained a secret. But she feared the lady's mind venturing to the tower room door, so she swiftly replaced her book to tiptoe down the stairs, softly closing the door behind. The coast was clear on either side of the corridor, but she needed to have some explanation for her whereabouts or another scolding would be in order.

"*There* you are!" Lady Nora shouted, returning from around the corner.

Hazel pursed her lips as she realized the woman had heard the door close after all. She cast her glance downward and clenched her hands together behind her back as her guardian approached.

"So, you've taken to hiding from me in your chambers again, have you? And I'd thought I'd removed all your little hiding places when you were a wee wench." She raised a severe brow. "Don't tell me you've stooped to crawling beneath the bed now? Really, at *your* age…"

Hazel's mind raced. Lady Nora assumed she'd come from her bedroom. All was safe. "You… required me for something?"

The woman released a sigh and started forward. "*Yes*, follow along, girl. It seems you're in for a rare treat and I do hope you've matured enough to appreciate it. It seems Dianna and the other young people wish to begin a game of Affrontery but are in need of a sixth. They've requested you especially."

Hazel's mind raced as her ears began to roar again. Affrontery was not so much a game as an excuse to verbally assault others in an effort to draw laughs from their audience. Whoever vacated the room first was proclaimed the loser and left to pick of the pieces of whatever pride they left with. She'd played it once before and had, after all, been the first to leave... in raucous tears. Lady Dianna and her ladies had never let her live it down. As there was no required number for the game, their desire for her was not only unnecessary but... calculated. They had a purpose in mind.

"Oh, Lady Nora, I beg you would excuse—"

"You *beg* to be excused a game with *friends* yet again? *Really*, girl, you shame me. You make no effort to find companions and now *my* ward is a known recluse throughout Castlehaven and expected never to marry." She turned then and took Hazel by the arm, digging nails into her flesh. "I cannot tell you all I have done in an attempt to salvage what reputation you had left after your parents... No, no, I cannot even speak it." She raised a brow. "*Tell me I will not have to...*"

Hazel's eyes seized the floor as she worked to rein in her tears. Lady Nora was well aware of how she hated to be reminded of what her parents had done, especially when it was spoken of so loudly with others in earshot, as many of the servants were now. This was an ultimatum for her to refuse to play the game or pay the consequences.

"Very well," she said resignedly.

Lady Nora released her and smoothed the lace of Hazel's cuff to cover the impressions her nails had made. "Show me compliance like that more often and we may just make something of a match for you after all."

Lady Nora picked up her pace until they approached the library door. Hazel loathed that one of her least hated places in the castle was about to be spoiled for her. Dianna was so diabolical that Hazel couldn't seem to put it past her that she'd selected it accordingly.

"Here she is," Lady Nora announced. "I do apologize for the wait, but you know Hazel."

Hazel's stomach dropped when she realized who was present. As expected, Dianna's ditsy cohorts, Stacia and Rebecca, were at her side. Even Theo, one of Dianna's suitors, often took part. But it was Armond—*dear* Armond—whose presence made her ill. He never played the game. Hazel was certain this was not because he could not take a jab but because he hated to dish them out. Yet, here he was.

Somehow, Dianna had conjured his presence. Unfortunately, she'd discovered Hazel's feelings for him some time ago. This had been another point of ridicule, though it wasn't as if every other young woman was not guilty of the same feeling. Armond was something of a lady's man, though it never appeared to be by any effort of his own. Not only was he the childless king's only nephew, making him next in line for the throne, but he was simply beautiful and utterly enthralling. Without effort, he lit up a room with his easy, open ways and talent for putting everyone at ease. He'd even been kind to Hazel a time or two. The fact he was about to witness her humiliation was the handsomest icing atop the Affrontery cake she'd ever been compelled to eat.

As Dianna stared her down with that pretty, wicked little smile, agreeing with Lady Nora over Hazel's peculiarities, Hazel raised her chin and gazed back... unflinchingly.

3

Armond's thick brows were especially sympathetic as he caught Hazel's eye. He had perceived the subtle jabs exchanged between Lady Dianna and Lady Nora at her expense. Most people either didn't notice or didn't care. But he had offered her these glances on occasion, proving she was not imagining the insults and that they were not acceptable. He looked away, but as one of the other girls joined in with, "Hazel is such a pitiable little dear," his over-wide jaw flexed with the clenching of his teeth. Even his vulnerable brown eyes shone with irritation. As Hazel studied him through her peripheral, she recalled those who had described him as too handsome to be taken seriously—not a good trait for a future king. But beyond his looks, he possessed easy compassion. To her, that was something to be prized.

Soon, the six were seated in a circle of green chairs and the velvet satchel was passed. The names scrolled across pieces of paper had already been prepared. Now, they would each retrieve one and that designated the person they must criticize. Hazel discerned Rebecca had retrieved her name when her eyes glistened merrily as she showed the note to Dianna. But Hazel could live with this. Rebecca was a petty girl who easily felt threatened. Once, she had caught Armond passing Hazel one of his sympathetic glances. Ever since, Hazel had sensed from Rebecca what next to no one had ever felt for her before: jealousy. It was ludicrous for the girl to feel so. She had wealth, upstanding parents, fine gowns. And Hazel was… Hazel. But in the end, the young lady was not very clever and Hazel doubted she could wound her very deeply.

At last, the satchel was in Hazel's lap, a single note remaining. She hated this moment, the moment she would discover whom she was expected to shame so deeply they would escape the room. But she was not about to let herself be utterly shamed before Armond. This time, she would survive the game. She would press someone else to leave if she had to.

But how she *loathed* the notion of wounding others. She had no desire to make anyone else feel as she did on a daily basis. More selfishly, she did not wish Armond to think her as cruel as the rest. Even so, it was the game.

With a breath, she plucked up her paper.

Armond.

She felt her face flush pink. How could she harm him? Could she even conjure up anything *resembling* a taunt about him? This might be the first time someone had lost because they couldn't insult someone. It made it impossible for her to pay any mind to the others assaults upon one another, though she noticed Armond's stab at Theo was really more amusing than cruel. Yet, the others acted as if he had done well.

"Hazel, you must take your turn," Stacia urged.

"Very well…" she began. But she had nothing. Armond was perfect. The best jabs were the ones that made others laugh, so one usually sought to form one that would both shame the victim and send laughter through the room. She would aim merely for the latter.

"Well?" Dianna pressed with a taunting brow. She *wanted* to see Hazel hurt Armond.

Horses. He was known for his love of horses, namely his favorite gelding, Chutney. Not a very decorous name, but he'd chosen it as a boy, thinking the gelding the very hue of his favorite spread. More than once, she'd entered the stables to the sound of him chatting aimlessly with the animal, who, she had to admit, appeared to be taking an interest.

"Prince Armond—"

"Please, drop the title," he interrupted.

She went pink again. "Armond... speaks so often to his dear Chutney, one might often imagine he heard responses from the poor animal... if, indeed, Chutney can be bothered to attend his longwinded master at all."

Theo and Stacia chittered.

It wasn't very good, but it had drawn laughter from a crowd who didn't care for her. Armond did not appear wounded in the slightest, but reading it was the best she could do, he bowed his head. "I hadn't realized others were near enough to hear..." he murmured in humiliation. But before she felt too poorly, he tilted his head in her direction and sneaked a quick wink.

Hazel could not conceal the smile that beamed from her, even when Rebecca glowered.

"My turn!" the girl said a little too excitedly. "Hazel, my dearest little girl, you are so full of yourself, it is the best explanation for why your face is so very swollen."

Hazel raised a brow. She hadn't expected much, but she had anticipated more than this. She knew very well her face was, contrarily, quite hollow—even sickly looking at times. Her guardian said it was a lack of sunshine and exercise. She wasn't wrong. But Hazel was fairly certain her eternal lack of appetite had more to do with it.

Despite the shortage of trueness to the jab, the other girls giggled beside her.

"Oh, enough of this *politeness!*" Dianna demanded as she restored the name-pieces to the sack. "You all know very well this is not how the game is to be played and we will be stuck here until someone leaves the room. Now, choose again."

The sack was passed. Hazel withdrew... Dianna's card.

This could be dangerous.

"I'll start this time," Stacia offered. "I got Theo."

The group howled in amusement. As Theo was something of a jester, he was easy to tease. Hazel had thought him amusing once, even charming. Then he'd shot a slice of beef at her face during the king's birthday celebration. It had been sauced and had landed squarely between her eyes. Needless to say, it was too humiliating ever to find anything altogether attractive about him again. Even so, he'd grown up a decent enough fellow, though why he should so value friendship with Dianna was beyond her understanding.

"I must admit," Stacia began, "I thought Theo very handsome... *once*." The group made humorous noises, anticipating what was to come. "That was when I was too young to know any better."

Laughter was drawn from all but Hazel, who took no pleasure in anything the people in this group but Armond had to say. But even Theo gave a small chuckle... unfortunately proving Stacia had not gone far enough.

The girl gave a half-smile before opening her mouth again, "Indeed, he's but a gargoyle beside Armond."

All laughed but Theo, Armond and Hazel. It was clear this was a tender point.

Stacia was known for her bluntness. She wasn't stupid, like Rebecca. She was intelligent—too intelligent. She knew precisely where to strike in a way Theo would feel it. She'd done the same to Hazel many times before. Where Dianna was vindictive and Rebecca jealous, Stacia truly thought Hazel an idiot... and it showed quite effortlessly.

Hazel wished Theo would just leave the room to rescue her from the remainder of this torturous game. But though red in the face, he remained.

Armond was next. "Rebecca, my friend..." he began jovially. "I'm afraid I must chastise you for spending far too much time flirting with the royal guard... when you are meant to be betrothed to the son of a Bashtiian noble."

There were intrigued "ooohs" and a few laughs. But it was clear Rebecca took little offense. She was a known flirt and proud to be. Moreover, it was well-known how little the girl liked the match her parents had made for her. Though it was a fine one, it meant she would have to move east and across the sea, to the kingdom of Bashtii. The country was famed for its beauty and had been around longer than the Kierelian dominion, making it much wealthier in numerous respects. But it was also known for its peculiar cultural differences. For instance, the nobility often went without shoes when in the Illuminas Palace of the capital city. Kierelians were far too straitlaced to appreciate such a practice.

"It is my turn," Dianna volunteered smoothly. Her eyes went to Hazel, eagerness burning behind them.

This was the moment—the *calculated* moment. It was the reason Hazel had been entreated to join.

"I overheard something the other day," Dianna began almost offhandedly, "which I would like to share with the lot of you."

Hazel gripped the edges of her seat. Whatever was spoken, she would not leave this room. If she was forced to tears, she would remain.

"King Zephuel was speaking of you, Hazel," she said lightly, as if this was a special moment for her.

It started Hazel's gears turning. Why should the king be discussing *her* of all people? And to whom had he been speaking?

"I confess I'd always wondered why you were housed within the castle, made a burden upon dear Lady Nora."

Dear Lady Nora indeed, Hazel thought.

"As it happens, it was the king's idea."

A few gasped. Hazel had always known this, of course. She'd been made to show her appreciation for the favor as often as possible. But the gasps revealed that others had actually questioned her presence in the royal fortress... had wondered why the daughter of the king's would-be-assassins was welcome.

Already, this was beginning to ache.

"Yes," Dianna continued. "As it happened, seventeen years ago, he gazed upon your wee, child-face and was certain he saw your parent's blood burning through your veins... that murderous desire for his head."

The room was actually silent. Hazel closed her eyes. But, swiftly, she opened them again, as if it were a mere blink. She would stand her ground... or sit her seat.

"When he saw that," Dianna continued with a half-smile, "he decided it was safer to keep his enemies close, to keep watch over you the whole of your life, waiting for the day you would emerge his foe, that he might deal with you swiftly."

At that moment, Hazel wished more than ever that her parents had not abandoned her when they'd been banished into the ruddy kingdom, the Deep South, which lay beyond the southern tribes. It was known for its savage people and was the number one enemy of Kierelia. She had always told herself they thought she'd be safer in Kierelia than in such a land... but it was difficult to feel convinced of it just now. Now, she understood the purpose of her welcome in Castlehaven and the revelation induced the intended result. She felt like scum. She couldn't catch her breath. She was falling through the floor.

But she stayed her seat.

4

"My turn," Hazel returned, blood boiling under her skin.

Something shifted in her. She squared her shoulders on Dianna, who glared back with a dark smile. But Hazel perceived the girl's surprise that she had not raced from the room. She also noted that no one had laughed, revealing they were either too stunned by the revelation or even they thought Dianna had gone too far.

"Dianna would have us believe she is the delight of all who behold her," Hazel began in quiet fury, "that she is proud and self-assured. But I once overheard her sobbing to her mother, 'Oh, *why* does Armond not love me as he should?'"

Hazel sat back in her chair to survey her effect. No one had ever done such a thing to Dianna before, in the game or otherwise. People feared her as much as they worked to convince themselves they liked her.

"The truth is," Hazel continued suddenly, *"no one* really likes you… and you know it." It was a sudden revelation. "They're *afraid* of you."

The red-faced Dianna leaped to her feet and shoved her finger in Hazel's face. "How dare *you* of all people—*worthless and unloved as you are*—speak to *me* as if I am *anything* as despised and pathetic as *you*."

"Now, now, now," Armond butted in, drawing Dianna back by the hand that had been about to strike Hazel across the face. "It is only fair, you know. It is the game. You've had your turn; she's had hers. Let us move on, shall we? Perhaps this really ought *not* to be played anymore."

Dianna turned to him with flashing eyes, as if *he* had just dealt the real blow of the morning. She spun from him to face her friends, thrashing the velvet sack across the room. "Well, I *never*…" she sputtered as she took each of her ladies by the arms and led them from the room.

The three who remained stared after them.

"I suppose… this means I won?" Armond said humorlessly. Turning to Hazel, he added, "Or we might share the win."

It was not meant as a rebuke, merely something to say—the truth. But it made Hazel stand miserably from her seat. "I don't care for winning this game," she said with something like a sob, feeling lower than low.

"Nor I," he replied with understanding. "We shall both be wiser in future, I suppose. Affrontery is a senseless pastime."

But Hazel had no say in whether she played or not. If they should go to Lady Nora, she must. And she couldn't hide from her guardian any more than she already did.

* * *

Hazel raced through corridors, taking care to avoid Lady Nora. She resisted the urge to fling wide the door to her tower, instead checking the hall before softly opening and closing it behind her. It was the window nook into which she threw herself as she crumbled into a pile of tears.

Could it be true the king viewed her as an enemy—had decided so from the moment he'd gazed upon her child-face? There was every chance Dianna had been lying in an effort to heap misery upon an already dissatisfied life. Problem was, the knowledge of this story only made everything about her life make more sense. She'd been told it was an honor to be made a ward of the king's sister… but that sister did not conceal her cruelty. The king had to be aware Hazel was not gently treated, yet he paid no heed. And why should he, if, rather than her caretaker, Lady Nora had been assigned her jailor? If Hazel knew Dianna, the story would be all over the castle before day's end. The moment she arrived in the banquet hall that evening, the murmurs would begin. "There goes Hazel, the king's *prisoner*."

Fresh sobs rang through her, but it was from more than this revelation. She had played the very game she so despised and she'd reaped no winner's reward. She felt twisted and hollow inside. She'd always been able to read others like a book, to understand what they felt, their fears, what they worked to conceal. She'd never dreamed she'd use that intuition to cause someone pain.

Why had Dianna waged this war on her? Why did she loathe Hazel so? Surely, she had much more going on in her life than to think of ways to harm her? Yet, for years, she'd taken a special interest in Hazel. Of late, it had been more like torment.

"My dearest girl," a voice sounded behind her, "whatever is the matter?"

She shot up from her windowsill to face the intruder.

"*Prophet?*" she gasped, batting tears from her face. "You're *back*." Cheer nearly reached her until a thought occurred to her. "How did you find me here?"

His eyes sparkled as he tapped his head. "This head knows many things it oughtn't."

She grinned back. That was enough when one was speaking to him. And she wasn't likely to receive more anyway. Her grin grew as she surveyed the oversized brown garments he wore, the very ones he never seemed to change from no matter whose company he kept. Nor was his long white beard ever trimmed. He cared not for the estimation of others and she loved him for it.

"I suppose you won't tell anyone about my tower... will you?" she asked.

"I should say *not*. A turret like this would lose all its charm if it were uncovered to all. Now, you were sobbing and I am longing to know just why." He offered her a seat upon her own nook, then sat beside her.

"I-I've been *cruel*," she forced out, unable to say more.

"As difficult as I find that to believe, I think it must be so, else you would not be so broken up. But I will say, it is that very brokenness that makes you of such value to the Great Entity. And it is why everything will be all right."

She pulled a kerchief from his pocket and asked, "But why should *I* be of any value to a *god?*" *Especially when I am of no value to anyone else.*

"Oh, I think the stuff you are built from could make you of more value to a great many more than you realize."

She grew quiet. Wouldn't the stuff she was built from be her *parents*, the infamous traitors? Or did he mean something else?

"Now, back to this cruelty business," he said. "You've looked yourself in the mirror and faced your wrong-doing. It is noble that you have done so. Repentance is as valuable as water in the desert."

"If you say so."

"I do."

"Well… where have you come from this time?" she asked, desiring to change the subject.

He raised his brows with intrigue. "If I told you, I would have to have you imprisoned."

That jest cut deeper than he'd intended due to the recent revelation, but she brushed it aside. "Then I beg you will not," she said with a small smile. "What has brought you back to us?"

"The Great Entity, whom I serve with my life, sent me. I have yet to discover just why. Even so, it is always pleasant to come and see my favorite young lady."

"Prophet," she said almost scolding. She would never understand why he was so kind.

"Don't 'prophet' me, Lady Hazel. Can I help it if you are the most unaffected person I know? Indeed, you have been baptized in the fires of life and grown-up shining."

Hazel chewed her lip. "I… wish others saw me as you do. I think there must be something wrong with you."

"Oh, there are many things wrong with me, but being fond of you is not one of them. I simply see through a vein of experience others have not been afforded. In the end, considering you as anything less than a diamond signifies there is something wrong with everyone else."

* * *

Hazel had not been wrong. Her entrance into the banquet hall induced a quiet stir, but on the arm of the prophet, she found she could bear it. Moreover, she knew the prophet's presence was part of that stir, especially as he was the one escorting her. She gripped his arm in the least ladylike fashion imaginable, but he merely patted her hand with care.

Upon being seated, she found Dianna was across from her. For the first few courses, the girl acted as if she hadn't noticed Hazel. But about halfway through, Hazel sensed eyes on her and glanced up in time to find that dreadful grin. As Hazel well knew, a Dianna smile was not a happy one. It was scheming. Hazel dreaded what this one might mean. After all, she'd mortified Dianna as none had before.

She began to feel she was in the clear when the meal concluded and most everyone retired to the entertaining room. Considering the gossip she knew was going around about her, the evening had been surprisingly painless. As usual, she selected the most comfortable chair in the darkest corner and opened the book she'd been carrying in the concealed pocket of her skirts.

Before delving in, she offered the room a final glance. Armond and Theo laughed at something Stacia said. Lady Nora entertained a group of noblewomen. There was a good chance she was complaining about her young ward... or captive, everyone knew now. Most intriguing of all, however, were the king and prophet huddled together on the far side of the room, discussing something both private and upsetting, if the prophet's face had anything to say about it. She might even have conjectured he was harboring disapproval toward the king, possibly chastising him as a father would. She would dearly have liked to know what was discussed, but as that was out of the question, she began her reading.

It was three piano recitals and two vocal performances later when she overheard her own name being discussed by a set of ladies mostly unknown to her.

"But isn't it dangerous for the king to keep the Lady Hazel about when she is... *what she is?*"

Hazel's stomach turned and she gripped the edges of her book as if begging them to absorb her into them.

"Of course it is, but he is a man of wisdom. One can only imagine he has prepared for what might arise. And after all, you've seen the girl. She is sickly in appearance. I cannot envision her accomplishing much against such a king."

With laughter, they moved on, but Hazel's reading had been spoiled. She glanced up to find Dianna's smile on her again. Had she heard what had been discussed? Likely not, but anyone could guess. This was proof that what Dianna had spread was on the tip of every tongue in the room. More than ever, Hazel was grateful she had moved her chair into the shadows where few would notice her... unless they specifically searched her out.

"*Hazel,* foolish girl, there you are," Lady Nora chimed as if on cue. "I've been looking for you everywhere. Why did you not consult with me before adding your name to the list of performers this evening? Really, I cannot tell you what poor timing this is to be putting yourself forward. And yet, they are now summoning you, so I've no time to resolve the matter."

Hazel's mouth dropped open. "L-lady Nora... I did not put my name on that list. Surely, you must know that."

"Know that? *Know that?* Why ever should I when your name is there clear as day? Now, *come along."*

Hazel yanked against the hand that wrenched her. "My lady, I beg you... I have *no desire* to perform."

Indeed, from the moment Lady Nora had discovered that her ward possessed some talent in singing, she had worked to press her into the spotlight on a number of occasions, likely hoping some gentleman would come along and take Hazel off her hands. But from the first instance Hazel had been compelled to do so, she'd learned to hate it. She'd been scarcely able to open her mouth, let alone remain standing before a crowd of eyes who already disapproved of her. She'd run and never again relented to her guardian's urging.

"Are you *really* going to heap shame upon shame, girl? I will not allow you to humiliate me yet again. You *will* perform. I command it."

Lady Nora continued to drag her unwilling ward through the crowd of those who chittered on about her even as she moved among them. Of *all* evenings to attempt another performance, this was the absolute worst. How on the planet Kaern had her name ended up on that wretched list?

"I must wish you good luck," Dianna whispered as she sidled Hazel with something like a hug. "I'm sure you will do *wonderfully.*" Her brow flew severely high and Hazel received the answer to her question. This was Dianna's idea of revenge.

She'd done *well*.

Heaping humiliation, all the room watched her, their whisperings rising to a crescendo until she was nauseated.

"Oh, Lady Nora, *please*," she begged quietly, near tears now. "I know as well as you do what is being spoken of me this evening. *Please*, make my excuses. Just… say I am ill!"

The woman appeared surprised but said calmly, "Then you know how important it is you perform well. Perhaps you might just manage to lift some of the disgrace you have cast on my household." With that, the woman abandoned her, though she remained near enough to keep an eye on her prisoner.

Never in her life had Hazel felt so at the end of her rope. It was an unbearable moment. The pianist began and she worked to keep herself from losing her dinner on the crowd. She missed her cue. The pianist began again, louder this time, annoyed. Impossibly, Hazel caught it the second time around, ringing out a long, tremulous note that nearly silenced the crowd.

It was a curious thing that, at the very end of her rope, dwelt a relief from caring what these awful people thought of her. The fear dissipated. But it was well Dianna had selected a song about rejected love, for she felt tears racing down her cheeks. Still, her voice grew stronger—stronger still when she found the prophet watching on from his corner with the king. He was both concerned and gratified. She was performing well. How could she have known that at her breaking point, she would find a new kind of strength? Yet, with it dwelled every moment of heartbreak throughout the years and it poured into her song.

It was then Dianna stole Armond by the arm and guided him through the room until he was standing before Hazel. Her voice stumbled a moment before catching the pureness of the melody again. He did not appear to understand the cruel girl's purpose, instead looking upon the performer with an expression that reminded of the prophet's.

It was at this point that two things occurred. Hazel's blood seared under her skin, frightening and strengthening at once. But almost at the same time, Armond began to rise... into the air. So gracefully did he float that he did not take notice. But at the moment Hazel's voice pierced the atmosphere with her clearest soprano, he soared toward the ceiling with a yelp. All the room gasped and shouted. The instant Hazel's note cut short, he dropped.

From the center of her soul, she knew what was to be done. She sang out again, cradling him in the arms of her high C just before he hit the floor. Gently, she laid him upon the floor. The room backed away from him, then turned to Hazel... and backed away from her.

The next moment, the prophet was beside her, racing her through the crowd and from the room.

"P-rophet, what just happened? I didn't..."

"You did, my girl."

"Hazel!" Lady Nora shouted as she stormed after them. "What on *Kaern* was that *demonic* spectacle? Is that what you've been doing behind my back?! Consorting with the dark arts?"

The prophet stood between them, an action Hazel would never in her life forget. Neither would Lady Nora, by the looks of her. "Good woman," he said, "I think you must take a moment to regain your composure before throwing accusations of that kind around about this young lady who is, after all, meant to be under your *care* and *protection*."

Somehow, his words reached the lady. After blinking back at him several times, she said calmly, "Come along, Lady Hazel. We must get you away before that crowd decides to storm after us."

Utterly disoriented, Hazel searched the prophet's face for an answer, but he offered nothing and she was made to follow. The entire march through the castle, not a word was spoken to her. There was no more questioning, no scolding. When they reached the door to her bedchamber, Lady Nora merely opened the door and ushered her inside.

"You will remain here until we discover what might be done." With that, she turned on her heel and closed the door. Hazel believed the change in her guardian was true to heart until she heard the lock turn from the outside. The woman was as constant as ever.

In the quiet of the room that followed the turning of the key, Hazel stood frozen, left to consider what could be *wrong* with her? The prophet had assured it was her who had performed that awful feat. But *how*? What if poor Armond had soared through the ceiling and been *killed*. She dropped upon her bed. How she hated to be left alone without a single answer, no one to speak her racing fears to.

After a time, she realized no one would come either to or for her that evening, so she changed into her nightdress and pulled herself under the coverlet. Sleep felt impossible at that moment, yet it was not long before she found herself in dreams.

A yip sounded from her lips as she was ripped to consciousness by the sight of Dianna hurled against the ceiling of the entertainment hall, her lifeless body hitting the ground with a splat. Hazel had never been so grateful for the soft bedsheets beneath her, but she threw them off and sprang to her feet. She would do no more sleeping this night. The nightmares promised more woe than her waking thoughts. Gazing to the large set of windows at the wall, she observed what a bright, starry night it was. It was warm, too—warmer than it had been in the evening for some time.

Kneeling before the window, she rested her arms upon the sill. It was then the chapel bells began to chime, informing her it was mid of night. She'd been correct in thinking no one would seek her that evening. It was like her guardian to make them wait until morning when Hazel longed to come to an understanding of what had occurred as soon as humanly possible.

She recalled how her blood had burned when she'd hit that note—the soaring one. It had not even sounded like her. It had been bold, purposed. Apparently, it had purposed upon tossing Armond into the air. It… was as if it had reacted to her feelings for him. It was getting him away from Dianna, from the performance…

The more she pondered this, the more she believed it to be so. The note had *obeyed* her. Yet, she ought not to be thinking of it as if it was something apart from her. *She* had produced it. It was her.

A groan escaped her as she buried her face in her hands. It was all too much. She was *already* scorned, scrutinized even more than usual because of the rumors of the day. Any latent hopes of ever garnering acceptance from her peers were nonexistent now. If she was even allowed to remain at the castle, she would be the *aberration*. It didn't help that the very one she'd lifted had been the most beloved man in the kingdom... and heir to the throne.

She raised her head and her hand went to the back of her neck. Impossible as it was, she had endangered *the heir to the throne.*

She would be what her parents were: an enemy of the crown.

The sound of carriage wheels sounded in the courtyard, coming to a halt before the castle entrance. What could this be in the middle of the night? She leaned out to further view the spectacle when something stopped her: a red glow behind her. She turned, expecting to find her guardian come for her. Instead, light emanated from the four rubies that crowned the tops of her canopy bedposts. She realized they'd been blazing for some time before she'd thought to turn to them. They had appeared just before the carriage. No, this light... had arrived with the carriage. Moreover, it had never occurred before. Leaping upon the bed, she stood to touch one of them, but they began to ring as if bidding her not to. Obediently, she moved her hand away and considered.

She sensed they meant to warn her about that carriage. And she knew she should be frightened that she was about to be spirited away in the dead of night. Even so, she felt her shoulders relax as she accepted this fate, whatever it may be. Somehow understanding she had no time to change, she reached for her morning coat and fastened it over her nightdress. Then, she stood at attention before the door.

It wasn't long before Lady Nora's key entered the lock to the room she now knew to be her prison. It was clear that the woman was startled to find her standing in readiness, but was stunned further by the glowing bedposts, whose lights began to dim.

"What on *Kaern*...?" Lady Nora murmured. "What have you conjured *now*?"

The prophet stepped around her, shaking his head. "It is no conjuring. You must be aware of the rubies from the Bashtiian mines—the ones they ceased trading when it was learned the stones were nearly extinct. The gems become devoted to whomever they spend their life with." He turned to Hazel then. "They are concerned and have alerted you in their way."

Hazel looked back in wonder of the gems she had long taken for granted. But if it *was* meant as a caution, she wondered what was before her.

"Come along, girl." Lady Nora gestured before starting down the hall. The prophet placed an arm of support about Hazel's shoulders as he accompanied her.

"What is to become of me?" she asked.

"As for the becoming of you, that is for you to decide. This evening, you are to call upon the Assemblage of the Wise, who will gather in the Clarion Citadel upon Mount Tier. There, you will be questioned—studied even—but no harm will befall you." He rubbed her shoulder. "You think I would let anyone hurt you, my Lady Hazel?"

With a trusting smile, she shook her head. Though he was most often away, the time spent with him through the years had been meaningful. He had earned her trust and she had won his.

Upon packing her into the carriage with a plush blanket over her lap, Lady Nora offered her a questioning look. Hazel would have liked to tell herself the woman was concerned for her welfare but she knew it stemmed from the conundrum of what her ward was turning out to be. Certainly, the woman had not signed up for this. Wishing Lady Nora was the sort from whom she might garner courage, Hazel turned her attention to the prophet instead. He knew what she needed and grinned at her before urging the driver on.

"Prophet…"

"Yes."

"This Assemblage of the Wise, I have heard some particulars about them. I know you are among their number. But what sort of people are they? Are they all like you?"

"Not in the least. They come from various kingdoms—Kierelia, Bashtii, Croy, even the faraway land of Lwyss. You will find most carry themselves rather imperially. They are an egotistical bunch. Even so, they possess enough humility so as not to impede their great wisdom. They are men and women of truth, science, philosophy... I think you will find them interesting. And, in the end, I do believe your visit will be a short one."

"Why is that?"

"Because I do not believe you are finished... shall we say, cooking?"

"Pardon?"

"We shall see."

* * *

Moonlight shone upon Clarion Citadel, once built to keep watch over the old border before the kingdom expanded. Now it was a retreat for the most brilliant minds upon the continent. Together, they invented, composed, developed and merely enjoyed one another's company—or so she'd been made to believe.

Torches burned in the windows, revealing these great minds were wakeful, likely awaiting her arrival. The carriage rolled to a halt before the entrance. The prophet stepped out and opened the door wide for her. Upon leaning out, she found what she felt must be the entire assemblage standing upon the steps just outside the oversized door. Could whatever was wrong with her truly be so dreadful as to warrant this eager reception? She recalled Armond's body dropping from the ceiling. Yes, yes it could.

Stepping from the carriage, she followed the prophet up the stairs as gracefully as a girl in a nightdress could manage.

"Greetings, prophet," a large, dark-skinned man voiced deeply.

Hazel realized not even these comrades were aware of the prophet's actual name.

"Evening, Auras," the prophet replied. "It has been some while since you have been to see us."

Others of the group eyed Hazel as they followed the two men into the citadel.

"I have only arrived this very evening," Auras informed, "I was summoned by your Great One."

Hazel drew beside the prophet and noted the rising of his brows. "I suppose that was rather shocking for you, was it not?"

The man nodded and shared a grin. "I should have known better than to doubt a one as distinctive as you."

"High compliment, indeed."

Hazel followed the men into a cozy room with stuffed chairs and a blazing fire. This high in the mountains, the warmth did not reach them as it did below.

"Lady Hazel," said a woman with long curling lashes and tiny lips, "we would be honored if you would make yourself comfortable upon this lounge. We wish you to be as relaxed as possible while we learn you."

Learn her? She blinked. "As you wish." But it was difficult to lie comfortably when a room full of astute people drew into something of a circle around her.

"Is this really necessary?" the prophet asked of the assemblage.

"Prophet, she isn't ready," the woman of the long lashes stated as if offended. She turned to Hazel. "Will you not sing, Lady Hazel?"

Hazel's eyes grew wide. "Prophet?" she squeaked out.

"I know very well she isn't ready," he said, "but King Zephuel requested the estimations of this council."

"Ready for what?" Hazel inquired fearfully.

The prophet knelt beside her and took her hand. "Will you sing for me, my Hazel, so these intellectuals may judge you?"

She caught that wondrous sparkle in his eye, the one seen in those of loving fathers when they gazed upon their children, or uncles when with a favored niece or nephew. It took no more than this to wrangle her.

Her voice was shaky, but, for the first time, she allowed herself to embrace the fact it was rather stunning. Yet, it neither sounded nor felt anything like it had during her performance. Whatever had occurred did not mean to appear a second time.

"Why did her gift emerge so early?" a black-haired dwarf inquired.

The prophet gazed on Hazel with soft eyes. "I believe she was under acute emotional duress. Likely, she is very near the time of emergence, then tensions boiled high and it culminated into a rather public reveal."

Hazel closed her eyes as she recalled the moment she'd realized *she* had been the cause of Armond's flight.

"Lady Hazel," the long-lashed woman said, "will you not tell the tale from your point of view?"

Hazel cleared her throat, satisfied she was not being asked to sing again, and relayed it. It was somewhat humiliating to divulge the more sensitive details (such as her feelings for Armond), but they were unwilling to settle for less than every emotion endured at the time.

At its conclusion, Auras turned to the prophet. "I believe your hypothesis is sound. We must surmise that this young woman possesses the gift of our southern neighbors, that wild strain of powerful blood we'd thought too diluted to emerge again. It is claimed it has not been seen for a lifetime or two, but I would be interested in hearing from one of their number on the matter."

Hazel was more acquainted with details about the southern tribes than most Kierelians, thanks to the book the prophet had given her. The southern tribes were considered unruly by Kierelia's standards but had grown more peaceable than in previous years, thus the reason Kierelia trusted them at their border. In fact, the tribesmen were known to be matchlessly honorable, likely the reason King Zephuel and his predecessors felt it dishonorable to attempt leeching them. Not to mention, they acted as an adequate cushion between Kierelia and the Deep South.

The tribal ancestors had not been so accepted. It was true there were legends of great power that came from one's voice. There had been a time when such gifts had been used rather savagely. In early days, before Kierelia was an established kingdom, the people who lived upon that land greatly feared the "beasts" of the south, as they were called. It wasn't until the southern gift began to diminish that the neighboring landsmen accepted them as allies. But if word were to get out that she not only shared their *blood* but that cursed gift of old…

The prophet gazed down upon her as if reading her thoughts. "That is correct, Auras. I have knowledge of a nearly forgotten marital alliance in her ancestry."

Hazel blinked up at him. Not even her guardian, who so loved to mortify her, had mentioned such a thing.

"Hazel, I knew your great, great, *great* grandmother, who was offered in marriage as a motion of alliance between an early Kierelian settlement and a southern tribe. It seemed the tribe wished to learn the settlement's ways by sending one of their gifted-less to live among them. In exchange, they offered their protection. Your grandmother, Hanzel, was the, er, seal upon the deal." At Hazel's wide eyes, he continued with, "I know it sounds a bit barbaric, but it is very like our royal alliances by marriage today. Moreover, I know for a fact the two fell quite in love and lived long, contented lives."

"Did my… did my parents know of this?"

"It is the darkest secret of your mother's family."

Many of the group drew up chairs as a conversation over matters concerning her bloodline and the possible extent of her "gift" continued. But it was apparent she had fallen asleep when she awoke to a rather alarming statement.

"Then she isn't ready to be weaponized," someone stated with disappointment.

Hazel forced herself to remain calm. She must continue to appear unconscious in case they should not wish to discuss it while she was awake.

"Yes, but an attack from the Deep South is not likely due for another year or so."

"I have read that many of the old tribesman's gifts did not emerge until well into their twenties. How can we be certain she will be gifted in time, let alone trained?"

"I cannot for the life of me understand why the Deep South does not attack *now* when they clearly have the means."

"My sources say they will not count themselves ready for another year."

"But will our *girl* here be anything like ready by that time or shall we tell King Zephuel to continue looking for other options?"

"I do wish you all would cease referring to Lady Hazel as some kind of weapon," the prophet spoke at last. "I have seen glimpses of what she may become should her life's journey permit it and I believe, if the Great One sees fit to empower her against any future enemies, he will do so in his timing. Kierelia was established under his blessing and, as far as I am aware, it remains so."

5

Due to the lateness of the hour, Hazel had fallen asleep again and been carried to the carriage where she slept soundly until they drove over a fallen branch. Having tumbled to the floor, the prophet helped her back into her seat where, by her preference, they sat in silence. Her mind raced over all she'd heard of impending war and the possible weaponization of her. She was more than glad that she was "not ready." She could not bear the idea of battle.

"I heard what they said," she said at last.

"I know. Your eyelids twitch when you're awake."

"But I fell asleep again… What is to become of me?"

"For now, you return to Castlehaven."

She raised a brow. "And then?"

"My girl, you're going on a journey."

"What?! Where?" A variety of emotions flooded her. She had

never left Castlehaven before.

"That, I will tell you when it has been approved by King Zephuel."

She eyed him. "Should he consent, when will I leave?"

"This afternoon, likely."

Her stomach twisted into knots. "You *really* won't tell me where I may be going?"

He shook his head.

* * *

Hazel raced through the forest that surrounded Castlehaven. She'd always found solitude here. And though it wasn't more than once a week that she was released into it, she knew it like the back of her hand. Just now, she had a specific place in mind—a place she very much hoped to meet the only friend she possessed, though he was a severely concealed secret.

At last, she came to the place where rock met grass and river. That rock eventually grew into a mountain, but from this view, it was merely the bearer of a small stream supplied from the runoff of melted snow. The stream flowed into the steady river, not large but very handy for dipping one's feet into. Throwing off her slippers and hiking up her skirts, she sat upon the bank and did just that.

"If your Lady Nora could see you now...." a voice spoke behind her.

She grinned. "She'd have me locked up for the rest of my life."

She heard the sound of stockings and shoes cast off before the young man sat beside her on the bank, his feet entering the water next to hers. "That would be less than you deserve," he said reverently.

She shoved him. "Dorian, if my guardian knew *you* existed in my life, she'd have me locked away in my beloved tower forever."

The young man with gray-black hair and wideset eyes merely shrugged. "I'd toss bits of food up to your window from time to time. Maybe even climb the very walls of Castlehaven, if only to see how happily you were getting on with your books."

Though Dorian was low-born and was—when she allowed herself to admit it—likely a thief who worked with a whole gang of criminals, he spoke as if he understood firsthand every detail of her life. Indeed, she had described every nook of her tower and he understood Lady Nora as well as she did. He was actually acquainted with the prophet. The man had come looking for her once and happened upon the two in their favorite spot, this place where they met as often as possible. In fact, there were many days when one or the other waited hours, hoping the other would arrive. Dorian, she knew, did most of the waiting. He had a free and easy life, from his descriptions, and he loved the woods as much as she did.

"I'm afraid I'd probably prefer you toss up books for consumption," she said. "I cannot imagine reading the same ones over and over for the rest of my life."

"And here I've never read a one."

"Not true, per se. I've read some to you. And there was the one the prophet read out to us." The prophet was the only one who knew of their forbidden friendship and the only one either of them could ever have stood entering their association. As it happened, Dorian knew the prophet nearly as well as she did, for the older man always made certain to visit Dorian when he went to town.

"True," he said with a nod. "His was the best."

"You always say you like mine."

"I do, but it is not always the case. After all, legendary romances are not usually the sort a man of my caliber takes an eager interest in."

She sighed. "Dorian, I have to tell you something."

"I'll try to listen."

"I'm serious. Something... something's wrong with me."

He skipped a rock. "What is it, little one?"

She stole the rocks from his hands and tossed them into the river. Then, she told him her story right down to the moment the prophet told her she would be traveling.

"Hazel... that's *crazy*. People don't lift other people with their *voices*. That's a tall tale, a legend. It must have been a lark."

"But it wasn't. I *promise*."

He stared thoughtfully into the water. "So... if the king consents, you *have* to go."

She nodded. "I confess, I was nearly excited when he spoke of it, but I woke with little courage this morning. After all, I have no idea where I'm to be sent, nor for how long.

"The southern tribes," the prophet spoke behind them.

Hazel spun about. She would be ridiculed for this trip, for yet *another* scandal in her heritage. But what did she care... really? Her life couldn't get much worse. And to be away from *Lady Nora?* PARADISE. "Wait, will I be staying... forever?" Wonderful as forever away from Lady Nora sounded, the thought of living with such a people sent shivers down her spine.

"Nay, it will be a short trip... Just long enough to convince the Assemblage of the Wise that you are being trained there... and for the rest of the kingdom to believe you've been cured."

"What does that mean?"

"It means it is a charade. The gift is not something to be driven out of one. But thanks to King Zephuel, all of Castlehaven will believe the tribes developed a way to abolish it. As far as training goes, it cannot be done while the gift is dormant. Though I do have a friend there who may be able to teach you more about it, I have other motives. While you slept, I heard from the Great One himself that you are to travel to a wood in the south where a cabin of logs will be waiting for you. Within, you will meet a woman."

"Who?"

"She is a prophet, much like me. Her name is Wynn. I have never met her, but she will have known me well."

Hazel blinked back at him. "That makes no sense whatever. Why must I meet her?"

"She possesses something I cannot give. That is all I know."

"Very well. It's better than the dungeons."

The man appeared distant. "When you meet this Wynn," he said pensively, "Tell her hello from me."

"Hold on, *hold* on." Dorian stepped between them. "We're talking about a trip to the *southern region*. Not only are they feral and uncivilized, but the vicinity's said to be crawling with sorcerers and the like." He looked to the prophet. "She can't go there."

The prophet put an arm about him. "Thank you for volunteering, my lad."

Dorian sent him a sidelong glance. "For?"

"Taking her protection under your personal consideration." He looked to Hazel. "The king will send a guardsman, of course, but..."

"You don't think a guardsman can be trusted to care for me?" she questioned.

The prophet didn't nod, but he didn't shake his head either. "Clearly, Dorian will be much more invested in your welfare than some king's guard."

Dorian stepped out from under the prophet's arm. "Much as I am loath to admit it, I am as concerned with Hazel's safety as you are... But I can't just drop everything to go traipsing off with her."

The prophet raised a brow at him and crossed his arms. "What precisely holds you back?"

The defiant shimmer in Dorian's eyes faded. "...Plans."

The prophet smirked. He knew as well as Hazel that Dorian's plans weren't likely to be... above board. "The two of you will leave as soon as you are packed. Dorian, you will be recompensed for your trouble from the king's own treasury. It will be good for you to experience the earning of an honest wage."

Dorian raised a brow. "I won't stoop so low as to take payment for protecting a friend."

The prophet smirked and started away. "Yes, you will," he called back.

Hazel eyed Dorian. "Are you certain you wish to come?"

Placing hands in his pockets, he replied with a huff, "It'll be an adventure."

* * *

Hazel smothered a grin as Dorian tugged at the sleeves of his new clothes, a gift from the prophet—likely more for her sake than his. After all, matters between Kierelia and the southern tribes, though currently amicable, had never been smooth. As a representative of her kingdom, it would do her credit to appear with a personal servant who was well-dressed enough to make her appear like the noble she had never much felt herself to be.

Dorian caught her eyeing him. With the widening of his eyes, he pointed to the baggy lace at the cuff of his sleeve. "You're not telling me the men of your class wear such frivolous garments?"

She shook her head. "But the high servants do. You're apparently here to wait upon me."

He leaned back, crossing his arms. "That's not happening."

She grinned. "Of course not, but you must look like an official of some kind and it is prohibited for you to dress like a royal guardsman."

He shook his head. "Never in my life did I think I'd be headed south to visit the tribes."

"Nor I..."

"You're frightened."

"I am."

"You've no reason to be. I won't let anything happen to you."

She grinned widely this time. Dorian didn't usually speak this way—didn't much care for sharing any kind of sentiment in general. "Thank you, Dorian."

Uncrossing his arms, he shrugged. "It's what I'm paid for."

Hazel had known it would likely be nightfall by the time they arrived at the most northern of the southern tribes, but she hadn't realized they'd be forced to sleep in the carriage most of that night. It wasn't until dawn that the transport entered an ill-worn forest path.

The forest was mostly painted with the green of cedar tree leaves, but it possessed splashes of teal moss up and down nearly every tree trunk, with a gold moss draped from lower branches. The gold appeared purposely placed and she concluded it must possess some use.

At last, she caught sight of the first log structure, before which stood a fur-clad giant of a man with arms crossed and a bow and arrows slung over his shoulder. He did not appear genial. Her heart leaped into her throat when the carriage was drawn to a stop before him. With almost too much gusto, the door was flung open and a great, gloved hand reached in. It was a moment before she realized she was expected to take it. The true girth of the fellow was revealed as he aided her from the carriage steps and onto the dirt-laden path.

"So, *you* are meant to be one of *us*, are you?" he asked with hands on hips.

She gaped up at his form and nodded. "I..." She cleared her throat. "I am."

A moment he eyed her before throwing his head back in laughter. "Well, I have my doubts," he said at last, "but we shall see." He then stole the trunk from her guardsman and started down the path. Uncomfortably, Hazel looked to the stranger, then to Dorian, who remained to gather the rest of their belongings.

"Come along, Lady Hazel of Kierelia," the man called after her. "I will show you the sights."

She looked once more to Dorian, who raised an amused brow and gestured for her to follow the stranger.

"You... are the prophet's friend?" she asked once she'd caught up.

He nodded. "Blythe is the name, in case you hadn't heard it. And this..." He used his elbow to gesture down the path before them. "...is the Clan of the Galmoira."

A line of log cabins stretched before her as the path dwindled into smaller ones, none of which they followed very closely. What she noted next were the draping lines of rope strung throughout from which hung more of the gold moss. As it was altogether unattractive, she couldn't imagine why this was done.

Outside many of the dwellings were blue-moss covered stumps from which tiny-leaved ferns sprouted, while every cabin was covered with ivy vines. This made it almost difficult to recognize the village for what it was. Moreover, it was not sizable, at least by her accustomed standards. It contained but eighteen shelters.

More interesting than the natural landscape were the people they passed, dressed in fur clothes adorned with draping strands of beads and feathers, with bow and arrows strapped upon nearly every back. Never in her life had she seen people sport leather gloves and boots, trimmed in still more fur. But it was the short fur skirts on many of the men that made her brows draw upward.

Moreover, her kingdom rarely saw a bow, let alone these long ones. The sword was the favored weapon of Kierelia, prized above all others. Yet, not one person here carried one. Her poor guardsman would stand out like a sore thumb.

"Galmoira, you say?" she inquired of her guide. "Who is that?"

She caught his smirk, revealing the Galmoira must not be a person at all. "You will see," was his reply.

When they reached the smallest of the cabins, the man hoisted her trunk onto his shoulder and opened the door wide for her. "This, my lady, is where you will reside."

Stepping inside, she was surprised by its pleasantness. Lit by many candles—ten total—it possessed but a small wooden desk and chair and a Kierelian bed layered with frothy furs. This was the extent of the décor, but it somehow put her at her ease.

"This is where your king would be housed if ever he was stalwart enough to venture into our territory," Blythe commented.

She turned back as he set her trunk before the foot of the bed. "The king?"

He nodded. "It is an extravagance to possess a single-man dwelling in our region. Considered wasteful to house no less than two families a home. We have received but your king's lowest ranking emissaries, so they were sheltered along with other clansmen. You may as well know it is considered an insult that King Zephuel has not paid his visit of yet, though he has sat upon that throne two-hundred-thirty Kierelian seasons." He looked to her as if expecting an explanation from her.

"I confess… I have little to do with King Zephuel's affairs. But I am greatly honored to be lodged in this fine structure. It is very appealing."

The man shrugged. "You are the noblest-born emissary we have received. As its first guest, I should hope you'd feel no less."

She merely nodded, uncertain of how to respond.

The large hand was held out to her. Placing her tiny one into it, hers was vigorously shaken. Before stepping out, he drew near once more with, "We will soon determine if you are truly kin."

She blinked after him as he strode back down the path. What if she wasn't? Had there been a threat in the statement? Would the king pay for her lack of their blood? For the first time, she *hoped* the prophet had been correct... that she would not prove a disappointment. And he had called her noble-born, a notion that had not occurred to her. Her own people did not treat her as nobility. She was not even certain she still was, given her parents' banishment. After all, their lands and riches had been seized. She had begun to feel herself merely a homeless orphan-prisoner.

6

Hazel spent hours alone in her small cabin before Dorian arrived with bread and a berry spread, along with a portion of dried pork. This came from Blythe's wife as a mid-day repast.

"Try the meat, I'm telling you," Dorian said, stealing a chunk of it. "I've got to take some of this back. Could sell it for a fine penny. And have you noted how bulky the men are here? My boss would pay men like these handsomely. Of course, they'd have to drop the skirts... or skelts, as they're called. Seems they're meant to display their muscular legs... and the hairier the better."

Hazel had to chuckle at that but was cut short by her owns concerns. "I don't think they like me being here."

"I agree. Bread and berries in your cabin don't make for the warmest of welcomes."

This had been her thinking.

CHRONICLES OF THE CHOSEN

"Blythe doubts I possess their blood. I would as well except… Did you notice their skin?"

"Dark… almost a tint of green."

She held out her own arm. "You see, mine is not so dark, but it has always had that sort of tint in contrast to, say, the creaminess of a typical Kierelian."

He examined her thoughtfully before, "I suppose I had noticed you look different somehow, but as you are so pale, I couldn't put my finger on it." He examined his own arm. "I am also browner than most Kierelians."

She nodded. She doubted her skin was proof enough of the shared bloodline anyway. Perhaps it was easily diluted… though it had survived in enough wholeness to bestow her with a "gift" that was supposed to be extinct.

The two spent the remainder of the day in the cabin. Dorian had tried to convince her to explore with him, but she lacked the courage. Knowing how he hated tedium, she had packed a set of chess, so they were not without entertainment.

When night fell, a knock sounded at the door. Dorian answered to a group of giggling girls not much younger than Hazel. They were tittering over the sight of her friend, which discomfited her until she realized they must find him handsome. With his gray-black hair, he was quite unique to them, as he was in Kierelia as well. But he also possessed bright, amiable eyes and a quick smile for a group of silly girls.

"I don't suppose you affable ladies are here to escort us to some nourishment?" he asked, perhaps more amicably than was necessary.

The girls giggled again before the tallest (a head and a half taller than Hazel) stepped proudly up to her. "Lady Hazel of Kierelia, evening meal is served."

The girls started off. Hazel's stomach growling, she wasted no time in following after them. But she froze as she beheld the spectacle overhead. *Now*, she learned why the suspended ropes of moss. Upon them hung hundreds of stunning winged-creatures who, like lanterns, glowed to illuminate the whole village.

She raced up to the girl who had announced supper. "What are these… these *things*?" She gestured to them.

"Galmoira," the girl replied. "Their feet favor the gold moss, so we make it plentiful where light is needed. They shine all the night long until the sun rises again."

Hazel surveyed them with wide eyes. "Absolutely *fascinating*."

The girl grinned. "We are the only clan that provides a resting place for them."

Hazel nodded with eyes alight. Thus, it was the name of their clan, was what they were identified for. She could see why. It was enchanting—like legends of the fairy-world she'd grown up reading about.

But the spectacle only increased in beauty when she arrived at a dining area with tree stump seats surrounding numerous bonfires. Above this were dozens of golden ropes upon which the greatest number of the Galmoira illumined the diners below.

Dorian gasped, so taken by the spectacle that he bumped into her as she halted to take it in.

"How have we not heard of this in Kierelia?" she murmured.

"Well, *you* know…," he said. "Kierelians do not visit the south for fear they still secretly possess your gift."

"We are fools," the guardsman, whom Hazel had yet to meet, spoke behind them.

She turned to him with new eyes. He was older than most guardsman, she knew, but she had not considered what that had to do with his being selected to escort her south. Seeing his eyes full of as much wonder as she felt, she was certain he'd been the sort to volunteer for the journey.

"I am Lady Hazel," she said as they were led to a firepit at the center.

"I am well aware," he replied with a smile. With a bow, he added, "I am Guardsman Gunther."

She curtsied. "Pleasure to meet you, Guardsman Gunther."

Taking a seat upon the stump beside her, he replied with sincerity, "The pleasure is mine, Lady Hazel."

Soon, skewers of uncooked food were offered to them and they were directed to hold them over the flames. The first of these was a chopped meat glazed in sticky sauce. Once cooked, it warmed the insides with its piquant seasoning.

Hazel closed her eyes as she relished another bite of the scrumptious meat, so tender it nearly slipped off the stick. She was still groaning over the luscious dish when an older clansman sat at her other side. Along with him were a set of young men whom she guessed to be his grandsons... perhaps great-grandsons. He was well-furred but did not sport the skelt. Likely, his legs were to frail from age.

The man smiled at her ecstasy over the morsel. "You like the sauce?" he asked.

She nodded eagerly.

He pointed her attention to Dorian and the guardsman, who appeared to be in discomfort and were discreetly spitting out the food.

"*Dorian,*" Hazel chastised, "whatever is wrong with you? This is *delightful.*"

He only grimaced and offered her his skewer.

"It is too bitter for them," the old man informed.

"But... it is sweet and..."

"Spiced," he supplied. "It is a seasoning that northerners detest. Seems you are the exception."

Hazel had to wonder why it had been offered to them when it was known the Kierelian guests would detest it. Was it some kind of test for her? Or did they not care if guests enjoyed their stay?

The man appeared to follow her thoughts as he said, "Northerners should learn to appreciate what they are given—*too spoiled.*" The last word was accompanied by his spitting into the fire.

To her surprise, she was taken in by his behavior. She smiled and finished Dorian's skewer.

Next came spits of chopped squash, purple root and sprouts. The vegetation charred on the outside while their centers remained fluffy and tender. Hazel thought it nearly as delicious as the glazed meat but pitied her Kierelian attendants when she realized it was coated in the same seasoning as before.

This issue was remedied, however, when a sizable, speared fish was brought to each of them. This was left completely unseasoned, for it possessed its own sweet, creamy flavor. Dorian and Gunther ate it ravenously and asked after second and thirds.

Plucking flakes of meat from his fish, the old man turned to her with pleasure. "You enjoy our southern offerings?"

"Perhaps more so than that in Kierelia," she said easily.

At that, the man released a bout of laughter and beat his knees. "You *are* a great lady, a *great* lady."

She grinned in confusion but happily accepted the next skewer as it was brought to her.

"*That* you will like most of all," he informed. He proceeded to watch her until she had taken her first bite of the shining, sticky sphere.

"*Oh…*" she gasped as the warm fruit hit her taste buds. "It is an *apple…* dipped in toffee!"

The old man nodded with satisfaction and ate of his own dessert, revealing this was a personal favorite.

Once the meal was complete, the elderly man drew to his feet, then held out a hand to help Hazel to hers. "You are most welcome in the Clan of Galmoira, Lady Hazel."

Blythe approached then, offering to see her back to her cabin.

"Thank you, Sir Blythe," she said, feeling content after the pleasant meal.

He snickered and shook his head. "Only Blythe, no 'sir.' We do not hold to your Kierelian customs here."

She nodded serenely and worked to keep up with his long strides.

As they walked, she noticed the people they passed searched her with much more curiosity than they had earlier.

"You have earned favor," Blythe explained.

She turned to him in disbelief. She'd hardly left her cabin that day. "I… do not understand."

"Our most respected elder, Sharin, was pleased with you. Also, you like the havari spice."

Hazel raised her brows. She'd never expected merely *liking food* could assist in her welcome among these strange people.

"Sharin is well-known for his detestation of northerners. He feels they're arrogant and offensive. You, however, were courteous. He will spread the word and it will aid you well."

* * *

The following day, she was awoken from a satisfying slumber upon her fur throws by a hammering at her door. Splashing water over her face, she went to answer.

"Dress, Lady Hazel," Blythe commanded. "You must sing."

She rubbed her eyes. "Sing… I-I don't…"

"You must," he said. "We sing with the birds. I will send your serving-man to escort you." With that, he left her standing in the doorway, heart hammering. Who would she be singing for? Was it customary to awaken one's guest to make them perform? Once Dorian came to fetch her, she would find Blythe and make clear to him she could not perform as ordered.

In a surprisingly short time, Dorian appeared for her. "Your hair is uncombed? How long does it take a maiden to be ready?"

She scowled past her yawn. "It is early."

Dorian soon led her through the village to the place they'd eaten the evening before. The Galmoira had vacated and the fires were but ashes. Half the number who had attended the night before returned that morning. Without any ado whatever, Blythe took her hand and led her to the center. Then, he sat and nodded for her to begin.

This wasn't right. She could not just awaken and do the one thing she loathed more than anything: perform before an audience. But looking to Blythe, she realized he simply would not be foiled. Her mind raced for what to sing. The only song that came to mind was the one she'd sung when her gift had prematurely emerged. She did not like to sing it. She did not like to sing at all. But when she began, it flew from her lips.

Straightaway, she shut her eyes to those around her and her voice came out easier. Singing came naturally to her, so she relied on what flowed instinctively from her lips without any grandeur. Her voice was a little breathy due to nerves and the early hour, but by the end, she knew she'd done well enough.

Moments after her last note, she opened her eyes. Dorian was smirking. Her guardsman appeared about as eager as he could, though he didn't strike her as a man of music. It was a moment before the southerners began to whistle, not in time nor to any specific tune. Uncertain as to what this meant, she gave a weak curtsy and took a seat beside Dorian.

"How come *I* didn't go flying into the air?" he asked as another of the crowd strolled to the center.

She shrugged. "The prophet said I'm not done cooking. I don't think my gift was meant to surface when it did—not until I'm a little older."

"I was joking."

She chuckled but was diverted by the sound of the new voice. It was strong, bright, perfectly pitched at every note. She'd never heard a voice like it before. It easily put her own to shame, but she didn't care. She absorbed the moment for as long as it lasted until it concluded to a myriad of whistles. This, she gathered, was their way of showing appreciation. They responded with the same practice for the next few singers.

At last, Blythe took to the center. Hazel was surprised. He had not struck her as a singer. But when he opened his mouth, the smoothest baritone she'd heard in her life escaped his lips. It was the best of the morning. No one could follow him, nor should they. In fact, she noted a peculiarity to his tone that none other had possessed. She'd heard it before. It was that silver sound of the gift that had rung in her own voice those nights ago...

She raised a brow.

His audience not only whistled but stood and stomped their feet in exaltation. Blythe took no bow but turned to depart from the gathering with the rest of them. Hazel bid Dorian wait for her as she raced after Blythe.

"It's a lie," she said to him, not thinking before she spoke.

He turned on her. "Pardon me, my lady?"

She shook her head. "It is said your people no longer possess the gift, that you should not be feared any longer... But I heard it in your voice just now."

Looking about, he swiftly pulled her aside. "I am the last, to my knowledge."

"Is that why the prophet sent me to you?"

"He hopes I can offer some guidance, but I offer only this: Should it emerge in you, truly, make *no* use of it. Conceal it. And, *certainly,* do not create another spectacle as you did before."

"*You* do not use it?"

"I have not used it in its truest nature since I was a boy. It is not prudent in this age… It is too dangerous, too priceless. I apply it only enough to enhance the beauty of my voice for its listeners."

"I don't understand."

"As you must know, one with such a gift is considered a threat. To some, it is a great weapon. Either way, it is perilous."

"Don't your own people know you possess it?"

"Only two friends from my youth."

"Do you… know the extent of the gift? Is it like the tales of old?"

"About all I can do is sway a few tree branches as if by the wind. But if the tale of what you did is true… that is like the old ones. Should it surface in you, *quench it.*"

Hazel was not surprised by this advice after what she had heard in the Assemblage of the Wise. Their first thought had been to weaponize her. She did not want that.

"Even so," he continued, "you are highly favored of the Great Entity. You must understand that it is a pronounced honor to possess the voice."

Her head dropped. "I confess I am not an exceptional person by any stretch, not at all liked among my own. If I do possess the gift… I believe it was a fluke."

He grunted. "The Entity does not make mistakes. Your people are supercilious, godless…" He paused a moment to study her face. "Not getting on with them does you credit."

* * *

It was many days before Blythe informed her that he would have her taken to the place the prophet wished her to visit. "It is revered ground among our tribes. We wished to see that you could be trusted to be respectful of it."

"What makes it so sacred?"

He eyed her a long while before shaking his head and answering, "Visions."

"I see... May I take Dorian, er, my manservant, along?"

He nodded.

It was some time before Hazel, Dorian and their guide, the youngest grandson of the elder with whom she'd eaten her first evening, arrived before an ill-kept cabin. Though it was, like all the others, made from logs, its construction varied from the rest.

"Your people did not build this?" she inquired of their guide.

"None know its maker and none go to live in it."

Hazel nodded as if she understood, but it was becoming an absorbing mystery to her. She approached the windows. "It's empty," she complained. There was not within but cobwebs and piles of dust—not a single stitch of furniture.

He nodded. "None go to live in it."

But the prophet told her she was to meet a woman named Wynn. Though the place was dirty, dusty and utterly vacant, someone must be concealed within... or this was not the correct place.

"Are you certain this is where the prophet meant me to go?"

"It is the hallowed dwelling."

Hazel shook her head and looked to Dorian, who cared little for their errand. Even so, he stepped up to the front step and tried the doorknob. "It's locked."

Hazel rubbed her chin. "Knock."

He did so.

Nothing.

The two turned to their guide, who shrugged. "It has always been so."

Hazel followed Dorian as he made his way around the house.

"Here's another door," he said before waltzing up to try the knob. It swung open. They looked to one another with raised brows.

"It's a corridor," he said, stepping inside.

They made their way through until they came upon a sight that made them both fall back a step. What had previously appeared as an empty room from the outside glowed with a lit hearth before which rested two wooden chairs that held a duo of knitting women.

"Oh," Hazel gasped, looking back to their guide, who had just marched up behind them. He froze, wide-eyed and mouth agape.

At her sound, the ladies looked up from their knitting to find the three standing in the hall.

"Er…what can I help you with, you silly dears," the redheaded woman, who could not be any older than Hazel, inquired. When none answered, she added, "Since you have already helped yourselves through the back door, you are most welcome to enter."

Hazel and Dorian did as told, but their guide remained in the hall.

"Um…" Hazel began in confusion. "I-I have come to see the prophet, Wynn. I require her aid."

Upon these words, the two women before the hearth eyed one another with near smirks. They then tossed their knitting into the fire, leaped to their feet and strapped swords around their waists.

Marching to where Hazel and Dorian stood, the redhead inquired, "What is the matter? A dark dragon attack? A broken leg? Sick child, perhaps?"

Hazel took another step back, shaking her head. "I must but meet this Wynn."

The redhead smirked and settled into her boots. "I am she. Who has sent you?"

"Oh, pardon me... I am Hazel and this is Dorian. We hail from the kingdom of Kierelia. I have been sent by King Zephuel's prophet."

The dark-haired woman sauntered up beside Wynn.

"Ivi..." Wynn started in confusion, "Was not King Zephuel in rule over a *hundred* years past?"

Ivi nodded, then turned to Hazel. "I'm afraid you have traveled to us from another time. The land upon which you stand is, in fact, now part of the Kierelian kingdom. And as for the prophet of whom you speak, I do believe he is both my great, great-grandfather and her mentor..." She gestured to Wynn.

Hazel lifted her brows. This notion was preposterous. "We cannot have passed through *time*. We have merely passed through a *door*."

"Yes," Wynn agreed. "But you have passed through the door of a very peculiar cabin."

At her words, the fire in the hearth snuffed out.

"I mean it is *special*," Wynn corrected as if she'd affronted the dwelling. "And the door through which you passed is especially so. It is a portal that leads to a variety of places... Though I have yet to witness a passage through time until now."

Dorian stepped up. "It cannot *really* be that you could know our prophet, if indeed we have somehow traveled through time. He is *very* old already. He cannot live for another hundred years."

"Oh, he doesn't," Ivi replied. "But he did..."

"Much like this house," Wynn began, "he is a very peculiar man."

"Look," Hazel said, "the prophet sent me to meet you, claiming you had something for me, something he could not give."

Wynn turned to Ivi, consternation on her face. "You don't think...?"

"That it should be sent back in time? That *would* be awfully queer."

"But perhaps that is how *you* receive it… in the line of time?"

Hazel was quite lost at this point.

"You might place it in her hands," Ivi suggested. "See if anything happens."

"But she is so… little."

"As if you can talk, friend."

Indeed, Wynn was shorter even than Hazel, though much more sturdily built.

"What *is* it?" Hazel asked, now more curious than ever.

Wynn appeared loath to do whatever it was she felt she must. Squinting as if in pain, she pulled a crystalline ruby sword from the scabbard at her side… and held it out for Hazel.

"Oh," Hazel gasped, holding her hands up. "I don't *want* it." The term "weaponize her" raced through her mind.

Wynn nodded. "Take it into your hand."

Hazel raised a brow and slowly held out her hand. When the hilt hit her skin, the tip of the blade dropped to the floor, but it was the sudden burst of light that stemmed from the touch that caused her to release it entirely.

"Oh, you must be *kidding*…" Wynn muttered toward the ceiling.

With an amused smirk, Ivi said, "Well, Hazel of early Kierelia, it appears you are the blade's subsequent master."

"When that angel, Viijelyk, said it would not be mine forever…" Wynn said, "I did not realize I'd have to give it up *so* soon. I have had it but a *year*…" She picked it up and looked at it as if it were her child. "Well…" she sighed out. "I'll go find you a scabbard." She exited and returned with a very worn one. "I know it isn't much, but I'm not giving you my good one. It was a gift."

"What was a gift?" a fellow—even taller than Blythe—inquired as he traipsed through the front door. Seeing Ivi and Wynn standing before Hazel and Dorian, with their guide standing yet wide-eyed in the hall, he placed hands on hips and released a bout of laughter. "Well, it didn't take long for the two of you to give up your trial at ordinary life," he said to Wynn and Ivi.

Wynn scoffed. "Phillip, it was awful. I shan't try it again." She thrust the scabbard containing the ruby sword at Hazel. "It will serve you well, whatever your need may be."

Hazel accepted it but dreaded the idea of ever actually needing it. Really, what had the prophet been thinking, sending her through time—if she truly had done such a thing—to fetch a *weapon*? Hadn't he been the one to stand up for her against such a notion?

When it was clear she was having trouble strapping it on, Ivi knelt to help her. "How is he... the prophet, I mean?" she asked.

"He was well when last I saw him. Oh, he said to say hello from him."

"Well..." Wynn spoke from behind Iviana, "that isn't much."

"The *prophet?*" the tall man inquired with an edge of emotion.

Wynn nodded. "A younger version of him. They've come from the past. He doesn't know us yet."

"Oh, but he knows *of* you," Hazel said in an attempt to comfort. The three seemed to need it. "He said he would one day know you well." She didn't mention he'd really only said this of Wynn, but it was clear he would one day know all of them.

Phillip grinned. "Peculiar man."

"Wait," Iviana said as she stood to her feet. "You say you are from the time of King Zephuel's reign?" She appeared concerned. "How are... things?"

Hazel's stomach soured. "They are well enough... Why do you ask?"

"It is no matter," Wynn put in swiftly, eyeing Ivi. "You ought to get back to it, Hazel of a younger Kierelia, and... well, good luck to you."

With that, Hazel found herself and the two with her pressed out the back door. Before she knew it, the three strangers were waving with forced smiles as the door was slammed in her face. In a moment, it disappeared altogether.

Gasping, Hazel raced to the front of the house to peer through the windows. Absolutely nothing. She tried opening the window next and, with Dorian's aid, was hoisted inside. *"Nothing!"* she called back. She popped her head out the window. "What was all that business with the concerned expressions and wishes of good luck?" She leaped to the ground.

Dorian raised his brows. "Beats me. I'd as soon not know. If a thing is meant to happen, it'll happen, I should think."

But the guide only gazed upon the shelter, eyes enormous.

"Er... what did you say your name was," Hazel inquired, jostling his hand a bit.

The young man snapped to attention. "It's Kai... Did we just, did that really just... was that the red-haired maiden, *truly*?"

Hazel raised a brow. "What do you know about the redhaired woman?"

"Visions of her are often seen by those who enter this part of the forest. For generations, she's been known. But no one knew *who* she was—if she had been, was to come, or was but a wood nymph... Now, *I* know." He looked into her face. "I thank you, Lady Hazel, for the pleasure of escorting you."

Well, that was quite a change from his attitude coming in. "We must tell Blythe what we have seen."

He pointed to the sword at her side. "And show him *that*."

Hours later, Blythe studied the delicate blade in his hands. "We do not use such weapons. Still, it is clear this is a fine specimen." Setting it down upon Hazel's desk, he said, "Lady Hazel, you have done what none other of the tribes has. You have met the redhaired maiden… and received a gift from her. Surely, you possess the blood of the southern tribes."

Hazel wasn't entirely certain it had anything to do with her bloodline, but it would do her good to be accepted among the clan. "I am honored you believe it is so."

He appeared amazed at the thought she might think anything else. "We must perform the ceremony of rights—the right to kinship with the great southern tribes. Even as you travel back to your kingdom, you must remember that your homeland is with us and that you take our loyalty with you."

Astonished by these sentiments, she curtsied deeply. "Truly…" she began, clearing her throat at her sudden emotion. "I am made speechless by such an oath." She bowed again. "I thank you and promise my loyalty in return."

"That may be a difficult promise to keep when among your people," he said with a half-smile. "But I do not believe you will break it. You are not of that sort."

At evening meal, Hazel received more attention than she had the whole of her life. Many actually fought over seats around her bonfire while others crowded around to cook her food. In the end, the entire clan gathered to hear her recite the tale of her journey through time. By the end of her story, the crowd whistled their appreciation.

After this, they performed the ceremony of rights. Blood was not drawn from her, as she'd feared. She was only made to wrap her wrist around the end of a teal ribbon as Blythe wrapped his at the other end. Then, they sang together. Though they'd had but a short time to practice a song that was utterly new to her, their voices blended in harmony that sent the hairs of her arms on end. It was resplendent. When they'd finished, the crowd both whistled and stomped their feet and even Gunther, her guardsman, applauded.

Hazel remained only another seven days, during which time she and her traveling companions were included in the everyday activities. Among these people, Hazel found acceptance she'd never experienced and it brought healing to the wounds of her past. Indeed, the longer she remained, the smaller Dianna and her cronies appeared. Even Lady Nora seemed so much less grand, someone Hazel felt she could stand up to.

So, it was with a heavy heart that she received the news she would make the journey home. As a parting gift, she was presented with a fur blanket, bow and arrows and a caged galmoira. She was grateful for everything, but when presented with her own *galmoira*, along with a large basket of the golden moss, she was brought to tears. To have her own glowing pet of the southern clan would be like taking them with her. Whether or not she was ever permitted to return again, she could never forget this "untamed" people, nor the love she had developed for them and they for her.

Once the carriage started off, Dorian pointed to the cage in her lap. "That, I believe, is all the proof you need that those people *adored* you by the end."

She nodded, batting tears from her cheeks. "I rather liked them too."

"Not that I desire to lose your company, but… why don't you just stay with them?"

She shook her head. "I was not asked to. Moreover, I do not know that I could become accustomed to living as they do for the rest of my life. Though I share their blood and love them greatly, I have been raised in a completely different way of life."

He nodded. "That is sound—perhaps even wise. But now… *Lady Nora*."

7

azel realized she had not experienced the true wrath of Lady Nora until she attempted to say *no* to her. She'd often made small, hopeless efforts. But when at last she put her foot down... she found herself shoved against a wall.

"I will be speaking to my brother, the *king,* about this!" Lady Nora shouted, proceeding to lock the bedroom door behind her.

But Hazel's newfound spirit was not broken. After all, she *liked* to be alone in her chambers and always kept a trove of books under her bed. She'd taken to doing so when her guardian had learned her fondness for them and began to remove them as punishment. Therefore, Hazel paid her cleaning maid with teacakes in order to keep them hidden under the large bed. Now, she was forced to crawl under, but coming out swathed in dust was well worth it.

Laying upon her bed, she opened the book but paused as the realization hit her that Lady Nora would speak to the *king* about her. Yet, not even this thought could sway her. She meant to make changes to her life and that included saying no when she felt it was appropriate. As it was, Lady Nora was only asking her to watch over her youngest daughter—"the little tyrant," as the castle called her. Hazel had often done so and, in fact, had something of a knack for handling the child. But when she realized it was meant as a punishment for having too much enjoyed her trip to the southern region, she could not bear to give her guardian the benefit of easy compliance.

Her eyes went to the ruby bedposts. For the first time in her life, she felt them watching her, in their way. They reminded her of something… the sword Wynn had given her. She wished it was not stashed away in her tower room so she might examine it alongside them. Could it be that it was truly formed of ruby? Could it even be that it was *Bashtiian* ruby? After all, it had glowed in her hand. Unable to do anything more about discerning its make-up, she shrugged off the thought and started into her book.

* * *

"King Zephuel wishes to speak with you, Hazel," Lady Nora said two days following. By this time, Hazel had not been fed since the morning she'd been locked away and her initial spirits had greatly dwindled. "He is in the confrontation room."

With a sigh, Hazel drew to her feet.

"Tell me you do not think it appropriate to make a special visit to the king dressed in that rumpled gown," Lady Nora reproached. "I will select something for you."

To Hazel's astonishment, the woman pulled out the wine-hued, crushed velvet gown. She'd been told it had been her mother's. Certainly, she'd never thought to wear it, nor would her guardian have wished her to. Slipping into it, she realized Lady

Nora by no means wished her to make a good impression upon the king. She was to be looked upon in the darkest light... the light of her murderous parents, whose blood he'd seen in her child-face that had made him decide she must be raised as a fortunate captive.

A hundred retorts entered her mind, but she found her spirits more dwindled by the last two days than she'd realized. If she had not had the company of her galmoira (which most often hung from the rope of moss she'd constructed in the rafters with the help of a manservant), she would've been worse off still.

Her guardian planted her before the mirror, placing hands on her shoulders. "You see what you are, don't you?"

My, how Lady Nora detested her. Yet... Hazel was forced to conceal a smile. For the first time in her life, she *liked* her appearance. She'd gained color during her stay with the clan and the hue of the gown was becoming to her. She no longer appeared ill. She looked *well*.

"It is your *mother*," Lady Nora hissed. "Keep *that* in mind when before my brother."

Hazel did smile then, though her back was turned as she started for the door. She *would* keep in mind what she'd found in the mirror. But her thoughts raced over precisely what the king would speak to her about. Total submission to her guardian, certainly... But she had not seen him since the evening her gift had emerged. Thus far, none from the castle had spoken to her about. After all, she'd been away some time. And she was meant to be cured. But King Zephuel was one of the few who knew otherwise. She felt certain he would confront her about it... in his confrontation room.

At last, she came to the door and gave it a weak knock. Shaking her head at herself, she knocked again, solidly. At the king's behest, she entered.

The coziness of the room was startling. She'd always imagined it like a room of interrogation, complete with torture devices. Instead, there were cushioned chairs placed on either side of a small table.

King Zephuel sauntered toward her. Taking her by the hand, he led her to one of the seats. "Lady Hazel, how well you are looking," he said warmly.

It was all she could do to keep her wits about her. Of course, he had no recollection of whose dress she wore—not like a woman would. He was thus far treating her with more consideration than ever before.

"Good morning, King Zephuel," she murmured.

"Please, we are cousins. When alone, I hope you will call me Cousin Zephuel."

Her brows shot to her forehead. "Yes, your majesty."

He smiled. "What have I just said?"

She closed her eyes in embarrassment and corrected, "Yes, Cousin Zephuel."

Pulling his chair beside hers, he said, "Now, I've no wish to beat about the bush. Your Cousin Nora wished me to speak with you and so speak with you I will. Unhappily, I have heard the rumor going around… about why I chose to keep you here when you were a child."

She swallowed. This was not the turn she had expected. Was the charade of niceties to fail now? Would she be cast into the dungeon?

"I…" he began. "Well, forgive me, but I must verify its authenticity."

She shut her eyes to him, swallowing the pain of this moment, when her seemingly kind cousin, who'd never spoken an ill word to her, turned on her to her face. "I understand, Cousin Zephuel."

He shook his head. "The conversation that was overheard was only part of what was spoken. As it happens, I was speaking with the prophet about how *proud* I am to see how you've grown. You've utterly debunked my embittered expectations. You are patient, unassuming, meek." He paused here as if to gauge her response.

"Cousin Zephuel, I... don't know what to say..."

He smiled warmly and patted her hand. "And then there was that day the prophet summoned you to our council. The word of wisdom you offered about the lumber was not only well-spoken but the perfect solution. Truly, I must do something I very much loathe... and that is to admit I was *wrong*. You've grown into a pleasant young woman and I am proud to call you my young cousin."

Hazel's eyes filled. What agony she had suffered since that fateful game of Affrontery. Why, if she could have known there'd been more to the conversation Dianna had overheard, she would not have been so emotional that evening and her gift might never have emerged.

But upon that revelation, her mind hit a snag... The tears dried on her face.

"Cousin..." she began slowly, her mind racing. "You are a noble king, well worthy of the post you more than adequately fill. That such words should come from you means the world."

With a large smile, he stood and led her to the door. "I am glad you receive them so easily. After all, I cannot imagine how painful it has been to have such nasty gossip spoken about you. I will do my best to stifle it."

Bowing low before him, she said, "I hope you will not trouble yourself too greatly." Presently, she strode from the room and listened as the door locked from the other side. Grasping her neck, she froze where she stood.

He was afraid of her. She turned around and stood as if to gaze through the door, recalling the generous countenance of the man beyond it. He feared what she might one day be capable of. That meeting had been his way of gaining assurances, checking in on the girl he'd always feared would one day turn against him. It had seemed a good plan to keep her about. He'd just never dreamed she might come to possess power as had been displayed in her voice.

His fear... was absolutely erroneous.

Contrary to his apparent belief, she'd always felt profound loyalty for him, *stubbornly* so. Perhaps it was only a kind of useless revenge against her parents and all they'd stood for in her life. Yet, she knew it went deeper than that. Despite how the castle, the kingdom, felt about her, she was deeply invested in its wellbeing. It was true she did little to contribute. But she loved the very ground they walked on, the trees of the forest, the rock from which the castle had been built—the very stone stolen from Mount Tier. She treasured the animals, even the people (though far preferring the common folk to the nobility).

Well, King Zephuel could *drown* in his fear for all she cared. But he need *never* suffer her betrayal—not even if her parents offered to swoop in and rescue her from the dreadful place. But even after these thoughts... she almost wished she'd chosen to remain in the south. Even so, there was something in her that remained devoted to *this* land, felt a kinship with *this* place, even if not with its people.

She had to wonder if anything he'd just spoken was even true. Had he noticed she'd turned out nothing like her parents, that she was truly—how she hated the word—meek? Or had that been an attempt to cover up what he'd never meant her to learn? He'd claimed he was speaking about her to the prophet. When next she saw her friend, she would inquire.

Lady Nora swooped around the corner. Seeing the state her ward was in, a smirk crept onto her face. "I trust your meeting was beneficial?"

If only her guardian had witnessed how the king had treated her. If only she knew the king was *afraid* of her. "Indeed, it was... informative."

8

It was the following day when a maid entered Hazel's bedroom with wide eyes. "My lady, I... I'm afraid your presence is required in the royal throne room."

Hazel startled. *"My* presence... in the throne room? Whatever for?"

The girl appeared concerned. "I'm afraid a lad has been found guilty of thievery and treason... He claims *you* will speak for him."

Hazel couldn't imagine who would make such a claim, but a terrible possibility came to her as she made her way through the halls. She had always known in the back of her mind that Dorian was often up to no good... even illegal activity. But to have been found guilty of treason? She couldn't imagine it of her friend. She moved faster, hiking up her skirts as her heart began to pound. There was none other who could claim her loyalty. It had to be him.

At last, she strode through the double doors of the throne room. She had but a moment to cast her eyes upon her gown and be grateful she had dressed in a finer one than usual. If one was to come before the king on his throne, one must present themselves accordingly.

These thoughts proved inconsequential when the fears toiling in her stomach were validated. Marching past the incarcerated Dorian, who looked to her with bright, pleading eyes, she stood before King Zephuel.

"Your highness," she said breathlessly, bowing low before him.

The warm nature he'd possessed in their meeting of the day before had turned cold. "Lady Hazel, what is the meaning of this?"

"King Zephuel, I-I am not aware of why I have been summoned."

"Aren't you? Then you are not a friend of this *vagrant?*"

"Er... yes... I am." The room was suddenly buzzing with gasps and whispers. "But I am in no way familiar with why he should be found here," she added quickly.

The king bent forward. "It has been discovered he is part of a conspiracy against the crown. This very day, he was found stealing from the royal coffers, along with those whom we have recently been made aware were storing up weapons to use against me. Do *you* know anything about this?"

Hazel's head was spinning. She had never been the fainting sort but feared she was about to become it. "I do not," she said through a strained throat.

"His group is part of an underground organization which seeks to remove the current royal line from rule."

She shut her eyes to these words. It simply could not be. It was a lie. First, her parents. Now, supposedly, her dear friend. She turned to Dorian.

Stepping toward him, she murmured, "Dorian… is this true?" It came out in a sob.

His eyes, which moments before had been pleading, fell to the floor. His head hung low. This was her answer.

"Oh, how could you?" she whispered. "How *could* you?"

He offered no response.

"Lady Hazel," the king spoke, redirecting her attention to him. "This young man is due a lifetime in prison for his part in this treason but says *you* will speak for his character… that he is redeemable."

Hazel was sinking through the floor. This was a test of loyalty. King Zephuel assumed she was part of this underground conspiracy. Defending Dorian in any way would paint her guilty. In the end, her heart chose her response. And it was bleeding.

"Your highness…" she gasped. "I have known this boy for some years only as a friend from the forest. I… confess to loneliness." She swallowed and stood straighter. "I am now of the opinion this has clouded my judgment. I *cannot* speak for him. Indeed, I discover I do not know him at all." It cut her to speak it as tears pooled down her face.

Astonishingly, the king's eyes softened ever so slightly toward her. "I thank you for this insight, Lady Hazel. You are free to go."

He *believed* her. She was saved. But Dorian's destiny was set in stone and she had made no attempt to save him. She worked not to look at him when she turned to leave, but her peripheral told her he watched after her, trying to communicate something. Did he hate her? Of course he did.

Racing through the castle corridors, she cared not who saw her. She could not see them through tear-filled eyes anyway. At last, she found where the door to her tower room stood that day. Rather inconveniently, it was just outside the passage to the dungeons. She glanced a moment down that dark stairwell, utterly terrified for Dorian to live out the remainder of his days in such a place. She'd been there but once, having sneaked down in curiosity. It had been desperately cold, dirty and filled with the howls of prisoners. It was true, the kings of Kierelia ruled justly, so there were no torture devices to her knowledge and it was not so foul as it might have been. But it was a something in the atmosphere that did one in. It was demoralizing.

Shaking her head at the compassion that wrung her heart, she thrust open the tower door and raced up the stairs. It had been some time since she'd visited and a soft cloud of dust was illuminated in the sunlight that shone through the window. Though she had always found such a sight attractive, she took up her dust rag and began to clean with more vigor than she had in her life. No matter what chore Lady Nora had put to her, nor how angry she'd been with her, she'd never abused furniture and floor the way she did in the time it took her to set the room to shining. Once finished, she hurled the cloth against the far wall.

Dorian... more than a criminal, a *traitor*... just like her parents. All three were traitors to the very land she so loved, though she could never say just why. She supposed loyalty was in her nature in a way it was not in theirs.

For Dorian to have supposed she would *speak* for him, save him? He had outed her before the court within her home that was already full of those who looked down on her. Had he not considered how it would look? What danger he might put her in? He knew of her struggles to overcome her history, to get past the rumors about why the king had allowed her to stay. But he had been selfish.

Yet, the extent of his self-interest could not be discerned until she'd spoken with him. And speak with him, she must. She could not rest until she'd gotten some answers. First, she must settle herself. This endeavor required a clear mind. She must be prepared to read his face. She had no idea if she'd receive any truth from him the whole of their friendship. She had no idea if he'd ever been true. Her mind raced over the years she'd known him. Some of it had to be real... didn't it?

* * *

The sun had set before she was prepared to descend from her tower... and into the dungeon below. The passage was dim, lit only by torches spaced perhaps too far apart. She wondered if this had been done in an effort to inspire dread in the prisoners who descended. Even she was filled with trepidation.

A guard stood below. When she relayed who she wished to visit, he did not stop her. Perhaps he'd been told to expect her or perhaps he simply did not care. Having been informed that Dorian was held in the cell at the very end of the prison, she was forced to travel past dozens of prisoners. Their behavior was like a nightmare, but she continued forward, ignoring them as they howled and hooted after her.

At last, she came to the cell containing the silent prisoner. He was crouched upon the floor with arms wrapped around his knees, his cheek pressed against the wall.

"Dorian..." she said softly.

Slowly, he raised his head. "I didn't expect you'd come," he said numbly.

"Just tell me it isn't true... that *some* part of it isn't true."

He smirked, but it held no joy, only a sort of drunken hopelessness. "I can't do that."

"But *why* did you do it?"

He crawled closer to where she stood. "How can you be so surprised? Surely, you hold no love for a king who thinks so ill of you? Who your own parents wished to see dethroned? Don't tell me you've never considered they had good reason?'"

"I couldn't care less what their reasons were in so much as it concerns whether their actions were correct. I have never for a moment been in agreement with what they attempted. I am thoroughly ashamed of them."

"And you are ashamed of me as well, now?"

"*Indeed*, I am. How can you think King Zephuel deserves to be robbed and betrayed like this? He is fair with the poor, with all his subjects. Every king in his line has been so."

"You think it is fair he lives in splendor while the rest lead thankless lives?"

She shook her head. "I cannot fathom your thinking at all. Are you saying you wish him and his kind brought to your way of life or you raised to theirs?"

"Why should one man get to lord it over a bunch of regular folk, make them pay taxes they could be putting to better use?"

"Dorian, there is a price to being a leader as well, I assure you. You shake your head, but I have seen it—the toll it has taken on my cousin. That's right: *my cousin.* As in, I am one of those whom you despise. He has aged considerably. Only a man in his forties, the gray upon his head grows daily. I have read in my books all about what a terrible responsibility it is to be king."

"Oh, your *books*... the very things you use as an escape from *these people.*"

"I *am* 'these people,' whether either of us likes it or not. You are *so* selfish! Has it ever occurred to you to *earn* a better place in this world rather than to take it?"

Slowly, he scooted away from her, back into the shadows. If she knew him at all, his mind was open to what she was saying. He had acted a fool, but he wasn't one deep down. But it was too late now. He had received his sentence.

"Dorian, did... you befriend me to gain information about the castle workings?"

Silence.

"I need an answer."

"It wasn't my idea."

Her world really and truly spun then. She sank to the floor.

"But it wasn't like that," he protested. "At least… not after a while. Yes, the gang put me up to it, to befriending the lonely girl who passed time in the forest… But it wasn't long before I felt true friendship for you. You're the only friend I've ever had, the *best*. I even stopped feeding the men information you gave me."

She gasped with sudden revelation. "Did you agree to go south with me in an attempt to recruit the aid of the tribes?"

"I…"

She leaped to her feet. "And you say I am your friend!"

"I *meant* what I said about protecting you. I wouldn't have let anyone hurt you."

"But *you* have hurt me… more than anyone else ever has. All these years we've known one another, I thought you were *my* only friend. Turns out I had so much less than that. I had a backstabbing, conniving…" She caught herself. She wasn't that person. She didn't have it in her to go there. She stole a moment to breathe. "I truly cared about you. Sickening as it is… I still do," she spoke the last with a sob. "I will come see you from time to time… see how you're doing."

"Don't come," he spat.

She grasped the bars of his cell, wishing she had the strength to shake them. "You're seriously going to reject me *now*?! I'm *trying* to be a friend to you!"

"I don't deserve it."

"You think I don't *know* that?!" Dropping her arms, she huffed and started away. He wasn't worth the trouble.

"I *mean* it, Hazel," he called after her. "Don't come back."

She clenched her fists. He didn't understand. Of course he couldn't. He was scum. But he was scum who had been her friend... all she'd had outside the prophet. It had been them against the world. Her enemies were his and vice versa, at least verbally. The thought of losing that completely, no matter how make-believe it had been, made her feel utterly deserted.

* * *

"You sent for me, Lady Nora," Hazel said as she entered her guardian's private quarters. Rarely, was she summoned here, as if her presence might sully the finery. This evening was an exception as Lady Nora was being readied for the banquet that evening.

"I thought, after all that has occurred of late, we were due for a chat. Take a seat beside me and polish my nails."

Hazel took up the buffer and did as told.

"You have shamed me time and again, girl. Yesterday's event... has nearly undone me."

Hazel's brows rose. The woman certainly didn't look undone. But even for an unloving guardian, she could well understand why her cousin was ashamed of her. "I am sorrier for my friendship with that young man than I can find words to express."

"Yes, well, I wouldn't wish to hear it anyway. What's done is done. You've displayed this reckless power, affronted poor Dianna, even resisted my authority. It really isn't worth mentioning your having been found a relative of the southern tribes... Not forgetting, of course, the disgrace of your *parents'* blood, which we have never quite been able to overcome, have we?"

Hazel's blood boiled. If she had to hear about her parents' sins one more time, she would wring someone's neck.

Lady Nora ripped her hair from the maidservant's hands to face

Hazel. *"Really,* child, I cannot think what else is to be done with you."

Hazel dropped her head in an effort to conceal the burning behind her eyes. Many times, she had endured discussions like this. For whatever reason, she had been gifted with the patience to stomach them, to persevere under such remarks. This evening, however, it was difficult to maintain the attitude expected of her. Yet, with the traitorous Dorian having outed her as his friend, she felt it all the more important to behave. It gave Lady Nora too much to work with should the notion occur to her to have her cast into prison beside him.

"We must have you off my hands," the woman said at last. "I cannot bear the burden of you any longer."

Hazel stopped her buffing and looked up with wide eyes. *Would* her cousin have her imprisoned?

"I've got your attention now, have I? Well, it's about time. This evening, we will adorn you more splendidly than you have ever been."

This was not what Hazel had expected.

Lady Nora took hold of her chin and turned it from side to side. "Surely, there must be something to be done to make such a face becoming enough to hook a Galfreen duke."

Hazel blinked back at her. "You *wish* me wedded to a duke?" Then, the country of which she spoke set in. Galfree was across the sea and on Bashtii's opposite border. The thought of going so far filled her with trepidation.

"I do if it will reward me handsomely… and it will. Moreover, it would send you far away from me. I have heard the duke has had trouble landing a bride in his own country, so he seeks one here and offers sufficient remuneration."

"But that's akin to-to… *selling* me."

"You've no dowry, girl. You'll take what you can get. And it's more than you deserve. Let that cursed 'gift' of yours be Galfree's problem. We want none of it here."

Hazel flung the buffer down harder than she meant, sending her guardian to her feet.

"How can you be so ungrateful for this chance I mean to win you?" Lady Nora asked as if truly incredulous.

Hazel glared back. She was near eruption. If her guardian forced her to answer, she would. But it would cost her, she was certain.

"Shall I escort Lady Hazel to her chambers and have her prepared handsomely for the banquet?" the maid asked.

Lady Nora's eyes glowered over Hazel, but she relented.

Hazel released a breath as she followed the maid, Bretta, from the room. "You saved me," she whispered to the girl, uncertain if she would even wish it referred to.

The maid offered a small smile but said nothing.

Hazel had always thought the girl truly loyal to Lady Nora, being the lady's favored maid. But though she may be as loyal as ever, she possessed compassion enough for Hazel. And she was certainly loyal enough to Lady Nora as she scrubbed, lotioned and beautified Hazel to her utmost. By the end, Hazel was both stunned and horrified by the spectacle of herself in the mirror. She was *glowing*. Dressed in white, her hair twisted this way and that, her skin warmed by the southern sun, she looked well indeed.

"I wish I could thank you for this," she said to Bretta.

The girl offered a pitying smile. "I must do as I am bid... as must you."

That was a piece of advice Hazel was in no mood to receive. Her only hope of the evening was that either this duke would find her unattractive or she might find him, in the least, kindly. As it was, she knew nothing of him but that he'd been unable to find a bride in his own kingdom. And, he was willing to purchase a bride.

That was a disturbing concept.

9

Visions of a far too portly, perhaps grossly unattractive gentleman played through Hazel's mind as she made her way to the evening meal. Qualms of excessive drinking or cruelty worse than her guardian's also contributed to the sour stomach she suffered.

"There you are," Lady Nora said amicably, taking her by the arm more gently than ever she had. The woman had a part to play this evening and she meant to earn her reward. "My dear, you look *lovely*," she said so those nearby would hear.

Hazel could not seem to muster the smile she knew her guardian desired. She merely nodded a thank you and awaited her fate. With a brow raised, Lady Nora led her through the crowd, stopping to ask someone where she might find Duke Fredrick of Galfree. The gentleman pointed and the woman lost no time in dragging Hazel that way.

Clearing her throat, Lady Nora proceeded to tap the duke on the shoulder. She was all smiles, prepared to promote her ward as she never had before, but she faltered when he turned around, a look of irritation written plainly on his face. Yet, it was not his expression that made the woman momentarily speechless. It was the fact he was nearly better looking than Prince Armond.

After a moment, Lady Nora regained her composure and pressed on. "M-may I present my distant cousin and ward, Lady Hazel." As he held out a hand to greet Hazel, the guardian looked between them as if reconsidering what she had purposed for her shameful ward.

The man bowed congenially enough but did not appear to be harboring much interest in the introduction. But it was clear Lady Nora had recalculated the reward, for she bid the duke escort her ward to a seat beside him at the feasting table.

Hazel did not know what to make of this turn of events. Surely, there were far more important aspects to a person than their appearance, but that he should be utterly unable to find a bride to the extent of requiring a reward was quite beyond her. After all, he possessed both looks and fortune as well as a title, even if Galfree was a tiny kingdom.

"Is… this your first visit to Kierelia, Sir Duke?" she inquired, proud of her effort to overcome her timidity.

"Indeed," he replied, making no attempt to further the conversation.

Starting into the first course, she shrugged. It was just as well he held no interest in her. Not only did she possess no desire of moving so far from her homeland, her heart was spoken for, though none knew it. She glanced down at Armond flirting with Lady Clarice and contemplated whether she preferred this to his consorting with Dianna. Clarice was a benevolent, graceful girl and would make a fine future queen of Kierelia. She supposed, if it came to it, she'd rather he end up with someone who could actually make him happy. But as it was, Armond was beloved of every lady he met. The conversation she witnessed likely meant nothing.

Noticing that the gentleman on the duke's left made no attempt at friendliness with his neighbor, Hazel concluded it fell to her to make another attempt at civility. It was queer none seemed interested in speaking with him. She put it down to the fact he had appeared in their kingdom prepared to *purchase* a bride... That did not reflect well.

"So, what do you make of our great Kierelia, Duke Fredrick?"

The man turned to her with a strained face. "I cannot say I care for it."

Hazel worked to conceal her offense. "Oh... why ever not?"

"I have been treated with nothing but contempt by king and gentry from the moment I arrived. It is not at all the reception I expected."

She was not surprised to hear this, but that he should have no idea as to why proved him irredeemably blind. "I apologize, sir, for the ill-treatment. I am certain it is not meant personally."

"I'm afraid I must disagree," he persisted, near losing his temper. "It has come across perfectly personal and I cannot understand it. I should think your kingdom would wish to *protect* its alliance with mine."

Was that a threat? If so, it didn't pack much punch. Galfree was a minor ally and was, moreover, a whole kingdom's distance apart from them.

"Do you mean to make trouble, sir?"

He looked to her with fiery eyes. "Make trouble? I should think Kierelia would fear more than the notion that I may 'make trouble.' Indeed, that is the understatement of the decade, what with your enemies in the Deep South planning to swoop in at any moment."

Hazel dropped her utensil at that, sending a slightly disruptive rattle through the room. "Do you mean to say you would *aid* our enemies?" she asked in a whisper.

He appeared as if he would laugh at her. But mirthlessly, he said, "Certainly *not*. I mean to say that, if war should reach your borders, I would think our support would be *indispensable*."

She raised her brows, knowing not how to respond to this claim. He was a right fool if he believed Kierelia looked to *Galfree* for any means of defense when it came to war.

When the third course was brought, she focused on avoiding any further conversation with the man. Consequently, it was silence for the lot of them, for neither his neighbor nor hers showed any concern for attempting a dialogue. The silence was burst upon, however, when a woman of the gentry, whom Hazel knew to have recently lost her fortune, introduced her daughter to the duke, making it painfully clear how amiable the girl was in character, if not appearance.

With red face, the duke concluded the conversation as swiftly as possible and turned back to his plate, his breathing heated as his temper appeared to be brewing again.

"And that is another thing," he began, "I have never had *so many* ladies proffered to me in a single day as I have this. For heavens, are there not men enough to be had in your kingdom, Lady Hazel?"

Her face flushed. This was a personal complaint now and one she'd had no control over. After all, she'd been dreading meeting him from the moment she'd heard of him. Moreover, she well understood why he'd yet to find a woman willing to wed him.

"Perhaps," she began, working to control her own temper, "you should not have arrived in Castlehaven with so much on offer to its ladies. And perhaps those young ladies are no more interested in being hoisted upon you than you are in appreciating them."

His brows rose higher than she'd have believed they could. "You think I have any control over what I offer? I am what I was born to. I should think *you* might understand that."

Slowly, she turned to him. "What precisely do you mean to say, Duke?"

"That I have overheard all about you this day and am shocked King Zephuel would allow his own sister to hoist such a maiden upon me. That you were born of traitors and have since grown to be one is a circumstance on every tongue, leaving me unable to imagine why you are yet welcome in this court. I can only conclude they wish *me* to take their problem off their hands."

Hazel stole a moment. She felt the heat rising in her face. This time, it was from deep-seated loathing. Taking a long breath, she said at last, "Duke Frederick, you have insulted this kingdom beyond belief in your attempts to buy a woman from her courts. It is clear why you have been unable to find a bride, for you have lost the only person at this table who might have been willing to converse with you. Good evening." With that, she excused herself and quietly meandered into the entertaining room.

Now perfectly empty, she wished beyond belief it would remain so. But with but a final course to be served, she would soon be joined and ignored by hordes. Her only hope was that she might be able to remain long enough to satisfy her guardian and sneak out as soon as possible. It was beyond her belief that the first people to enter the room should be Dianna and her ladies, soon followed by Armond.

"Why, it is Lady Hazel," Dianna said in a light tenor. "Tell me, have you tossed any more unsuspecting princes about since last we met you?"

Hazel couldn't help feeling the embarrassment of this. "The prophet says it was a fluke..." She did not add he said it would return one day.

"Oh, I'm *sure* it was. We all toss poor boys about like rag dolls from time to time."

Hazel felt her face redden for the third time that evening. It was beginning to grow far too hot for her.

"But how is your dear little criminal friend?" Dianna started in again. "Have the two of you been plotting his escape so you can finish what your parents started—"

"Dianna!" Armond admonished. "You are being most unfair. Really, this behavior does you no credit whatever."

Dianna rolled her eyes. "Armond, you are so naïve. She almost killed you."

"She did *not*," he replied. Looking to Hazel, he added with a wink, "Always wondered what it would be like to fly."

Hazel held no hope of concealing the grin that beamed from her face.

"How *can* you smile, knowing your little compatriot is locked away in our dungeon," Dianna pressed. "Really, I cannot for the life of me imagine why King Zephuel allows you to remain here."

Armond physically stood between them. "I won't hear any more of this, Dianna. Just walk away."

Dianna chortled with her ladies, but her smile dropped as he crossed his arms, awaiting her submission.

"Why… is that an *order*, my prince?" she teased weakly.

It was a moment before he nodded as if it had never occurred to him what a command from him, the heir to the throne, might mean.

"As if she's worth it anyway," the girl muttered, trotting away as slowly as possible in a feeble effort to prove it was of her own volition.

Armond turned to Hazel then and bent over her, his hands resting on the arms of her chair. "Are you quite all right, Lady

Hazel?"

No, she was not all right. She was breathless. She gulped. "I, that is, er, yes, I am all right… or I will be."

He sparkled a smile down at her and stepped back. "Always the trooper. But it seems to me you've had a rough time of it lately. Tell me, how was your journey to the southern tribes?"

"O-oh… it was pleasant, actually. I'm afraid we in the north have labeled them falsely."

He folded his arms. "I am surprised to hear that. Have you told my uncle of this?"

Her mouth nearly dropped open that he thought she possessed knowledge pertinent to the king. "I have not," she murmured, eyeing him speculatively. It was queer how similar his treatment of her was to his uncle's. But Armond's attention was not born of fear. It was his nature and it was why she cared for him.

"There you are," a voice that made Hazel cringe sounded from the doorway. Just as she'd feared, it was Duke Frederick marching toward her. "I must speak with you about the accusations you put to me if you don't mind."

But Hazel did mind. That she should ever have to speak with such a gentleman again made her ill. She was certain all the rose that had entered her face from talking to Armond was flushed out now.

"I am afraid Lady Hazel must retire early," Armond intervened, standing between them as he had with Dianna. "She is of a frail disposition, you see, and must often do so. Lady Hazel, shall I see you out?"

Floating on a cloud, it was all she could do to nod. Without further ado, he helped her to her feet and had her whisked from the room before Fredrick could bat an eye.

"I hope you don't mind," Armond said when she was free. "I couldn't bear to see you forced to speak to such a brute, especially when you appeared so discomfited by him."

He had noticed her discomfiture at the table? "Then you have heard of the reward he offers?"

"Who has not? I'm afraid he will have no luck here."

"If anywhere. I was forced to sit with him at banquet. He is a true fiend."

"Well, if the patient Lady Hazel cannot bear him, I shall not attempt it. Shall I see you too your rooms?"

"Oh, er, no. That is, it is very kind of you to offer, but I am accustomed to making my way alone."

"So, I've gathered," he replied with another of his quick smiles. "I bid you good evening, my lady."

* * *

It was all Hazel could do to stop her head spinning as she lay in bed. Such a chaos of emotion raged through her: anger, humiliation and then such joy and… love. She was hopelessly and endlessly in love with Armond. How very kind he was—so thoughtful and observing. No one but the prophet treated her as he did.

And then there was the wicked, awful, hateful duke of Galfree. What if her guardian should force her to meet with him again? Or worse, to be civil toward him, even affirming to any proposal of marriage he may make. After all, he was desperate.

But she would never acquiesce to such an offer. She would run away without a moment's hesitation if it were forced on her. To the south, she would run—away from him, Lady Nora, Dianna, the king, the entirety of the court… Dorian. She sat up. She *wanted* to go, to escape the place that had of late been so difficult to cope with, even more than in all the years past. Everyone was against her but for such a very few: the prophet and… Armond.

Oh, to be forced to run from him made her ill. Yet, she found it did not stop the racing of her heart as she thought out a plan of escape. It had been easier in years past. She used to manage to get by unnoticed, to hide away in her nooks and crannies. She'd been everyone's little helper, but a helper no one really cared existed. It had been agreeable enough... but things had changed.

But how would she ever get to the tribes? She had no horse that belonged to her. She was not the best rider, anyway. She knew nothing of traveling, possessed no coin nor any sense of direction. She'd had no idea how helpless she was until this moment. Always, others had come to her for help with their chores and projects. She'd felt herself capable and it had given her a sense of purpose. Now, she saw how little she could help herself.

A weight lay upon her that not even memories of Armond's treatment could lighten. She felt herself sinking, sinking, sinking. Something must give or she would lose her grip... on sanity, perhaps. There must be some way to be free of the misery of accusations made against her of late. There must be someone she could turn to.

It came to her—the sensation she'd had upon leaving The Mirror so many days past. She recalled how light and burden-less she'd felt. She simply must be allowed entrance again. Now the thought had gripped her, she considered sneaking in that night. But it was forbidden to enter again without express permission from the king himself.

10

Hazel stood before the door to King Zephuel's study. He was famed for disliking interruptions here, but she had no choice. Lady Nora would never help her gain an audience with him. She must take her chance. She lifted her fist... and knocked.

There was a shuffling of papers and the clearing of his throat before he inquired, "Who is it?"

"It is Lady Hazel, Cousin Zephuel."

A moment's silence followed before the door was opened to her. "Cousin Hazel, I am surprised to see you. Won't you come in?" He was neither so warm as in their prior meeting nor so harsh as when she'd been summoned to his throne room. She took comfort in both these factors.

"Your majesty, I will come to the point," she said as she accepted the chair proffered to her. "I beg a second visit to The

Mirror."

He sat down across from her. "The Mirror... a second time?" He appeared to be deliberating as he reorganized the parchment before him. "Lady Hazel, I... I cannot begin to tell you how disappointed I was in your friendship with the traitor."

She gulped. Would it cost her the visit? "I can never convey how *dreadfully* sorrowful I am that I was fool enough to be taken in by him. I wish I could make you understand how much I would never wish you or this kingdom harm."

He looked at her with surprisingly vulnerable eyes, then released a sigh. "I believe you, Hazel."

She cast her gaze to the desk. He had used no title before her name. This was something only close family members practiced. But she looked up to find his face had hardened again.

"Even so, you must realize I cannot be showing you favor after what has been revealed."

She held her breath. To her horror, a tear streamed down her face, followed by another. She tried and failed to regain her composure as she said, "Don't you see it is why I feel I must go there? Everything..." She sobbed. "Everything's falling apart. I have no one."

Clearly softening, he drew his chair around the desk to sit beside her. "But why would visiting the mirror room help you? Most find it very unpleasant."

"Yet, none actually recall what occurred within," she said, sniffing as her tears slowed. "I emerged from it refreshed and strengthened."

He raised a brow. "Do you *recall* your experience?" She couldn't tell if it was curiosity or accusation with which he inquired, as if she possessed some other power he might fear.

"No, but I know the one who dwells within must be... *wonderful*."

He released a quick breath and turned away from her, rubbing at the back of his head.

"What is it, your majesty? Have I spoken irreverently?"

"Oh, it is nothing… nothing that concerns you." He turned back to her suddenly, as if grasping at something she may possess. "I have gone there many times… I leave with nothing. Nothing at all since my first appearance as a young man—just emptiness, as if nothing and no one has taken interest in me, as if the Great Entity has turned his back on me." He caught himself and appeared almost to regret the admission. Even so, he continued, "But… you met him?"

Hazel considered. She had not even realized it was meant to be the Great Entity. All she recalled were the keeper's words: *Mind your thoughts in there. He can hear them.* "I must have."

"Then…" Here, he paused. "Will you ask him something for me?"

"Of course, *anything*… But I cannot promise to remember the answer."

He rifled for something in his desk, then pulled out a parchment upon which he wrote a swift note. He then packed it, along with quill and ink, into a small satchel. "Take this and come out with an answer."

Disoriented, she accepted it along with a signed document to allow her the second visit.

Swiftly, she strode through the corridors. For the first time in her life, she was on a mission for the king. He had chosen to confide in her, depend on her for an answer from the very god of their land. She hoped beyond hope the one within was the sort of entity that one dared ask questions of and further hoped she would actually be allowed to take his answer down on paper. After all, hadn't others thought to attempt such a thing before?

Showing her pass to the keeper, the woman raised a brow at her satchel. "It is against Kierelian law to take anything in with you."

Hazel froze. "Oh, but I…"

"You are extremely fortunate to have been granted express permission."

She relaxed. He must have included it on her pass.

Entering the room, it was peculiar to know she'd spent time there, yet remember so little about it. It struck her how dim and bare it was but for the large woven carpet in the center. Setting down her satchel, she gazed nervously about.

"Great Entity?" she whispered.

Had he even been present when last she'd been there?

"Great Entity?" she tried again.

With no response, she turned to the carpet again. A depiction of a girl with singing symbols floating from her mouth drew her. She bent closer to examine it and had just moved on to the dragon casting flame upon a poor king when a warm breeze brushed her face. She looked up. From where could a draft be coming in a windowless room? She made her way to the wall as the wind persisted. It came from between the cracks in the stone pieces. Her hand met warmth at the touch. She drew her hand away and scratched her head. It could not be that there stood a fireplace or even chimney on the other side, else she'd smell smoke.

She leaned against the wall, contemplating it, as an irregular peace filled her. It was as if it was born of the warmth. Slowly, she slid down the wall and sat upon the stone floor. Resting her head against it, she felt her eyes drooping. It wasn't until a knocking at the door that startled her from her slumber that she discovered she'd wasted her chance. But the knock had sounded in a familiar rhythm and it was this that revealed what was cajoling her into serenity. The wind was omitted through the wall in a rhythm… like the beating of a heart.

The knocking at the door continued. Unaware of how long she

had slept, she knew she must leave. But not only had she not received any kind of encounter to bring her comfort, she had not acquired an answer for her cousin. She raised her head. What *had* his question been? He'd written something down on the parchment within her pack. Removing it, she puzzled over its contents. It read,

Has your favor been lost to me forever?

Well, she had no answer for him, but she did have this thrumming wall. Perhaps whatever lay beyond would hold a kind of answer for them both. Scribbling on the note, she turned to face the exit. It was a shame to have so squandered her precious visit. Was the room's Entity offended she'd dared to sleep in his chamber?

The feeling of all recent memory lost to her was no less discomfiting than the last time. Though she did not feel as light and free upon exiting as before, she did sense the embrace of peace. In fact, she might even be a little warm... perhaps too warm.

"We've other visits to be had today, missy," the keeper reprimanded. "What could you possibly have been doing in there?"

"I cannot say..." she replied, wondering how much time she'd spent.

"Well, what does the note say?" the keeper asked with curiosity.

Hazel peered down at the foreign parchment in her hand. Seeing first the king's writing, she realized this must have been his question. Peculiar. But underneath was her own writing.

"The room behind The Mirror," she read aloud. She glanced back at the mirror room.

"The castle always changes it," the keeper snapped. "Today, it's just a pantry containing linens."

Hazel raised a brow. "Well, I suppose I must but examine it.

Down this hall?"

Following the woman's direction, she drew before a plain wooden door. Opening it, she found, as promised, a pantry. Nothing out of the ordinary. Merely cold gray stone. With a shrug, she stepped out but was caught by the expanse of the corridor. This could not be the room behind The Mirror. There was too much space between where this wall came and where she was sure the mirror room's wall ended. This pantry's wall did not share that of the other.

For some time, she raced through corridors. In the end, she found there was no room behind The Mirror at all. Checking her parchment again, she discovered no further clue. How foolish she'd been not to give more details of this ill-begot quest.

"Good gracious, girl," Lady Nora's voice descended from behind her. "Where have you been all morning? I'd begun to think you'd run away to your woods without permission and was near sending a guardsman after you."

"I apologize, Lady Nora. The king wished me to visit the mirror room. It seems I spent more time there than intended."

"My brother wished it? I suppose he hoped the Entity would find some fix for your... vocal quandary."

"It isn't a problem yet, Lady Nora. The prophet said so." How she wished the king had not insisted her guardian be among those who knew the claim of her cure was a falsehood.

"And yet, the prophet sent you south for training from your dreadful relatives. Tell me why he should do that if you are no longer the pebble in my shoe?"

"I suppose he fears it may return..." she said quietly.

"And there you have it. Something that requires fixing. In any case, I have a real treat for you. It seems Lady Stacia is having trouble with her needlework. Her mother requested a tutor and, naturally, I thought of your aimless little self. Come along."

Hazel nearly balled up the parchment in her hands and threw it at her guardian. The last thing she needed this day was to be anywhere near Dianna. That included her cohorts. Stacia would take no lesson from her in any case. The girl thought her a pathetic halfwit. Even so, Hazel was aware of how equipped she was to aid anyone with their needlepoint. Through the years, Lady Nora had forced hours upon hours of it upon her until she had quite mastered it.

"I apologize for the wait, Lady Stacia," Lady Nora sighed out as they entered the sitting room. "Lady Hazel's been dillydallying again. I hope you will attempt to have an influence on her, won't you?"

Stacia offered a cheerless grin but did not reply. This was her way, making her different from Dianna and Rebecca. They would have leaped at the chance to please the king's sister. But Stacia was a clever, no-nonsense young lady… and about as arrogant as they came.

Taking a seat beside Stacia, Hazel leaned over to see what they had to work with.

"I beg you, take this mess from me," Stacia groaned, casting it to Hazel.

"Mess" was the perfect word for what Hazel found in her hands. But with an experienced eye, she set to work untangling it, picking her needle through it with proficiency.

"If you moved that fast in everything," Stacia said, "you might not be so late all the time."

Hazel ignored her. Knowing Stacia, it wasn't even meant as a gibe—just a fact. But the reason she was so often late was because Lady Nora volunteered her for things without telling her. Not once had she awoken to the reading out of an itinerary as other noble ladies did.

"What were you up to anyway?" Stacia inquired, though her

tone revealed little interest.

"I was in The Mirror."

"Really? Haven't you already been through that ordeal?"

"I have."

"Whatever took you there a second time?"

"I... was looking for answers."

"And...?"

"That is all." She had no intention of relaying her business to anyone, let alone this girl. "Here you are." She handed the stitching back to Stacia.

Stacia laughed, turning to Hazel with new eyes. "Lady Hazel, you are a wonder. I don't think another woman in this castle could have brought order to my chaos in twice the time."

"Oh, well, I've performed my share of needlepoint."

"Don't I *know it*. Lady Nora is always showing it off to my mother, who, in turn, shoves it in my face in hopes I will improve myself. But it hasn't any effect, I'm afraid, for I couldn't care any less."

"My... cousin shows off my work?"

"She simply dotes over it."

Huh... Hazel fell back into her chair with folded arms. Something near a smile was attempting to cross her face. *So*, she wasn't completely lacking in virtue, after all. She could *sew*.

"Do you actually like this... stuff." Stacia held up her current project.

"Not at all."

"Then why do you do it all the time?"

"Lady Nora."

"Ah. I can imagine your guardian seeks perfection in all you do, since she is so flawless herself."

Hazel raised her brows, intrigued by the girl's intuition. "You are correct," she replied, working to conceal her astonishment.

"Of course I am. I do not speak unless I feel quite certain I will be."

"Because you wouldn't wish your reputation as a brain to go amiss." The words were out of Hazel's mouth before she realized.

Stacia chuckled. "It seems we have been skimming through one another's mail."

Hazel could only gaze off with a concealed smirk. Stacia was being pleasant. If she'd have known her gift for fixing needlepoint fiascos could earn her an element of respect, she'd have raced about the castle doing just that a long time ago.

"I'm beginning to think it's rather a pity Dianna hates you so much," Stacia began. "You're really not as senseless as I had you pegged for."

Hazel couldn't begin to think how to respond, but her heart began to race as a question occurred to her. Dare she ask it? "Why *does* she hate me so?"

"Mm, that's never really been clear to me," Stacia said offhandedly, as if she had no idea what her answer might mean to Hazel. "But I do know Armond was to blame for the whole *Affrontery* vengeance."

"Armond?"

"Dianna was speaking ill of you one day, mocking something or other she'd seen you do—don't recall what. Anyway, Armond stepped in, much like he did last night. Said we ought to make a friend of you or something... *Oh*, yes, I remember. We'd been making fun of your... well, I'm afraid we'd been going on about how little effort you put into your appearance. But I suppose you couldn't care less..."

Hazel did care, somewhat. Lady Nora simply did not provide very attractive attire for her, nor did Hazel possess her own maid for beautifying. Most often, she attempted something fashionable herself, but it was a gift she did not possess.

"Anyway, he said *he* thought you a pretty little thing and we ought to be making an effort to include you in our circle. And, well, I suppose Dianna took that notion into her head the wrong way and invited you to that game of Affrontery to make you look a fool before Armond. Didn't work out well for her, as I recollect."

Hazel couldn't reply. Her heart was racing... in the happiest way possible. Armond had not only stood up for her, he'd said he thought her pretty... had actually attempted to get the girls to befriend her.

"You bear feelings for him," Stacia said with a grin, now utterly abandoning her needlework.

"Oh, *no*, er, I, of course not."

"Of course you do. Everyone does. But you, my lady... well, funnily enough, I'd say you might actually have a chance. After all, I've never heard him call a girl pretty before."

"I-I don't know..." The familiar blush flooded her face.

"You should tell him!" Stacia said with real interest now. It seemed if one wished to bond with a Dianna-follower, one must possess skill with a needle and speak of potential admirers.

"I *couldn't*."

Stacia took up her needlepoint again. "Suit yourself... but *I'd* tell him if I thought I had a chance."

* * *

Days later, Hazel yet contemplated her conversation with Stacia—the rarest and most unexpected one they'd shared. Since then, whenever they came across one another, Stacia raised a daring brow at her, pressing her to speak to Armond. Why Stacia cared, Hazel could not fathom... except that the girl must be weary of her own love life. Then again, there was always the chance she meant to press Hazel into humiliating herself before Armond. But even as this was the likeliest possibility, she did not believe it so. Unexpectedly, she and Stacia had become... friendly. To further the notion, she was certain she'd witnessed Dianna about to come after her for the usual round of insults, but Stacia rerouted her elsewhere. It was impossible, of course, but Hazel's intuition informed her it was the case.

On the other hand, every time she saw Armond, she ran for the hills. Though she'd always been timid with him, the idea of facing him, knowing he saw her as more than the pitiful girl with the shameful background, terrified her. He thought she was pretty. And she had no idea how to respond to that. After all, he'd defended her three times now, that she knew of. To her, that looked like he took special interest. Then again, he was thoughtful without even trying. It was his nature.

How she wished she had some trusted friend she could discuss the dilemma with. If the prophet were at court, she might venture enough courage to speak to him, but he was off nobody knew where, as usual. Customarily, she would speak her mind to Dorian, tell him all about her latest Armond news. And he would have advised her. He offered surprisingly sound advice. But now...

She froze. Her feet had escorted her to the passage that led to the dungeons. This had not been done of her conscious volition and by no means would she follow where her feet itched to go. Turning away, she froze again.

He had told her not to come. She had meant to listen, to take this last piece of the soundest advice he'd ever given her. Even so, it was curiosity and (if she admitted to herself) her *heart* which made her start down the dark stairwell. Once again, the guard did not stop her from making her way down the maze of delirious prisoners.

At last, she came to his cell where he lay asleep on the stone floor.

She cleared her throat.

"As if I wish to be awoken for more of that *gruel*."

"It's me."

Instantly, he sat up. "What are *you* doing here?" he accused.

"Appeasing my curiosity. You look horrible." Indeed, there were deep shadows beneath his gray, dreary eyes. His hair was a mess of dust and oil and his clothes were caked in dirt. "Don't they feed you, clothe you?"

"Who cares?" he said, falling back against the wall to cross his arms in a cheerless motion.

"I don't know..." she replied, turning her gaze from him. "I guess I had always heard the king treated his prisoners with... well, unmerited leniency."

He shrugged.

"What's wrong, Dorian?"

"I'm in prison."

"There's something more..."

He shook his head.

"Dor—"

"I killed a guard."

"What?!"

"I tried to escape... Turns out I hurt someone, shoved them too hard. Their head smacked the stone floor."

"Oh..." she gasped dizzily. "H-how did you find this out?"

"The guards pay me regular visits now."

She didn't know what to say. She couldn't help wondering which guardsman it had been, if she'd known him.

"I didn't mean to," he admitted, emotion creeping into his voice. "I never intended—it was an *accident,* I swear... not that you have *any* reason to believe me."

She stepped forward, grasping the bars.

He was crying.

"I know you didn't mean to…" And she did. She had no doubt.

"You were right, Hazel. And I was wrong. I should never have got caught up with the underground… They're a bunch of greedy thugs grasping at clouds in a senseless attempt to find… I don't know what."

Not wishing to rub it in, she carefully searched for how to respond. "How did you get caught that day you were found robbing the king?"

"Some of the men and I were in the treasury. When we heard a guardsman sound the alarm, it was chaos. We'd been getting away with it for so long. Everyone else had escaped through the hidden tunnel but me. When they heard the guardsmen shouting, they closed it off."

"So, they just left you behind to be captured…? You could have been *hanged*."

"I deserve no less."

"Dorian—"

"You know it's true."

"I-I don't… I wouldn't want you to be hanged."

"Of course not." He turned away from her. "You're soft." He looked to her face again, his eyes clearer than she'd seen them since before his capture. *"Don't* be soft, Hazel. *Don't* come to see me anymore."

She gripped the bars. *"Armond said I was pretty."*

"Wh-at?"

"And Stacia thinks I should tell him how I feel."

"Stacia?"

"I don't know what to do. I *want* to tell him. I want him to know. I want to know if there's a chance…"

"With pretty boy?"

"I have to know in case I find a way to get back to the southern region… in case I have to escape the Galfreen duke."

"Why would you have to escape a duke?"

"He's looking to purchase a bride. Lady Nora is looking to sell."

He stood then, striding to the bars. "You're *not* going to be sold to some duke from godforsaken Galfree. You love Kierelia."

"I do… It's why I'm looking for a reason to stay."

He gazed at her a long while, thinking what, she had no idea. At last, he pulled away. "Tell pretty boy how you feel. He'd be a chump not to care for you."

11

Armond was in the garden. This was her moment. She would tell him all. But his dark hair shining in the sunlight made it difficult to move forward.

"Hazel," he said when he found her in her hiding place. He looked pleased to see her.

She offered a weak smile. "How are you this evening?"

"I'm well enough. Just been to see my uncle, the king. He isn't in one of his pleasanter moods."

"Oh, I'm sorry…" She wondered if it had something to do with the fact that she hadn't been to see him with the answer he'd asked for.

"It is quite all right. He is often in a temper of late."

It surprised her to hear he'd been upset with someone other than herself, even his beloved nephew, whom he loved as a son. It made her position in the king's eyes seem much less disastrous.

He smiled at her then. "But how have you been faring since last we met? I do hope that duke ceased hounding you."

"Thus far, he has."

"Good. I believe he took his leave of our kingdom yesterday. You ought to be quite safe now." He eyed her a moment. "I am surprised Lady Nora would even consider you for such a match."

"How did you know?"

"Things get around... not to mention you were sat with him at banquet that evening."

"You noticed?"

"Everyone did. He was the talk of the evening. Anyway, I do hope my aunt will find someone better for you than that mercenary."

"I... hope so too." Silence commenced as Hazel's heart and mind raced. "Armond... I must admit I came looking for you for a purpose."

His brows rose. "Is there something I may aid you with?"

"Not necessarily, I—" Her stomach leaped into her throat. She gulped it down. "I came with a confession."

"That sounds serious," he said with concern. "Shall we sit?" He gestured to the stone bench behind her.

"That may help."

The sun cast a hazy glow over the flowers and shrubs surrounding. The perfection of the moment made her all the more anxious. Suppose Dorian and Stacia were wrong? She couldn't do this. There would be no going back. But if she left for the tribes without knowing... well, she simply wouldn't be able to leave.

He took her hand, his eyes urging. "Hazel, unburden yourself."

She plunged. "Armond, since I could remember... I've cared a great deal for you. I've admired and esteemed you. You've been... a kind of role model. But of later years... my-my feelings have changed—deepened, I suppose. You see, you're rather wonderful.

Your consideration for others, your feeling heart. I suppose... what I mean to confess is... I have feelings for you." It wasn't quite what she'd meant to say. She'd held back.

Searching her face, he gave her hand a squeeze... then released it.

It dropped into her lap.

"I don't know what to say," he began tiredly. "I really hadn't expected this of you."

"Why-why not?"

"I didn't think you were like the rest."

Her eyes shone. Why did she *always* have to be so different?

"Aw, don't look that way. I just... think you're so much cleverer than them."

She stood, working to cover her trembling hands behind her back. "You think... it wisdom that I *not* recognize your admirable qualities?"

He rubbed at the back of his neck, more perplexed than she'd seen him. "I thought you were something above the girls who're always pining after me."

She froze, the most surprising irritation settling in. "And now I'm *not* because... I think you're wonderful?"

He shook his head. "I am sorry, Hazel. It isn't personal. I harbor feelings for no one just now. I suppose I just thought I was safe with you."

She stood and nearly dropped but caught herself against the bench. "Well... I apologize for being such a disappointment to you." Unable to take a breath, she stood again and turned on her heels, fleeing the accursed golden garden. Stacia must have known this was how it would turn out, that she would humiliate herself and somehow fall even lower in his estimation. Something above the other girls? Was she only worth something to him if she did *not* love him? It was the most bewildering statement she'd ever heard.

Shame for having confessed her feelings—for having felt them all those years—coursed like hot fury in her blood. Her hands shook as she made her way through the corridors. Eyes blurry with tears nearly shed, she could not seem to remember the castle's order for that day and kept bumping into walls. Angrily, she tore down the tapestry before her and used it to wipe the wet from her eyes. At last, she found where her tower door stood and raced up the stairs.

Upon reaching the landing, she froze.

The door had opened again.

"What on the planet *Kaern* are you doing up there, girl?" Lady Nora called up after her.

Hazel remained where she was, hands shaking.

Lady Nora drew beside her to survey the room. "What is this place?" As if as a villain in a nightmare, her gaze fell upon the bookshelf. She strode over to it, proceeding to pull a volume from the shelf. "I gave you this last year..." She thumbed through it. "Seems you bothered to give it a read." She replaced it and met her ward's eye. *"This* is the hiding place, is it not?" She glanced around again. "Really made it your own, I see... How long have you been coming up here then? How often have you heard me call below and ignored my plea?"

"Never, Lady Nora," Hazel replied numbly. "I always come when you call."

"Yet, you never bother to remain in a place where I might find you should I require your aid. Did it ever occur to you to *desire* to be of service to those who sacrifice for you? To those to whom you owe so great a debt?"

"I believe I have done enough to earn what you've given me, Lady Nora."

The woman's flawless brows rose into her hairline. "I see. So, you think *nothing* of living in this castle, allowed to dwell among the gentry, fed from the king's table, clothed by *my* pocket."

The fire raged hotter in Hazel's veins. "The *king's* pocket. You live by the mercies of your brother, as do I."

It was a single, silent moment before Lady Nora grasped a book and hurled it across the room. She marched up to her ward, pointing a finger in her face. *"You,"* she breathed, "have *no right* to speak to me that way."

"I have only spoken the truth, something that ought to be done more often... something I should have done long ago."

A hand smacked across Hazel's face, sending her vision into starry night skies. Before long, her guardian had slammed the tower door shut following her exit. She proceeded to call after one of the guardsmen. Hazel couldn't begin to guess at her aim until she heard a key turn in the lock.

She turned from the stairwell and sat in her window nook, resting her arms upon the sill. Kierelia's landscape rolled out before her in all its sunset glory. For the first time in her life, she couldn't bear the sight. Should her guardian ever release her from this tower (difficult to believe at the moment), she would flee the kingdom without another thought. With nothing more than the clothes on her back and her caged galmoira, she would walk out the front gates and not stop until her feet hit the southern forest.

* * *

Her ears were ringing. No, someone was singing, far away. She sat up, shaking her head after the deepest sleep she'd ever experienced, likely due to the disappointments of the day before. No, someone was shrieking at her. She'd heard it before: the ruby bedposts in her bedroom. Though her bedroom would be on the other side of the castle, they managed to reach her ears.

"I've *heard* you," she murmured, rubbing at her ears.

They ceased.

But there were still shrieks below and... there was a haze in the room.

She stood to observe outside but saw little through the haze. Taking a chair to the window, she smashed it through to have her deepest fears confirmed. Smoke billowed from castle windows and turrets, from the trees of the forest surrounding. Castlehaven was aflame. Ducking back inside, she searched for a cloth to hold to her face, regretting her decision to burst open the window as smoke flooded the room. Soon, the atmosphere was so thick, she could not see where she went. She nearly toppled down the stairs when a bright light pierced the smog. Still in its sheath beneath her stuffed chair, the ruby blade lit the room.

She drew it up and worked the buckle around her waist. Then she withdrew the heavy weapon and drug it down the stairwell, using its light as a guide. But the door at the bottom wouldn't budge. Of course. Lady Nora had locked it.

Panic set in.

"Help!" she screamed, coughing over the smoke. *"I'm trapped!"* But even a few minutes more banging and screaming did not aid her. Either no one could hear her or they didn't care. Racing back up the stairs, she raced to the window, using an old fan to blow away the smoke. She glanced down the length of the tower. There was nothing whatever beneath her but yards upon yards of stone wall. She could never climb down.

She flew back down the stairs again, pounding and screaming with all her might. Before long, she fell to the ground in a fit of coughs. That was when she saw it. The smoke was beginning to billow in from underneath the door. Soon, she would either burn in her prison or pass out from smoke inhalation.

The ruby bedposts sang out again, thundering in her ears. This time, she realized how they reached her. Laying her ear to the sword at her feet, she found the song was somehow channeled through it. That was when she comprehended what she had. Taking up the weapon to hack at the doorknob, the sword sliced through it like butter and the door swung open.

She stole a moment to gaze incredulously at the crystal blade in her hand before scrutinizing the vicinity. There were no immediate flames, but the gloomy smoke made the light of her sword all the more necessary, almost slicing a clear path as she went. The first corridor she tried raged with flames. It was two more corridors and not a person in sight before she at last spotted a door she hoped led to her freedom.

12

Hazel stepped out into hazy, sunlit chaos. People darted about madly, shrieking and flailing in terror. She turned to survey the damage to the castle and found parts of it in ruin. But how could all this be? How could a fire consume the castle so fast? And why was no one working to put it out? Surely, the frantic shrieking was unnecessary.

Racing around the fortress, her breath was stolen as she witnessed the source of havoc. Towering as tall as the castle itself was a great black beast that breathed torrents of flame over all below. As if dissatisfied by the state of the castle still standing, it threw itself upon it, smashing her home beneath its weight. As royal guardsman worked to assail it down below, it continued to crawl over the fortress that buckled beneath it.

Hazel's hands flew to her face as she screamed, praying all had escaped. But her concern only grew as she considered the few around her. Where was everyone? A sudden fear sent her flying to the other side of the castle, searching for a window into the dungeons below. A crumbled opening was revealed and she raced over to cry, *"Dorian!"* Desperate shouts were returned but none were him. Despairingly, she hiked up her skirts and made ready to shimmy in, but the stones of the fortress swayed as the beast came crawling over. It wasn't until she was some distance away that she realized terror had sent her to flight. Scolding herself, she raced back, searching for any faces she might know.

The monster came tumbling down the wall and Hazel's hopes were renewed as a group of guardsmen and a few nobles charged it. These men were well trained. They had only to slay this mysterious adversary before they'd lost everything. A shout diverted her attention and she spotted Armond also racing upon the scene. When she returned her gaze to the guardsmen, it was to her horror that she could no longer find them. She fell to her knees as she realized they'd either been killed or had run in terror, just as she nearly had.

Yet, both horror and hope remained as Armond dashed toward the beast. But he stopped short upon discovering what she had. Those he'd gone to aid were gone; he was alone. The creature drew up on hind legs and roared like nothing she'd ever heard before. The sheer volume of it sent Armond to his back, with the shadow of the monster towering over him. The hairs on the back of her neck stood on end as she witnessed the thing bowing over the quaking prince.

"Armond, run!" she shrieked, hands clenched into fists at her sides.

He lay frozen upon the field.

Unthinkingly, she flew after him. It was just in time that she rolled him from harm's way as flame coursed over her own body. Agonizing heat flushed through her, but the flame itself did not reach her flesh. For the first time, she gazed up into the creature's face, but it was not gazing back. It was watching something. She turned.

Armond was fleeing as swiftly as his legs would carry him. Perhaps out of a love for the chase, the beast tore after him. As its shadow fell over him, Armond turned in a fit of shrieks and fell once more to his knees before it. Hazel's ears suddenly ringing, all other sound fled her. She gazed down at the sword at her side. Drawing it by the hilt, adrenalin helped her carry it across the expanse. At the nape of the beast's neck was a cut one of the guardsmen must have managed. Without questioning whether she could achieve what she set out to do, she flung her sword and squealed as it met its mark, piercing the vulnerable place.

But rather than slaying it, she knew she had only caused it pain, for it suddenly turned on her, teeth bared in rage. She nearly buckled at the sight, but at that moment, something like the determination she felt when sorting the mess of someone's needlepoint entered her. Like the very needle her hand so proficiently guided, she sailed upon the dragon's back and darted up its leathery exterior. It seemed not to understand to where she'd disappeared and started after Armond again. But in another moment, she grasped her crimson blade and struck it deeper into her assailant's flesh. The giant lizard-like beast bellowed and stumbled forward. At that moment, her legs lost their grip and left her hanging by the hilt of her blade as it went tearing down the monster's flesh.

Like an earthquake rippling through the ground, their enemy's body dropped and she was tossed not far from it, her teeth jarred by the impact. Sword still in hand, she was lucky it had not been thrust into her own flesh. Such relief lasted but a moment as her skin seethed from the scorching blood of her victim. Frantically, she dashed for the pond in what was left of the castle garden. She scrubbed at every inch of her skin until she was clean enough to ascertain that she was not severely burned.

It was the scene to which she turned to survey that made her nearly throw up the contents of her empty stomach. As people wandered back from various regions, come to view the slain beast, she realized just how much they'd lost. The castle was in absolute desolation. She gasped out a sob, mourning the transformable fortress that had been like a clandestine friend.

It sickened her to contemplate who might yet have been inside as it had toppled into ruin... some who might yet be alive within the rubble that they must now sort through to seek survivors and... she hardly knew. She turned her back to it and sauntered over to where the others gathered around something beside the monster. It was Armond, kneeling in the dirt, his head in his hands. He couldn't help them, help her. But help her with what? Comfort? Well, that had certainly been decided against even before all this destruction.

"What of King Zephuel?" she asked a guardsman.

Glaring at the ground, he shook his head.

She moaned. The *king* was gone. This was why they all stood looking to their helpless prince. But why would anyone stand around such a pitiable sight for hope? She noted the sword beside him, then studied their faces. They were perplexed but... grateful. They couldn't understand why he acted this way when he had just slain their foe. They looked to him for leadership, but only Hazel understood they would not get it.

She searched the crowd for anyone who could tell them what was to be done, someone to take initiative. There were guardsmen, servants, villagers... then there was she and Armond. In the vicinity, that was *all*.

Her eyes fell upon a horse. Ignoring its master's shouts, she leaped upon it and sent it racing for Clarion Citadel... to the

Assemblage of the Wise. The prophet. If he was there, he would know what to do. He could lead them out of this mess, the horror that had become their kingdom.

It was a briefer ride than she recalled, perhaps because it had not been made within the confines of a carriage or perhaps because she had ridden recklessly. But she began to realize she had taken a wrong turn when she could not locate the towers of the citadel. She had almost given up when she saw it: the rubble.

"No..." she gasped. Leaping from her borrowed horse to approach the wreckage, she reached the steps that should have been. She knelt to steal up a chunk of stone. Had the assemblage been within when it was decimated? Where was her dear prophet?

"Hazel!" he called from her left.

"Oh, *prophet*," she yelped, racing toward him to throw her arms about him. It was her turn to shake, to cry, to breakdown.

The two stood there for some time before he finally pulled her back, smoothing her hair from her face before taking her cheeks into his hands. "What of Castlehaven, my girl?"

She looked to the wreckage of Clarion Citadel. "It is as you see this... Only, I don't know if any nobles survived. Just... Armond and me, a few servants, villagers and guards." She looked into his face. "The assemblage?"

"They had traveled to Bashtii for a conference with its future king. King Claros passed recently. His young cousin will take the throne now... if the dragons haven't traveled that far."

"Dragons?"

"The fire-breathing creatures."

"There are more...?"

His eyes looked pityingly on her. But there was something else there. Guilt. "There are *many* more," he said soberly.

She narrowed her eyes. "What do you know about this?"

He pulled away then, running a weary hand down his beard.

"Not as much as I used to. It has been too long. I *can* tell you that these dark dragons were, not long ago, peaceful, even thoughtful creatures. They were beautiful, graceful and—"

"*What* are you talking about?" She would never embrace the notion that these dragons could be *beautiful*.

"It isn't what it seems," he defended. "They were lured to Kierelia by a sorceress who exposed them to flame conjured by the dark arts. That curse sent them on their rampage all over the kingdom."

"All over…?" she gasped, nearly dropping.

"Sit, Hazel. I must confess something to you now."

She found a flat piece of rock and sat down, anxiety fuming in her stomach.

"This is all the doing of your cousin, King Zephuel."

"Whatever can you mean?"

"I only just discovered his transgression some days ago. I returned to speak with him, to remedy what he had done. I was too late." He swallowed, then started again. "For some years, since you were very young, Hazel, he has been colluding with a sorceress… the sorceress Maera. And, no, not the one who released the dark dragons. It seems he went to her for defense against our enemies in the Deep South. He was afraid… and he did not trust the Great One. Instead, he placed his faith in the dark arts…

"What the poor fool did not understand is that, once one has made an agreement with a sorceress, it opens a spiritual door to the Dark One of the Nethers. King Zephuel rejected and therefore lost the favor of the Great One by making an agreement with the very one who wishes this kingdom destroyed. For, one day, Kierelia is meant to be the *greatest* upon the planet Kaern."

Hazel struggled to comprehend his claims. She knew little of sorcerers or this Dark One, let alone *spiritual* doors… But she did begin to understand the king's behavior of late, why he wished *her* to seek the Great Entity in The Mirror, why he'd seemed afraid, ashamed even. "How have you learned all this?"

"That… is why I had you sit down."

She raised her brows. What he'd already told her wasn't enough?

"Since your parents were banished, I've searched far and wide within the Deep South. I'd nearly given up hope ever finding them alive. In the end, they were only in hiding."

Her parents… were *alive.* And he'd found them.

"Having known them as well as I had, I'd always contemplated their motives behind the assassination attempt. They weren't the mercenary sort, despite what you've been told all these years. It is why Zephuel had felt so betrayed. They were the kind of people one trusted."

Hazel gripped her skirts in between her fingers, her heart pounding in her ears.

"It seems they were aware of the agreement made with the sorceress and they understood what it would mean for the kingdom. They strove to alter the king's decision, but when he would not budge… they decided to handle matters their own way. Granted, it was a wrong, *disastrous.* But they felt they had good intentions… and they were right about the risk."

Hazel reeled. Tears burned down her cheeks. If this was so, the lie she'd always told herself about why they'd left her there wasn't true. She'd thought it was because she'd be safer in Kierelia than in the Deep South… But they'd known the curse of King Zephuel's decision was upon the kingdom. They'd known better than anyone that danger was imminent. "Why did they *leave* me here?" she bawled out, a shaky hand working to stifle her sobs.

"That, I do not know, my girl."

How could he not have asked them? Didn't he know it was the question that had plagued her from the moment she'd been made to understand about their banishment?

"They wish to see you," he said quietly.

"Oh, *do* they?! Well, I do not wish to see them. *Ever*."

He nodded. "I thought as much. I would not send you anyway."

Pulling a pile of debris into her hand, she chucked it at the horizon. The sun was setting upon her kingdom and it was in shambles, with more dark dragons wreaking havoc elsewhere. They were done for.

"Oh, prophet, you must come back to Castlehaven with me. There are some survivors, but Armond is in no state to lead us. We require your guidance. It is our only chance in this plight."

For the first time since she'd known him, he dropped his chin.

"What is it?" she questioned.

"I thought I could stop this," he said. "I *knew* it would come, but I thought we would have more time. I had *plans*, I..." He swallowed, his eyes darting back and forth. "This is where I must bow out."

Hazel bit her lip, working to rein in her temper. "Prophet..." she said shakily. "You would leave us *now?* We *need* you. Has King Zephuel really let you down so much that you cannot bear the sight of us? We cannot do this without you."

"It is *I* who have let this kingdom down, Lady Hazel... twice over."

"...What does that mean?"

He looked into her eyes, his own sparkling with tears, and offered her the smallest, most pain-filled smile. "That is something I rather hope you never discover, sweet one."

In the blinking of her eye, he was gone. The wind whistled around her. She shivered and hugged her arms about herself. She was alone. So, so alone. She shook, she sobbed, but in the end, she stood to her feet.

After all, when had she ever not been alone?

* * *

Things were no different in Castlehaven when she returned. Armond was precisely where she had left him, but those who'd looked to him for courage had since moved on. Many sought the solace of weeping, others stood deliberating—mostly guardsmen who were likely deciding where they would go from here. She noticed a group stealing away with chickens and baskets of food. She rode after them. Resting her hand against the hilt of her blade, she said, "You will return to Castlehaven with those."

"*What* Castlehaven?" one of them spat.

"Return it and remain there until you are given further orders, do you hear me?" This time, she unsheathed her sword, working to conceal how unnatural it felt in her hand.

They knew who she was, she was sure. And certainly, they questioned whether it was worth obeying her. But in the end, they returned. She rode after them and watched on as they approached other villagers, likely complaining she would not even let them eat after such devastation. But she thought wrong.

An older woman approached with, "Wilfred says you have plans. Where will we sleep? All the nearby villages have been laid waste to."

Things were already worse than she'd imagined. And now, quite suddenly, this woman was looking to her for help. "Remain here. *All* who come for aid are commanded to remain..." Her mind raced. "Tell them we will rebuild. But as for tonight... I will speak with the guardsman about what may be done."

Riding up to the group of them, it was clear they were astonished to see her.

"Thought you'd run away for good, my lady," one spoke.

She shook her head. "I left in search of help. Didn't find any.

Way it looks now, it's just us. What do we do for shelter? The nights are too cold for sleeping comfortably and these people require rest."

They looked between them, shaking their heads. "We cannot say what is to be done for them. We were… wondering if there was even a kingdom left to serve."

She rolled her eyes. "Do you see the ground beneath your feet? That is your kingdom. Until it is gone, you will serve it." She glanced over their number—twenty in all. Speaking to the first ten, she said, "Why don't you put yourselves to good use and seek out materials with which to manufacture tents. Build more than you can imagine we'd need, as more will be coming. As for you…" She gestured to the other half. "You ought to be sorting through the rubble, searching for survivors." A sudden grin—the first of the day—broke upon her face. "Guardsman Gunther… I am pleased to see you."

To her surprise, he grinned back. "At your service, my lady."

"May I trust you to oversee these projects?"

"Yes, my lady," he replied with a bow. Turning to the men, he shouted, "You heard her. Now, get a move on. We haven't got all day."

Hazel felt reassured that she'd selected the right man, which was fortunate since she'd merely chosen him because he was the only one she knew. Next, she gathered the servants. "Bretta," she said to Lady Nora's favored maid. A shadow crossed both their faces as they looked to one another, understanding what they'd lost. But Hazel could not afford the time to discern how she would mourn her guardian just then. "I am glad you are safe," she ended. Turning to the lot of them, she continued, "Search for something to wrap Prince Armond in. Then bring him water and food. You may have to force-feed him. Then get him into the first tent that's built. And watch him, Bretta." Leaping from her horse to draw the maid aside, she added, "Inform me when he has returned to his senses."

"*Will* he return, my lady? He's been muttering strange speeches since we found him."

Hazel nodded with an assurance she did not feel. "He will if I have anything to say about it. And remember, he is our king now. I leave it to you to do your best to make him whole."

"Lady Hazel," said Laurene, Hazel's favorite cleaning maid whom she'd bribed with teacakes to keep her books concealed beneath the bed. The girl drew a small cage from behind her skirts. It was the galmoira.

"*Oh,* you saved him!" Hazel cried, looking upon the girl with teary eyes. She'd been forcing the poor creature from her mind since the catastrophe occurred.

Laurene grinned. "This fellow and I have grown to be friends since you brought him to stay. Was the first thing what entered my mind when I knew we must escape."

Hazel hugged the girl, though she was not embraced in return. Indeed, the maid appeared quite rattled.

"W-well, I'll just set him in a safe place for now, if you don't mind."

"Laurene, you must keep him as your own. I did not cast him even a thought in my own escape. He deserves the master who best feels his worth."

The maid's face grew red as she curtsied, then curtsied again. "*Oh*, I *thank* you, my lady! I will prize him the whole of my life."

By evening, Hazel's throat was hoarse from giving orders. She was unaccustomed to speaking so much. The number of those gathered at the wreckage of Castlehaven had more than doubled as survivors arrived for help and guidance. It was with more speed than she'd expected that tents were erected. They were a welcome retreat from the winds that whipped through the camp.

It hadn't taken long for her to realize someone must be sent in search of food. She directed a group to take whatever they could find, whether from markets, farmland, surviving homes. Anyone sent out was to carry a message to survivors: gather at Castlehaven if they wished to endure. Considering she'd been hearing stories of more dragon attacks, some even slain, she did not think this would be disputed by anyone. Thankfully, all other dragons described were much smaller than the one that had destroyed the castle. Most were only a little larger than a horse.

As for supper that evening, she took cues from the Clan of Galmoira. Bonfires were built, over which skewers of food were prepared. The light they provided was a comfort and the comradery found around them drew even laughter from one of the groups. It brought Hazel hope that they just might make it out of this disaster, but it also made her ache.

That night, she lay awake in her tent. She'd been one of the few afforded her own, while almost all else were forced to share, even with strangers. But the people had insisted she and Armond, their only nobles, be afforded their own spaces. Hazel would have insisted Armond have his own, anyway. All evening, she'd worked to hide him. The people could not continue to see him in his current state. It made *her* ill as it was. Since she had actually been the one to slay the beast, she could not fathom why he responded thusly. But she supposed it had more to do with witnessing the destruction of his entire life than just the terror of the monster... the *dragon*.

The people had begun to call it that after she'd let it slip. She was certain they wondered why she knew what to call a creature none had ever seen before. She wondered, herself, how the prophet had known it. He'd claimed they'd been lured to a flame conjured by dark arts, but where had they come from before that? Had they been hidden?

Now, she could but hope the remainder of the dragons out there would keep away from the haven she was building or all her plans would be for not. She'd proclaimed Gunther in charge of the lookout and the guardsman were to take shifts keeping watch as the camp slept. She wondered if anyone *would* sleep that night, knowing there were more monsters out there, continuing to reap destruction—more that could come for the little they had left.

She sat up. They had no military. The Deep South could come for them at any moment to lay claim to the land. She lay back down. The remaining dragons would act as a deterrent. Even so, they required protection from their enemies, man or monster. But what could be done?

Blythe and the Clan of the Galmoira came to mind. He had called her family, had pledged loyalty to her. If he thought he could but spare some men, perhaps even rally a number from the other tribes, they might at least be able to aid in protecting the camp from the dragons while they rebuilt. Not to mention, she felt the use of a bow and arrow would make a more proficient weapon against them... considering one would not have to *race up their backs* to get a blade into them.

Someone cleared their throat outside her tent. *"Hazel,"* a man's voice whispered.

She crawled over to pull the flap aside. "What is it?"

"It's Dorian."

"Dorian!" She leaped out. "I thought you were *dead*," she sobbed, wrapping her arms about his neck.

He patted her back uncomfortably. "I should have been, but some of the stone wall in my cell crumbled and I was gifted a small hole through which to escape. I heard you've been giving orders. Thought that was impressive. I've been in the group of those searching for food since Armond slew the beast."

She shook her head. "It's not impressive at all. I'm just all we have right now... until Armond snaps out of his stupor. *Oh,* I'm just so relieved you're alive... and you're here. You didn't run away?"

"You thought I would?"

"Well, I don't know... you're technically still a prisoner. Once we rebuild, I don't know what will become of you."

"Well, I'm not leaving you now."

"Me?"

"You stuck by me in my darkest hour. I'm going to help as much as I can. When all is said and done, well, we'll see what happens."

She sighed. "You're a better man than I thought you were. That is, when I found out... everything."

"I'm no better. I'm just... returning a great favor. You have no idea what a bright light you were in those dungeons."

"But you always fought me! You told me to stay away."

"You didn't belong down there and... I don't deserve your friendship. But so long as I have it, I will aid you. Deal?"

She nodded.

"I have some... interesting news," he said.

"Yes?"

"Dianna and her ladies are alive."

"What? Where are they?"

"Hiding in a cave."

She raised a brow at him.

"They were, uh, visiting me in the dungeons when everything transpired—trying to gain information about you. Their escape route was cut off. The bars to my cell busted, so I was able to pull them out through my whole in the wall. I got them to safety when I saw the beast. But Dianna..."

"What about her? You said she was alive."

"Yes, but her hair caught fire. She's... bald. A few wisps here and there I guess, but... she refuses to come out of hiding."

"Are you kidding me? The kingdom just lost everything and she's afraid of people seeing she's lost her *hair?*"

He nodded.

Hazel could scarcely believe that of all the nobility to have survived, it had to be the most useless girls in all Kierelia. She swallowed her bitterness down. "Would you mind taking some food and blankets to them?"

"Already have. I think they are as comfortable as possible just now."

She nodded. "They will have to begin doing their fair share tomorrow."

"So I told them. Only Stacia seemed to take me seriously. Rebecca just whimpered and Dianna sat silently in her corner."

"Sounds like Armond."

"I've heard. These pampered royals don't seem to be primed for hardship."

"Who can be, really, for something like this?"

"You seem to be handling it in spades."

"'Seem' is an appropriate word."

He raised a brow. "I don't think you're giving yourself enough credit. You just built something here from nothing."

"Well... we'll have to see if it'll hold. I need to find Gunther."

"I'll fetch him. What do you need him for?"

"We must get a message to the Clan of Galmoira."

13

"Good morning, Armond," Hazel greeted as she entered his tent.

He didn't move. It was as Bretta had said. He was no better and the deep shadows under his eyes revealed he hadn't slept a wink.

She slapped him across the face.

"Aaaahow!" he bellowed, bounding back from her. "What is *wrong* with you, Lady Hazel?"

"Oh, good. You're awake. Listen, we need to make some plans."

"Plans? What are you talking about?"

"Armond, I need you to step it up. You are technically king now. You've been trained for this."

"Hazel, I can't! You don't understand. I've never seen or heard of anything like this. I don't know what we're going to do and... I have a confession."

"Don't tell me you've fallen in love with me," she said ruefully.

He blinked, not seeming to grasp the jest. "I didn't slay that dragon."

"I know. I did."

"*You?*"

"You don't have to sound *quite* so surprised." Though she had to admit, it was just as farfetched to her that a feeble, little needlewoman had done it.

"We have to tell people," he said quickly. "They all think I'm their hero."

"They have to believe it was you."

"They have to believe a *lie?*"

"It's the only factor that's made you appear like you're capable of leading us out of this."

"But I'm *not*. I'm so not. I was tutored to lead a *thriving* kingdom. Nothing prepared me for this. I just can't see us digging our way out. We are at the mercy of the Deep South or whoever comes for us first."

She slapped him again, thrusting a finger in his face. "Speak that way again and I'll have you fortuitously tossed off a cliff. We need you, you inconsiderate dolt. And if *I* have to work tooth and nail to see you do your duty, I will." She paused a moment, studying his face. He looked pitiable—nothing like the prince she'd so venerated. What were they to do? "From now on, you will follow my direction. You will say what I tell you to say until I feel you've earned your right to a voice. Do you hear me?"

He nodded, rubbing at his smarting cheek. "I'm so glad you're here, Hazel."

"You ought to be. You'd be dead if I wasn't."

Before long, he emerged from his tent. A wave of whispers followed as the camp watched him. Just as Hazel had anticipated, they expected some word from their king.

He turned to them. "I thank you all for your fortitude and generosity during this most distressing of times," he shouted. "And I..." He hesitated, eyeing Hazel with discomfort. "I thank the Lady Hazel for following out my directions while I have been unwell."

Applause ensued as glittering eyes looked to her. She'd been afraid of this. They'd already grown accustomed to turning to her. It was why she'd forced him to claim credit for her dealings.

"I know you will do all you can to help her and I see this kingdom back into harmony... and safety." He turned to the castle ruins and she saw his hand begin to quiver at the sight. He swiftly concealed it behind his back as he re-centered his feet. "We will *rebuild* and will grow stronger than ever because we have endured this fire. We have been tested and we will prove ourselves worthy to call ourselves Kierelians."

The crowd applauded, causing a smile to creep onto Hazel's face. She'd known they would like that. They loved their kingdom as she did. They loved the land and the land was what they had left. They were at their lowest point but could only grow from there... that was, if they survived.

The remainder of the day was spent much like the one before. Hunting parties were sent to continue garnering food. Men and women were set to sorting through the rubble that would one day be their fortress again. Whenever a fortunate survivor was discovered in the wreckage, it was proclaimed to the whole camp and all came running to celebrate them.

Before long, Hazel discovered they were fortunate enough to have an architect among them. Along with Armond, they went to work designing a new stronghold, stronger than the last and to be built as swiftly as possible. It would be smaller, but they would construct further in future. Just now, they required a home base.

They also planned for new homes to be developed around the

castle, as there had been before. These would be erected even more rapidly in order to shelter the people while they completed the castle. They couldn't be expected to continue living in tents after all. The weather would soon turn and the season of rains would begin.

Hazel and Armond met with all the remaining guardsmen and even promoted some of the fittest villagers to join their number. It was imperative they have protection from the dragons that might yet come to decimate what they worked to restore. Hazel relayed her request for aid from the southern tribes—something that was deliberated over. It seemed no matter how much she assured them that the tribes were nothing like they'd grown up believing, the well-established anxiety remained.

It was the grace of the Great Entity, she was certain, that no more dragons were spotted in the vicinity, though more and more villagers arrived with reports of destruction. Once, someone had declared they spotted one of the winged creatures soaring overhead, but as no one could attest to the trueness of the claim, they were left to watch the skies with trepidation.

It wasn't until they had nearly ceased work one evening that the survival of The Mirror was discovered. Great boulders blocked off the entrance, but the etching above the door made clear what it was. Hazel raced up to the lone structure and pressed her face against it. Inside... was hope. The late King Zephuel may have lost the Entity's favor for his kingdom, but they could regain it. Perhaps they already had, if this room's survival was any testament.

"This will be the heart of the new fortress," she announced. "We build from *this*, the soundest of center stones." With eyes shining, she looked to Armond, who clearly could not grasp her elation—what the room's existence could possibly mean for them. She scarcely understood what it meant herself, considering she couldn't actually recall anything that had ever happened within.

Recalling the note she'd written herself about investigating the room beyond, she went to that wall and ordered the workers to help her clear the rubble away. Before long, they revealed something like an altar or shrine. But unlike The Mirror, this was destroyed.

Squinting her eyes, Hazel knelt. In the center of the small space were the remains of a large purple stone—dull, cracked and... lifeless, she found herself thinking. Beneath this was a black amulet. She gathered these up into her hands.

"Does anyone know what this is?"

"Queer stones, my lady," a villager responded.

"Yes, but you can see there was a small room here. I know for a fact it possessed no entrance. Does anyone know what the room was for?"

None present possessed an answer. This only furthered the mystery of The Mirror. Dropping her findings into a skirt pocket where she used to conceal books, she determined to ponder it later.

"Hazel," Dorian said as he approached. "Are we to abandon the great ladies to their cave again tonight?"

"They still haven't absconded it? For heavens, they've no right to sit back while we do all the work." Her mind raced for what to do with them. "Take Armond to them. Tell him I want them here and put to work or they shan't receive another morsel of food. If they refuse, the two of you may drag them here to me and I will deal with them myself."

He nodded and turned to go, but hesitated. "Do you... have something that could be used for a headscarf?"

"For Dianna?"

He nodded, perhaps a little meekly.

She couldn't help admiring his thoughtfulness of such a selfish person, but this did not alleviate their dilemma. There was not much spare cloth to be had. At last, she gazed down at her skirts and tore a piece from it. "Use this for now. We will fabricate something more suitable later."

* * *

"Someone is here to see you, my lady," Gunther reported one evening.

"I'm terribly occupied, Gunther. Who is it?"

He leaned in close. "It is the southern tribes."

"Oh! Has Blythe sent some of his men?"

"Some? That depends on how many he had to begin with."

Quirking a brow at him, she strode in the direction from which he'd come. Entering what remained of the surrounding forest, she found Blythe standing with hands on his hips, the customary bow and arrows over his shoulder. What she saw behind him stole her breath away.

"Blythe, what is this?"

"This, my Lady Hazel, is what is left of the southern tribes."

"What is left?" She estimated their numbers and guessed at about five hundred people complete with gear and baggage.

"Aye, the beasties came after us as well. It's all gone. Well, not the whole forest. Just our homes. All the same, we come to you not as refugees but allies. We will remain until your kingdom is on its feet once more. Afterward, we will restore our own homeland."

Hazel was speechless. "Y-you *all* came to help us?"

"We have come to the aid of you, our kin, Lady Hazel."

"You all came for *me?"* she squeaked.

"You requested our aid and we repay that faith with our protection. We are a robust people, accustomed to the elements. We will make our home in this forest until we have seen this through."

It was in a daze that she led Blythe and another of the tribal leaders through the camp and to Armond's tent. When she relayed the news to him, he fell into his seat.

"I didn't think we would make it," he said, dumbfounded. "But... how are we to feed and house everyone?"

"We feed and shelter ourselves," Blythe replied proudly, slightly offended. After all, he hadn't brought his whole region only to be considered a burden.

"Armond is only in shock," Hazel explained. "But we are more thankful for your thoughtfulness and sacrifice than I can ever put into words. Truly, when the restoration is complete, we will send a number of our people to aid in yours."

Blythe shrugged. "We shall not need it, but you may do as you wish."

A commotion outside the tent sent Hazel to the opening. She feared the worst: that a dragon had been sighted. Instead, glowing in the evening atmosphere, a wee galmoira fluttered in and rested on Blythe's shoulder.

"It is your galmoira," he said, deeply pleased.

Hazel only smiled, neglecting to admit she'd gifted the animal to a servant.

"Now, you possess one of the rarest creatures on the continent," he said dejectedly. "It was... clear the fire-beasts acquired a taste for the galmoira. They'll be extinct by now, short of this fellow."

Hazel's heart bled over this. She couldn't imagine the southern region without them. "I am so very sorry. It is a *sorrowful* loss."

He looked her in the eyes. "Thank you, Lady Hazel. It pleases me you regard them as we do." He appeared to shrug this off as he said, "At any rate, my people will make camp in your forest this evening. You may use the time to assure your people of our well-meaning. Tomorrow, we aid you in whatever respect we can be of use."

Hazel glowed as bright as a galmoira at night as she looked to Armond, who seemed only to sit stunned by this turn of events. They had protection, they had manpower, they had builders. And they had *allies*. She widened her eyes at him, urging him to say something.

"I must thank you, Sir Blythe, for a debt I may never rightly be able to repay," he said.

Hazel nodded happily.

* * *

Before the sun had scarcely risen the following morning, Hazel was awoken with a start.

"Lady Hazel," Gunther whispered outside her tent.

"Come in," she said groggily. Sitting up from her makeshift bed.

He opened the flap but only set foot in the doorway. "I apologize for waking you. We have a situation."

She rubbed her eyes. "What is it?"

"Two of the smaller dragons have been sighted not far from here. It is believed they will soon find us and... do what they do."

She blinked at him, her mind racing for what to do.

"Shall I... wake the king?" he asked.

The very fact he'd come to her before Armond was a concern. It revealed that Gunther knew the king was not in charge.

"Yes. I will come with you."

Armond stood stricken upon hearing the news. Hazel stepped on his foot to which he leaped and righted himself.

"Shall we send guardsmen?" Gunther suggested.

"No," Hazel replied. "Armond will wish to handle this himself. He is the dragon-slayer after all."

Armond looked to her with a raised brow.

She eyed him.

"Uh, aye… I… will go," he said weakly.

Gunther looked between them, clearly skeptical. "Very well, your majesty." He bowed out of the tent.

"Are you cracked?" Armond hissed. "I can't face off two dragons on my own!"

"First of all, they're small. Secondly, I will be coming with you. I'll meet you at the edge of the cliffs and we'll go in together. The people need more assurance you are a capable leader and this is our chance."

"First of all, I'm *not* a capable leader. Secondly, *you're* no fighter."

"I slew the big one."

He nearly grinned, shaking his head. "How ever did you do it?"

"I raced up his back, stabbed my sword into his neck and hung on for dear life as it tore down his flesh."

"That…" he began with raised brows, "is a stunning feat. *Well done,* Hazel."

"I don't need your adulation," she replied shortly, her memory momentarily jolted back to the day he'd been so very disappointed she was like all the other girls. "I just need your armored rear-end in those cliffs by sunrise so I don't have to do this alone."

"What if I freeze up again?"

"Then I'll do it alone." She was impressed by her show of confidence in the face of her private trepidation. She only hoped "small" meant *really* small… and that Armond wouldn't freeze up.

* * *

It wasn't until she had fortuitously wandered into the very clearing where the dark dragon lay sleeping that she understood small really meant bigger than a horse. This, to her estimation, was quite large enough.

Silently, she backed away and hid behind the nearest bush. "This won't do," she murmured under her breath. And where was Armond? She worked to remind herself she'd bested a dragon many times this one's size. Why could she not do so again? And yet... despite the fact that one of its kind had obliterated her kingdom, she found it difficult to descend upon the unconscious beast.

"Hazel," Armond whispered.

She leaped, snapping a twig underfoot. The two peered over the bush.

No movement.

"Where have you been?" she scolded.

"It takes a while to get into all this." He gestured to his armor.

She peered down at herself in her filthy, torn dress.

"I suppose this isn't exactly fair, is it?" he said meekly.

She shook her head.

"So, what's your plan?" he asked.

"*My* plan? You're the one who's been battle-trained."

"But you're the one who has actually done this before."

She quirked her head. He was right. Recalling a book she'd read about a king who'd lopped off the head of his enemy in his sleep, she worked up both her stomach and her courage. Stepping out into the clearing again, she directed Armond to warn her should the creature awaken. Then, she tiptoed toward the creature until she faced its back, carefully avoiding the end where the fire blazed out.

Raising her crimson blade, she made ready to strike when the weight of the unfamiliar weapon sent her toppling backward. Into the pile of dead leaves, she went and *up* went the dragon.

With its barred teeth mere inches from her face, she reached for the fallen sword... but it was too far. Taking a last look at the animal, she dove for her weapon. That was when the flame surged.

But when she turned over, she found it had merely singed the end of her dress. Taking up her sword, she leaped up in time to find Armond standing before the beast, hindering it from reaching her. *At last,* he had discovered his courage. But as she waited for him to make some move, he stood motionless.

"Armond! Either move out of the way or attack, but *do something."*

She soon regretted this direction when the sound of her voice diverted the dragon's attention. As it reared back on hind legs, Hazel did not realize it meant to leap until it was in the air, springing toward her.

"Armond, *now!"* she cried, recognizing he had the perfect opportunity to spear its fleshy underbelly.

In moments, it was atop her. She screamed and it was many moments before she realized it was not moving. At last, it was hoisted off her. Armond held a hand out to help her up. Leaping to her feet, she observed the beast. As she'd directed, Armond's sword stuck out from its flesh.

The two looked to one another, smirks slowly spreading on their faces.

"We did it!" he announced, leaping to sweep her about in a circle.

Laughingly, she spun, but quickly she drew away. "So we did," she said with satisfaction.

"I only wish *that* had been me the day of the first dragon attack. I might actually feel like the hero everyone believes I am."

Hazel couldn't say he had been *altogether* impressive, but she let it slide. "At least now it'll be the truth when people call you dragon-slayer."

His eyes widened.

"Well, it's true…" she defended.

He shoved her and drew his blade from the beast's side.

Mouth open in shock, she followed his gaze to where the second dragon stood over its companion. It nearly stole the breath from her to witness the pain in its eyes. She hadn't realized how intelligent they were. For a moment—and despite the accursed fire that had altered its makeup—it *felt* the loss of its kind. Though it pained Hazel to do it, she leaped beside Armond, sword at the ready. But this one was faster, angrier. It swept them aside with its tail before they knew what was happening.

Armond drew back onto his feet while Hazel reeled from smacking her head upon a rock. The dragon lost no time in responding, casting seething flames over them. Armond tripped over Hazel's legs in an effort to escape. With no other choice, Hazel rolled until she struck a tree. The pain of the impact jarred her hip. She turned over in search of Armond.

He was unconscious. Had he been hurt? Had he fainted? She worked to stand but it was difficult with her tender hip. Her sword was nowhere to be seen. This was it. They were done for. As the dragon surged toward her, she closed her eyes to her fate before she heard the thud of a body hitting the ground.

"Armond?!" she screamed.

She opened her eyes.

But it was the dragon, an arrow in its neck. She turned in elated expectation of a southern tribesman. What she found instead was… another dragon?

14

The beast floated down through the trees, nearly landing atop Hazel. She flung herself out of the way, then leaped to her feet, sword at the ready. But she stopped short.

This dragon possessed a rider.

The passenger leaped from the dragon with hands raised. "Hold your horses there, young woman. This dragon means you no harm."

Her sword remained ready as she glanced beyond him to this new beast. It eyed her a moment before turning to a nearby tree and extracting a batch of leaves from it. Then, it chewed.

"It eats... leaves?" she muttered in confusion.

"Anything green," the stranger replied. "As does every dragon who has not been possessed by the curse of the dark flame."

She studied the stranger, who appeared a decade or so older than herself. This man had answers. She sheathed her sword and stretched out her hand. "Lady Hazel of Kierelia."

"Latos," he said, taking her hand, "Realm Leader of the Greater Archipelagos, a neighboring realm."

Her hand froze as she studied him with a dubious eye. "I have heard of no such realm."

"By realm I mean world… or perhaps planet. It is complicated."

"Are you claiming you come from the stars?"

He shook his head. "More like an alternative layer of your universe. Yes, we travel from a portal in the sky, but—You know what? Yes, from the stars."

She had never heard of men who came from planes in the heavens. "…Prove it."

He eyed her. "That is a very difficult instruction, Lady Hazel." He pondered a moment. "You have inherited the gift of voice, which… means you perform great acts with song through a power embedded in specific intonations of your vocal cords."

She blinked back at him. "How can you know that? Do you know the prophet? A southern clansman, perhaps?"

He shook his head. "I possess a keen ear for the Great One's voice. I listen for what he would say and hear more clearly than any other. It is *my* gift and it is one of many bestowed upon the people of my world. This, I'm afraid, is all the proof I can offer."

"I have sung in the way you describe but once."

"You will again."

She shook her head. It was unnerving to have a perfect stranger claim to possess knowledge from the god of *her* land.

"He is God to us all," he said as if hearing her thoughts.

She blinked at him. "You remind me of someone…" she murmured, considering the way he spoke, his appearance. "Ah! It is the prophet." Though, this man was much younger than the other.

Latos appeared surprised. "You possess a *prophet* in this land?"

Armond squealed, alerting the two to his consciousness. The dragon ate from the branches over his body.

"It is all right!" Hazel cried, racing to him. "Do not harm it. I think it must be this man's pet."

Latos chuckled. "He is Tragor, my *friend*."

The dragon eyed her.

Hazel glared back until she softened against her will. It *was* beautiful. "These dragons…" she began, "they are of your world, I gather?"

Shame crossed his face much as it had the prophet's. But what could the two have had to do with this predicament?

"I'm afraid that is why I have come… I must speak with the leader of your kingdom at once."

Hazel hoisted Armond to his feet. "This is the man you are looking for. He is king now."

Armond looked to her. "And who is this?"

"Claims he is 'Realm Leader' of another planet. And he *knows* things."

Without further ado, Latos fell to his knee before Armond, his right arm drawn across his chest. "I have come to bear responsibility for the destruction of your kingdom, King Armond." Raising his bowed head, he said, "In a fury, I cast my problem into your world and your people have paid the price. I must now pledge the legions of my realm to the destruction of this strain of dark dragons. I give my word that I will not take my leave of your kingdom until every one of them has been obliterated and the sorceress who created them taken in hand."

Hazel bent to raise him to his feet. She was not one for ceremony, even if the sentiment was so sincere. "Explain yourself, man."

He sighed. "A woman by the name of Aradia professed love for me. As a married man, I rebuffed her. When she attempted to kill me in retaliation, I banished her to your world. From what we have been able to gather, she consorted with the sorcerers of your realm and was taught the dark arts, something never heard of in my domain. In any case, she is the woman who created the dark flame that summoned the dragons from my world, the Greater Archipelagos, and possessed them with the Dark One's daemonkind."

Hazel looked to Armond, who was wide-eyed and appeared to understand little of what was said. Certainly, he knew not how to respond.

"This is a sorrowful tale for both our worlds," Hazel replied. "I deeply regret you thought Kaern, let alone Kierelia, an adequate prison for your foe... But I esteem your accountability, as well as your willingness, to attempt to amend the calamity. Truly, I am uncertain what we would do without it."

The man bowed again. "I thank you for your understanding, Lady Hazel." He looked to Armond, working to read him. "King Armond."

Armond raised his brows and nodded. Clearly, he was unused to being called king. His own people scarcely did as yet.

"How many warriors have you brought with you to slay these beasts?" Hazel inquired.

Latos pointed to the skies. Squinting past the rays of the sun, she realized that what looked like hundreds of dots in the sky were actually dragons with riders.

"Those are all *your* men?" Armond gasped, possibly envious.

"Men and women, yes."

Hazel looked to Armond with concern. "Our people will attempt to slay those dragons should they come near, riders or not."

Latos appeared greatly concerned by this. "That is not acceptable. Perhaps you might leave the slaying of dragons only to my people."

Armond looked to Hazel questioningly.

She shook her head. "That will not do either," she said. "Our people will find it difficult to entrust their whole safety to strangers. I think you must put forth a directive, Armond. No dragon shall be slain who is marked by..." She searched the dragon before her. Though it possessed none of the malevolence of the dark dragons, it was fairly indistinguishable from them. "Sir Latos, I wonder if you could have your dragons wear some kind of flag about their necks to denote them as benign."

He considered her suggestion before nodding. "That is an astute solution. We will do so immediately and commence our undertaking."

Hazel bowed to the man who claimed to be leader of an entire planet among the stars and tugged at Armond to do the same.

"We wish you the favor of the Great Entity and admire your accountability," Armond pronounced, appeasing Hazel with his diplomacy, even if he had all but mimicked her own words.

The man bowed low to each of them before leaping upon his dragon as it lifted into the sky.

Later that evening, Hazel lay in her tent, astonished by the events of the last few days. She and her people had lost everything. They were devastated and compromised. But for the first time since the upheaval, she might enjoy a peaceful night's rest.

Though the prophet had claimed King Zephuel's foolishness had lost them the favor of the Great Entity, she began to feel the Entity's recompense for all they'd lost. The entirety of the southern tribes had come to their aid and now they'd acquired a battalion of protectors from another world. They had so much more than her sheer stubbornness and a king who boasted more beauty than ingenuity. Yet, Armond had demonstrated his potential that day. Not only had he stood between her and a dragon, he had helped her slay one. Surely, that was evidence of greater things to come.

15

It had taken but a year for Kierelia to unite, erect a new royal fortress and provide homes for most of its citizens to see them to this day: Armond's coronation. Though he had been called king for some time, the occasion was imperative. It would dissuade any uncertainty that he was, indeed, ruler of the land.

This was something that had been whispered about as Hazel had been helping to direct things, encouraging the people to work in harmony and labor well for their future. But her intimate involvement had generated an unfortunate consequence. It had made the people wonder if perhaps a *queen* upon the throne would not more effectively safeguard the future she had been inspiring them toward. The moment Guardsman Gunther had relayed this talk to her had been the moment she'd told Armond it was time he had his own voice. From there, she'd stepped back as much as possible.

Thankfully, Armond had already been contributing in unexpected ways. He was gifted with settling disputes, reminding Hazel of his old nature. He also visited the elderly, supposedly to comfort them after all that had occurred but really to garner what wisdom they offered. Furthermore, he understood much more about the dealings of soldiers, something Hazel was ill-equipped for.

Despite this show of his capabilities, it was not in the kingdom's best interest for her to step away completely. After all, she'd been the one working with the architect on the plans for the castle's reconstruction, along with the other facilities. A sizable kitchen lodge had gone up first, where many could gather to be fed during their appointed shifts. The food was prepared by an unpaid staff, who were often employed all the day long. Stacia and Rebecca were among them. After trying them in a number of other duties, it was the only one that had at all suited and they began to show real promise. In fact, Hazel was quite certain they delighted in the task. After all, it was one of the few chores that rescued one from the mercies of the weather.

Dianna was another matter. She refused to leave the room she'd been given in the future inn. This made finding a task to make use of her quite difficult, especially as Hazel refused to visit her in order to make demands. But eventually, it was discovered she possessed something of a gift with the needle. Before long, she had sewn up new clothes for nearly every refugee. Moreover, she did it more swiftly than was reasonably expected.

In an act of desperation, Hazel appointed Dorian as her own assistant. She had very soon found herself the chief answerer of questions and solver of difficulties. Moreover, it was challenging for her to allow others to perform work she could very well do herself. But when, one day, Dorian had found her in a state of exhausted tears, he'd insisted she allow him to take on some of her duties. But not only did he become assistant to the king's chief advisor, he got himself named the kingdom's secondary dragon-slayer. Possessing a keen eye, he was often the first to spot danger on the horizon. Without alerting anyone, he crept off to handle matters himself. The first time he'd informed Hazel of this, she'd turned to him with annoyance.

"How could you go off without me? What if you'd been killed? We'd never have known what had become of you!"

He quirked a brow at her. "First of all, I don't see why I'd take *you* along. Second of all, I did not find it difficult. As all else has reported, it was a smaller dragon than the one that destroyed the fortress."

Since she could not very well reveal her aid in the slaying of the first three, she was forced to concur with his argument. And as it was, his slaying of the four following became a matter of routine, earning him the honored title.

By this time, hundreds of surviving Kierelians had come to live and work at the castle site. They shared food and shelter as both small and large cottages and inns were erected. And with her own hands, Hazel helped their people lay stone after stone of the new royal fortress. Before she had been forced to give it up, the matter furthered her reputation as their resolute leader. They couldn't help but admire her for dirtying her hands beside theirs.

To make matters worse, she'd been proclaimed their good luck charm. In fact, she'd developed a title of her own: Lady Fortune. This had arisen out of a strange occurrence. Unthinkingly, she had taken to singing as she worked, which brought joy to her listeners and helped to bide the time until day's end. One day, she yipped, releasing a stone from her hand.

"Was that a *spark*, my lady?" the woman working beside her questioned.

Shaking her hands, Hazel nodded with a self-deprecating smile as she picked up her broken brick. It wasn't until the following day that she endured the incident again. In fact, with nearly every slab she lay, a tiny bolt sparked between it and her fingers. Before long, she'd almost learned to disregard the occurrence. But this was not so for the workers as it was eventually considered a good omen.

"Twill be a *blessed* fortress now, Lady Fortune," they decreed.

Over the days that followed, she realized it only occurred when she handled the *old* stones—the ones whole enough to be used. To add anxiety to peculiarity, it only happened when she *sang* or even hummed.

Strange enough as it was, she told no one of the sensation that occurred in her own body. In time, she sensed that she was either depositing something *into* the bricks... or taking something out. She could never be sure. Either way, a transference occurred and it frightened her, especially when the sensation of carrying it around with her continued even after she'd given up the labor. Questioning if it had something to do with the gift she was meant to possess, she relayed her troubles to Blythe.

"I've never heard it's like from our people," he said. "I'm afraid you, Lady Hazel, contain something unknown."

"Why must it be that I *contain* something?" she asked, both exasperated and frightened.

He shook his head. "I cannot say, but... a spark can only emerge from within... or be making an entrance from without. I instruct you to be leery."

This conversation had done little good, but it *had* put her in mind of something she'd been meaning to discuss with Armond. She approached him later that day with, "It is in both regions' best interest that we convince the southern tribes to join the Kierelian kingdom."

He looked to her in astonishment. "I cannot believe that has not occurred to me. Will you have their leaders brought before me at once?"

Pleased, she promptly did so and sat at the back of the tent to survey her king at work.

"Southern tribesman," Armond began.

A meager salutation for the leaders of a proud region but acceptable.

"It is with great pleasure that I offer you a place under the rule of our fine Kierelian kingdom."

Hazel froze.

Wyse, the leader of one of the largest tribes, spat upon the floor. "You think we will leap at the chance to place ourselves under another kingdom's rule? Let alone one so *highfaluting*—"

"Wyse," Blythe cut him off. "We do not insult our neighboring king, no matter the provocation."

Armond appeared like a deer in sight of an arrow. "I-I thought you would be pleased... to become Kierelians. After all, you've sown so much into—"

"Precisely," said the third leader with a glimmer of humor. "*We* have helped *you*. Perhaps it is you who should come under our rule."

"Kierelians under the dominion of tribesman?" Armond asked, genuinely unsettled.

Hazel leaped from her seat to stand beside him. "Revered leaders of the free tribes," she said with hands folded neatly before her. "In truth, we are in great need of not only an alliance with your people but a closer bond. Already, yours and ours have established marital unions, many more have formed intimate friendships. Moreover, your protection and work ethic over these past six Kierelian seasons have been unquestionably indispensable." She turned to Armond with, "Dare we say it?"

His brows rose and he nodded without a hint of understanding.

"Not only could we never have gotten where we are today,"

she said, "but I do not know that we will, in the end, survive as a kingdom without you."

Blythe grinned at her, knowing full well that, though she meant every word, she presented the proposal rather... artfully.

"I understand you desire both our population," Wyse began, "and our guardianship over the border to the Deep South. But what precisely can *you* offer *us*?"

Hazel stole a moment to clear her throat. "It is true we already owe you so much and have promised to aid you in the rebuilding of your own lands. But you are aware that, with your land between us and the Deep South, you are just as vulnerable to them as we are. In order to take us, they will take you."

When the leaders appeared displeased by this turn, she continued with, "Do not misunderstand. I have heard tell of how victoriously you've held them at bay in the past. In fact, you're fairly famed for it in Kierelia and the surrounding kingdoms. But there *will* come a day when we will need one another... quite equally. Why not rally together and merge as a united force now, that we may be thoroughly equipped when that day arrives?"

After long looks exchanged between the leaders, Blythe stepped forward to take Hazel's hand. "We acquiesce to your proposal, for your sake, Lady Hazel. *You* are our blood as well as our neighbor. Now, we are closer than neighbors. We are fellow countrymen. It appears... we are *Kierelians.*"

But her rapture over the moment had been short-lived. Not long after, a gentleman dressed as peculiarly as Latos, the Realm Leader of the Greater Archipelagos, arrived to speak with her.

Bowing low before her, he said, "My report is of a dual purpose. Firstly, I have come to make you aware that my people have, to the best of our ability, completed the promised task. Every dragon has either been slain or fled into deep hiding and not likely to be seen again for some time."

"Oh!" Hazel exclaimed. She had noticed the dragon sightings had diminished. "Oh, you must send my thanks to Latos. It is a fine man who will keep his word, even to the extent of keeping away from his own land for so long in order to do so."

He bowed his head. "That is the other matter I came to report. You see, it is why *I* stand before you rather than he."

Hazel's stomach twisted.

"Some weeks ago, when he felt he'd done all he could for your land, he took it upon himself to face down his foe, Sorceress Aradia."

"He went *alone*?"

"My lady, he is the greatest warrior our people have ever seen. And when he insists upon a thing, one does not question him. That said, it is with great remorse I report that he has, in fact, been bested by the witch… that he has passed on to the world beyond."

Hazel's hand went to her throat with emotion. She'd scarcely known the man, but he'd walked, spoken and acted with *greatness*. She mourned for his people at such a loss. Clearing her throat, she said, "Please convey our deepest sorrow to your people. He was an estimable person. I am so very sorry his end was met in the aid of our kingdom."

He bowed low again. "He would not have had it any other way, to be certain, Lady Hazel. I thank you for your sentiment and will pass it on to the rulers of the Greater Archipelagos."

After that, he lifted away atop his dragon.

Now in her freshly-completed chambers, Hazel was caught frowning when Anna, her lady's maid, broke into her remembrances with, "Though I imagine they'd wait all day before starting the coronation without you, it would be courteous to appear *on time*."

Hazel fully agreed, though she carefully avoided the mirror as she vacated the room. She'd been dressed as she never had before—as royally as any queen, she was sure. It made her uncomfortable, but Anna had insisted it was correct. As Hazel was one of the very few remaining nobles and was, after all, the best-loved, it was required she do her part. Thus, it was in a gleaming green gown, gold slippers and delicate, vine-like tiara that she descended the stairs.

She knew it was self-centered to feel so anxious. After all, it was Armond's big day and she well knew how apprehensive he was. She'd spent the whole of the prior evening bolstering his courage not only for the ceremony but his reign. In the end, it had been Dorian's assurances that brought peace to the king nearly crowned and released them all for an evening's rest.

"Hazel, by the birds in the sky, you look a right vision," Armond said with a genuine sparkle in his eyes.

She knew her deep red blush would have utterly spoiled the effect had she not just spent the entirety of the last year under the effects of the sun. "And you look a stately king—*quite* regal."

It was clear this satisfied him as he stood all the taller. Offering his arm, he asked, "Well… are we ready?"

"Are 'we' ready?" She chuckled. "This really has nothing to do with me."

His expression transformed. "Nothing to do with you?" He leaned in close to whisper. "I wouldn't be here without you. Furthermore, it was quite a distinction that they requested you act as crowner."

Her nerves spiked again. "Thankfully, I was not asked to perform the ceremony." As it was, an old friar from the eastern border had arrived eager to aid their new king. He was an unpretentious, elderly man who had become Armond's assistant as Dorian had been hers. It was well he'd come to understand Armond's weaknesses and self-doubt. But he was judicious and empathetic enough to offer wisdom without overstepping.

Needless to say, he was a godsend by Hazel's estimation and had been, by her meddling, appointed royal priest, though the kingdom had not possessed one for decades.

"Armond, dear, I'm afraid you must release my arm and escort yourself to that other entrance," she said

"Oh, I'd already forgotten. And we only just rehearsed last night!" He raced for the other end of the hall.

Chuckling to herself, Hazel was about to enter through the secondary entrance when Gunther approached.

"We have a problem," he said soberly.

Her stomach turned at sight of his anxious face. "Well, what is it, man?"

"Castlehaven is under attack."

"Attack?" She had to question this. She'd heard no battle sounds whatever. She did, however, begin to perceive the clopping of hooves.

"They have not made their move as yet, but there currently resides a sizable battalion of foreign soldiers outside the castle gates, commanded by a man I do not recognize. I... surmise they may be our enemies from the Deep South."

Hazel felt she would drop through the floor. But then, she stopped herself. She had toiled too laboriously for this day. They all had. It was too late for anyone to turn up to take them now. She simply would not allow it.

Marching on ahead of Gunther, she disregarded his pleas that she await the protection of a personal guard and threw open the double-doors. Her breath was immediately caught by the great legion of knights before her. But at the head of them was not a stranger from the Deep South. It was Fredrick, the *wretched* duke of Galfree.

Marching up to his horse like a man weighted in armor, she threw a finger toward him and roared, "How *dare* you appear here after all we've done to pick ourselves up from the ashes only for you to steal our kingdom away from us. And on *this*, the coronation day. I *will not* have it, I tell you!"

To her utter dismay, he responded by throwing his head back in laughter. Her face heated. She understood his amusement. What could a lone woman possibly do to stop them? But she had slain a towering dragon. She could sort any needlework catastrophe put before her. She'd learned she could produce treaties between kingdoms. This man was not yet acquainted with her tenacity.

When at last he had composed himself, he said, "I'm afraid you harbor a misunderstanding, Lady Hazel. We are not here to prevent the coronation. Over the last year, we have been inundated with tales of how Kierelia rebuilt itself from nothing. Though already allied, our admiration for your kingdom has multiplied.

"As it stands, after learning of rumors that the kingdom of Stlock had plans to cause trouble for your king this day, we decided it was in our best interest to attend. In other words, we are here to *safeguard* the coronation."

Chewing her lower lip, Hazel crossed her arms and stared up in bewilderment. Part of her was grateful… if his tale was true. But she was perplexed as to why he considered them allied with Galfree. Furthermore, why should he have any interest in Kierelia's welfare after the way he'd spoken of it when last they'd met?

"And what business is it of yours, Sir Duke?" she questioned. For, truly, she began to realize how unusual it was that Galfree possessed such a mighty battalion. Moreover, why had they not offered to aid them when they'd *truly* needed it all the last year?

He raised a severe brow despite the glimmer of good humor in his eyes. "That is crowned *King* Fredrick of Bashtii to you, Lady Hazel."

Hazel's arms flew to her sides. "Bashtii?" Her mind raced.

"I... I was of the understanding you were Duke Fredrick of Galfree."

He shook his head and, quite suddenly, a bright smile dawned upon his face. "When last I was here... was *everyone* in Castlehaven under that impression?"

Meekly, she nodded.

He raised his brows. "That explains a *great* deal. I *was*, at the time, Duke Fredrick... but of Bashtii. I am acquainted with this Fredrick, the duke of Galfree, and now comprehend perfectly the lack of hospitality I received here. Indeed, I do believe he was meant to pay a visit to Kierelia about the time I did but had unearthed himself a bride before his departure. I, however, arrived because my cousin, King Claros, had recently passed away. I was meant to relay this news to King Zephuel and inform him of my approaching coronation to the kingship. But I was unable to obtain a conference with him before I... took my leave."

Hazel shook her head in disbelief. *"King* Fredrick," she began, sweeping him a deep curtsy, "I beg your pardon for the ill welcome you received on your visit. I assure you, had the king known your true identity, your stay would have been an entirely different occasion. Up to a year ago, your kingdom had been our greatest ally. We were pained that you turned your back on us in our hour of need. It is now abundantly clear as to why the friendship waned.

"I thank you, on behalf of the kingdom, that you have taken such care to arrive at our aid this day, despite our treatment of you in past." She hesitated a moment before, "But as things are becoming clear, I must state again that I do not understand this consideration." Bearing in mind what ill will he had likely harbored, she half-feared it was all a ruse to storm the gates.

With a smirk, he relaxed in his saddle. "I'm afraid I am a lazy king. If Kierelia does not thrive and the land becomes obtainable, I will be forced to enter into war with another nation over it. I simply prefer not to go to war." With a shrug, he added, *"I know. I am a discredit to my dynasty."*

She worked to with-hold the smirk that so desired to creep onto her face. "Crowned King Fredrick of Bashtii, I earnestly invite you to witness the coronation of your allied king this day."

He shook his head. "I have brought my men all this way and will remain here to perform my duty alongside them until the ceremony is complete."

Her eyes drifted to the soldiers' faces behind him as they dutifully sat upon their steeds, bringing utmost honor to their leader. "I do not believe a word of your laziness," she said. "I have a feeling in the short time you've been king, you have proved a judicious one."

16

To Hazel's right and left sat the crowned kings of Kierelia and Bashtii. This was a moment she'd never thought to dream of let alone desire. As it was, she found she did not like it. It drew the eyes of the room to her, making it difficult to enjoy the feast at her ease. Even so, she took pride in the moment. Her king was now officially the crowned and rightful king of Kierelia, and the leader of their greatest allied kingdom was in attendance.

The rest of the nobility consisted only of the friar turned royal priest, a few lords who'd been discovered to have survived the attacks on their lands as well as a handful of former peasants who, through the loss of kin, had inherited wealth, land and titles. Lastly, there were Stacia and Rebecca. Hazel wasn't certain where Dianna was.

"King Fredrick," Stacia began, "I heard a tale about a 'golden king' who rules a kingdom across the Bashtiian sea. Could that by any chance be you?"

Hazel glanced at the king beside her, easily reconciling why Stacia believed he may be. Not only had he arrived in a golden suit of armor, but his hair, eyes and skin were various hues of gold as well.

To the surprise of both ladies, he nearly blushed. "I am afraid it is."

"But that must bode well of your people's adoration," Stacia said. "It is said the golden king is considered a godsend."

He shook his head. "It is clear the people and I are on good terms, but I have only been in rule but a year." Then, he shook his head and leaned in with. "Now, *you* must point out this Lady Fortune we've been hearing so much about."

Stacia raised an amused brow. "I am afraid, King Fredrick, you've been sitting beside her the last three courses."

His brows rose. "You mean to tell me that you are she? I had not realized! Why, it is a great honor to have made your acquaintance."

Stacia chuckled. "Nay, you dear man. It is Lady Hazel."

Slowly, he turned to Hazel with new eyes. "We have been hearing stories of the Lady Fortune and her king and how they conquered all... I had not dreamed *you* were her."

"How flattering," Hazel said with a curt nod.

Not catching her drift, he continued, "As I said before, you have the admiration of Bashtii. You, Lady Fortune, are a hero to our young women... to *all*, really."

She blushed, once again grateful for her bronze complexion. To think her name, or her *nickname*, was known to people of a kingdom she'd never even been to. "I'm sure my part in the story must have been exaggerated," she said. "I am no hero."

"Did you not help King Armond orchestrate the restoration in but a year?"

"Well, yes, but there are still homes to be built, particularly in the newly acquired southern region."

"That is another item of interest. It is said the tribes were assimilated because of, well, their love of the honorable Lady Fortune, whom they consider to be as close as kin."

Hazel blinked as she realized he was actually looking at her as if *he* admired her as his people did. His marveling eyes on her were nearly unsettling. "Well… that is because we *are* kin. A portion of their blood runs within mine."

He raised his brows. "You possess the wild, tenacious blood of the tribes? No wonder you've got cheek."

"She is bold because she is Kierelian," Armond said with an irritation Hazel found difficult to comprehend. He looked to her with bright eyes. "And because she is *Hazel*, a most capable and brilliant lady."

"Couldn't agree more." Fredrick raised his glass. "To Lady Fortune, who raised her kingdom from embers."

Armond raised his glass as well. "And who has been my closest and most trusted confidant these last six seasons. May we be worthy of her."

"Here, here," Fredrick added.

They drank then, eyeing one another over her head. Hazel glanced between them. There was something entirely male happening in the subtext of the exchange that she could not quite grasp. It was unhappily clear to her that they did not much care for one another, which was a pity if they wished to remain close allies.

"So, Lady Hazel," Fredrick said. "What are your plans now the work is finished? A woman so capable as yourself must have impressive ambitions."

"I have never been ambitious," she replied easily. "And the work here isn't close to complete." She caught herself and turned to Armond. "That is, I feel certain the king has arrangements to continue piecing our kingdom back together. We're working our way out of a deceased economy, there are inquiries on whether taxes ought to be collected any time soon... and much more. We must see the kingdom flourishes swiftly in both trade and population."

With raised brows, Fredrick looked to Armond. "You must greatly appreciate possessing such an asset, King Armond. Having been crowned but a year ago, I easily confess I wish my kingdom boasted a Lady Fortune. It has been a difficult journey finding those whom one may trust."

"I am certain she is appreciated by all, but by none more so than myself," Armond returned. "She is a boon... and a charming one at that."

Hazel passed him a bewildered glance. "I may be called many things, but I think none would necessarily call me charming."

"And that," Fredrick said, "is a charming response."

Hazel very nearly rolled her eyes. It was time for a change of subject. "So, King Fredrick, I have heard Bashtii experiences fine weather this time of year."

Light entered his eyes as he described his kingdom. It was clear he loved his as she did hers. But as the evening progressed, she worried Armond would grow irritable from being ignored. But contrary to her last meeting with Fredrick, he was interested only in conversing with her—Lady Fortune.

"Where is Dorian, I wonder?" Armond said suddenly.

Hazel tore herself from Fredrick to search the room. "Gunther," she called to where he stood guard. "I don't suppose you know anything of Dorian's whereabouts?

"That's something I meant to discuss with you after the festivities. I'm afraid he is in the dungeon."

Her brows furrowed. "Whatever *for?* Surely, you did not

require him to return to his cell after all he has done to aid us?"

Gunther shook his head. "He is of another mind. He had *himself* re-imprisoned just after the coronation."

"What on Kaern is going on in that man's head?" she cried. "And who saw fit to yield to his appeal?"

"It was me, my lady, "Gunther admitted, "but only after I could withstand his relentless petitions no more. By the end of his speech… I'm afraid he had me convinced he was correct."

"And you did not think it your duty to seek *my* opinion?" Armond asked from beside her.

Hazel turned to discover unexpected annoyance on his face. For the first time, he was responding like a king without her urging.

Gunther bowed. "He was insistent it be done with haste and I did not wish to disturb your celebration. However, I had every intention of relaying the situation to both of you later tonight."

Hazel's hands tightened into fists at her sides. "I'm going to see him, the *fool.*"

"You'll have to excuse us, King Fredrick," Armond called, placing a hand on Hazel's back as if to escort her.

She nearly froze as she realized that the passive rivalry between them might just be over *her*. Irritated over Armond's juvenile conduct, she shrugged his hand away and marched from the room.

As she made her way through the new castle's passages, she was filled with unexpected sorrow that it no longer shifted each day, as the old one had. Even so, she had to admit it was handy to know precisely where one was going. She had just reached the bottom of the dungeon stairwell when a sudden warm gust swept her off her feet.

"Tell him," an adamant voice whispered.

"What?" she called from the floor, hoping Armond had spoken from behind her.

"Are you all right?" he asked, rushing down the stairs to where she lay.

"Who's there?" she shouted as she was aided to her feet.

A deep laugh echoed through the corridor, bouncing off walls, echoing over and again through her mind. *"Tell him... of my benevolence."*

"We will have to put some kind of handrail on these stairs," Armond muttered unhappily as he surveyed her.

The laugh continued to echo through her mind. It was a knowing sound. Somehow, it both discomfited and delighted her.

"Who *was* that?" she asked.

"What do you mean...? Did someone *push* you?"

She shook her head. "There was a gust from below and... a voice."

Armond took hold of her shoulders, examining her face. "What is your name?"

"...Hazel?"

"Do you know where you are?"

"I'm standing in the Castlehaven Keep with a king who thinks I'm batty."

He released her. "You're well enough. But you ought to be seen by the physician."

"I didn't fall, Armond. I... floated."

He raised a dubious brow.

She shook her head. "Let's just find Dorian."

Her mind raced over what had transpired, who the voice could possibly have been. In the end, it came down to but one possibility. Could it have been the voice of the Great Entity, the god of their land and the spirit of the mirror room? Had he deigned to speak to her? But what might his meaning have been?

Tell him of my benevolence. Could it... have been meant for *Dorian?* But why should she have been selected as the Entity's mouthpiece unless she was correct about one thing: She *had* encountered him in The Mirror. She might even have... met him.

"Give me your keys, please," she demanded of the prison guardsman.

"I... can't do that...? *Oh.*" His eyes fell to the king behind her. He handed her the ring.

"Where is he?" she asked.

"Who, my lady?"

"Dorian," Armond supplied.

"Oh, he's at the end. Said he wanted his old one."

Hazel rolled her eyes, hiked up her skirts and marched.

"What in the world are you thinking, you foolish boy?" she demanded as she reached his cell.

He twirled to face her. "Now, Hazel, I knew you wouldn't understand. It's why I did it while—"

She punched the key into the lock.

"Hazel, *really,* I have my reasons."

She turned the key and threw open the door. "And they are?"

His shoulders fell. "I'm a traitor and a killer. I understand you think the last year earned me my freedom, but I only did it for your sake."

"And for the kingdom," she said defiantly. "I saw you fall in love with it, watching it work together to build itself back up."

"Precisely why I will fulfill my sentence."

"A lifetime in prison, never seeing the sky over Kierelia again?"

"I deserve no less... I helped steal half the coffers and killed a royal guard. I-I met his *wife*—a lovely woman. She told me she *forgave* me. But if she, of all people, won't hold me accountable, someone has to. *I* have to. Now, close the door... *please.*"

Hazel was breathing hard. She was angry. It was true she was not so desperate for his friendship as in past, but she wanted it just the same. And she wanted what was best for him. With the folding of her arms, she walked away, the door left wide.

"Hazel!" he shouted.

She stopped, remembering what the voice in the breeze had said. "The Great Entity grants his pardon."

Silence. Then, "How would you ever know that?"

She turned around. "It is difficult to explain, but I think I know him. He told me he forgives you. He, the god of all the land, grants you emancipation from your wrongdoings." She walked into the cell and took his hand. "Please, come out of here with me."

"I don't understand why a god should be concerned with me..."

"Neither do I," she admitted. "But he is... enough to knock me flat on my back. I think he must be something of a conundrum... and a god of *pronounced* benevolence." She was uncertain why she felt so free to speak this way about an entity she did not rightly know. But the words were planted in her heart and from her mouth they flew.

"As is your king," Armond said, stepping forward. He drew his sword and for a moment Hazel panicked. Then, he laid it upon Dorian's shoulder. "I dub you *Sir* Dorian, knight of my guard and a member of my personal watch. During our most difficult time, you proved yourself worthy of my esteem, even inspiring me to step up a time or two. There are few in this world I have left to trust. You are one of them."

Dorian fell back a step, appearing as if he might weep. He turned to Hazel, his face searching hers. "Does... the Great Entity know *all?*"

She raised a brow. It was a peculiar question, but she nodded. "Of course he does." Or so she assumed.

Shaking his head, he released a charged chuckle, then let them escort him away.

Taking his arm as they walked down the hall, Hazel said, "Run to your room and see yourself into something more presentable. I want a turn with you when the dancing begins."

"You do realize I haven't a clue how to dance."

"Neither have half the people up there. Trust me, it'll be fun."

When they parted ways, she turned to Armond. *"Thank you."*

"Of course. He deserved it. He isn't the same man who went into the dungeons to begin with."

"I know. Sometimes, I feel I scarcely know him… until he does something stupid like this. That is *very* him. But what can I say? I love him."

Armond jerked away from her and proceeded to march out the nearest door into the garden. Incredulously, she followed after.

"Armond?"

"You're in love with him? I thought you were merely friends?"

She couldn't help laughing. "I'm not *in* love with him. He is more like a brother than anything—a very rascally little brother, even if he is a few years older."

The cloud over his head appeared to disperse as a small smile stole its way in.

"Well, I don't see what you have to be so pleased about," she said dubiously. "It isn't as if I'd have abandoned you to run away with him. Moreover, don't go about thinking you have some sort of ownership of me."

"W-what do you mean?"

"Don't think I didn't notice the way you acted around King Fredrick, as if him speaking to me was somehow treading on your toes. I cannot begin to fathom what got into you."

"I'm in love with you."

Hazel stepped back. In love with her? But then… she paused. "Why?"

"Why?"

"What makes you think you're in love with me?"

"How could I not love you? You've been remarkable. I always knew you were special, that you had a dignity about you. But until... *everything*, I had no idea who you were."

She glanced at their surroundings as he spoke, shaking her head as she realized they were in the very garden in which she had confessed her own feelings. The pain of that day returned. She had poured her soul out to him. And he had dealt his rejection in the most mortifying terms. It still made her face burn to think of it. "Well, I'm very disappointed in you, Armond," she bit back. "I had no idea you were 'just like all the other boys...'" She turned from him, ready for escape.

"Wait," he implored, stealing her wrist. "Please don't hold that *stupid* day against me. I was blind and childish and... *Marry* me, Hazel. Be queen of Kierelia. I can't imagine doing this without you."

So, *that* was it. *"Of course* you can't imagine doing it without me! And *of course* you suddenly want to *marry* me. You're terrified of doing this on your own because you know we'd never be *here* without me. And you're *so* right. But you're not in love with me. And whether or not we marry—we *won't*, by the way— I'll be here to help you in any way I can."

Armond swallowed, folded his arms and cast his gaze to the floor. He looked pitifully exposed. "You don't know that..."

She took a step toward him and gently patted his hand. "Neither do you."

Feeling more burdened than she liked to admit to herself, she returned to the coronation celebration. But it was to her dismay that she heard him call after her. It couldn't be that he hadn't given up, could it? Well, she could not face him again. Not tonight and not when she was not even completely aware of her own heart.

Seeing Fredrick, she took hold of him like a lifeline. "Do you care to dance, King Fredrick?"

Flinching, his gaze fell to her hand on his. "I forgot my gloves."

Armond had nearly arrived.

"Come, Fredrick, you do not require gloves to *dance.*"

He wrenched his hand away. "I don't dance."

She peered up at him. "The *golden* king of Bashtii does not know how to dance?" she asked lightly. But suddenly, she caught the consternation on his face. It brought to mind the first time they'd met. He'd been insulted by all the eager guardians attempting to cast their daughters upon him. She'd thought everything that had happened that night had been part of their misunderstanding. Apparently, that was not the case.

She stepped back. "I wasn't proposing *marriage* to you, or even desiring it. Truth be told, I was only working to avoid someone else. I apologize if consideration from a woman of my inconsequential status and tarnished reputation has offended your propriety yet again."

At last, Armond reached her, taking her hand into his. "I'd like to finish our conversation," he beseeched.

She turned to him, partly confused over their conversation not having reached a close but also finding the sight of him so much less disturbing in comparison with the alternative. "Oh, *come on,* Armond. Let's have this next dance."

It had been some time since any of them had danced and Hazel had scarcely done so in her youth. But it mattered little. They were in a room of rich and poor alike with few nobles present to critique.

"Are you going to tell me what that was about?" Armond asked.

Avoiding his gaze, she said, "I don't know what you mean."

"You went from fleeing the sight of me to fleeing *with* me... and from the *golden* king of Bashtii."

She peered up into his face in time to discover a smirk there. It was true he was jealous, but at this moment, he was only teasing.

"It was nothing of consequence, I assure you," she replied lightly.

"Well, whatever it was… good for him."

"Are you saying you're *pleased* he insulted me so I would dance with you?" she asked, feigning irritation when what she was beginning to feel was… flattered?

"He *insulted* you?" He ceased dancing and moved as if to confront Fredrick.

Swiftly, she took hold of his sleeve and towed him back into the dance. "The last thing we need is a feud between allied kingdoms," she said laughingly.

It was a moment before he could shrug it off, but he was soon smiling down at her. "Well, if he doesn't stop flirting with you, we may have one anyway."

"Flirting? Hardly!"

He chuckled. "Yes, *flirting*, my lady. Have you not been shown enough special attention in your life to understand when you're receiving it?"

She grew somber a moment. Thinking over her life, she certainly had not.

"I'm sorry…" he said softly, staring down with the old consideration, as if he knew her thoughts.

"I don't want to be pitied by you," she said. It was truer now than ever. It had been that pity that had made her believe he felt for her more than he had all that time ago. Of course… now he actually was claiming to possess feelings. But she had some serious misgivings.

He appeared surprised by her response and said soberly, "You *do not* have my pity, Hazel." In his tone, she read how much more he felt. She did not think it love. It was admiration, respect, esteem. As a girl, she'd wanted others to find her beautiful. But he honored her for who she was and she found that reached her much more significantly… crawling under her skin in a way she dreaded.

* * *

It was difficult to fall asleep that evening. Her mind spun with the events of the day—astonishing confessions, exasperating insults. But she was so proud Armond was crowned king. And his first decree had been to pardon Dorian by making him part of his personal guard. It did Armond credit that he recognized the quality of man Dorian had become, and had even seen fit to pardon the past by offering him a very promising second chance.

As for her sentiments about Armond's admission, she hardly knew what to think. She still firmly believed his sensation of feeling was due to his need of her. It was true he owed her much, she would not deny it. But she could not believe he was any more in love with her now than he had been before, even if so much had changed since then.

As for the state of her own heart... It was such a mess of emotion, she hardly knew how she felt. It was true: something of the old feelings for him had re-awoken when he'd spoken to her. But she could not bear to let it take root again. His prior rejection had cut deeply. She'd felt her world had fallen apart. The next morning, it actually had.

The look on Fredrick's face when she'd asked him to dance flashed into her memory. It was a little humiliating to know he'd thought her chasing after him and had so detested it. But why had he shown her such attention only a short while before if she was so far beneath him?

She pounded her fist into the mattress as she realized it must have been in response to Armond's little rivalry over her. How could she have believed he truly esteemed her? Well, she would do all in her power to avoid him until he went away again.

But then... she remembered why he'd come, how he'd arrived with a whole *battalion*. Surely, there was kindness in him... but that did not mean *she* had to concern herself with it. That was up to Armond, as was negotiating the renewed alliance. In his treatment of Dorian, Armond had proven to her how worthy he'd grown of his crown. This negotiation was his chance to prove himself to the *people*.

17

That night, Hazel awoke to a burning in her chest. Upon peering down, she found the place from which the pain stemmed was... glowing. With a squeal, she leaped from the bed and raced to the full-length mirror. It continued to burn as she watched it work its way toward her throat. Another gasp and she was singing. It was nearly involuntary, but she found it helped, so she continued wailing out her obscure note. When it hit her throat, the note was cut off and she bent over, choking and heaving. Finally, with a guttural hack, it flew from her mouth.

Taking up the skirts of her nightdress, she raced to where she had heard it crash. Relief of being free of the unidentified object washed over her as she knelt before what appeared to be a radiant stone... a diamond? But how and when had she swallowed it? And why was it glowing? She reached for it but hissed when it seared her fingers. Nursing the burned hand, she reached for a nearby kerchief and used it to take up the stone to examine more closely. It was large and, if she knew anything about gems, pristinely cut. But how on Kaern had she ended up with it *inside* her? And what was she to do with it?

"*Go,*" the voice she'd heard in the prison earlier in the evening whispered into her ear.

"Who is it?" she cried out, frightened now.

"*Go. The door.*"

Hoping beyond all hope this voice meant her no harm—that, indeed, it was the god-Entity of the land—she went for the door.

Abruptly, it struck her: the day they'd discovered The Mirror had survived. There had been evidence of another room behind it. Within it had been a stone much like the one she held, but it had been broken to pieces. She still had it in the drawer of her nightside table.

"The Mirror... is that where I must take it?" she asked the air.

The stone shone hotter, sending her feet racing. It struck her that the room behind The Mirror had not been rebuilt. Who could have foreseen a purpose for it? Now, what was she to do when she got to the mirror room and could not place the diamond in its rightful place? Moreover, why was it to be put there at all?

The Mirror's door was before her. It possessed no keeper. It was all but forgotten to them at the present. If noble eighteen-year-olds were no longer forced to enter, what was its use to anyone? Stepping in, she found a somewhat familiar feeling carpet in the center of the room.

"Great Entity, I am here. But what am I to do?"

As if lifted by the great gust of wind that followed, the far wall rose into the ceiling. Another room was revealed—one they had not built. Within it, stood something like a fireplace, but set higher so its hearthstone reached her waist.

"What on *Kaern*..." she whispered.

The diamond burned severely through her kerchief, so she swiftly emptied it onto the hearthstone. But it did not feel right to her. Mind racing, she came to the conclusion that the diamond burned because it was meant to act as a fire-starter within the hearth. But hot as it was, it wasn't nearly hot enough for that. Some other act was expected of her.

Placing hands on hips, she nearly leaped as she looked to her waist. Somehow, her scabbard containing the red sword had been fastened around her. She had some small recollection of having done so before she'd picked up the stone in her bedroom, but she'd not been conscious of what she'd done at the time, nor even why.

Nervously, she withdrew the ruby blade. It glowed in answer, fully knowledgeable of its use. On an inkling and with great apprehension, she touched its tip to the diamond.

The explosion hurled her back into the mirror room where she was caught safely in the arms of the wind. She coughed and waved at the smoke as she worked to regain her breath. After the haze dissipated, she wandered to the threshold of the secret room.

An enormous fire blazed from the place, white at the center, then purple, with a red ring on the outside. It was the strangest flame she'd beheld and hotter than any usual fire. It made her feel alive, *rambunctious*. Its heat pulsated through her body, into her heart, beating in time.

That was it… that was what she was hearing. It possessed something like a heartbeat. The diamond at the center beat like a live heart. That was what made her feel so lively. The flames pulsated in time. Within them, she saw visions of kings, knights and ladies performing all sorts of deeds—some wicked, others courageous and awe-inspiring. The images flashed so fast, she scarcely grasped a moment of it for her own recollection. But when she gazed down at the carpet piece, she recognized some of those heroes and villains as the men and women within the embroidered chronicle.

A woman with her mouth open and music streaming from it caught her eye. She bent to touch it and suddenly the wall to the diamond's room slammed shut. She raced to it, touching her hands to its stone. It was already warmed through. With the raising of her brows, she suddenly recalled the note she'd left herself the last time she'd visited the room. This, then, was what she'd been searching for, this peculiar room with no doors except that which could be opened by the room's Entity.

With a sigh, she turned away. Approaching the exit, her hand went for the doorknob. She paused. Like always, she would not recall what had occurred within. But perhaps she might piece it together in time. After all, she would not forget the stone nor from where it had come. That, along with her note about the wall all that time ago, might be enough. Not to mention, the Great Entity had spoken to her twice in one night... *outside* of the room. His attention to her would not soon be forgotten.

* * *

Shouting sounded throughout the castle for some time before Hazel peeled her eyes open. The sunlight in her bedroom revealed she'd awoken later than she'd meant. She was utterly exhausted, though she could scarcely recall why. There'd been a burning in her chest... *Oh!* That got her out of bed. She'd coughed up a *diamond*, and then taken it to The Mirror. After that... she'd crawled back into bed. Swiftly, she dressed and patted her hair into place before opening the door and nearly colliding with her maid.

"Oh, my lady, you mustn't go about with your hair like that. And you missed breakfast, so I brought a tray for you. Perhaps you'd like to sit at the little table on the balcony. It is a fine morning."

But Hazel stood eyeing the hall outside her door. It wasn't a hall at all. It was their meager library.

"*Yes,* my lady," Anna said, "as you see, the castle is up to its old tricks. Took me some time to locate your chamber. In the end, it was a poor guardsman who found you. I'm afraid it was with an embarrassment he will not soon forget, waltzing into your ladyship's room while you were fast asleep."

"But… I do not understand. We were meant to believe the old castle had been *built* to alter itself each day. We certainly did no such thing with the new one."

"Then we must believe it was—is—*enchanted,* just as the 'fools' always believed. In any case, it has come back to life, though none can gather just why. It's driving everyone just crackers. Well, only those who did not secretly miss it. But since it *is* a new fortress, with all new rooms and corridors, you cannot blame them being troubled. No one's got the schedule yet. It's been knocking upon door after door all morning until we learn its ways again."

Hazel bit her lip as she sat to breakfast. Could it be that whatever she had done in the mirror room had altered things? Could it be her fault that the poor guardsman had gone waltzing into a lady's bedchamber—that they must all spend weeks learning the new fortress' ways?

Looking up at its walls, a smile crept onto her face. It was *back*—her old friend. Despite it all, she was *grateful*. If it had been her doing, she was delighted. Their slain stronghold had returned from the dead.

Once finished with her meal, she wondered how she would use her time that day. She knew there was much to be done, but as Armond had not officially offered her a position now he was king, she wasn't certain what she had a right to dictate to. It was not in her interest to overstep. Even so, it wasn't long before much of the castle staff were coming to her for answers. She sent as much as she could on to Armond, but she thought it her duty to the promise she made to him to continue helping as best she could. And as the staff were so accustomed to coming to her, it would not hurt to aid in the more menial tasks... That was, until she made her way to a quiet corner and heard her name uttered.

"...They're saying it doesn't bode well for the alliance," said a woman's voice.

"Which is exactly why the king must be ousted, and the great Lady Hazel crowned in his stead," said the other.

"That's what everyone's wanted all along. It was only due to her loyalty to him that we went along with the coronation."

Hazel stepped out from around the corner, hands on hips. "And my loyalty to him does not waver."

The serving maids leaped and flushed shades of red.

"But, m-m-my lady—"

"Let it be known," she interrupted, "I've no intention whatever of entertaining notions of taking the throne for myself. If King Armond should be ousted, I go with him."

"*Yes,* my lady," the first gasped with a deep curtsy, the second not far behind. The two scurried on their way.

Hazel shook her head. This would not do. How could anyone imagine *her* upon a throne? Why, only the year before, she'd been despised for who her parents were. Her parentage had not altered since then. She was not ruler material.

Working to subside her anger, she recalled an invitation to do needlework with Stacia and Rebecca. She'd not thought to take them up on it, but as she thought it in everyone's best interest that she retire from aiding the staff until arrangements could be made with Armond, she supposed returning to her old pastime might be a comfort.

The ladies were more than pleased to see her, just as they were every time they met. It seemed she was a favorite of theirs, which was more discomfiting than complimentary. Always, they wished her to accompany them in whatever menial project they meant to perform. But for a girl who was accustomed to being both useful and alone, it was a bit much.

"We were just discussing how difficult it is to return to courtly life after a year of utility," Stacia said.

"But not too difficult," Rebecca added.

Hazel and Stacia exchanged silent smiles. Despite everything, nothing could change Rebecca.

"But it *has* been scandalously dull of late," Rebecca continued. "Even at the ball last night, there was scarcely a dignified partner to be had. If it hadn't been for that gorgeous Bashtiian king bringing all those knights, there wouldn't have been a one."

"Speaking of King Fredrick," Stacia said, "he seemed rather taken with *you*, Hazel… as did Armond."

Hazel blinked. "I don't think they—"

"You were hogging them," Rebecca blurted crossly.

Stacia laughed. "If merely being herself is hogging them..." She looked to Hazel with understanding.

Hazel smiled back. She had once thought Stacia had got her to announce her love to Armond for the pleasure of seeing her rejected. But as the lady continued to encourage her about him, she reconsidered. It wasn't as if the two were going to be the closest friends, but it was nice to know one of the old foes had grown to respect her even before she'd become "Lady Fortune."

"I'm not sure what I wouldn't have given to be sat where you were, Hazel," Rebecca said.

"To have not one but two king's fawning over you..." Stacia added. "I can't say I've ever been hugely fond of Armond myself, but he does have rather astounding eyes."

Rebecca sighed. "I was never allowed to pursue him with

Dianna around." She perked up. "But she's not around anymore." She turned to Hazel. "I don't suppose you've laid claim to him?"

Hazel was stunned by the notion that, at her command, Rebecca would consider him off-limits. Things certainly had changed. "Where *is* Dianna these days?" she inquired. "I didn't see her at the coronation."

"She doesn't leave her quarters," Rebecca said. "Cannot bear being seen by anyone but us and a single maid."

"Doesn't even like seeing *us* much," Stacia added. "Not that we relish the idea of spending all day every day in that drab little room of hers, anyway."

"I don't understand," Hazel began. "Hasn't her hair grown back?"

"No," Stacia said with sudden sorrow. "The flames seem to have damaged her to the follicles. It only grows in wispy patches."

Hazel's brows rose. That did put matters into another light. Even so, it should not stop the lady from living. "All she's lost is her hair. Her legs work fine. And her face is still... as it was." She couldn't bring herself to call the girl beautiful when she possessed such a cruel heart.

"Indeed," Rebecca replied. "But a woman's hair is her pride, especially when hers was such a brilliant auburn. Thinks herself grotesque without it."

Hazel refrained from rolling her eyes at the inane statement about a woman's *pride*. "But a headscarf of some kind was offered?"

"It does no good," Stacia said. "You know Dianna."

Hazel did... but not as a friend. Even so, it was not difficult to imagine her too vain to be seen in her current state. She could almost pity the girl, but she was not there just yet.

As she completed her first stitch, a peculiar stiffness drew her attention to her right hand. A smear of gold gleamed back at her.

She worked to wipe it away, but it would not budge. What could it be that it refused to part with her skin? It was unpleasantly tight. She would have to scrub it away later.

She stopped short as something the maids in the hall had said resurfaced to her memory. "Have you ladies heard anything about how things are going with the alliance negotiations?"

Stacia's brows rose. "You do not know? The king of Bashtii has unceremoniously taken his leave of us. We're all hoping it was because things went that smoothly, but... there are rumors Armond may have bungled things."

Hazel leaped to her feet. "I must see to this."

Entering the hall, her eyes fell on the very man she wished to see. "Gunther!" she called after him. "Is it true King Fredrick has taken his leave?"

He nodded. "King Armond has just sent me to fetch you."

"But why was I not sent for the instant King Fredrick elected to depart from us?"

"It was unannounced and, therefore, not discovered until he was quite gone."

"How I wish you were joking. Well, perhaps... perhaps things aren't as they seem. I shall go to Armond."

But the sight of the king with hands wrung through his hair as he sat at his desk did little to soothe her.

She took a step toward him. "He's left then?"

He looked up as if he had not even noticed her enter "He has?"

Her brows rose. "Some hours ago. You've not been told?"

"Nay, well, I supposed he would be leaving when he stormed out in that absurd fit, but I'd not thought so soon."

"So, he *stormed* out? Why should he do such a thing? That isn't at all stately."

He shrugged. "The man is arrogant, won't see reason and won't compromise. We didn't get on at all."

"I understand, but... we cannot afford to lose Bashtii. Something *must* be done."

His eyes darted back and forth as his mind raced. Finally, he looked to her. "What if I should promote you to royal diplomat, send you on to meet with him in Bashtii?"

"Well, I..." It was precisely what she'd been thinking. She'd be hanged before she'd let that stuck-up prig of a Bashtiian king run off without a new agreement. *She'd* never have let him march from the room. "I suppose that would do just fine."

He sighed. "That's what I was afraid of."

"Afraid?"

"Well, to send you away... to him."

It was difficult not to smile. In the end, she failed. "You will have the priest, and Dorian."

"You know very well that's not what I meant."

"Well," she said, desperately working to conceal her grin, "when do I leave, oh, king?"

"With all those horses, they must take the Dreyen Peninsula. It's a much longer journey than simply crossing the sea by ship. Upon their return, we shall send a messenger to request a welcome for you. Once we've received it, you may be on your way—in a few days, I suppose."

"That should do very well. Gives me time to pack and leave instructions with the servants. Speaking of, I wonder if you should appoint me head of staff. That way, anytime I direct them, it will be by your order."

He nodded. "You may be Kierelian emissary, my chief advisor and head of staff. I shall have it written up and signed before the day is out."

"You don't think that's too much?"

"Not for you," he said with a smirk.

Eyes shining, she curtsied and pulled open the door.

"Hazel," he called.

She turned.

"Has it never occurred to you to just go ahead and *take* the throne like everyone wishes?"

It stunned her that he was aware of the talk. Furthermore, she was saddened that he knew he was not wanted. "Of course not."

His brow rose. "You know that makes you something of an eccentric, Lady Hazel?"

With a chuckle, she curtsied again. "You certainly know how to charm a maiden."

"Hazel, you… you won't go falling for *him,* will you?"

She bit her lower lip to keep from smiling before swiftly turning about to conceal her failure. She played at straightening the tapestry on the wall. "There is little chance of my falling for that pompous so and so, I assure you." She gave it a final tug, then turned to search his face.

He looked to her with a stunning grin. "And I suppose they *do* say absence makes the heart grow fonder."

She rolled her eyes and bounded through the door. "I suppose I'll see you this evening," she said over her shoulder.

"You can be certain of that."

Hazel retreated happily but stopped short as the cleaning maid outside returned her smile. It was rather pointed… to the extent of making Hazel uncomfortable. Had the woman overheard Armond, er…paying her special attention?

18

Hazel breathed deeply of the sea air that rifled through her hair. Never in her life had she been aboard a ship, let alone a royal voyager. She closed her eyes and soaked up the overwhelming scent of salt, so fresh and obscure compared to anything she'd experienced. Not only was she traveling across the sea to the popular Bashtiian kingdom of which she'd heard so much about, but she went as an ambassador for her kingdom. So much had changed for her in the last year. She'd gone from a rejected, miserable caged bird to royal dignitary on her way to negotiate an alliance. She was at her leisure.

Guardsman Gunther pointed to the forward horizon. Goosebumps of excitement flooded her skin as the white and gold flags of the harbor rippled in dramatic welcome. The closer they drew, the more eager she became until she was leaping up and down at the hull of the ship and leaning so far forward, Gunther begged her to step back. Reminded that she had a job to do for king and country, she worked to settle herself. She gathered all the stubbornness within her for her meeting with Fredrick.

At last, they entered the frenzied port. Gunther directed her to retire to her cabin until he was prepared to escort her from the ship. Immediately, her maid scrambled her into new garments—a sophisticated gown in burgundy with a veiled headpiece to match. This, she easily recognized, had been designed by Dianna's adept fingers. But even that fact could not bring her down.

Thrilled to finally explore the docks, she was disappointed by the scarce peek she attained before being ducked into a closed carriage that started off with haste. When she turned to peer through the back window, she was certain the large party waving after her chanted, *"Lady Fortune!"* Could it be that the driver thought it wise to get her away from them? If so, what danger did they afford? They looked like a friendly lot. Even so, her driver sped swiftly onward until they had entered more private paths.

"Gunther," she began, "were those people—"

"The driver informed me that the city has been celebrating since they heard of your coming. Their excitement was so great, King Fredrick thought it wise you were spirited from the public posthaste."

"As in... their eagerness might cause me *harm?* But I have not heard of such a thing except in books! And I cannot imagine they've never received a visitor from Kierelia before."

He raised a brow. "It is not that you are Kierelian but that you are Lady Fortune. Seems you're a legend on these shores."

Her eyes grew wide as she gazed outside the window with embarrassment. How exaggerated had her story become that this was her reception? It was clear some mistake had been made.

Soon they were passing through a populated street. This was where those of the middle class dwelled, or so she guessed by the edifices. It struck her how much freer these people were than those of her kingdom. Kierelians were a self-possessed, decorous lot. But many of these went *barefooted*. They laughed boisterously, argued in public streets, cried in public streets. Well-dressed children ran about as Kierelian urchins did.

As they continued, it became clear that even their poorest lived by fairly comfortable means. They were a wealthy country, after all. This made them relaxed and, therefore, carefree—like a lot of children. But then, there was a sturdiness about them. It was in the way they were bodily built but also in how they worked. Those who went about tasks did so with determination, with a satisfaction in what they lay their hands to. Yes, they were undomesticated compared to Kierelians, but they were content with their lot and happy to do their duty... or so she imagined as she passed.

With a gasp, she caught sight of what had to be the illustrious *Illuminas Palace*, standing erect and gleaming in a polished, terracotta-hued sandstone. Featuring dozens of grand, sparkling windows, it was further adorned with chiseled etchings in an ancient pattern, alluding to the kingdom's boasted maturity. The structure easily dwarfed Kierelia's new, swiftly built fortress. The wheels in her mind began to spin with plans for further construction, but she fairly gave it up as she noted the fountains lining the main drive that sent blue water soaring to the very heights of the castle itself.

"Gunther, have you ever seen the like?"

"I have not," he murmured almost enviously.

At last, the carriage halted before the marble steps of the imposing entry. Hazel was promptly aided from the carriage by a man who introduced himself as Harrin, a high-ranking member of staff. She was a little disconcerted by this, as she'd expected to be welcomed by Fredrick.

"Lady Hazel," he said with a low-sweeping bow, "what an

honor to have you within our gates… *truly*."

With a small smile, she nodded, unsure of what might be expected of her.

"Please, follow me and I will escort you to your chambers until his majesty returns."

Returns? With a brow raised, she did as directed but had to inquire, "When can I expect to meet with King Fredrick?"

"Almost directly after you have made yourself comfortable, my lady. He had every intention of welcoming you himself but was called into the city to settle a matter of importance to its citizens."

Well, she could not blame him for being concerned for his people. She often wished the trait came more naturally to Armond. But if she knew him at all, it would come in time. After all, the way the two kings had come into their crowns differed vastly.

"*Oh…*" Hazel sighed out as she was shown into her chambers.

Harrin turned. "Is this not adequate for your needs, my lady?"

She nearly laughed but shook her head instead. "It is *perfectly* suitable."

Her rooms in Kierelia were but a bedchamber and a closet of a sitting room. Here, she was afforded a three-room accommodation, all oversized and luxuriously decorated in a style utterly foreign to the simplicity of Kierelian convention. In fact, she'd have called the suite too extravagant if she weren't eager to spend time in it. The space made her feel like a real royal (even if she was but a distant one) and revealed that Bashtii meant to honor their Kierelian guest.

After Harrin departed to show Gunther and her maid, Anna, to their accommodations, she further surveyed the rooms that were superbly adorned in the terracotta palette and accented in periwinkle and ivory. But it was the view of the Bashtiian Sea outside her sizable windows that made her grin. Yes, she could bide her time here until Fredrick was prepared to meet with her.

* * *

"Lady Fortune!" Fredrick cried merrily upon entering his study.

Hazel had been made to wait far longer than she felt was appropriate, but she merely stood unsmilingly to offer her hand. Her frown deepened when his gloved one easily took hers, reminding of the last time she'd seen him.

His openness diminished as he released her, clearly picking up on her ill mood. "I must convey my deepest apologies for returning so late to meet you. I assure you we'd have had chaos in the streets had I not soothed matters between our merchants."

Hazel humbled. "I understand. I do hope all came to rights."

"It did," he said confidently. "This has been a matter I'd been hoping would work itself out, but there comes a point when one must become more involved. In any case, I do beg your pardon and hope your welcome was gratifying."

"It was," she admitted. "The rooms are… more than adequate. I thank you."

"Oh, please do not. It is no less than you merit."

This was spoken so genuinely it made her blush. Even so, she recalled her purpose. "I must say," she said, lowering her voice, "I am astonished you so easily revoked the alliance between our kingdoms."

"Oh, the alliance isn't *revoked*," he said almost tiredly. "Should Kierelia ever regain its former strength, it would be too significant an ally to lose. But I'm afraid I must stress what a petulant, childish king you have placed on the throne. Brought me to the absolute end of my patience."

Her temper flared at his insults, but she gulped it down. "In the time I've known you, that hasn't seemed entirely difficult to do."

He laughed easily. "I'm sure it *does* seem that way. But I assure you, I am known for my patience. Even so, I do not stand for extended disrespect and that is all I ever seem to receive from your kings."

"So, you let me come all this way just to tell me you do not mean to end the treaty?"

"I let you come here so you and I could negotiate the arrangements of that agreement, something King Armond and I *cannot* do."

She sighed. "We already had an alliance between the previous kings. I do not understand what can have been so difficult for the two of you to sort out."

"For starters, he wants a fourth of my military at his disposal indefinitely... with nothing in return but promises for a bright future between our kingdoms. He would accept no less."

She froze as she felt her face flush red. She should never have trusted Armond to handle this on his own. His management of the southern tribal leaders had shown her that. But he'd displayed such confidence when making Dorian part of his guard, it had gotten into her head that the officiality of the coronation had put things to rights in his head. Unhappily, she recalled how people used to say he was too handsome to be of much use, but she would not give up so easily. "I think we should be able to negotiate something much more amenable to both countries."

"I rather thought as much," he said with a grin.

They spent the remainder of the day working on the treaty. Hazel was pleased to find it much less difficult than anticipated, as Fredrick was more generous than Armond would have had her believe. Well, she supposed not everyone could be expected to get along, but when it came to the leaders of neighboring monarchies, something would eventually have to be done. She would not tolerate their tantrums forever.

As she peered above the plans Fredrick explained to her, she studied his expressions, absorbed his intonations. She recalled the way he'd arrived to protect Armond's coronation even after he had been so dishonored in his prior visit. Could it be that Armond alone had been in the wrong? Yet, he was a feeling man. Surely, he had shown some reason. And after all, Fredrick had revealed his arrogance in his treatment of her at the coronation ball. No matter how polite he was with her now, she must assume it was all for the good of himself and his own kingdom.

"I suppose we should stop here for now," he suggested, "so our aids do not throw their backs out readying us for this evening."

"This evening?"

His brows rose. "Surely you were informed about the ball to be held in your honor?"

She shook her head, her mind racing as to what that may entail. She had hoped for a quiet dinner and then early to bed in her comfortable rooms.

"So many of my people were anxious to make your acquaintance that it was resolved you would be received with a ball. I'm terribly sorry you were not informed. I suppose I'm the one who ought to have done it. But I am certain your servants will know all about it."

She nodded, dearly hoping this was the case.

On her way back through the halls, she was astonished to find the rumors about nobles who did not bother with footwear were true. In fact, she began to feel out of place in her slippers. Could it be she was expected to dance with exposed feet that evening?

She rather hoped so.

19

Upon the landing of the ballroom staircase, Hazel stood in a gold gown, her hair curled and cascading down her back. Her frothy skirts sparkled with golden dust and her hair glittered with Bashtiian crystals. Not even for Armond's coronation had she been so elaborately attired. But the gown had been selected to honor the "golden king" of Bashtii, so wear it she must. Shakily, she took her first step onto the case.

To her horror, she nearly lost her footing when the room suddenly broke into applause. Whistles and shouts of "Lady Fortune!" besieged her so that it was all she could do to bite her lip, ignore her burning cheeks and survive the remainder of the stairs without tripping. She had nearly reached the bottom when she glanced up in time to find King Fredrick grinning up at her, clapping his own gloved hands as he released a sort of breathless huff. A sigh of admiration? She would not fall for that again. He appeared supportive merely to appease his country's perplexing adoration of her.

At last, her bare foot hit the floor and her fear of tripping down the stairs was behind her. But after righting her skirts, she looked up to find Fredrick standing over her with glimmering eyes. Upon noting her annoyance at his presence, he sobered. Yet, it was with a scarcely concealed smirk that he said, "As I am certain you relish no further compliment from me, I merely say you do your kingdom credit."

What was that supposed to mean? That he was amazed she hadn't fallen down the stairs? That the clothing she'd been provided with aided her façade as a royal emissary?

"Er, well, thank you," she replied self-consciously, lifting her skirts in readiness to escape him.

He held out a hand. "Won't you share a dance with me?"

"Oh, I wouldn't wish to inconvenience you. I am certain there are far more suitable partners to be had here."

He stepped in front of her retreating frame. "Then why do I find you are the only lady I actually wish to dance?"

She raised a brow at him. "That is a very good question considering our last ball."

All signs of a smile fled his face. "Look, I never thought you beneath me, nor even that you were trying to pursue me."

"Then why did you refuse to dance?"

He fidgeted with his glove. "It is complicated."

"Do you possess some fear of dirt?" she asked, glancing at the gloves. "I assure you, I clean often."

He threw his hands behind his back. "I fear nothing more from you, Lady Hazel, than that you will never forgive me. Truly, I endure great remorse that I caused you pain."

"You didn't cause me *pain*... only insulted me."

"And I am sorry for that, too. Please, let's have this dance, else I shall sit out every one on account of you and every lady here will despise you."

The corner of her mouth turned up. "Are you such a commodity, then?"

He shrugged. "I *am* king."

She chewed at her lower lip, considering. "I will dance with you," she said at last, "if you will remove your gloves."

Though his every feature remained composed, the sudden white of his face betrayed him.

"I… cannot," he said.

Absently, she worked at the golden mark on her hand. What was the matter with this man that he would practically beg for her forgiveness, then reject her the next chance he got?

He snatched her hand into his.

Her eyes flashed. *"What* are you—"

"This…" He pointed to the golden blemish. "How long have you had it?"

She worked to regain her appendage but found it held fast. "I cannot just say. But I assure you, it is no proof of my uncleanliness. It simply will not remove."

"Would you say it appeared the evening of the coronation?"

"Why, yes… I discovered it the following day."

Keeping possession of her hand, he whispered, "Come with me," then proceeded to pull her through the room and to the nearest exit. It was all she could do to take up her skirts to keep from tripping.

Once in the hall, she wrenched her hand away. *"Where* are you taking me?"

"The armory." He continued onward.

She blinked after him, weighing her options. In the end, her curiosity won out and she raced after him. "Why are we going there?" she asked, breathlessly trying to keep up with his pace.

He opened a large door and sauntered across the room of armor until he came upon an ornate suit, the one he'd worn to defend the coronation. Standing before it, he turned to her and crossed his arms. He was breathing hard, as if angry.

"What *is* it?" she pressed.

"You see what makes this suit special?"

She nodded. "It is gold, for the 'golden king,' I suppose."

"Ask me how it was made," he gasped out.

"Er, I suppose a very fine armor maker..."

He shook his head.

She crossed her own arms. "Then how?"

"I did it... by accident."

"Oh, well... it is fine work."

With a huff, he shook his head and searched the room until he finally tore a small piece of fabric from his own tunic. He then ripped off a glove with his teeth and took hold of the cloth with his bare hand. "Come see," he said.

Slowly, she stepped forward, squinting her eyes—not trusting them. What she witnessed was impossible. The fabric was transforming into gold, stemming from where his fingers held it. When the job was done, he took hold of her hand with his gloved one and dropped the piece into her palm. She thumbed it around and at last raised a brow at him before biting into it. Sure enough, it was solid.

"That's what would happen to you if I touched you long enough without my gloves."

She shook her head incredulously, eyes wide. "That's... *extraordinary.*"

He laughed bitterly. "You wouldn't think it so amazing if that gold speck on your hand had spread any further."

She re-examined it. Her actual *skin* had turned to *gold*. She wondered how deep it went and whether it would always remain or if it would eventually… chip away? "I see…" she said, looking up at him and, for the first time, feeling she understood him. "You cannot control it?"

He shook his head. "Caught a butterfly as a child. It dropped to the ground, lifeless and hard as precious metal."

"So, you've not touched anyone with your hands since?"

"Tried not to, a brush here and there, but it doesn't seem to take effect that quickly."

"But when I took your hand at the coronation ball, that wasn't all that long…"

"It activates more quickly when I'm nervous."

"You were nervous you'd turn me to gold?"

He eyed her. "…Yes."

"You say you've had this gift since you were a boy? Were you born with it?"

He nodded. "So my mother said."

"What she must have thought! And how difficult bringing up a child you couldn't touch much longer than a moment."

He grinned a little at that. "Well, she could touch any part of me but my hands. That's where the power stems from. I didn't even know I had it until I tried to catch the butterfly."

"You weren't aware of it any sooner than that?"

"Well, she always had me in the gold-lined gloves. Unusually, my power is stunted by gold itself."

She thumbed at her golden speck. "Have you ever… turned anyone to—"

"Certainly not. We were always very careful."

"You and your mother?"

He nodded.

"But isn't turning things to gold rather handy?"

"Not when people find out."

She nodded. "Suddenly, you're their personal treasure trove."

He appeared surprised by her understanding. "Yes… ruined my relationship with my father. As a boy, my mother kept it secret. When I discovered it, she made me promise not to tell anyone… But he was my father."

"His greed grew?"

"As you said, I was his little fortune-maker. After a while, it was all he could see when he looked at me."

"But your mother?"

"Loveliest woman I've ever known. Made her a golden rose once. She tossed it out and made me pick her one with a gloved hand. It hurt her to have my father see me as he did. She wanted no part in it."

"So, is this why you're called the golden king?"

He shook his head. "The people don't know. No one does now my parents have passed. I *hate* that nickname, by the way. Came because of my armor. Thoughtlessly put it on with my bare hands once and was forced to wear it out to battle. As the battle was so victorious, I was deemed 'the golden king.'"

"So, you have never told anyone aside from your parents?"

He nodded.

"Then…why have you told me?"

He kicked about a pebble underfoot. "Hated the idea of insulting you again… not to mention it completely spooked me what I did to your hand. I am most dreadfully sorry about that."

"Well… it's no harm, Fredrick. Sort of special, actually."

He offered a sad smile. "It's nice of you to see it that way."

"Rather than the fact you could have turned me into a glistening statue, to be remembered forever as Lady Fortune and no more?" She smirked up at him.

He bit his lip, then relented to a chuckle. "Yes… that would have been rather sorrowful."

"Honestly, Fredrick," she began, taking a step toward him. "It's actually really quite *splendid* what you can do. Not for the riches, just… for the sake of such an impossible ability. Where do you suppose it came from?"

"The deepest flames of the Nethers, I suspect. It has done me no favors. I cannot even act in my full capacity as king because of it."

"How can that be?"

"Have you ever heard of the Cave of Nielsas, from where the lively rubies come?"

"Not the cavern, but I used to have my own store of such rubies."

"Truly? I don't suppose you bonded with them?"

"I did. They saved my life during the dragon attack actually."

He eyed her awhile. "The cavern was formed by our first king, who was said to possess the power to produce those rubies."

"That sounds familiar."

He nodded. "But he's the only king, let alone person, in the whole of the kingdom who performed anything like it. At any rate, it is where the heart of our kingdom lies."

"The heart of Bashtii?"

"Indeed. The cavern possesses ruby hand-pieces that every ruler is meant to form a bond with by touching them with the naked palm and speaking to the god within. He then provides protection and favor for the land. But every time I try to touch it…" He stopped abruptly, considering her. "Why don't I show you?"

"You mean now?"

"Well, no. I suppose tomorrow will do."

"Very well. I would like to see this cavern. It sounds a bit like our mirror room."

"So I've heard. I think you would like it there and… perhaps you can help me."

"How could *I?*"

"You bonded with your rubies. Scarcely anyone is able to

procure kinship with them anymore."

"Really? That's sort of—"

"Special," he finished with a smirk. "At any rate, you may be able to help me form a connection with them."

She raised her brows. "I suppose so."

"Well, I… suppose we should get back." He offered her his arm as he asked, "May we have our dance *now?*"

"Oh, *very well*, but it had better be an awfully good one after all this."

* * *

Fredrick lit the sconces, sending the walls of pure ruby ablaze and shimmering. Goosebumps soared down Hazel's arms as she moved from the dark tunnel into the cavern. She watched as the dazzling light shining off the gems sent crimson rainbows over herself and Fredrick. But more significant was the viscosity of the atmosphere, so full of something she could not grasp it made her emotional.

"I had no idea…" she murmured, her voice echoing throughout.

"Is it similar to The Mirror?"

She nearly laughed but stifled a sob instead. "Not quite."

"Over here. These crevices are where I am to lay my hands."

"And why is it a problem? Do you fear turning it all to gold?"

He shook his head, then removed his gloves and rolled up his sleeves. He reached for the crevices, then paused. "I… would stand over there if I were you." He pointed to the far wall.

"All right."

He looked to her with more soberness than she'd ever seen him wear. "What you are about to see cannot go beyond these walls."

She nodded in anticipation.

At last, he adjusted his feet and slowly moved his palms toward the placements, his hands shaking with nerves Hazel could not yet grasp. The moment his flesh touched gemstone, he was hurled backward, his head smacking against the wall.

"Fredrick!" she squealed, racing to his side. She knelt over him and patted his cheeks as if it held some hope of waking him. Brushing back the hair from his forehead, she lifted his head to feel for blood but found it miraculously dry, possessing just a small bump she hoped would not grow larger.

"Fredrick..." she whispered. Was *this* what he had meant to show her? Why would he put himself through such an ordeal? He must be desperate for help, but how could she possibly aid him in this issue?

Angrily, she stood and turned to the crevices.

"This is a good man!" she shouted. "He cannot help his golden touch!"

The gleam in the gems rippled, but she shook her head. It had to be a trick of the light.

She turned to check on Fredrick but was caught by the sound of singing, similar to that of her ruby bedposts. She took another step toward the crevices and the sound grew louder. Another step and its beauty enraptured her, visibly swirling around her. When she blinked, the sight disappeared.

It startled her to discover she had taken the last few steps to the wall. The music drenched her in itself. It was a call, a summons. The rubies desired her touch. It made her heart race with excitement and then fear as she watched her arms reach out. Forcibly, she tore them back and the music ceased.

Breathing hard, she peered over her shoulder at Fredrick. He still did not awaken. She should be concerned for him but turned back to the wall instead. Her eyes were watering. Her heart was aching. She moved her hands near the placements again, not touching them... but longing to. Everything in her missed that wondrous music and wished to answer its plea.

Releasing her breath, she shook her head and stomped her foot. She could not touch the wall. It was meant for the rulers of Bashtii. *They* must bond with the rubies, not some unloved girl from a kingdom across the sea. It was in no way her place and may produce dire consequences.

"*Oh!*" she gasped upon suddenly finding herself in a habitation that possessed *such* beauty as she had never imagined possible. It was only then she realized what she'd done.

Physically, she staggered under the atmosphere. Goosebumps flooded her body as she shook. Sweat dripped down her face and neck, soaking through her garments. What had she *done*? She ought to find her way back to the cave somehow, but her eyes wouldn't budge from the figure at the center of the room.

He appeared as a man, sat upon a sapphire throne atop a floor of clear glass. Beyond the enthroned figure were curtains of emerald-rainbow luminescence and from him burst blazing bolts that set the room to quaking as they struck. His eyes, hair and clothes were ablaze with a glorious substance that sent Hazel's face to the floor, her body laid out helplessly. She was both thrilled to have found this place and shrieking to be away from it. This realm was not meant for her. She was not supposed to have touched the rubies. She was not worthy of facing such an… entity.

Utterly overcome with the surge of understanding that struck her, tears burned down her cheeks and onto the crystal floor. This… was the *Great Entity*. So grand, majestic and glorious did he sit. She had to *escape* him, to escape all he was in his wholeness before her. But she lay plastered to the floor.

A touch upon her shoulder drew her attention. She possessed just enough strength to turn over and view the humanoid creature with three sets of wings who offered her a burning coal. "Eat."

She scanned the creature's eyes and found astounding purity in them. Surely, those eyes could mean her only good. She took the coal, eyed it, then swallowed it whole. The act felt strangely familiar. But more importantly, she felt *relieved*. The glory of the Entity at the center of the room had not lessened, but she felt strangely able to stand upon her feet again, to further assess her surroundings and to wonder at it all.

Surrounding the throne were beastly creatures she could never have dreamed up. Some were flaming and possessed many wings, others possessed the faces of animals or were covered in eyes all over their flesh. Still others were sat upon smaller thrones that encircled *the* enthroned one. Unexpectedly, they stepped forward as one, stole the crowns from their heads and cast them at the feet of the Great Entity, proceeding to fall prostrate before him.

"You are worthy, our God," they cried, *"to receive glory and honor and power. For you created all things, and by your will, they were created and have their being."*

It so moved her that, if she had possessed a crown of her own, she would gladly have followed suit. She was gripped by the longing to offer something to he who sat in a kind of magnificence that no earthly king might ever possess. It was clear the Entity was a king, yes, but he was a king of quite another sort.

At long last, he locked eyes with her. She felt she would melt through the floor. Then, he looked to the creature who had offered her the coal.

"He summons you, Hazel of the Many Kingdoms," the creature said.

Hazel of the Many Kingdoms? She could not fathom what this meant but it mattered not as her feet at first tiptoed with hesitation and then raced to the feet of the God at the center of the room. Pressing her way beyond the creatures of this ethereal world, she was at last before *him*.

"Hello again, sweet Hazel," spoke the encompassing voice

she'd heard in both the prison and her bedroom some evenings past.

"H-h-hello…" she croaked.

"Do you know who I am?"

She nodded. "The Great Entity of The Mirror."

"I am the inventor of invention, the creator of creation. I am the God of *all* worlds and all things, for *nothing* exists apart from me."

She crumbled to her knees. "I am so sorry for having referred to you in such minute capacity, Wondrous Entity," she wailed.

A hand raised her chin until she was drawn to her feet. She was stunned to discover it was *his*. "And you… are one of my *prized* creations."

"Me?" she gasped, tears cascading down her face.

"You, Hazel, possess a rare quality. Under pressure, you transform coal into diamonds. Your scars become your strength."

She shook her head, working to grasp that the Entity of all things saw such attributes in her. "I should not have touched the ruby wall," she said guiltily. Her unworthiness burned at the center of her person at the same time that his words overwhelmed her with acceptance.

"I *asked* you to," he said.

Her mouth dropped open. That certainly explained why the call had been so undeniable. Who could resist him? "Whatever for?"

"Because I chose you."

"You chose me to bond with the rubies in the cavern?"

He chuckled, a sound that was like tolling bells. "Do you recall when we met in what you call The Mirror?"

She was about to shake her head until one of the many-winged creatures touched her. The memory of the encounter dawned in her mind. She looked to the Entity with new eyes. He was so different from the one she'd met then, the one who'd called himself H.S. At the same time, it was clear they were comparable.

Suddenly, the seven lampstands that, in all the wonder around her, she'd not thought to pay much mind to, twirled and drew together. In a fit of smoke, they converged as one and she was cast off her feet by the force. The room rumbled and when the haze dissipated, H.S. stood before her.

"Long time, no see, Lady Hazel," he said, "... for *you*, anyway."

She accepted the hand he held out for her and drew to her feet. "You are... the Entity as well?" she asked him in bewilderment, looking between the two.

He nodded. "One and the same. I am his essence, his spirit. So, you see, you and I were already bonded before you ever entered the Cave of Nielsas. We are old friends now, are we not?"

Unable to help herself, she grinned and nodded.

"But there is one other you must meet before we may be considered well and bonded."

Before she could question him, he began to spin. Soon, he was twirling so fast he appeared as a spiral of wind. But as it slowed, she perceived a new figure in his stead. When at last the man faced her, it was not her H.S. at all, but another entirely.

"I am sorry to be late, dear Hazel," he said. "I was paying a visit to another world just now. But upon the cry of my Father, I appear when summoned, either to sit beside Him enthroned or to visit one so beautifully fragrant as you."

"Your... father?" She glanced to the Great Entity behind him.

"Indeed, I am his only son, the Anointed One."

"The Great Entity has a *son*...?" she questioned in astonishment. Her hands flew to her mouth. "Oh, *pardon* me," she murmured with a low curtsy.

He only laughed. "Indeed, I am his son, once sent to the realms of man to vanquish the penalty of the ancient law, the one that makes you feel so unworthy to stand before him in this place. He does not like edifices between himself and those he cares for."

"But… if you vanquished it, why do I still feel so—"

"Because you have not accepted this chalice as yet." He withdrew a lovely gold one from behind his back and held it out.

Eyeing it eagerly, she reached for it, then swiftly drew her hand back. "Is that…?"

"Blood." He nodded. "It is mine which I shed so you could accept it as freedom from the clutches of justice."

"Must I… drink it?"

He shook his head. "Only take the cup, dear Hazel, and pour it over your head."

"Over my…?" She gestured to her head, swallowing in discomfort at the thought.

The room quaked and thunder echoed. Her eyes flew to where the Great Entity sat in all his majesty. His eyes held hers, daringly. How could she refuse him? Accepting the chalice from the Anointed One, she felt it spark in her hands until she at last raised it above her head… and poured.

More liquid than could have been contained in the chalice coursed over her frame, so warm and inviting that it felt as if she had plunged into a hot bath. The aromas of frankincense and myrrh arrested her senses and she soon found herself, inexplicably, giggling at the sensation. It was very like the presence of her friend, H.S.—that lively, raucous feeling he produced. She felt liberated in a way she had not since meeting him for the first time.

At last, the blood cleared and she looked down at her gown, now glistening, white and new. In awe, she sighed up into the face of the Anointed One. "Are we quite bonded now?" she asked.

He laughed and stole her hand to give her a twirl. *"Quite,"* he replied. But in the next moment, he was spinning into the vortex he had arrived in until H.S. was in his place once again.

"Miss me?" he asked.

Smilingly, she nodded at her friend. "But, why will you not allow Fredrick to bond with you?"

"That is not *my* doing. The Entity and his son were not the creators of those rubies, but the creators of their creator. Therefore, we cannot alter them, due to our own ancient law."

"But… can I *help* Fredrick somehow?"

"A better question might be, can you help *me*?"

"Oh, *yes*, of course!" she cried. How she yearned to offer him something, anything, he might value.

"Sing."

She hesitated, taken aback. "Was I summoned here to sing?" she asked incredulously.

When she gained no response but the twinkling of his eyes, she knew there was naught else to be done. As he stepped aside, she gazed up into the fiery eyes of the Great Entity and obeyed his command.

She sang of all he was here in this place. Her voice swelled through the room, echoing off the walls and causing the towering pillars to shake. Soon, every beast and figure joined in her song.

"Hazel!" Fredrick cried.

She leaped about in search of him, overjoyed he'd found his way into this magnificent realm after all.

"Hazel!" he called more vehemently.

Her eyes fluttered open and she was met by his frightened face above hers. She was still singing when she asked him what the matter was.

He appeared almost relieved but a brow went up as if confused. "Hazel?"

She sat up, a tune still floating from her lips as she peered up at the ruby walls of the cavern. The torches had sniffed out but the room was alight with a red glow omitted by the gems themselves. When she stopped singing, the radiance dimmed but did not entirely flush out.

"You touched them…" Fredrick said beside her, "and they have chosen to bond with you."

"The Great Entity summoned me. And *he* has not rejected you. Only the gems created by the first Bashtiian king have."

"And you know this… how?"

"I asked the Great Entity."

His brows met his hairline. "Did he say how to fix it?"

"He… told me to sing."

"Well, what I just heard from your mouth was astounding, but I do not see how that may help me."

"Nor I."

"But, does this mean *you* are the one now bonded with Bashtii?"

Her stomach sank. It could not be. She was not Bashtiian. "I don't imagine so… What if I sang again—asked the rubies to accept you?"

"I would not mind hearing that voice of yours again."

She closed her eyes and sang out an obscure tune. Immediately, the gems glowed in response. She asked them to accept Fredrick's touch, then gestured for him to attempt contact. But as his hands went up, the rubies sang back in alarm.

"Wait!" she cried. She did not relish the notion of watching him be knocked unconscious again. "They do not listen."

His head hung as he gazed at his hands. Then, he looked up. "Hazel, ask for rain."

"What? Why?"

"Bashtii's plains have been thirsty for some time. Ask for it."

"I don't see what good it will do for me to ask, but…" She did as bid.

Fredrick took her hand and led her through the tunnel system. When they reached the mouth, the downpour was evident. He turned to her with a sad grin. "You did it," he said. "You bonded with the Cave of Nielsas, with the one who reigns over our kingdom. *You* are now bonded to the land of Bashtii, not I."

Her mouth fell open. "F-Fredrick… you cannot be correct. I am no Bashtiian ruler. I am not even Bashtiian."

"Yet, the Entity responded to your plea, just as he has with our past rulers."

"But… what does this mean? What are we to do? We must transfer it to you."

He shook his head. "There is nothing that will break the bond apart from death. Bashtii is at your mercy, Lady Fortune."

She stood, breathing hard. "I am *so* sorry, Fredrick. I never meant—"

"Of course you didn't. You were called. I have read the story many times."

She released a long breath. "Well, I… I will always be at your disposal… should you require *anything*. I promise never to overstep your command or use it for Kierelia's gain. I—"

Taking her by the hand, he scanned her eyes. "I trust you, Hazel. We will work this out."

When the rain lightened, they agreed to walk back, their horses loyally following along behind.

"My ancestors used to trade those rubies for galmoira from the southern tribes," Fredrick explained. "But then the Kierelian kingdom was formed and trade relations with the tribes ceased so we could be allied with Kierelia."

"Which is somewhat ironic now the tribes *are* Kierelia."

He nodded. "But I wonder if that was why the gift of voice ceased emerging in their people. I've often questioned whether it was originally activated by the lively rubies."

"What are you saying?"

"Well, it is written that the rubies of Nielsas were considered a most prized commodity in the tribes, but I do not believe they ever thought to link the gift with them. When trade relations between our countries ended, the rubies they yet possessed would have eventually been traded for goods with various other nations. Then, over time, their vocal giftings diminished. When you sang in there, the stones were quick to respond. Of course, you don't possess the gift, but your voice is rather enchanting..."

Hazel wasn't about to correct him. She hadn't thought to suppose her gift had anything to do with what had just occurred. She wished her gift might never emerge again. Trepidation that the incident may have altered something sent her heart racing.

"So, you know my story," he said, interrupting her thoughts. "What is yours?"

"Well, I don't turn things to gold."

"I'm sure you've experienced life despite that."

She chuckled. "Not much of one. I was just the unofficial errand girl, expert needle worker... that sort of thing." It was mostly true.

"So, nothing terrible in your past?"

She shook her head.

"Nothing at all?"

She looked up at him with a brow raised.

"Really don't want to share with me, do you?" he said with a grin. "I mean, I heard all kinds of things about you on my first trip to Bashtii."

"Oooh, that's right. And you used it to insult me."

His blush surprised her. "That wasn't a proud night for me. But after hearing so many stories about you in the year that followed, then meeting you, I can't imagine much of what I originally heard was true."

"Like my being a traitor to the crown?"

"Right… that's clearly not the case."

"No, it is not. A friend of mine had been part of a rebellion and used me for information."

"Sounds like a virtuous friend."

She sighed. "It's difficult to explain. We're as good of friends now as ever."

His ensuing expression bewildered her.

"What?" she asked.

"Oh…" He appeared almost embarrassed, a surprising trait on such a self-possessed man. "I suppose I was thinking you must be very forgiving."

She turned away, inspecting herself. "I suppose I am. But…"

"But?"

"Oh, nothing."

"But what?" he pressed, darting in front of her with a smirk.

She huffed. "At the time, I just couldn't bear to lose a friend."

"Even though they'd betrayed both you and the king?"

She dashed around him. "As I said, it's complicated."

He raced after her. "I see," he said, perhaps having mercy on the fact she clearly did not wish to speak of it. "Well, I also heard rumors about your parentage…"

That wasn't a much better subject but one she was far more accustomed to. "Probably all true," she replied.

"They tried to kill the king and were banished?"

She nodded.

"But—forgive me—why aren't you with them?"

"I really don't know."

From her peripherals, she watched him eye her. She couldn't imagine what he was thinking. Had he picked up on her annoyance?

"Perhaps King Zephuel wouldn't let them take you," he said somberly, as if working to soothe her. But how could he understand her doubts?

"Perhaps," she replied, though she knew it wasn't the case. She'd been but a burden to King Zephuel.

"What are you thinking?" he pressed.

She raised a brow. "That you ask a lot of questions."

"It is called trying to get to know you." When she did not respond, he added, *"I* revealed much to you."

"So, now I owe you?"

He nodded mirthfully. "Honestly, I'm just trying to learn more about you."

"More like trying to figure me out. I see you eyeing me over there, wriggling your way into the innermost trappings of my mind."

"Well, you are fairly difficult to decipher," he said with a huff. "You must have been well trained to conceal your feelings."

Stopping short, she turned to look at him. He was right, though she hadn't realized it until that moment. Turning away, she continued forward again.

"What?" he plagued.

She shook her head.

He sighed again. "So... what would please you for evening meal?"

"You wish *me* to choose? That is not customary, is it?"

"Answer the question."

"Well, I don't know... I don't suppose you grow turnips here?"

He laughed. "We do, indeed, so turnips it shall be." He bit back a smile, shaking his head.

"Now what?"

"Nothing at all. If you won't share your thoughts, I'll return the sentiment."

"Fine," she replied with a returning grin. He wasn't acquainted with her patience.

20

It was a fortnight before Hazel and Fredrick felt the alliance had been drawn up in fairness for both countries. It had felt like tiring work but both understood such things usually took much longer. Of course, if Armond did not agree to it, it would all be for naught. But she felt certain even he would be content.

In the end, it had been a surprisingly pleasant visit. After Fredrick had exposed his secret to her, their relationship acquired a new tone. No longer did she think him arrogant and stuffy. She came to find he rather esteemed her, just as he had seemed to at the coronation celebration. In fact, it had taken some doing for her to assure him she was perfectly ordinary, despite the stories.

"If you're just like everyone else," he said, "what are these rumors I heard about your possession of the gift of the southern tribes... that you once chucked Armond across a room with your voice?"

Her mouth fell open. She'd not realized he'd been acquainted with that point of gossip. She liked to think it a secret since all believed she'd been cured. And why had he not just fessed up to knowing about it when last they'd spoken about the gift? "I did *not* chuck him!"

He sat forward, crossing his legs where he sat upon the windowsill. "But you did do *something...*"

She restrained a smirk at the state of him sitting with intrigued eagerness. But the memory of that night easily sobered her. "I was asked to sing. Though I hate performance, my guardian..." She gulped, the memory of her guardian's death hitting her with new force. She could not honestly say she missed the woman, but she wasn't heartless. "Lady Nora insisted. At some point, something in my voice changed and Armond went flying."

"Flying? But how could you have known *you'd* done it? For that matter, how did he get back down?"

"Well, I stopped singing and he dropped."

"He... dropped? How *high* was he?"

"High enough. I caught him with my voice and he reached the floor without a scratch."

He rubbed at the back of his neck with wide eyes. "That is incredible. I don't see why you don't make use of it all the time. I know I've annoyed you a time or two. You have my full permission to send me flying whenever necessary."

"I would, *of course,* but it did not occur again after that."

"I don't understand..."

"I guess it only emerged due to the culmination of great emotion I was enduring. It wasn't supposed to happen for another couple of years. I was even sent to the south to gain what knowledge I could. But how much can you learn without practice?"

He eyed her. "How did it make you feel?"

There he was at it again, watching her closely, attempting to decipher her. It drove her a little mad, always to be under his scrutiny. Was there something wrong with being a private person? And after all, she *was* sharing. "It was frightening, but it hasn't returned, so all is well."

"Would you sing for me now?"

"What? No."

"Please?"

"I do not like to perform."

"Well, it's only me."

She shook her head. "I do not care to just now."

"What are you so afraid of? I won't judge you. Or... are you shy of me?"

He was daring her and she knew it. But when she felt her face grow hot, she couldn't bear to have him believe she cared so much about what he thought.

She sang.

It was a clear, sweet note. Fredrick's mouth dropped open as he stole a sudden breath. She thought it a peculiar response. Surely, he'd heard plenty of singers before. Of course, there was the chance he was not a singer himself so was more easily impressed. Still, as his eyes brightened, she couldn't help feeling... flattered? Unnerved?

Without a thought, she sprang forward to cast him aside as a poker from the fireplace went flying toward his head. It scarcely missed the top of her own—probably taking a few hairs with it— before it struck the wall.

Fredrick sat up with a long whistle, looking to where it stuck out of the study's formerly immaculate wall. "I never realized how much I rifled your feathers, Lady Fortune."

She marched to the fireplace. "Who threw that?!"

He turned to her with wide eyes. "It was you."

She shook her head. "No... No. I didn't feel anything." Or was too distracted to realize.

"Didn't you know you were lifting and dropping items all about the room?"

Absently, she rubbed at the gold bit on her palm. "I didn't..." She looked up at him, feeling more vulnerable than she had in a long while. "Was I really?"

He nodded, eyes bright with incredulity.

"But-but I don't see how..." With the stomping of her foot, she gasped, *"That cavern...* the rubies. Or the *Entity.* Something about something there... or the combination—perhaps the gems themselves. They *awoke* it." Her hands went to her throat as if she wished she might rip her vocal cords out.

Fredrick stepped forward to take possession of her shoulders, lightly shaking her. "It is a *gift,* Hazel." He released her then, taking a sober step back. She watched him suddenly relate to how she felt. He, of anyone, should know how such a peculiarity made one feel. But then he looked up. "You have a truly spectacular voice. Even without the gift, it would be an anomaly."

"But I can never sing again—not now!" She fell to the bench before the fireplace. "And I do *love* to sing."

He sat beside her. "You didn't seem to..."

"I like to sing *alone...* when I'm bored, gloomy, content. If I were trapped in a dungeon with naught else to do, I would be satisfied so long as I could sing."

She looked up at him as he watched her with that look, only this time he was over the moon she had opened up, even if completely by accident.

She stood. "I-I'll retire to my chamber for a while, if you don't mind."

"Very well," he answered with almost exasperating understanding. "I will see you for evening meal?"

She shrugged, then curtsied and exited the room.

* * *

Hazel awoke in The Mirror. She sprang to her feet, unable to remember how she might have arrived there. She did not in the least recall journeying home. The memory loss was meant to occur once one *left* the room—not while within.

The door opened behind her and she turned to find a beautiful woman enter as if she owned the place, or would like to. After her, came Armond, who looked about the corner one last time before entering himself.

"We're fortunate I haven't appointed a new keeper of the room," he said quietly, as if afraid someone might hear.

"Armond?" Hazel said dubiously.

The two walked past her, up to the far wall.

"As king, *you* must command it to open," the woman said.

"Command what to open?" he asked. "There is no door."

"Armond?" Hazel spoke loudly. But when she attempted to take hold of his shoulder, she found her own hand went through him, as if he were a ghost... or she was. *Was she dead?*

The beautiful woman who stood nearly half a head taller than the rather tall Armond said with a grin that worked to conceal her irritation, "If you do as I say, you will understand."

Armond raised his brows and then obeyed.

The center section of the stone wall lifted to reveal a secondary room. Within it, stood a hearthstone with the most curious flame Hazel had ever seen. At its center, she was almost certain, glittered the diamond she had choked up those nights past.

"How did you know this was here?" Armond asked the woman. "I was not aware it was in the architect's plans."

"It wasn't. It never is. It constructs itself."

He quirked a brow at her. "How can that be, my lady?"

"Of that, I have never been certain," she said with the shake of her head. "Now, did you bring it?"

As a look of discomfort crossed his face, he withdrew a black amulet from his pocket. "I don't see why you required something from Hazel's chambers for this."

"It wasn't hers to begin with," the woman said almost angrily. "She stole it. We're merely replacing it."

Hazel gasped as she took a closer look at the amulet. It was the one she'd pulled from the debris after the castle's destruction. It had been found beneath the pile of broken gemstone. She'd gathered both the stone pieces and this amulet into her pocket and then stored it safely in a satchel which she now kept in her night table. Now, it seemed, Armond had taken it from her quarters. She raised a brow at him.

"But what do we do with it?" he asked.

"You must drop it directly into the center of the flames. It will take over from there."

Hazel observed this woman with new eyes. Who was she and why was she ordering Armond about, getting him to meddle with things he did not understand? What was their intention?

Armond stepped up to the hearth, his head held back as the heat overwhelmed him. Then, he centered the amulet above the fire... and released it.

Immediately, the flames transformed. Where they had been white, purple and red, they were now blacker than black. It was like a dark void.

Hazel looked to Armond. *"What have you done?"* Though she could not rightly understand what had just occurred, it could not bode well.

The stranger smiled. "And there you have it. Guaranteed protection of Kierelia for all time."

As Hazel gazed between them, she watched Armond transition from himself to his uncle, King Zephuel, and back again. She blinked. What could all this mean? How was that dark amulet going to protect Kierelia? And why had she seen King Zeph...

She froze. King Zephuel had cursed his nation by consorting with a sorceress... She peered into the woman's enchanting face. Could this be the infamous Sorceress Maera, who was said to have lived nearly as long as the prophet?

Had Armond just repeated history?

She awoke with a gasp, sweat dripping from her face. It was a moment before she realized she was in a Bashtiian bed in the middle of the afternoon. Had it all been a dream then? Only a nightmare? She stole several relieved breaths. Armond had *not* just cursed Kierelia again. They were safe.

...But were they? It had felt *so real*. Something in her did not sit right. She stood from the bed to pace the floor, considering what she'd just witnessed. It had been a *dream*. She had to let it go, ignore it. But she could not.

She had to go home.

***

Hazel had not intended to appear for supper. An early bedtime was necessary if she was to catch the first voyage the following morning. But the thought of leaving without speaking just once more with Fredrick was out of the question. Somehow, somewhere along the way, he had worked his way into her meager collection of friends. Though it often unnerved her, he cared very much about the things she said, about learning who she was. She thought that a rather rare quality in a world where most cared for naught but themselves—especially nobles.

After the meal, many retired to the entertaining room where

they chatted until the performance began. It was much like an old evening in Kierelia, though they'd given up the tradition since the calamity. Hazel found she did not miss it.

"Enjoying yourself?" Fredrick asked as he sat down beside her.

She nodded. "And you?"

He shrugged. "I've heard better."

"Oh, I think he's talented."

He tilted his head to eye her. "Falls a little short of what I heard this morning, but it will do."

She played with her hands. "I asked your staff to inform you of my departure on the morrow."

"I was made aware," he said with a huff. "I had planned to show you a few more of the sights, but if you are so homesick for *king* and country…"

"Well… perhaps one day I'll see them."

His brows rose. "The sights? You plan to return?"

"I'm not inviting myself, but you never know."

Silence commenced between them and she began to wonder if she'd offended him. It had been discourteous to decide to return home without first speaking with her host, who happened to be an allied king.

"I am sorry I was so hasty in booking my departure," she said. "But I must see that all is well at home."

He nodded. "I would like to write to you if you don't mind."

She smirked. The notion satisfied her. After all, one did not share such secrets as these two did with just anyone. "I would not mind that at all."

21

"Oh. You're back," Armond murmured, scarcely looking up from his book.

Hazel blinked. "Yes, I just thought you'd like to know things went smoothly."

He offered her a quick smile. "Great."

Silently, she huffed, her mind racing back to when last she'd seen him. Hadn't there almost seemed to be... something between them? Maybe even something like feelings that might have inspired a king to propose to a nobody?

"Well," she said, not concealing her vexation, "I've got the agreement ready for you to sign whenever you have time to go over it."

He nodded.

"It may take some time, so be certain to block out an afternoon and let my maid know."

He looked up and nodded before returning to his book.

Widening her eyes, she turned on her heel and had nearly stepped out when she heard, "Good to see you finally back where you belong. I'm sorry you had to be bothered to return at all."

Silently, she took a few steps toward him. "Are you... offended I stayed so long?"

He shook his head. "Your time is your own. It's not as if you're a servant."

She huffed. "You realize it wasn't actually that long for an alliance negotiation?"

He didn't give her the satisfaction of looking up, but she did note the doubt in his eyes. "We've been hearing the rumors."

"Rumors?"

"That you are to be engaged to King Fredrick."

"What?"

He raised a brow.

"I have no idea where that came from," she said with irritation, "but I assure you nothing of that nature was at any time considered... nor even hinted."

His face softened, but her heart did not. She'd been looking forward to seeing him all the while she'd been away. She'd missed him, had even sent letters, to which she'd received no response. "At any rate, let me know when you're ready to sign."

Then, she did leave the room.

A hand took possession of her wrist. "Hazel, wait," he urged.

She stole it back. *"What?"*

"I'm... *delighted* to see you."

"I don't blame you. Now, you've got someone to pawn your work off on."

His face fell. "You really think that's what I do—how I think?"

She released a long sigh. "No, I just... I was looking forward to seeing you again and you're being so... asinine."

"Asinine?" He raised an almost mirthful brow.

"Irritating."

"Are we in for a round of Affrontery now?"

She shook her head. "I'll see you later."

He took hold of her arm again. "I really, *really* missed you, Hazel."

She gazed back, speechless—both angry and flattered. And completely swept up in his bright eyes despite herself. But then she recalled why she'd returned. Biting her lip, she looked up into his face. "Have you visited The Mirror of late?"

His eyes rose, briefly betraying him before he could say, "Does anyone visit that place anymore? It doesn't even require a keeper."

"Which would make sneaking in with a renowned sorceress nearly effortless."

Her heart hammered as he gazed down at her in astonishment.

"How can you know that?"

How could she know it? It was a good question. Even so, her heart sank. *"Armond,"* she said fiercely. "Tell me you did not consort with Sorceress Maera."

He drew her back into his study and soundly closed the door. "It isn't what it seems. *She's* not what she seems. She's—"

"Very beautiful."

"No! That is, she is, but... she came to *me,* offering protection from any and every danger we might face, Hazel. Dragons, the Deep South, even Bashtii, if it came to it."

"Bashtii?! Armond, can I not leave you alone for one moment before you..." She stopped herself. No matter how angry she was, he was her king. "First of all, I assure you Bashtii is the opposite of a threat. Secondly, what you have done has not vouchsafed the kingdom. It has sentenced it! Your uncle's involvement with Maera was what lost us the Great Entity's favor in the first place. I

firmly believe it was why the dragons were able to wreak such havoc on us."

"You firmly believe? But you don't really *know* anything. And what do you mean my uncle was involved with Maera?"

"What you have done is merely a recurrence of what he did. It was... it was why my parents tried to have him, er... dethroned."

He raised a brow. "Are you considering the same?"

Her brows shot up. "How *dare* you ask me that?"

"It's not as if you'd have to kill me. The throne is yours if you want it and you know it."

Stealing a breath, she took a moment to settle herself before drawing him beside her on the settee. "What can I say to assure you I will never do as you fear?"

"I don't fear it, I..."

"It doesn't matter. We must fix what has been done to the heart of the castle."

"The *heart* of the castle?"

She shook her head. "You don't remember what you did in The Mirror?"

"Well, I know we were meant to deliver some amulet, but I recall nothing that happened once within."

She stood and held out her hand. "It is time you understood the innermost workings of your fortress, Armond."

* * *

That night, they crept into The Mirror. Hazel wasn't certain why she felt the need for secrecy or whether it was at all necessary. But even Armond had seemed to agree that their dealings ought not to be known. Then again, he *would* be the one to wish it concealed.

"Hazel, I have no memory of where I may have put that

amulet," he said, lifting the center carpet to peer beneath.

"In my dream, you asked this wall to lift and there was a room behind it."

"I'm sorry—your *dream*?"

"Oh," she said sheepishly. "I didn't mention that was how I knew what you'd done?"

He planted hands on his hips and shook his head. "How can you have dreamed about my actual whereabouts, Lady Hazel?"

She shook her head. "I cannot say. I feel… that is, I wonder if it might not have been the doing of the Great Entity."

"Are you trying to tell me an old god is tattling on me to you?"

She nearly slapped him. "He is not merely an old god, you *fool*. He is *the* God, the creator of all existence. And he is absolutely *beautiful*."

His brows met his hairline. "Are you trying to tell me you've actually seen this Entity?"

She calmed, not having meant to reveal her experience in Bashtii. "Just tell it to open, will you?" She pointed to the wall.

He patted the stones warily. "All right, here goes… Wall, open."

Instantly, the wall began to rise into the ceiling, revealing the hearth in the small room beyond.

Armond's hand went to his head. "Curiouser and curiouser," he murmured.

The black fire that billowed like a void was not welcoming.

Hazel handed Armond the tongs. "Fetch it, oh, king."

"I see nothing but blackness. How am I to find it?"

She shrugged. "Feel around."

He lifted the tongs.

"But *carefully*," she quickly added. "That is where I believe the heart dwells."

He looked to her as if she were mad, then slowly reached in. In a moment, his brows lifted and he withdrew the amulet. Instantly, the two were thrown back and smoke filled the chamber. Gasping and coughing, the two drew to their feet as it diminished.

Hazel raced to the hearth room to find the fire was now white, purple and red again. The glittering diamond burned eagerly at its center.

Armond dropped the tongs to peer into it as best he could. "There really *is* something in there."

Hazel picked up the amulet from the floor. "Now, we must determine what is to be done with this nasty beasty."

* * *

The last thing Hazel wished to do was journey from her newly built home once again. But journey she must, this time with both Armond and Dorian at her side. She had experienced yet another dream concerning the amulet. In order to display their total renunciation, Armond must return it to its maker: Sorceress Maera. It had long been rumored that she housed within the southern region. Indeed, many of the tribes rather esteemed her, while still others either fear or loathed her. Blythe saw to it that his tribe was included in the latter. This made it all the more convenient for them to stay with his clan. There would be merely complete understanding, or so they hoped.

Hazel's eyes watered when they came to where the mossy forest should have been, where instead there were mostly charred trees and stumps. The beautiful mosses had all but vanished. She and Dorian exchanged dejected glances. Its beauty was quite gone. Even so, she already spotted saplings of fresh vegetation. One day, the forest would gleam in glorious beauty again.

It wasn't until they reached a largely tented area that they realized they'd arrived. Before it stood a cluster of people whose greeting greatly differed from her last visit. This time, an assembly met them at the carriage, where its door was flung open by Blythe.

"Welcome, King Armond!" he said heartily. To Hazel, he spoke in a satisfied whisper, "And *welcome* Lady Fortune, singer of enchanted song."

Her eyes flashed. Could he tell, somehow, that her gift had re-awoken? When he raised a brow at her expression, she knew she'd just given herself away. But the crowd was eager to welcome them, so from the carriage, they were escorted. Soon, they were carried upon the hands of the people and into the large green tent.

When they were at last set upon their own feet and could view the spectacle, it was clear this was where the whole of the local people slept. It was so very, very different from her prior visit that it at first saddened her. But then she gazed upon the faces of the cheering people, busily smiling and shouting over one another. They were *happy*.

"Come," Blythe said. "I must see you to your tents."

Hazel's relief was two-fold. She was more than ready to escape the noise and clamor of the crowd and she was satisfied that they were offered private tents. She couldn't really imagine Armond sleeping within a crowded one.

Her own shelter was much like the one she'd kept during the year of construction. It possessed a tiny desk to one end with a small mattress on the other. Upon it, lay a pile of furs. She smiled. These people may have lost much, but not their love of hunting.

"Many other tribes have begun to rebuild," Blythe explained. "We have been focusing our efforts there before seeing to our own edifices. You may regret not agreeing to stay with another clan."

Hazel shook her head. "We wouldn't think of it."

That evening, they gathered around bonfires and were fed much as in Hazel's prior visit. Armond and Dorian didn't care for most of what was offered but Hazel relished every bite. Again, she noted a new kind of jubilation among the people. The tragedy had drawn them closer. She hoped the countrymen of northern Kierelia felt similarly, but she doubted it. It seemed hard circumstances only made these southerners more determined to resilience and selflessness. Though she had meant to urge Armond to send more builders to aid them, she decided against it now. She would not rob them of their hardship if it produced such priceless camaraderie.

Toward the end of the meal, an elder stood upon the center tree stump to declare, "Now, we will hear song from the Lady Hazel."

Hazel's stomach dropped. She glanced at Blythe. To her surprise, he appeared to share her apprehension. This was further proof he'd guessed her secret. She looked to him to rescue her when a pair of children took her by the arms and brought her to the center.

Standing before the awaiting crowd, she swallowed. How could she do this now that her gift had re-awoken? She could not bear another scene. Her mind raced for what to do as the crowd cheered for her to begin. Her eyes met Blythe's. He gestured to his heart and shook his head. Do not sing from the heart. This was his instruction. It made sense. If she could control her emotions, she could better restrain the power inside her.

She recalled an old tune that had always bored her. Her palms were damp. It had always been difficult to perform, but knowing what might happen made it almost unbearable. Even so, she worked to shrug off her nerves. She must remain as emotionless as possible.

Hazel opened her mouth and... nothing came out. She choked, swallowed, smiled embarrassedly at her audience and began again. This time a few notes were choked out before she found she simply could not go on. She tried twice more before finally gesturing to her throat, shaking her head and rushing to her seat.

"What has happened to me?" she asked of Blythe as he walked her to her tent that evening.

"I have."

She turned to him in bewilderment.

"I hummed in my seat and was able to send enough of my gift to choke out your vocal cords."

Her cheeks burned. "But… why would you do that?"

"I told you once to keep your gift hidden. I meant it."

"Well, what was I supposed to do when a whole village demanded I sing?"

"Just as you did. I simply did what I could to aid you."

She considered this, supposing it was better to be accused of stage fright than possessing the gift. "Thank you."

"Do you wish for aid?"

"With my gift? Yes, I suppose. But we are not meant to be here long. Our dear priest cannot be expected to hold things together on his own for more than a night or two."

"But this is important. Do you not agree? Unless you plan never to sing again."

She sighed. Prudent as that may be, she did not believe she was capable. "We will make time."

* * *

It was Blythe himself who led Armond, Hazel and Dorian through the forest. And it was to Hazel's dismay that he said, "Follow this path and you will come upon the sorceress' dwelling."

"You're not coming with us?" she asked. She hadn't realized how frightened she was of the task at hand until that moment.

"I have a past with the sorceress. It would be unwise for me to go with you."

She eyed him dubiously.

"I was... in love with her as a younger man, before I realized just what she was. She has since made attempts to ensorcell me into returning to her."

Hazel's brows shot up. She could not argue with that, but it did nothing to dissuade her trepidation.

"I will await your return just here," he said, "so be certain you return by the same path. If you have not come by noontime, I may send a rescue party for you, so be swift about your business."

Hazel clenched her fists as they stepped onto the path. She had never experienced fear as she did now—except when facing the giant dragon. She couldn't begin to fathom just why this endeavor got under her skin. Perhaps it was because two kings had been so easily fooled by her. Even Blythe had. How could she expect to remain more clear-headed than they? She supposed it helped that she would not be captivated by the sorceress' enchanted beauty as they had been.

Dorian came to walk beside her. "You are frightened?"

She shrugged. "The woman is capable of things we may not yet have dreamed of."

"Yet, you are on speaking terms with the God of all things. We should be fine."

She questioned this, uncertain it could be considered 'speaking terms,' though they *had* spoken. Then her mind was transported to that majestic throne room, his very presence set before her in fathomless brilliance. She breathed more easily. She *did* know the Great Entity. It was his protection they required and she swiftly sent up a petition for it.

Two giant, winged men appeared on either side of the path. She yelped before realizing that neither Armond nor Dorian took notice of them. Furthermore, the giants reminded her of the angelic beings in the Entity's realm.

"Dorian," she said. "Look to your left and right."

He did so, then eyed her.

"That's what I thought," she said.

"What is it?"

"We have company."

He looked about with a suspicious eye and nearly withdrew his sword when she shook her head. "They are of the Eternal Realm... the land often referred to as Paradise."

He continued to scan the vicinity but only shrugged. She could not imagine why she was able to see them while her friends could not. Perhaps because she had set foot in their realm? Well, she was simply grateful the Entity had not only heard her mental plea but had answered it.

Next thing she knew, the forest began to spin. Woozily, she fell to the ground, unable to stand until it ceased. But in exchange for the trees that had surrounded them moments before, they were met by a vividly bright scene of a decadently colorful forest with ethereal sunrays.

"More of the Entity's work?" Dorian asked.

She eyed the new scene with skepticism. It made her queasy. "I think not."

Armond, who'd been walking a little way behind the two, caught up to them. "This is awfully enchanting, isn't it?"

"Indeed," Hazel said dubiously. "That is just about the word I would use."

She couldn't understand it, but something about the endeavor sent her right back into childhood again, desiring to hide in corners and avoid run-ins with Lady Nora, attempting to escape evening meals so she wouldn't have to face Dianna... even trying *not* to gain Armond's attention in case she should do something embarrassing. This mission—the very thought of facing the sorceress—intimidated her. What had ever moved her to become the kingdom's go-to girl for handling dragons and sorcerers? She'd gone from being the girl with not a care in the world but Lady Nora to practically balancing a whole kingdom on her shoulders. And now she had to walk through this ensorcelled wood with the goal of seeking a malevolent witch. If, years ago, anyone had told her that she'd find herself *here*, she'd have hidden away in her tower and never faced the world again.

An arm went around her shoulders. "Little sister, you are shaking," Dorian said with far more concern than ever he'd displayed before. "Surely, we will come upon no harm in a place such as this."

"I'll be fine, Dorian," she muttered with more confidence than she felt. "Do not forget that you are here to protect *Armond.*"

He looked as if he might weep. "I care only ever to watch out for you. I've only one little sister after all."

She raised a brow at him. Certainly, she felt close enough to be like a sister, but he'd never spoken as if he actually considered her family.

Suddenly, Armond was between them. "*I* will see she is safe. I am the love of her life after all."

Hazel nearly choked. "You are *no* such thing, you foolish man."

He grabbed her hand and pulled her close. "Hazel, you need me as much as I need you—admit it."

"I..." She was speechless. Suddenly, his eyes were glowing balls of magnificent light. Why had she ever considered spurning his proclaimed affection? "Armond, are you truly asking me to—"

She screamed and fell from his embrace as one of the winged figures swiped his sword through the atmosphere. In the next moment, she was shaking her head, her mind clearer than moments before. Dorian and Armond appeared to be doing the same.

"This forest is under an enchantment," Dorian said solemnly.

"Indeed," Armond agreed. "The air is so thick it is difficult to think."

Hazel nodded. "But we are well-guarded. Trust to the Entity."

Dorian nodded but Armond eyed her leerily.

They drew around the nearest bend where a resplendent mansion resided. Crawling with wine-hued roses, their fragrance wafted after them, drawing them forward. It was all Hazel could do to focus on the winged giants to keep her head above water. The scent was nearly intoxicating, causing her eyes to water from their compelling richness.

"*That* is a witch's house?" Dorian questioned.

"Seems so," Hazel said.

Armond stood frozen in his tracks. It was a moment before she realized he was weeping.

"Mate, it's the enchantment again," Dorian urged.

Armond shook his head. "It could only be the dwelling of an *angel.*" He looked to Hazel. "We must be wrong. She could mean us no harm. We must not insult her by returning the gift she bestowed."

Hazel looked to the giants, who smiled before swinging the sword overtop his head.

Armond blinked, then touched a hand to his cheek in bewilderment. He examined the tear, then looked to the others. With the clearing of his throat, he started forward. "Let's get this over with."

Hazel's nails bit into her sweaty palms. The presence of the giant angels offered some comfort, but seeing that the atmospheric spell had been able to ensorcell Armond again made her anxious. What if they should all allow themselves to be taken in? The kingdom would be lost.

None of them moved when they came to the door. At last,

Dorian shrugged, unsheathed his sword and knocked. Hazel stood behind him, feeling the coward she suddenly was. What was it about the place that stole away all the confidence she'd gained in the last year?

A beautiful voice sang out and the door swung open. When no one was revealed and the singing ceased, Hazel was certain Maera had used *the gift* of the southern tribes... or had mimicked it. It made her feel completely powerless. If the woman could match what small gift she had, what chance did they stand? With a wave of anger, she shook her head and stomped her foot. She would not be daunted.

22

The house was dark within, nothing like the bright splendor without. Still, it was immaculately kept and smelled of the roses that crept inside the dwelling, somehow surviving without much sunlight. To be sure, they were conjured by the witch's craft and likely held a magic all their own. Hazel noted not to touch them, let alone their thorns. Who could tell their capabilities?

"H-hello," Dorian called out when no one came to meet them.

"This way," the immaculate voice sang to them.

The two men eagerly followed after that voice, leaving Hazel in nearly the coldest fear she'd endured in her life. Hatred for her floated on the very wings of the atmosphere. Every beam, stone and flower loathed her. But it *longed* for the two friends she'd foolishly brought with her. It was imperative Armond be present. It was his acceptance of the amulet that required his personal return and rejection. But why had they put Dorian in danger? Moreover, why did the house *want them?*

She hurried after them, taking each by the arm to yank them from their current stupor. They shrugged her off and continued forward. Helplessly, she looked about for the giants but found they had not entered with them.

She was on her own.

They arrived at a room that possessed the greatest number of buds. Here, a woman dressed in white lounged before a bright window. She looked like the angel Armond had claimed her to be, but Hazel's bones shook with rage and fear.

The roses' fragrance stung her eyes as they entered. Her lungs felt as if filled with smoke. Still, she forced herself to step up between the two lads. It was imperative that she was the one to face the sorceress.

"You are Sorceress Maera?" she asked smoothly, surprising herself.

"Hazel, is it? You're smaller than I'd expected."

Hazel lifted a brow. She'd not realized the lady even knew of her existence, let alone cared to expect anything of her. "And you're even more stunning than I expected… but then I suppose it is conjured." She began to feel she was playing a game of Affrontery.

"Your friends do not seem to mind," the woman said with a smile.

Hazel turned to find them dreamily gazing at Maera. She snorted. "They are under your enchantment. It has little to do with your looks."

Maera grinned. "You have not come for a *beauty contest* have you, little prophet?"

"Prophet?" Hazel questioned dubiously. She was nothing like the prophet… was she?

For a moment, Maera hesitated, realizing she'd spoken something she'd not meant to. Could it be their enemy knew her better than she knew herself? Could it be the dreams she'd had of late revealed more about her identity than she'd realized? She began to wonder if more had been unlocked during her encounter in the Entity's realm than just her voice.

But this was all meaningless. It was not what they'd come for. She turned to Armond, working to gain his gaze. "King Armond, return the amulet."

He hesitated before the sweep of a sword passed over his head. Hazel blinked. The angelic giants were still with them, though unseen except for in this action. Armond stole a breath of air as if he'd been unable to for some time. Then, he choked over the aroma of the room. Coughing still, he reached into his inner pocket and held the amulet toward the sorceress.

"Take it back," he said. "We want nothing from you."

"Why, *Armond*," Maera said in a charming tenor. "Why should you reject my protection? We agreed something had to be done to make certain nothing like that dragon disaster ever took place again, else the kingdom might finally witness how truly afraid you are."

He glanced up at the woman in confusion, then looked back at the amulet, eyeing it in contemplation.

"The castle possessed the amulet when the dragon arrived," Hazel reminded. "It did no good whatever. It may even have summoned the trouble."

Armond blinked and held it out further for the witch. "Take your dark talisman," he said as if it was difficult to speak. It revealed the extent of his inner strength that he was able to rebuff the spell. He kept looking to Hazel as if to keep himself rational.

Maera drew to her feet and stood before him, taking his hand into her own. She closed his fingers around the token and held it there. "I gave this to you out of the sentiment of my heart. I want to see you *safe.*"

His eyes grew large and sparkling and Hazel understood she had lost him again. She wondered what the giants were waiting for when she decided to take matters into her own hands. Reaching for his ensnared hand, she found herself thrust against the far wall by the sound of Maera's song. Neither Dorian nor Armond rushed to aid her as she drew gasping and shaking to her feet.

"Do you give me your word that you mean us no harm?" Armond asked with that same light in his eyes.

Hazel blinked. He sounded *rational.* He was under no spell—not currently anyway. He was merely… bewitched by the woman's beauty.

Maera smiled warmly. "With *all* my heart."

Hazel could practically see Armond's heart beating out of his chest. Desperately, she ran to him and flung herself onto her knees. *"Armond,* you claimed you love me. Was that *true?"*

Gulping, he turned his attention to her, examining her face as if to remember who she was. Hazel's heart raced. She'd declared it in an attempt to pull him from Maera's grasp, but… would it work? *Did* he love her?

As her eyes pleaded with him, her mind flashed through all the instances in her girlhood when she'd asked this question. Could Armond ever love her? Over and over, she'd told herself it could never be. And when she'd finally taken the chance, he'd rebuffed her as she'd always known he would. She felt herself that insignificant, insecure girl again as she knelt there on the floor, facing the man she knew she still loved, though she wished with all her soul she did not. She never wanted him to have that kind of power over her again.

At last, something dawned in his eyes. *"Yes,"* he declared. He yanked his hand from Maera's, leaving the amulet behind. "I *do* love Hazel." He spoke it with fresh feeling, as if rediscovering the sensation himself.

That was when Maera's true colors emerged. Her teeth sharpened into fangs as she roared and flung the amulet at Hazel It smacked her squarely in the stomach, stealing the breath from her. The room grew fuzzy as she crumbled onto the floor.

"You will regret this, young king!" Maera cried. "The Deep South has been seeking my aid in their schemes against you. I offered you my protection. Now, I promise my vengeance. It will not be long now. And your little love is no match for me."

23

azel was only aware she'd passed out when she awoke to the sound of her own singing. It was quiet, scarcely audible really, but she felt her lips moving. Upon opening her eyes, she found Armond strung up by rose vines while Dorian knelt before the witch, utterly entranced.

"You will be king, as was your destiny," the sorceress said to him. "And I will be your queen."

Hazel did not move. She could not simply race over as she had before. An actual plan was necessary... or perhaps merely a weapon was. She felt for the crystalline hilt of her ruby blade. Drawing it carefully, she attempted to bound to her feet before she realized something weighted her to the floor. Upon her stomach, the amulet had planted itself like a horse's hoof. She gritted her teeth as she attempted to remove it.

"Giants," she whispered desperately.

Promptly, the amulet was lifted from her. It then floated across the room and was laid silently beside the witch. Hazel sprang into action, half ready to hack the head off the sorceress. But that was when her voice sang out in fury. It was not from her throat alone from which it resonated, but the sword in her hand. As she sang, her song rose in volume as if, quite astonishingly, amplified *by* the weapon.

Instantly, Maera turned to her, throwing her own mouth open in song. Her melody reached Hazel's and she actually felt her own soundwaves being pressed back at her. Desperately, she increased her volume and the sorceress staggered. Ignoring the doubt within her, Hazel bodily pressed forward, drawing her sound nearer and nearer until it overwhelmed the witch's vicinity. At last, the woman dropped to her knees, covered her ears and screeched in furious agony.

Maintaining her hold over their enemy, Hazel focused part of her song after the vines clasping Armond until they crumbled into brittle pieces. Freeing Dorian was another story. He would not awaken. Instead, he threw his arms around Maera as if to protect her from Hazel, but when that did not work, he stood and withdrew his sword.

Hazel stepped back, uncertain of what to do. She could not call on his love for her as she had with Armond. Instead, her mind raced over their years of friendship, when he'd been her only friend, the one with whom she'd shared her every secret, had trusted so explicitly.

That friend started toward her and she fell back another step as she recalled how he'd been using her all those years. A flash of his face when he'd demanded she keep away from his prison cell sent fresh pain through her. But she had not given up on him then and she would not now.

His eyes were a blend of numbness and hatred as he seized her wrist to keep her from escaping. She nearly released her sword in disbelief. Instead, she roared out her heartache at him. Against her will, tears washed down her face. But the drops drew his attention to her eyes. At last, he staggered back. Releasing her wrist, he stared down at the sword in his hand, taking in what he'd nearly done.

It was then he leaped into action. Stealing Armond and Hazel from the room, he raced them through the mansion, out the front door and down the path. It wasn't until the three were thoroughly out of breath that Hazel made him stop.

He bent over to rest his hands on his knees as he caught his breath. "I..." he breathed, "nearly *killed* you."

She patted him on the back. "She almost *made* you kill me."

He shook his head. "Your voice... it's back."

Her eyes darted to Armond, searching for what he might think. A blush stole over her as she recalled what he'd said, what had broken the sorceress' power over him. He *loved* her... and he'd proven it. There was no doubting him now.

She was surprised to find an answering blush on his face. It was clear he'd just learned that he felt even more than he'd realized... and he was actually self-conscious about the fresh confession.

He offered her a glittering half-smile and asked, "Did you sing *through* that beautiful blade of yours?" He came to stand close beside her and took it into his hands. "Where ever did this come from?"

"A... friend of the prophet's."

His brows rose as he handed it back to her, his eyes conveying something he did not speak. He was seeing her in a new light. "You were our hero in there... yet again." Abruptly, his knees buckled and he cried out in pain.

Hazel dropped to her knees beside him. "What is it? What is the matter?"

He drew back his sleeves to reveal arms covered in thorns... the barbs from the enchanted roses. Just as Hazel had feared, they were poisoned—that was, if the green hue emanating from every tiny wound indicated anything.

"They're all over my body!" he bellowed out.

Hazel looked to Dorian as he examined the lesions himself. "We must get you back to the clan," he said forlornly. "Can you stand?"

Armond nodded and drew to his feet only to have them buckle under him again.

Dorian looked to Hazel. "You'll have to help me drag him. Take one of his arms over your shoulder and I'll take the other."

It felt an age before they finally met Blythe. With his great girth, he took Armond up over his shoulder and raced him through the forest. Armond screamed as the thorns dug deeper into his flesh and the toxin spread.

When they finally appeared at the village, Armond's face was green and the village healer shook his head. "Never seen a case like this."

Hazel leaned in close. "This is the king of your country now."

The man blinked at her. "I am well aware of who he is, young lady."

Huffing, Hazel left the tent as the healer explained that he must locate and remove every single thorn and then apply a salve purported to heal any ailment caused by witchcraft.

Not far from the settlement, she stopped to lean against a tree, stealing a few moments to breathe her emotions into submission. What would they do if the salve did not cure him... if he could not return to his throne? Who was the subsequent heir? She didn't believe there was anyone left of the royal family except... her.

She shook her head. She would never take his place. But... if he didn't make it... would she *have* to? She shook her head again. He *would* make it. She looked to the heavens where she imagined the Great Entity's throne room to be and prayed Armond's return of the amulet placed him under the Entity's favor again.

"Do not worry, Hazel," Dorian said, making her leap at his sudden appearance beside her.

"...I didn't hear you coming."

"I know. You were in your worrying stance. But he will be all right. I know it."

"How can you know it?"

"Because he returned the amulet. He is in favor again."

She bit her lip as she examined his silhouette in the moonlight. "How can you be so certain?"

He shrugged. "The night you told me the Great Entity had spoken to you about me... that he knew all and he offered his mercy... It was no small matter to me. If he could be so benevolent concerning my iniquities, he certainly will be with Armond."

She smiled at him, though he could not see it in the darkness. It was true. The Entity was more than a god—not just a distant, overbearing lord. He was a hero and one who cared more intimately over the workings of those he'd created than she would ever have expected.

"So..." he began. "Armond is in love with you."

She could hear the grin in his voice and couldn't help smiling herself. She was glad he could not see it. "So it seems."

"Well, he could not do better."

"But he is *king*. He must wed someone who can offer fresh strength to the kingdom."

He laughed. "Hazel, I don't think there is anyone stronger than you in any kingdom. I tell you, I adored you as the sweet, rejected girl you were, but you have transformed into a pillar of strength. I am *amazed* by you."

Her mouth nearly dropped open. *"Aw, Dorian..."* she said with a light punch to his arm. "You look *up* to me? I'm like your exemplar now."

He chuckled and lightly shoved her back to her tree. "Don't push it, Lady Fortune."

* * *

By the following day, Armond was fully alert and by the next, he could walk without aid. They remained a few more days to be certain he had all the rest he required. But by the end of six days, he was near pleading with the healer to bequeath him a sound prognosis so he could return to living again.

Even so, Hazel could tell every bump of the carriage caused him discomfort, making it clear he'd been exaggerating his wellness. She only hoped the journey homeward would not be too taxing.

Once Dorian has fallen asleep, Armond leaned forward with, "Maera says she will aid the Deep South in their upcoming strike."

"She would have helped them anyway," Hazel replied. "It is my belief that the 'amulet of protection' was only a ruse to weaken us for them."

"But don't you think she'll aid their cause more fiercely now?"

She considered. Maera did seem the vengeful sort. "Likely."

He swallowed. "And she said it will not be long before they come... I'm just not prepared for this, Hazel. What will we do?"

"It will test your role as king, I grant you. But we will see this through together. We will inform Gunther of what was relayed. He will prepare our troops. And we have an ally in Bashtii, don't forget. We will send Fredrick word as well and he will be at the ready."

Armond snorted. "He is a whole peninsula away should we need him. You know, I asked him for a portion of his troops—"

"I *know* you did, but he cannot afford to be without them for an indefinite period of time. It would be foolhardy when he is such a new king and will be considered untried by surrounding kingdoms. *Many* would like a chance to get their hands on Bashtii."

"But we are half the kingdom we were before and I am as untried as he is."

"Yes, but they are *his* troops—not ours. He will send aid when we have actual sightings of our enemy's approach."

"I don't like that we're forced to count on him so much."

"Well, he's all we have just now. We lost every other ally when we lost King Zephuel."

"Then why haven't we worked on that?"

"I don't know. *You're* the king. I just returned from salvaging the alliance we still have." She folded her arms and looked out the window, working to conceal her flaring temper.

"Hazel."

"Yes?"

"I'm sorry. The *last* thing I want to do is argue with you."

She glanced at him. "I don't want to fight with you either."

"And the last thing I want to do is keep discussing *him.*"

"Fredrick?"

"King Fredrick."

She raised a brow at him. That had been rather snappy for someone who claimed they did not wish to fight with her.

He smiled humbly. "Have I ever told you how gleaming your hair is in the evening sunlight?"

She rolled her eyes.

"I mean it," he said with a grin. Abruptly, his face lost its merriment.

"What is it?"

"I… was just remembering your gift."

She caught her breath nervously, fearing what he might think.

"Yes?"

"I heard Blythe discussing it with you during my recuperation."

She nodded.

"I disagree with him."

"Disagree?"

"I don't think you should train. What if someone should hear? I don't know what the people would do to you."

"Excuse me?"

"You *know* how they fear the idea of the singers of old. They love you now, but if they ever learned... I'd never let them do anything to you, but I still hate to think what—"

"Armond, I'm fine. I'll be careful. The training is only to make certain I can control when it is used... so it is never used again."

"Please make very certain." He sat forward and took her hand into his own. "After what happened at Maera's... If you weren't so capable, I don't know what would have happened to you. You're... so much more precious than I ever knew when we were young. I just want you *safe*, Hazel."

Her returning smile did not reach her eyes. She had always taken care of herself. She did not need him worrying over her. But in another moment, she softened. Perhaps she simply was not accustomed to someone caring. And someone to care for her was what she'd always longed for. Here, that person sat before her and she seemed only to bicker with him. She squeezed his hand. "The Entity will see me well."

24

Hazel swallowed. She was in the deepest, darkest part of what was left of the old castle. No one ever went there. It was rumored to have been an old torture chamber where the ghosts of its victims haunted. She rather doubted this. Even so, it provided the perfect place for her to determine how difficult it would be to train the gift out of her voice.

Taking a deep breath, she began with a tune she hated—one Lady Nora had so loved. Unexpected tears sprang to her eyes as the melody melted from her mouth. She recalled instances her guardian had requested she sing just for her. It had not been motherly or loving, but it had been a sort of appreciation. And Hazel had to admit it: She'd loved Lady Nora in some capacity, even if the woman hadn't been capable of loving her back. She'd worked so hard to gain the woman's approval to no avail. Now, she was gone from the world forever.

Hazel nearly gasped when she realized she was surrounded by a swirling cloud of torchlit dust. Her voice rose and it rose. As her grief mounted, it danced morosely, seeming to droop with its own sadness. At last, she ceased as sobs overtook her. How could one mourn someone who'd been so antagonistic? There had to be something wrong with Hazel that she could feel as she did. But then, she never had allowed herself to properly mourn *any* of the losses endured that fateful day. She'd marched forward, dragging the whole kingdom with her. Now, all the sorrow of that time returned and she fell to the ground under its weight.

The creaking of a door sent her back to her feet. She blinked several times. A new door had appeared, but... it was *not possible*. Those spiraling stairs with their gleaming handrail were too familiar. Slowly, she started up, running her fingers along the banister.

"Oh..." she gasped, drying her face with her baggy sleeve as she took in the sight of her tower room—her little home.

Racing to the bookshelf that still sheltered her books, she stroked their bindings. Somehow, the window she'd broken the day the fire was replaced. For that matter, the dust that should have caked every surface from a year's neglect was absent. By some miracle, it had survived. Anything she'd loved, she'd kept in this place and it was all *safe*.

"How?" she whispered out. She recollected the castle's structure from the outside and knew this tower was not present. At great risk, she unlatched the window and leaned as far out as she could. Just as she'd thought, the tower was a new addition.

"But *how?*" she laughed out, a hand going to her throat in a tumult of emotion. Could it be the castle had somehow... collapsed the room into itself... burying it safely beneath the surface?

Joyously, she threw herself into her favorite old chair and splayed her skirts out until she was comfortable. Laying her head back, she closed her eyes and inhaled the aromas. Though her life had changed so much now that she was more than welcome in Castlehaven, this place still felt the most like home—like a parent cradling her weary body after all the striving over the last year. Here, she was just Hazel and nothing more was expected of her than that.

"Argh!" she growled, leaping to her feet as she took in the placement of the sun. It was time for evening meal and she'd promised Armond he would see her there that evening. Every muscle in her body and mind pleaded for her to remain. But she was a woman of her word. Racing down the stairs, she shouted, *"Don't* go anywhere!"

* * *

Everyone present at evening meal was abuzz over the chairs that had mysteriously scooted about of their own accord. Hazel bit her lip as she caught Armond's glance. It had to have been her singing. Somehow, the gift's reach had far surpassed what she had surmised. She was only grateful she'd done no harm. But it was true, in the end. She could never sing again. If it could range through *stories* of stone, she had no idea what she might be capable of... and she had no way of practicing in private.

She did her best to plunge into the meal, working to shove out the discomfort she felt that it was she they spoke of, though they had no idea of it. Many believed the castle itself had performed the act since it seemed to possess a flashier personality than the previous one. But the meal became more enjoyable for her as the topic waned and other matters were discussed. That was, until she caught a quiet conversation between a nearby couple.

"They say there is a *secret* engagement between King Armond and our Lady Fortune. Though why it should be so private, I cannot imagine."

Hazel's face heated. She dared a glance at Armond and her agitation intensified as she realized he'd heard the conversation as well. He looked back at her thoughtfully, though she could not read what those thoughts might be.

"Can we talk," he mouthed to her.

Casting a glance about for any watching eyes, she replied with a subtle nod and the lowering of her gaze.

What could he wish to speak about? Was he bothered by the gossip? Did he blame her? She shook her head at herself. It could not be. She'd done nothing to reveal her feelings for him... so she hoped. Even so, it felt like a whole evening had passed before the supper ended and he drew her into his personal sitting room.

The moment the door was closed, he swiveled onto a knee before her. "Hazel... will you marry me?"

She drew her hand back before he could take it. "What?" Why was this proposal so much more surprising than the last? Was it because she'd not expected another? Or because it meant so much more now?

"*Marry* me," he urged. "Be queen of Kierelia and rule by my side. The people need you and *I* need you."

Turning her back on him, she marched across the room and fell into a chair. She well understood this was not the response he hoped for, but she needed a moment to regain her composure, to *think*.

Unwaveringly, he followed and sat close beside her. "What is the matter?" he asked gently. "Still can't bear the sight of me?"

She turned to find his half-smile upon her. It was *clear* he understood that her feelings for him had re-awoken. It was also a little frustrating. But they'd only *just* begun to change. Peering back into those eyes that had for so long been irresistible to her, she said, "I don't know if it is wise. I don't know that we would be *good* together… if I—"

"We would be *tremendous* together. Think of all we could do for the kingdom! Not to mention… I believe I could make you happy." His voice softened as he continued. "I remember how difficult things used to be for you. And then you worked so hard to help restore Kierelia. I just want to see *you* cared for, for a change."

Her head spun as her mind raced. Her walls were coming down and exhilaration flooded her. For a moment, curiosity about what Fredrick would think crossed her mind. She'd missed his company since leaving Bashtii, but though they had parted good friends, he had not kept his promise to write. Meanwhile, Armond, king of the kingdom she loved, the man she'd grown up adoring, offered her his affection and the promise of creating a bright future for their people. In the end… did she still love him?

"Yes," she said, "I will marry you."

25

The castle fairly pulsated when the news was announced the following day. There was to be an engagement celebration that very evening. Hazel's maid fretted over selecting the perfect gown for the occasion. After all, Hazel would be presented as future queen of Kierelia. Now and then, she found herself gripped with fear at the idea. Somehow, the part about becoming queen had not rightly sunk in when she'd accepted the proposal. At the moment she'd consented, she'd thought of him alone.

She shook her head, recalling a younger version of herself in all the years before the dragon attack. That girl would never have believed she'd find herself *here*, engaged to a man who would make her queen… *engaged* to *Armond*. It was utterly improbable.

When the hour of the celebration dawned, she was astonished to find the feasting room decked even more elaborately than for the coronation. The room roared with applause as she walked to her seat. When she drew beside Armond, who looked on her with pride, all shouted, *"Hail Lady Hazel, future queen of Kierelia!"*

It was all so much that she could scarcely eat when they were served. Her heart swelled. Never had she felt so accepted, so *wanted*. And it was not only by the people but by her future husband. Truly, the Great Entity had seen fit to favor. She glanced into the rafters to offer up her thanks.

Near the end of the feast, a servant came to whisper something to Armond. He nodded and then turned to her with ashen face. "It… seems the people are requesting you sing."

Her stomach sank. "You know very well I cannot."

A chant of, "Sing, sing, sing, sing!" rose from the assemblage.

Armond moved to speak for her, but she leaped to her own feet. If they were to be disappointed, she must do it herself. It was important she set this standard now: that she could not be expected to perform for them. They must forget she had ever loved to sing.

The room fell silent as they awaited her performance.

She cleared her throat and squared her shoulders. "I thank you all for the honor of wishing to hear a song."

They applauded.

She swallowed.

"I regret to announce that… my throat has been poorly of late. It is impossible for me to perform."

The room did not conceal its disappointment. She and Armond exchanged a look. When she was seated again, he leaned in with, "They will learn to accept it."

But the following day, Dorian met her in her room with, "I heard what happened."

"Well, you were more expectant of this engagement than I was, as I recall."

He shook his head. "Yes, congratulations. But I meant about the people wishing you to sing."

"Oh… well, they will learn to accept it," she said, mimicking Armond.

He lifted a brow. "What about the training regime you and Blythe discussed?"

"Did you hear about the chairs that moved on their own?"

He laughed. "That was *you*?"

"I was in the old 'torture chamber' and *still* it reached them. How can I train without taking the risk of hurting someone?"

"All you must do is take a horse far into the forest."

She eyed him. "Everything is so *close* to perfect just now. I wish I did not have this nonsensical gift to worry over. I'm terrified I'll ruin it all."

He patted her shoulder. "You'll do the right thing at the right time, Hazel. Train and get comfortable with yourself again. In the meantime, hail Lady Hazel, future queen of Kierelia."

Smirking unhappily, she shrugged his hand off. Even so, she took his suggestion to heart. Every chance she got, she sneaked away to a far-off corner of the forest. There, she sang… and prayed she did not harm any animals. As it happened, they were rather drawn to her voice. Often, she caught a family of deer venture near her clearing, the squirrels did not scatter and the birds sang with her. Never did she do them harm for rarely did her gift act out so erratically as in past. In fact, she found it perfectly natural to control. When she felt the power swelling, she sang more quietly, as if soothing it into submission. On the rare occasion she tried to lift something, it rose and fell according to the pattern of her voice. She found new delight in what she could do… until she invited Dorian along to witness her progress. In that instance, she cast his body flat upon the ground.

"Ouch," he murmured where he lay.

She flew to his side. "Are you all right?"

He nodded. "Right enough. But that's *some* left swing your

voice has got there."

She pulled him to a sitting position and plopped down beside him. "I'm sorry. I don't know what happened. I've been in total control until now."

"Maybe I'm bad luck."

"I think I'm nervous."

"Because of me?"

"Yes. People listening to me sing always makes me anxious. When alone and in the peace of this glorious wood, focus is effortless." She turned to him. "You're going to have to come along with me every time."

"You want to *use* me?" He patted a hand to his heart.

"I need someone to observe as I train."

"And what happens when you grow accustomed to singing before *me*?"

She chewed her lip. "I'll have to find someone else to practice with."

"Armond?"

She shook her head.

"And why not?"

"I don't know, I... think I'm embarrassed about what I did to him the first time."

"But he is your *betrothed*, you ninny. I am certain he can bear it. And after all, you said you sang before that King Fredrick."

She sighed. "You are right. Armond doesn't even know I've been training."

"Excuse me?"

"Don't look at me like that. I just wanted to try it on my own for a while to see how it went. He doesn't think I should be training anyway."

Dorian lifted a brow.

"He's afraid someone will catch me and the people will turn

against me."

"I don't think there's a thing you could do to turn these people against you. And Armond must not understand how much all that warbling means to you if he's so willing to see you give it up... Sort of rubs me wrong, Hazel."

"Oh, don't be cross with him. He just wants to see me cared for."

Laying a hand on her shoulder, he leaned in close with, "Then I dare you to *let* him."

26

azel found Armond leaning on the rail of his study balcony. She relished how the sun set his dark hair to glistening, how his thick brows drew together as he chewed at his lower lip. True, he appeared concerned about something. But, as always, it only aided his looks.

"Armond," she said from the threshold.

He spun about and immediately his face relaxed. "Hazel," he said as if the mere sound of her name satisfied him. "Where have you been?"

"The forest."

He took her hand to draw her beside him. "You've been spending a lot of time there."

She stole a long breath. This was her moment. "Yes… I've been meaning to tell you about where I am with my gift."

To her astonishment, he laughed. "You know, I was just

recollecting that evening you shot me into the rafters. I cannot tell you how petrified I was, but I have to say it is somewhat humorous to look back on. I guess you could say you swept me off my feet."

She tried to laugh with him. "Is… that what you were thinking about before I joined you?"

"I suppose it was."

She swallowed, recalling his somber attitude before she'd alerted him to her presence. "What about it, specifically?"

"I was just thinking about how, all this time, I'd thought the prophet had sent you to the tribes to be healed of it."

"I didn't exactly need *healing.*"

He raised a brow at her. "You know that's not quite what I meant…"

"Yes," she relented, releasing a breath. "It is my own discomfort that makes me touchy."

He took a step nearer and leaned on the rail. "Was there something you wanted to speak about?"

Her mouth opened in hesitation. "Er, no," she lied, disappointing herself. "I just wanted to see you."

His grin grew impossibly large, utterly knocking the breath from her. That was the smile of the old Armond, the carefree lad of her youth. But he grew suddenly somber as he said, "As for me, there is a small issue I meant to discuss with you."

Swallowing, she found she could not look at him. Had he found her out after all? How she kicked herself for not having confessed but moments before.

"It seems Dianna has not left her rooms once since she was originally introduced to them."

Hazel met his eyes with a mixture of relief and exasperation. "Why… that is preposterous! I was aware she hadn't left them before my trip to Bashtii, but I expected her to have emerged by now."

"The servant who cares for her insists it is true. Dianna has materials brought to her and continues to replenish the clothing supply of the *whole land*. But unless Stacia or Rebecca visit her, she sees no one. Hazel... could it be she is scarred from the destruction of all she ever knew?"

"Maybe partly... But I believe I have an idea of what this is really about." She patted his hand. "Leave it to me."

* * *

Hazel hesitated before Dianna's quarters. It wasn't a surprise visit, as she'd made certain the lady was forewarned. But though Hazel had so readily volunteered herself for the task, she could not help recalling the years of hostility—how effortlessly Dianna could make her feel like a shameful child. She'd always known how to pick at what would hurt most.

Straightening her shoulders, Hazel forced herself to knock.

"Who is it?"

A peculiar question considering Dianna ought to be fully aware. Then again, Hazel supposed she wanted no surprises.

"Lady Hazel."

A sigh sounded from the other side. "Come in if you must."

Hazel paused within the doorway. The room was larger than Armond's and exquisitely decorated in creme and pink. Noting how small the single window was, it was clear the bright hues were necessary. Somehow, it felt like sunshine.

It was also clear that Dianna had somehow bribed the architect into designing the room specifically to her needs. A small window meant there was less chance of being seen. The room was large and bright to make it pleasant despite the lack of sunlight and fresh air. But witnessing such forethought only increased Hazel's concern. This life of reclusiveness was premeditated. Dianna even possessed a small dining area complete with a larder of fruitcakes and biscuits.

"This is a... comfortable space," Hazel said as she approached.

"I find it so," Dianna replied, not looking up from her sewing.

"I believe you designed the dress I wore to the Bashtiian ball."

Dianna's eyes flickered up and she gestured to the chair across from her. "You loved it."

"Er, well, yes. It was exquisite work."

"I have exquisite taste."

Hazel sat down. "What are you working on now?"

"Hazel?"

"Yes?"

"I presume you've come to see me for a purpose. It's not as if we're old friends. I'd appreciate it if you'd get straight to the point."

"You're not leaving your rooms."

"Indeed."

"But... can't you see it isn't healthy?"

"As if I require wisdom from you, oh, Lady Fortune, future queen of Kierelia."

So, she had heard. That could make this conversation thorny. But Hazel had promised Armond she would handle things and she was a woman of her word.

"Dianna, do you really intend to remain sewing up gowns in this room the *rest* of your life?"

"No. I design men's garments as well. And I've been working on draperies and tapestries."

"I mean it. Surely, there are more important things than your vanity."

"Like what?"

Hazel groped for something. She didn't know what the woman's values were apart from making people miserable.

"*Helping* people is surprisingly satisfying."

"I'm clothing the whole kingdom from this room. Is that not enough for you?"

Hazel leaped from her chair and knelt before the girl, forcing her to look down at her. "Isn't there something more you require of life than *this*."

"You are literally the saddest, sorriest little orphan who ever attained a royal crown. Really, I cannot imagine how Armond can desire such a desperate little nobody for a wife."

Hazel released her breath. This was a defense mechanism, she knew. She'd heard stories of her treating Stacia and Rebecca similarly whenever they tried to get her out of her chambers. Then again, Dianna had always treated Hazel this way. And why? Stacia had once told her Dianna was jealous because Armond had stood up for her. But surely that could not stimulate *such* loathing. "Why do you hate me, Dianna?"

The girl thrust her sewing aside. "No matter what I do to you, you refuse to break. It is exasperating. What is wrong with you?"

Hazel blinked. "You want me to break?"

"I want you to not be *so* composed, so benevolent, so.... *ach*, I don't know! So *dignified*. Really, I don't see how you could have gotten this way with parents such as yours."

"You... think I'm dignified? And that's a problem?"

"Of course. How would you like to grow up alongside this graceful little goody-goody, efficient at everything she lays her hands to? You're even better at *needlework* than I am and it is *my* pride and joy! Not to mention, how you've earned Armond's attention... along with everyone else's. Even Lady Nora used to go on and on about you to my mother. Truly, you are insufferable. I don't see what you have to be so very *poised* about."

Hazel stared up at the woman. Surely, she'd never had the slightest clue that the Dianna who'd grown up hating her thought anything so complimentary. She'd always assumed Dianna saw her as an aberration. All the while she'd been—dare she venture—envious? "But you were always shaming me…"

Dianna appeared as if she'd only just realized all she'd divulged. "Because you were a joke… are—are a joke."

Hazel almost chuckled. "You know, you're the only girl I know who can pull off a bald head. I'm not trying to rub it in, but, hair or no, you're a lovely girl. I think, perhaps with a headscarf, you could still win any man you wished… And then maybe you could bring yourself to move on with your life."

"Are you jesting? How many men do you think go about in search of bald women?"

"Well, none. But that doesn't mean you can't find one who thinks you're beautiful despite it."

"That is doubtful."

Hazel had to admit she was probably right. It would take a certain kind of man to see past it. And Dianna wasn't exactly a woman of character herself. In fact, she was something of a royal pain. "This dignity you speak of, Dianna... I think it's called beauty on the inside. It is good character—humility, kindness, steadfastness. I think as we get older, we'll find it far more precious than that on the outside."

Dianna stared back at her. "I think you're full of it, Lady Hazel."

Hazel laughed openly. "Perhaps I am."

Silence commenced as the two sat in thought.

At last, Dianna ventured, "How is Armond?"

"He seems happy enough to me."

"I've been hearing things about the way he rules… that perhaps it doesn't come as naturally as it should, that he's… not the brightest?"

Hazel quirked her head to the side. "It was overwhelming to

lose everything. He's got to get his bearings."

She nodded. "I hope he finds them then."

"He will," Hazel assured, drawing to her feet. "Why don't you come with me to see him?"

"Why do you think I'd be willing to see *him*, of all people?"

"Because you're worried about him. And he could use clever friends." Despite herself, Hazel had to admit Dianna had always been quite bright.

"But if I don't want anyone to see me, he's the last…"

"He's engaged, Dianna. It's not as if he can reject you now."

"And you said you didn't want to rub it in."

"Suppose you start taking midnight strolls in the garden? You'd be surprised how beautifully it has regrown."

"If ever I'm despairing enough to take advice from you, I'll do just that."

Hazel laughed and had nearly exited the room when Dianna called, "Tell Armond to remember what King Zephuel always said… about how a king ought not to *rule* the people, but serve and, when necessary, govern."

Hazel nodded. She had to admit it was a sound reminder. She'd never have expected it to make a home in Dianna's heart, but it warmed her to think there was perhaps something of beauty inside the lady after all. "I'll tell him."

* * *

Weeks passed and still Hazel heard no word of Dianna leaving her chambers. Even so, she was too busy taking surprising delight in the planning of her upcoming nuptials. To her disappointment, it would not take place for some time, as long engagements were Kierelian tradition. All the same, the people were pleased to know the match was imminent. And, in the meantime, she and Armond spent plenty of time together going over the alliance agreement with Bashtii. This took much longer than expected, however, for he questioned everything.

"Armond!" she cried one day, finally at the end of her rope. "You have no idea how hard we worked to make this amenable for both kingdoms. I love Kierelia. Do not you think I would work tirelessly to make certain we made a good deal?"

"Yet, every other sentence, I find you speaking of the *wonders* of Bashtii."

"So, now I must be a traitor," she scoffed. "Is that it?" She rose from the table and went to the window, pulling the curtain aside to gaze out into the evening sky. The sun was setting in its most glorious array, but she had to admit it was nothing to a sunset over the Bashtiian Sea. It was true: She'd felt a peculiar pull to that other kingdom since she'd left. In fact, she missed it... almost *desperately*. She sensed it had something to do with that ordeal within the Cave of Nielsas.

"Hazel, I'm sorry," Armond said softly. "I've trusted you with so much. There is no reason not to trust you with this. I've just signed."

She twirled to face him. "You have?" She glanced at the document in disbelief. But of a sudden, disconcerting guilt flooded her. "Armond, I think there is something I must tell you."

He took a seat and invited her to sit beside him. "What is it?"

"It's about Bashtii."

He rolled his eyes but offered a half-smile. "Go on."

"Something... happened there that, well, I think it may be why I keep speaking about Bashtii. You see... King Fredrick requested my aid with a problem in the Cave of Nielsas."

"That is the cave created by their first king—the cavern with the infamous rubies?"

She nodded. "You've heard their kings must bond with those

rubies to form a kinship with the God of the land concerning the kingdom?"

He nodded. "My uncle informed me of something like that."

She swallowed. "Well… it seems that *I* accidentally formed that bond with Bashtii… instead of Fredrick."

He sat back. "Hazel, *how?*"

"I… touched them and met with the Entity in his eternal throne room."

A series of emotions crossed Armond's face before, "This could actually be quite *useful*. We can employ it in negotiations. I mean… you could make *anything* happen to them, couldn't you?"

"Armond, I have no intention of using it in that way. I gave Fredrick my word."

His eyes darted back and forth between hers as he considered. "And a promise made to *him* means so much?"

"It was a promise made to a friend, Armond. So, yes, it does. And do not you see that the very fact I hold such power over them but do not use it will only strengthen the relationship between our nations?"

He stood then and ran his hands through his hair. "I do, Hazel, I do. But… the Deep South is on their way. It will not be long now. We could use this bond just long enough to get hold of his troops so that we will actually be *prepared* when they arrive."

She well understood where he was coming from, but it changed nothing. "I am so sorry, but… I gave my word and I will not break it." She went to him then and took his hands into hers. "The Entity is with us now. We must trust him for the salvation of Kierelia. We are as equipped as can be."

He gripped her hands tightly for a moment, almost as if he would compel her to do as he bid, then released them. "Very well, love. I will trust you in this as well."

27

Hazel sang in her corner of the woods while Dorian lazed on the ground behind her. She had perfect control within his presence now. And it was so easy in the forest. The way the animals drew near, the sound of the warm breeze through the trees… It was utterly serene. She gazed up at those trees, so familiar to her from her youth. It was a miracle that so little of it had been destroyed by the dragons. It stood strong and would continue to grow and *grow*…?

"Dorian!" she gasped.

He leaped to his feet. "I saw it! I saw it!"

"They *grew*… Another foot at least!" She turned to face him. "I made trees grow."

He leaped up and spun her about. "If you can do that… I mean, what else could you do? You don't just have to *throw* things. You can nurture them."

"Dorian… what if I could heal people? That's something I read the voice of old could do."

"Well, try something else!"

"All right." Peering about in search of something to do, she was, for the first time, thrilled about her capabilities. Dare she admit she was proud of what was within her? After all, she was… *powerful*. She bit her lip a moment. "I have an idea."

"Go for it."

She looked to the clouds above and burst into vibrant song. Rain poured from the sky, saturating all in the clearing.

"Hazel, did you just…?"

She giggled. Never would Kierelia possess fear of droughts again!

"Hazel?"

She and Dorian spun about.

"Armond," Hazel squealed. Singing swiftly to make the rain cease, she ran to him. "How did you find us here?"

"Just lucky, I guess," he said, casting a quick glance at Dorian before returning to her with coldness in his eyes.

Hazel hesitated. Was he jealous she'd brought Dorian? "Oh… he comes with me sometimes. You know, old times' sake."

"Hazel…" he said slowly, "You just made it rain… with your voice."

She took his hands into hers. "I've been meaning to tell you of my training—tried to several times, in fact. I just had to have a better grasp on it before I felt comfortable…" She took a long breath, shaking her head. "There's no excuse. I'm sorry I didn't tell you."

He gazed back at her. Did she imagine the chill?

"I really *am* sorry for not telling you," she said quietly. "You deserved to know."

"Hazel… we need to talk." Casting another glance back to

Dorian, he added, "Come back to the castle with me."

With her head hung low, she followed after him in silence. She knew she should have told him, but surely... surely this was a little much. His face was red, his eyes fiery. He was *seething*.

Walking up beside him, she asked, "Armond, have I hurt you so much?"

"Let's just get back to Castlehaven."

Her stomach flipped over. His tone was so quick, so taciturn. And why shouldn't it be? She had broken trust with the man she meant to wed. Her mind raced for a solution to this problem until at last they were safe in his study.

"Oh, Armond, *please* forgive me," she cried. "I never meant to hurt you. It's just the way you talked about the gift as if it were a disease in need of—"

He shook his head. "That's not what upsets me. Not now, anyway. It may have before, but now..."

"What is it?" she said quickly. "Have I done something else?"

His jaw flexed as he clenched his teeth, staring her down. "You tell me."

She shook her head, blinking, her mind searching. She'd never seen him like this. "What is the *matter*?"

"While you were away in Bashtii, Priest Wilhelm and I saw fit to send a spy into the Deep South." He sat back, as if surveying his effect.

Hazel relaxed as her brows rose in pride. "Well, that was a *wise* idea. Have you learned something important then?"

"The scout immersed himself into their society until he gained the faith of their king. Now, perhaps you've some idea to what I refer."

Tears stung her eyes as she felt his coldness again, but she could not begin to fathom what any of this could have to do with her. "Did... did you discover when they plan to attack? They aren't on their way *now*?" Was he angry she had refused to use her Bashtiian bond?

With sorrow, he took her hand and sat her down beside him. "Hazel... *please*. Just talk."

She searched his eyes, her heart thudding in her ears. "I wish I knew what... what you wanted me to say."

He stood again and turned his back to her. "I want you to admit you've no need to wed me to become queen of this kingdom—that you've nurtured it all this time only to hand it over to your parents and their leader, King Rakutan of the Deep South."

She leaped to her feet. "Armond, what on the planet Kaern are you *talking* about?"

"My spy informed me of your parents' agreement with the southern king—that they've been making plans together since their banishment." He looked her square in the eyes. "I know their reward for aiding him is seeing their daughter crowned his queen. You plan to wed *Rakutan.*"

She fell back a step, her eyes searching his back. Could it be true? Had her parents truly betrayed their country so wholly? And did they really think she'd just marry some malevolent man she'd never met? And how could Armond believe she'd known anything about it?

"I knew nothing of what you speak of until this moment," she said hoarsely. "I only learned they were still alive when the prophet told me, not so long ago. And I've scarcely spared a thought for them since."

He spun to face her. "And just when did you speak to the prophet?"

"The day the castle was destroyed, just before he abandoned us."

"Hazel, what do you expect me to think? They're already planning to give you this position, second only to the king. Surely, they approached you at some point."

"I swear to you, Armond. No such meeting has taken place. I am loyal to Kierelia and her crown."

"Yet, you've undermined me from the beginning..." he said thoughtfully. She could see everything was falling into place in his mind. "From the beginning, you took over—even limiting what I could and could not say or do. Now, all of Kierelia wishes you were its leader. You've got them wrapped around your finger. So long as they can have *you* as their queen, they will accept King Rakutan as ruler. My uncle would say that looked like you'd prepared them for the reaping."

With a gasp, she cried, "Your uncle, despite what my parents had done and despite what Lady Nora told him, *always* believed me."

"Then why did he retain you here to keep an eye on?" he said with frustration. "It was clear he had some reason to fear you."

Pain like she'd never known coursed through her to hear *him*, of all people, describe her as a person to be feared. "I think... he was angry with my parents, angry further that they'd left me here as a burden to him. Perhaps he did feel they'd left me as a plant. So, when he looked at me, he saw only betrayal. But I swear, there came a day when he claimed he was proud of who I'd become. He even asked me to speak to the Entity for him."

Smiling bitterly, he shook his head. "My uncle never praised people like that, not even me."

She blinked back at him, fighting the tears that threatened. "Armond... you *know* me."

"Do I?" He shook his head. "I honestly don't know anymore..."

She watched him struggle. He always struggled when it came to matters in which the gift of wisdom would have come of use. He doubted himself too much. Now, he doubted he had read her rightly. He was growing confident in the most audacious of notions. She knew he had fully embraced these new beliefs when he looked up at her with deep pain in his eyes.

Brushing tears from them, he said, "Though I cannot say just why, I still *love* you… I cannot see you imprisoned."

She froze, the heat of her cheeks drying the tears. She knew what he would say next.

"I must banish you from this kingdom," he choked out. "Go where you will—to your parents if you wish. I will not stop you." Suddenly, he turned to rifle through a drawer in his desk. He plopped a stack of letters onto its surface. "Better yet, go to your dear Fredrick. He has not ceased writing to you since you returned."

Her mouth fell open. It was a large pile. Most of them were opened. She had wondered why Fredrick had not kept his promise to write. Now, she knew he'd more than followed through.

"You must leave my kingdom and never return," he continued, "…on punishment of death."

She pressed her lips together, restraining the fury that built like a tidal wave. Memories of how compassionate he'd been to her before the dragon attacks, before she'd told him of her feelings for him, flashed through her mind. This man was so different from him. Where she had grown in fortitude through that difficult year, he had become fretful, anxious and bitter. His easy compassion had given way to… *this person.*

"Armond," she whispered. "Please do not do this. Don't send me away from you. Don't send me away like my parents were." It would be shame beyond imagining.

His jaw flexed. He considered. Then he turned away. "Just go to them… *please.*"

She covered her mouth to stifle a sob. She forced herself to turn away from the man she'd been about to marry, from the man she'd aided through their harshest ordeals, the one she'd been so proud to see crowned. Once, he'd thanked her for all she'd done. Now, he thought it all duplicity. How *could* he? She had worked *so* hard. She'd taken on so much in his name to make him look the part, to provide him time to grow into it. Meanwhile, *he* was the one who'd been educated for the role while she'd merely grown up a glorified errand girl.

Seeing the figurine she'd given him on her return from Bashtii, she grasped it and smashed it against the wall. Without looking back, she slammed the door and raced to her bedchamber.

As swiftly as her body would move, she used shaking hands to shove clothing into a traveling bag. Then, she raced to her tower and threw in as many books as would fit into the remaining space. With a sob, she offered the room a final glance.

"Please, hide yourself again," she whispered. "I won't be back."

Racing down the stairs, she blinked and the door vanished behind her as requested. Then, she deliberated. There was just one more place she wished to see before her departure. She did not think Armond would know or care if she stole a few more moments and she just... *needed* it.

The Mirror still possessed no keeper. No one used the room anymore. Perhaps no one would again. It was terribly sad, really, to have such access to the God of all things and never to seek him.

She opened the door and stepped inside. For a moment, her heart warmed as she recalled her first-ever encounter with H.S.— the memory that had been afforded her in his throne room. But with that warmth came fresh pain. She rejected that pain, pressing it down, down, down.

Finally, she looked up. "H.S., my friend. Oh, how I need you now."

A light breeze washed over her.

"What do I do?" she asked. "Where do I go? Can I really

abandon Kierelia?"

The breeze grew stronger and with it she smelled the salty air of the Bashtiian sea. Oh, how she yearned to be there. The longing sent a shiver through her as goosebumps coursed over her arms.

"Very well," she whispered. She then scrawled the name of that kingdom onto her hand and held it before her face as she vacated the room.

Leaping upon the first horse she could find, she rode it bareback to the Kierelian dock, letting the wind dry her tearstained face.

"Is there a ship departing for Bashtii soon?" she inquired of a dock worker.

"Aye. If you can catch that one just there, you'll be there by evening."

She raced faster than she had in her life as she watched the ship pulling away. Pressing past onlookers and farewell-ers, she leaped from the dock and just caught the side, letting the ship workers do the rest in getting her aboard.

Righting herself, she faced the Kierelian shore, her eyes gazing beyond to the grassy hills and the golden setting of the sun. She ought to have fared Dorian well, but she couldn't have endured another moment on that soil. She would write to him and he would understand. As it was, she would see what Fredrick could do for her.

Turning her back on her homeland, she made her way across the ship and rested her hands upon the rail. She could almost imagine she saw the Bashtiian shoreline from there, though it was not possible. She took a deep breath and heard it quiver. Falling back upon the bench behind her, she drew the hood of her cloak over her face, letting the wall of the ship cradle her as she mourned all she'd just lost.

28

"Hazel!" Fredrick called merrily as he raced down the entry steps to greet her. "I heard you'd been spotted on our docks, but I wouldn't believe it." He hesitated. "Are you all right? Is Kierelia under attack?"

She shook her head. "I've been banished."

"Banished?" He halted where he stood, releasing a swift breath. "By *Armond?"*

She drew before him with a nod.

"But I thought…" He rubbed the back of his head uncomfortably. "Well, we'd heard you were engaged…?"

She shrugged. "Clearly, we're not now. Fredrick, may I remain here this evening?"

Eyeing the large satchel in her hand, he took it from her. "You may stay forever if you like."

Though she'd not really thought he would turn her away, she sighed with relief. "Thank you. It means… a lot."

She followed him as he led her through corridors. Numerous servants attempted to take the satchel from him, but he batted them away. Now and then, he looked back at her, sometimes sadly, others questioning. At last, they came to the rooms she'd enjoyed on her previous visit. With a peculiar feeling of homecoming, she fell into the nearest chair. "Thank you for this room. It feels…"

"Like home?"

She quirked her head. "Familiar."

He set her bag down and turned to search her. "Hazel, how are you in one piece?"

She shook her head. "I'm probably not, but… I can't tell you how grateful I am that I could come here. I don't know where else I'd have gone. I would have gone to the southern tribes, but… that's Kierelian territory now."

He shook his head. *"How* can you be banished? Surely, it is a misunderstanding."

"My crime is having been born of my parents," she said bitterly.

"Does he still blame you for what they did all those years ago now?"

She sighed and shook her head, hands going to her temples. "I'm sorry, Fredrick, but I must rest. Perhaps we can finish this conversation later. I promise not to trespass on your hospitality any longer than necessary."

He knelt before her, resting a hand on the arm of the chair. "I meant what I said earlier. It would please me to have you remain as long as you live. Your welcome here is irrevocable."

A painful smile worked its way in. "Thank you, Fredrick. I owe you."

* * *

Hazel found it impossible to leave her rooms the following day. As

Fredrick was called away, she had no reason to leave. Without asking, both meals and choccum (a Bashtiian teatime) were brought her. Other than that, she was left to her own company.

She spent hours reliving the last year, reflecting especially on Armond. How could he have gone from the sweet boy he'd been before the catastrophe... to the man who'd actually cast her into the same fate as her parents? He, above all but Dorian, understood what that would mean to her, what a knife to the heart it would be. She fancied it was worse than imprisonment until she cast her eyes about the comfort of her current space and had her midday meal set before her. It was not worse than prison.

Though the dragon attack had awoken previously unrealized gumption in her, it had burned away the very thing that made Armond so lovable: his heart. True, he wasn't heartless, per se. But he had acted heartless. She was his *fiancé*. They were meant to be in love.

And yet, though she'd spent much of the evening before in tears, she found herself unexpectedly tearless this day. She was broken but... *not* broken-hearted. She did not love Armond. She wasn't certain she ever had. All the feeling that was true were the remains of what she'd felt for him in childhood. *Not* for the foolish king he was now.

But she could only endure so much of this deliberation before she felt she would burst with sorrow. Therefore, it was with self-gratitude that she went to the shelf where a maid had carefully nestled her books. She selected a volume and when that was finished, she went for another. At last, the day was nearly over and she threw herself upon the bed, exhausted without ever having left her suite.

The following morning brought the same heaviness as the one before. But this time she pulled herself from bed and was clothed before the maid could arrive to help her. After breakfast, her hair was dressed and, at last, she turned for the door. She would leave the room, though everything in her screamed not to. But really, what could happen? Plenty. It was a wide world. However, from the reclusiveness of her youth, she well knew how easy it would be to fall into the old pattern. She would not allow herself that comfort.

When she finally stepped outside and closed the door, she deliberated upon how she would spend her day. She had no invitations from Fredrick, which was well enough for her for the time being. A stroll in the garden? Yes, the fresh air would do her good. She started that way when her feet veered in the opposite direction and she found herself entering the library instead. It was a vast one, as she well-remembered. And after all, Kierelia's had been burned to ashes.

"Hazel, my dear!" a familiar voice exclaimed.

Fire burned in her stomach. Her hands clenched into fists. *"Prophet."*

He strode across the room and placed hands upon her shoulders, studying her. "You have *grown.*"

She edged away from his grasp. "Really? You look shorter."

He continued to look her over with sober admiration. Pride even. "I have heard so many tales about you. I cannot say how glad it has made me to hear them. Why, King Fredrick cannot stop singing your praises... Speaking of, I've heard nothing of your voice. Hasn't it emerged yet?"

She crossed her arms. "Why should you care?"

He took a step back and released a sigh. "My dear girl... I am so sorry I had to leave you. I can only imagine how difficult it has been. But you have come through with soaring colors."

"*Had* to leave?"

Gently, he took her hand as if testing whether she would let him keep it. Then he led her to a set of chairs before a bright window. "Is he gone?" he asked.

She blinked back. " Who?"

"The other one. Er, Latos, the Realm Leader of the Greater Archipelagos."

Hazel was taken aback. "Yes… As a matter of fact, he passed away after saving us from the dark dragons."

He released a breath. "I supposed as much. I may return then."

"Prophet, why were you running from Latos?"

"My girl, I don't suppose you've ever heard anything about passing through time?"

"As… a matter of fact, I have done it myself, thanks to you. The cabin in the southern region?"

"That's right. Then you'll understand. You see, Latos has not actually died—contrary to popular belief. He has passed into a time before men tread our world. The sorceress who conjured the dark dragons sent him. And, well… he never died, due to an anointed agelessness bestowed him from having been Realm Leader. Therefore, here he sits before you as a terribly old man."

She choked, swallowing several times before, "You're positively *batty*."

He grinned. "Just so."

"You're trying to claim that *you're* him. You look nothing alike." Though, she knew it was a lie.

"Very complimentary, my dear. Age *does* have something of an effect when one has lived so long."

"But if it's true, what does his—your—younger self's arrival have to do with your disappearance a year ago?"

"Well, it is common knowledge to most time-jumpers that one simply ought not to exist in the same vicinity with oneself. It produces peculiar effect. I knew the younger me would arrive soon—having lived it myself all that time ago—so it was imperative I retreat. When I sensed he had gone, I returned to the planet to learn what I could."

"To the… planet?"

"Yes. It is true I must not be near myself, but really, I ought not to dwell in the same world. It is too great a risk. So, I've been realm-hopping. Seen some very interesting places. It was really quite enjoyable."

Despite herself, she watched that almost child-like face and believed all he said. "I wish you'd just told me all before you left. You wounded me greatly."

"I am very sorry, Hazel. I... didn't suppose it was the right time to attempt an explanation at time travel. Moreover, well, I was a little miserable, and I suppose quite thoughtless as a result."

"I see. But... you had to have *known* the dragon attack would come! You'd already been there, done all Latos has. Why did you not stop it?"

"I thought I could, truth be told. In fact, I tried! I made changes from when I'd come as Latos, hoping Kierelia might be better prepared for the attack. It was why I helped the Great One build a castle that could defend itself. But because of Zephuel's agreement with the witch, things did not go as planned. And, somehow, it all happened earlier than the first time... caused by some change I made in the timeline, I suppose. Time-jumping is sketchy that way. In the end, it caught me off guard and broke my heart all over again. I suppose the Great One willed that I should not be alerted for some purpose of his own, but... well, now you understand how much of the blame rests on me... *twice* over."

She released a long breath. "If the Entity had wished you to stop it, he would have aided you. I suppose the incident was not meant to be wiped from this 'timeline' you speak of."

He smiled back at her. "*There* is the understanding girl I know and love. Now! As it is finally safe for me to return to Kierelia, why don't you come with me? Or have you got business to finish here?"

"My return to Kierelia would mean certain death I'm afraid."

"*Death?*"

She eyed him a moment. "I'm banished."

He sat back. "I am so sorry, Hazel... I never thought Armond capable of such cruelty. Why has he done such a thing?"

"Apparently, my parents have plans for me. He heard of them and thinks we're in cahoots."

"Well, that is dreadfully foolish."

"I am aware."

"I see you must have friends here, however."

"Yes, Fredrick and I have grown in friendship."

"I see. Well, he is a *good* man. Don't know if you could do better than to have a comrade such as him."

Thoughtfully, she nodded. She'd not quite thought of him that way. She didn't know him as well as she might, but he *was* quite a unique person and he had been eager to support her in her hour of need. That meant more than her pained heart could fully fathom.

* * *

"Well, you look comfortable," Fredrick said pleasantly when he came upon her swinging in the garden some days later. He sat upon the ground before her.

"Oh, please, let me make room for you here," she urged.

"No, no!" He held up his hands. "When one is that comfortable, one must not adjust one's skirts to make room for an intruder."

She thrust her swing into motion again. "What brings you here?"

"I was looking for *you*, actually. Haven't been able to catch as much time with you as I'd like."

"It is all right. I have needed time to think."

"Of what, pray tell?"

"Oh, everything."

He opened his mouth as if to say something, then seemed to think better of it as he shifted his gaze to the shrubs behind her.

"What?" she pressed.

He lifted his brows. "Oh, nothing, I just... There's something I've been wishing to ask, but I do not think now is the time."

"Well, I want to know now."

He eyed her a moment. "I have been wondering how two people can go from engaged to one banishing the other."

She exhaled.

"You see, it was not a tactful question. You do not have to answer."

"I *thought* he loved me, thought we loved each other."

Fredrick shifted uncomfortably.

"But I think, when it really came down to it, he only wanted me to help him gain the people's love. I have to believe he could not think as he does of me now if he'd really cared."

"He should have taken your side. After all, the surest proof of love is serving another above oneself."

"He fell incredibly short of that ideal."

"Are you... are you heartbroken?"

She raised a brow at his intrusiveness but then thought better of it. "You're asking if I truly loved him. In a word: no. But I was not aware of it until I got here."

He froze. "...Here?"

"Yes, getting to Bashtii gave me room to process."

"Oh. I see."

"It revealed how sorrowfully shallow my feelings were. Moreover, I had fallen for someone who no longer existed. And I think I felt pressured to appease both him and the people."

"And now?"

"Now... well, I suppose I'm quite free, aren't I? I have the whole world before me. I can do anything. I just have to work out what that might be."

"You've no aspirations?"

"You *would* ask that question." Unfortunately, her former aspirations of building up a kingdom of strength with the value of helping one another had been obliterated with her banishment. "No, my future is an open book."

"I suppose being queen is off the table?"

"Well, of course. I'm not marrying Armond anymore, am I?"

"Ha! No. But it is a sorrowful thing. You would make a grand leader for any people. You walk in influence most dream of. I, for one, would delight in watching that kingdom flourish."

"Heavens, you're not trying to send me back to Armond, are you?"

"Not on your life."

She laughed. "You don't care much for him, do you?"

"For good reason, as is now clear. You worked hand in hand with him to rebuild your kingdom from next to nothing. Then, you agree to marry the swine and he just casts you away like—"

"I'm working on *forgiving* him for that, you know. Perhaps the matter should be dropped."

"Forgiving him? Why would you do that?"

"Why... I don't know. The bitterness sits ill upon me. I want to feel free again."

He stared back at her, a small smile forming.

"What?"

"I just like the way you think."

"Well, do you agree with me?"

He nodded.

"Then I like the way *you* think. Moreover, here you speak of all I could have been for Kierelia, but don't you go thinking I haven't heard stories of all you've been to Bashtii. These people adore you. And they honor you because you honor them. They say you take a deeper interest in their concerns than any king before you."

He raised a brow. "Are you saying you're impressed with me, Lady Hazel?"

Laughingly, she shook her head. "*Oh*, very well," she admitted. "I am."

"Well, imagine *that!* Lady Fortune has seen fit to bestow her approval upon the Bashtiian king. We shall be a favored nation now!"

"Oh, you can drop the nickname, *golden king.*"

"Touché! But listen, is it true your title came from magic that sparked from your fingertips as you helped place the stones of the new fortress?"

"*Magic?* Imagine!"

"You're not denying it..."

She diverted her gaze. "I suppose I did have a peculiar experience."

"Like sparks from your fingers?"

She huffed, not having realized such minute details had spread so far. "Yes," she admitted.

"Well, if that isn't the most intriguing... Why do you think it occurred?"

She shrugged. "All, I know is, is..."

"Yes?"

She eyed him, then sat on the ground beside him to lean in conspiratorially. "One evening, I awoke to the most irregular sensation in my chest. Then, before I knew it, out popped this gemstone..." She laid out the story as she knew it and they continued in the leisure of converse until the setting sun summoned them to supper.

29

A fortnight later, Fredrick rapped upon her door with an announcement.

"Er, Hazel... you have a set of visitors."

Her brows nearly rose to her hairline. *"Who?"* Could it be Dorian? She'd written but had not heard back. Often, she'd wondered if Armond had actually managed to turn him against her.

Fredrick stood in the door some moments before crossing the room to sit beside her. Softly, he said, "They claim to be your parents."

She sat upright, unable to move for some moments as her heart pounded in her ears.

"Do you wish me to send them away?" he asked.

She blinked at him, her head spinning. "No. No, send them in."

"It'll be a moment. I commanded they remain in my receiving room until I'd sorted it with you."

She offered a weak smile. "Thank you, Fredrick."

After two weeks of pleasant converse, exploring and sightseeing with Fredrick, she'd awoken that morning with the surprising sensation of *happiness*. It made sense that they should now come and traipse upon her contentment. She touched her hair to see that it was in place and rearranged her skirts, then chastised herself for hoping for their approval. It felt as if she had not awoken at all. Surely, she must still be dreaming.

A knock at the door sent her to her feet. She strode across the room but hesitated as her hand reached the doorknob. Part of her wanted to shriek at them to leave her alone with the little peace she had found. But she'd been bred to decorum and baptized in fire. Coolly, she opened the door.

Sure enough, they were the perfect likeness of the portrait she'd found of them before it had been destroyed.

"Do come in," she said serenely, holding the door for them.

They did so and the three were soon seated across from one another.

Hazel had no idea what to do next—how to begin. The situation was surreal. How could these people she'd dreamed about for so long suddenly turn up in her life like this? It felt as if someone had pulled the rug out from under her.

"What brings you here?" she asked at last.

The woman—her mother—smiled. "Oh, *Hazel,* you must be so stunned to see us after all this time. And I assure you, we are so very pleased to see you. You have grown lovelier than we had imagined. And we have heard so many pleasing things about you. You are *all* we could have hoped for."

Hazel swallowed. "It has been some time, hasn't it, since last we met? I was… an infant, I suppose."

"You were but a year, yes," her father said. "You are certainly not a little girl anymore."

"I am not."

Silence commenced far longer than was comfortable for

Hazel's guests. But she had no idea what to say to them. Moreover, she battled between ecstasy and fury... She worked hard to embrace something between both. But that meant pain—aching tenderness straight through her heart. These people had abandoned her, left her behind in a kingdom that would hate her, thanks to their ill deed.

"We couldn't believe it when we'd heard you'd been banished from Kierelia by that foolish boy-king," her father said abruptly. "It was wise of you to come to Bashtii. And it made it possible for us to safely pay this visit."

How she could feel defensive of Armond after what he'd done, she did not know. Even so, her eyes narrowed as she asked, "How did you know I was here?"

"We have a source."

Of course they did.

"Hazel," her mother said, "may I cut to the chase?"

"I wish you would."

"We've come to make up for the time spent without you. Furthermore, we've come to see you crowned queen of the new Kierelia by marriage to the unconquerable King Rakutan. You, from all we've heard, will make the *finest* queen Kierelia has ever seen, once our plans have come to fruition."

So, it was true. Hazel sat back in her chair, raising an intrigued brow. "But though Kierelia was once vulnerable, she has risen again. She is rather robust, in fact. And her alliance with Bashtii is that much stronger, if I do say so myself. How can Rakutan possibly plan to take her?"

"My dear, whose idea do you think it was to tempt the sorceress, Aradia, into luring the dragons? Much as you have worked to rebuild, you cannot convince us that Kierelia is as strong as it was before. Even so, you saved us a great deal of trouble in the long-run by re-establishing its economy so rapidly."

Hazel released a breathless, shuddering laugh to which they smiled and nodded with satisfaction. They thought her impressed.

What she was... was in shock. *Her* parents, who had claimed they'd wished to remove King Zephuel from the throne *because* of his relationship with a sorceress, had brought on the dragon attacks. She supposed things had changed once they'd been banished. Ethics had shifted. She swallowed and swallowed again, stealing a few moments to regain her composure. "Then... why did you not make your move when we were in ruin?"

"Why, we thought we'd have time. We didn't believe Kierelia could be restored after such a calamity. And we hadn't counted on that man, Latos, arriving to slay the beasts. We were scarcely able to salvage a few for our own use before he'd vanquished most of them. And then, when the rumors of Kierelia's rebuild reached us, we simply were not yet prepared for our assault. You see, we were well aware of the strength of Kierelia's alliance with Bashtii and our dragons were not yet trained."

Hazel choked. "You have *trained* dragons?"

"The few we captured, yes—four of the smaller variety. It was a pity we were unable to get our hands on the giant beasty the Kierelian boy-king slew."

"Even so," began her father, "the ones in possession are trained well-trained. They attack by mere whistles in specific intonations."

"Oh." Hazel murmured with interest. "Like with music."

"Precisely."

Her mother observed her a moment before moving to sit beside her. She gazed into her daughter's eyes with, "My dear, Kierelia shall by ours two days hence. That is why we came to you now. You must prepare. We will fetch you some days following in order to present you to the new court... and the unconquerable King Rakutan. He has already agreed to our terms. If we aided him, our daughter would be queen. But when he sees you, I am certain he will wish of his own volition to see you enthroned beside him."

Hazel gazed back at her mother, whose eyes yet held hers.

How she wished she saw love in those eyes, some kind of actual consideration for her wellbeing. But any dream that they may have had valid reason for leaving her behind had been destroyed when she'd discovered they'd lured dragons into the region... and neglected to see her to safety. Indeed, she was quite certain her part in their schemes had been an afterthought. It was likely they'd only thought to bargain for her crown once they'd heard the stories of her as Lady Fortune, beloved of the people. *Of course* they wanted her. With her, they might just accomplish what Armond had speculated. They'd win the loyalty of the Kierelian people.

It was time she provided a few confessions of her own. "Thanks to you, I have grown my whole life under the anguish of rejection from nearly all I encountered. But all that made me stronger, shrewd and resilient. It prepared me for all that was to come. You think some king can banish me and I'll just help you destroy all I built? Armond hasn't harmed me any more than you have. And with or without his—or anyone's—good opinion, I'm going to be all right... Because *I* like myself and so does the Great Entity. And that is enough." She spoke out the revelation as it dawned upon her and then she watched them.

Her parents exchanged a look between them. Her mother placed a tight grasp on her shoulder, as if holding her there would gain what she sought. "My girl," she said, "we could not carry you into territory that we'd heard so many terrible things about. Not to mention, we knew how clever you were. You were a *bright* baby. We discerned you'd take care of yourself and work matters to your advantage. It is in your blood after all. Now, you have gained much prominence—a status you would not possess had you come with us. We simply desired what was best for you."

The woman spoke so briskly, it left no room for Hazel to entertain notions that any of it rang true. At most, they'd left her there in hopes she'd grow into someone they could one day make use of, just as King Zephuel had feared. A child was but a pawn to them.

"I thank you for your... consideration." She worked her shoulder from her mother's grasp. "But I am not interested."

Her father cleared his throat. "We'd rather hoped we'd birthed a daughter of greater metal. You were such a spitfire as an infant. It is... disappointing to see you've grown so subdued."

"Well," she began, "I've heard all that before and lived through it. I will be fine without you." She was amazed by her own composure, how deeply accurate the claim was and the fact she was essentially dismissing them not only from the room but from her life.

They gazed back at her, utterly mystified by her genuine reserve. It was clear they could not begin to fathom this child of theirs. And for the first time in her life, she was *grateful* they'd discarded her.

"Hazel..." her mother began, "you simply cannot be serious. You will be *queen* of nearly the entire region."

"I was going to be queen before you came along and ruined it. And when I lost the chance, well, I couldn't care much less than I do now. I've no desire for the position. I shall be perfectly content without."

In disbelief, her father flew to his feet. "You *will* come with us. Like it or not, you are our daughter. You are required to fulfill the bargain."

With a polite smile, she stood to her own feet. "Mother, Father... depart from my chambers or I shall scream. I assure you, King Fredrick will respond accordingly."

Her mother stammered for words she could not find. She looked to her husband, who glared down at Hazel in quiet fury. It was clear he wanted nothing less than to throw her over his shoulder and bolt.

Decisively, Hazel screamed.

It was almost comical the way they spluttered and dashed from the room. Hazel fell into her seat again, gaping at the wall as her mind replayed the previous scene. Oh, how she'd missed them all those years, hoped they loved her, hoped they'd had good reason…

For a moment, she felt orphaned afresh and it was as if the walls would cave in. But then… she recalled the blood of the Entity's son that had been poured over her head within that eternal throne room. There had been something in the action that was more intimate than the embrace of a parent, more infinite than the care of any mortal soul. She could almost see herself in that place when she closed her eyes and it was there she desired to be above all else.

But she was startled from her reverie by Fredrick's sudden presence. He planted himself beside her, drawing her hands into his. "Are you all right?" he asked. "I've sent the guards after them. They won't make it out of Bashtii."

Hazel directed her attention to a face full of the most bewildering concern. "I am all right," she said dazedly.

He searched her face. "What did they *say* to you?"

"Not much more than I already knew."

He searched her again, then huffed and offered a small half-smile. "Are you *ever* going to let me in?"

Her brows flew up as he pinned her with eyes so wishful, so uncharacteristically vulnerable. Why should he so care to know her? No one had ever worked so hard for it, save Dorian. And most of his friendship had been a ruse to use her as a mole. Yet, here was someone who, as far as she knew, had no ulterior motive. He merely asked that she express how she felt.

"I… believe I'm in shock," she conceded slowly. It was some moments before she felt able to sort through her feelings. "I am so very disappointed. But I cannot say I am wholly surprised. They deserted me after all. And for no good reason. Just… callousness and hoping I could prove useful one day." Biting her lip, she realized she had gripped his hands so tightly that her nails had left red impressions in his skin. She rubbed at them with her thumbs as she continued, "But I mean it when I say I am all right. I've been through *much* worse." Surprised to feel a tear drop to her chin, she gazed up at him with a quivering smile.

His eyes were glistening with moisture as if *he* felt the pain she wasn't allowing herself to acknowledge... And he *cared*. A lot.

"What has gotten into you?" she asked in astonishment.

He blinked, suddenly self-aware. It was clear he surprised even himself. "Knowing your history, I knew what their sudden arrival here could mean, that they could hurt you. My first instinct was to banish them from the kingdom before seeing you. But then I thought you might be disappointed at missing the chance..." She could see his mind searching for answers, as if he scarcely understood himself.

His gaze dropped to their interlaced hands. Hers followed.

Inwardly, she cringed as she realized what they were doing, what was happening. Not but weeks prior she'd been engaged to another man—one she'd thought herself in love with. If Armond's betrayal hadn't been enough to squelch her affection for him, her own realization that she had not been anywhere near in love with him had. Now, here she was holding hands with a man who looked at her like she was the most precious thing in the world. She couldn't be doing this. It was foolhardy. Surely, she'd learned her lesson.

But those eyes, that held more empathy than Armond had ever felt, jolted to her face. He wrenched his hands away, eyes wide.

Of course. She'd been holding his *bare* hands... the hands that could have turned her to gold. It was fortunate his gift did not always initiate. Swiftly, he yanked his gloves from his pocket and pulled them on. Then, he sat back a little further from her with an almost amused expression. She was fairly certain he apprehended that her walls had flown up... And he found it funny? No, mildly entertaining... which was a whole other factor far more confusing than the rest.

No, it was him good-naturedly giving in to the fact that she was... complicated. She didn't like that notion. She hadn't even realized she did not easily let people in until he'd mentioned it on her last visit. It was clear it had been bothering him for some time and was something he'd been working to overcome.

"Why don't you tell me what was said," he suggested as if helping her get past herself.

But this only made her temper flare. She felt condescended to. Swallowing back a sudden desire to take out her tempest of emotions on him, she reminded herself that this was the only person sitting before her and *caring*. She stole a breath and considered where to begin. *"Oh,"* she gasped as sudden realization hit her. "They're... they're going to attack Castlehaven in two days."

"Your parents?"

She nodded. "They're allied with the Deep South. They just told me they plan to attack two days hence. I hadn't even realized what they'd just given me. I know all about their plans. They assumed I'd go along with them—even offered me in marriage to Rakutan in exchange for their aid." Pleadingly, she looked to Fredrick. "I *have* to do something. I have to go back to Kierelia and warn them."

"We have to do something," he corrected. "I'll ready the troops."

"The troops?"

"Yes, as defense for Kierelia."

"Oh, yes, of course. I forgot about the alliance."

"I'm not doing it for the alliance."

She flicked him a glance. He was letting her know he'd decided how he felt while daring her to acknowledge what he'd said.

Conceding to herself that something new was blooming in her heart, she sought the yellow route. "We'd better get going."

* * *

Hazel was astonished by how swiftly Fredrick gathered his men. Furthermore, he spared little for his own kingdom. They would bring almost the whole of the army with them. The sheer number of them upon horses over the expanse of the Bashtiian field made her proud to call Fredrick her friend, to call Bashtii a Kierelian ally.

Soon, they were off, with Hazel a few paces behind Fredrick. She was glad for some time to think. They were riding into a country that, by law, must kill her on sight. Fredrick had promised her his fullest protection, but it only did so much to ease her. Still, it mattered little. She had built Kierelia up and she would not sit back and watch it be torn down again.

It had been considered that she, Fredrick and a smaller legion might travel across the sea, which would provide for a swifter warning. But Fredrick thought Hazel ought not to appear without the whole of an army to defend her. It was then deliberated that he go by ship himself, but he insisted he could not feel her safe without his own eyes on her. Then, of course, it was contemplated whether a message might be dispatched ahead of them. But again, Fredrick disagreed. As had been made clear, his first concern was for Hazel's safety and he did not wish to give Armond time to make plans against her should he be so irrational. Therefore, Kierelia would lose a day's warning.

Some hours later, Fredrick drew back to ride along beside her. "I have taken every precaution, but I cannot imagine Armond would really wish you killed."

"Nor can I."

"Do you... think he may have changed his mind about everything in your absence?"

"He'd have written if he had. Unless he was uncertain of where I was..."

"He knows. Word of your arrival in Bashtii has spread."

She smirked to herself. "He thought I'd be going to my

parents."

"Whatever the case, he would be a fool not to hear you out when you arrive."

"Indeed," she murmured.

"But?"

"Well, I hate to say it…"

"He *is* something of a fool, isn't he?"

Unhappily, she nodded.

"Too bad you couldn't have wedded him after all, for Kierelia's sake."

With a frown, she glanced up to find him smirking as he gazed into the distance.

"Oh, yes…" she replied with a scarcely concealed grin. "It is a pity."

Swiftly, he turned to glimpse *her* face before relaxing into his saddle again.

30

Hazel couldn't believe her eyes as she sat surveying Castlehaven from the hill. It was surrounded by the whole of Kierelia's army—a pitiful sight, truth be told. They scarcely surrounded the castle in three rings. But seeing the militia standing in readiness made her question whether they needed her caution after all. Else, why should they be so prepared?

She and Fredrick's men rode swiftly across the field, but he bid them halt when Kierelia's ranks raised their weapons. He motioned for Hazel to join him at the forefront. "I think they must think we are an enemy. Perhaps we should not draw much closer all at once."

Hazel considered. She knew this meant he would ride on without her, but she had no way of knowing how ludicrous Armond's response would be and who knew better how to handle him than she did? She nudged her horse onward.

"Hazel!" Fredrick shouted, kicking his horse after her. "I was not planning for *you* to be among the number that approaches."

"I am aware," she said with a smirk.

He shook his head unhappily and called back for a small escort to join them.

When they reached the ranks of Kierelian soldiers, Armond shouted from a high tower, "So, you recruited the golden king into your schemes, Lady Hazel!"

Her stomach twisted as she realized what he was thinking, but she set her shoulders. "No, your majesty. This is the Bashtiian military come to offer you warning and aid due to an impending attack from the Deep South."

"We are aware of that threat, as you well know!"

"Are you aware they arrive on the morrow?"

His eyes grew wide. "How can I believe you are not part of their plot?"

"You might address the royal alliance between our two kingdoms!" Fredrick hollered. "However, if you continue to persist in this questioning, we will happily be on our way home."

Hazel twitched beside him. She knew he was bluffing... or hoped. But Armond had become so stubborn, there was every chance he would not allow them entrance. Must they, then, shout the remainder of their caution in this fashion?

"Very well," Armond called. "King Fredrick, you and a small number of your guard may enter for a brief conference."

Fredrick shook his head. "The warning you receive is from the Lady Hazel herself. I insist she be permitted entrance and that she be treated as a party of my personal council, rather than an offender of your kingdom. I must have your word she will not only pass unharmed but be regarded with the honor deserving of a Bashtiian emissary."

Armond shifted his weight from foot to foot, glaring down at

Hazel and Fredrick as he considered. "You have my word."

Hazel did not feel comforted.

It was strange to walk those halls, with the eyes of Kierelian servants and guardsman upon her. Certainly, all had heard of her supposed transgressions, for that was how one upheld a banishment. To her disappointment, it was clear most believed what they'd heard as they glared after her, whispering under their breaths to one another. It did not cease to amaze her how swiftly one went from national hero to scum. It pained her beyond conscious admittance. *These* were her *people*. She treasured them.

A servant spat at her feet. Fredrick motioned for his guards to seize the man, but Hazel gripped his arm and pleaded with her eyes. He motioned again and the imprudent servant was released.

What *precisely* had been proclaimed about her? Had Armond actually gone so far as to reveal her gift of song...? Certainly not. Not even he—

"Southern singer scum," another servant muttered under her breath.

Hazel's eyes widened. She'd known the woman personally, if not very well. The servant's eyes widened back and she cast them meekly to the floor. Perhaps seeing Hazel in person, as a *person*, had reminded the woman of her true identity. Or perhaps she feared Hazel would sing her into the rafters. Hazel kept her gaze lowered for the remainder of the passage.

They entered the conference room to find Armond sitting at the head of the table, the prior friar at his right, a lord at his left, with Dorian directly behind him as unofficial counsel. Hazel's eyes flew to her friend. Her stomach tied itself into knots. But his eyes softened with immediate pleasure. The knot released. She couldn't imagine why he'd not responded to her letters. Then again, the Kierelian king had a history of misplacing them...

Armond stood and bade them all be seated. Fredrick sat at the opposite end of the table and motioned for Hazel to sit at his right while his considerable circle of advisors filled in the remaining chairs. Hazel was certain their attendance at the table confused Armond, who would not yet realize these soldiers were Fredrick's closest companions *and* were, despite military rank, well-educated and selected for their estimable astuteness. Hazel was certain one of them had even been among the Assemblage of the Wise when she'd visited.

"Your soldiers are tired, I see," Armond taunted.

Hazel nearly convulsed and made ready to retort when she felt Fredrick's hand rest upon hers.

"My council is trained in all things, including combat," he explained. "Despite their regalia, these are my advisors."

Armond's brows rose. It was clear to Hazel how threatened he was by Fredrick. It surprised her she hadn't understood this before—why they couldn't get along. He well understood how small Fredrick made him appear without ever meaning to. And it was true: Armond looked a pathetic figure compared to him. Even Fredrick clearly understood the difference between them, though not in arrogance. It saddened her that, if they'd met before the dragon attack, they might have liked one other. But Armond had never quite recuperated from those losses. Nor had he ever, she was certain, recovered from his own faint-hearted response to the colossal dragon.

"Now then," Armond began. "You say we are to expect an army tomorrow. Is that all?"

Fredrick folded his arms and looked to Hazel.

She raised her brows, then began, "Apparently, they have an enormous one."

"As we well understand," Armond said with annoyance.

She kept her eyes from rolling—only just. "But they've also got dragons... trained ones that respond by command."

Armond drooped in his seat, all the color drained from his face. He was deflated. Dragons were his greatest fear. Hazel couldn't help but feel compassion for him.

"How many?" he asked hoarsely.

"Four."

He looked faint.

"They are the smaller variety," she assured, despite herself.

He looked on her with refreshed irritation. *"Four* trained dragons and you think their small stature will save us?"

"I think it may give Kierelia a fighting chance, yes."

Slowly, he shook his head. "That's it. They've got us. We may as well surrender now."

Hazel leaped to her feet in fury that he could give up so easily, but Fredrick spoke first. "Not necessarily. You've got two armies this time. I spared little of Bashtii's troops. They are at Kierelia's disposal."

Armond blinked at him. "I-I must thank you," he said humbly.

Hazel took her seat again.

"Problem is," Fredrick began, "my troops have never even seen a dragon—only sketched likenesses. You, King Armond, are dragon-slayer. What guidance can you give us?"

Armond blinked. "Yes, er, yes…"

Hazel kept her gaze from his. She had no mind to cast salt into his shame. Besides, he had helped her slay one of the small dragons. He might advise from that front.

But Armond only endured a few more moments' hesitation before, "Dorian, here, has slain far more than I. Dorian…" He gestured for him to address the room.

Dorian's brows rose in surprise, but he stepped forward to give what council he could while the room listened on.

Hazel glanced up as she felt the heat of Armond's gaze. She almost leaped in her seat at its intensity. *How* he detested her. Any semblance of their "love" had vanished. It was as if he blamed her for having slain the dragon, as if *she* had caused his inner turmoil, as if she had sent the dragons.

He cast her a renewed glare, though unconsciously.

With a gasp, she fell back in her seat. Fredrick glanced her way, but she ignored him.

Quite suddenly, she grasped precisely how Armond felt about her... what he had always felt for her. It was not *love*—never had been. Nor was it even dependence. It was jealousy. He envied her strength and ability. He coveted the way the people loved her, how they wanted her even above their crowned king, whose line had been in rule before Kierelia had been made a sanctioned kingdom. As his lack of understanding the workings of his own mind had kept him from realizing it, he'd acted to possess her as his own if he could not surpass her. It was probably true that he'd believed he loved her. Perhaps he might even have possessed real feelings for her if he had been more secure in himself. But in the end, the resentment had won out and he'd taken the first excuse to be rid of her without even realizing why he was doing it.

"Ouch," she mumbled under her breath.

"What was that?" Fredrick murmured to her.

The wheels in her mind continued to spin. Before the kingdom's destruction, when life had been well for Armond, he'd been gorgeous, self-assured and benevolent. She'd truly esteemed that man. The change had come when he'd cowered before the dragon. As nearly everyone else had done the same, it wouldn't have been a problem... had *she* not stepped up and done what he couldn't. Moreover, he'd had to watch her sail through the kingdom's year of rehabilitation and then arrive at coronation day with the tongues of the kingdom wishing *she* could be their leader, even when they had no conception that she was actually the original beast-slayer.

He'd not just altered because his life had fallen apart. He would never be the same while *she* was near... because *she* was his problem. She was the reason he had lost his confidence and grown envious... which had toiled around inside him until it had nearly killed his kindheartedness—the one good quality he yet possessed.

She'd sought only ever to be a support, to help pick him up when he was vulnerable. But somewhere along the line, she'd become his competition. Once, he'd admired her for not wishing to take the crown from him when she might so easily have done so. Now, like Dianna, he detested her all the more *because* she wasn't the type who would—because she was *good*. She nearly choked as she came to her next realization. The way he looked at her, spoke to her...

He thoroughly *hated* her. When had that happened?

The intrusion of a Bashtiian soldier stole the attention of the room. He bowed before Fredrick with, "I apologize, your majesty, but the army of the Deep South has arrived sooner than anticipated. They have nearly reached our ranks."

Fredrick sprang to his feet, his mind clearly formulating plans. "How can it be that we were not alerted?" he asked.

"It seems they took the time to arrive by a mountain pass from the bordering kingdom—Stlock, I believe. Kierelia's southern region have not been alarmed as expected... and, therefore, will not arrive to aid in the battle."

"That is a pity..." he murmured thoughtfully. "They are mighty warriors. How great is our enemy's number?"

"The whole of it has not ceased emerging from the pass, but I can tell you they will be greater than our armies together."

Fredrick rubbed at his chin as his eyes darted back and forth at the speed of his thoughts. "I assume you've led the remainder of our men down the hill to join Kierelia's?"

The soldier nodded.

"Very good." He turned to Armond. "I will make my way below and begin directing my men."

Armond nodded. "I will remain here to devise a broader plan."

Hazel did not conceal the snort that sounded from her. He meant to hide away in his castle during the whole of the battle. Even so, with a few of Fredrick's advisors remaining with him, they may just be able to come up with something viable. They would have to if any of them were to survive.

Hazel stood. "I'm coming with you, Fredrick."

The room went silent before Armond spoke what all were thinking. "What good is *your* presence going to do him? Your time would be better spent helping me establish a strategy."

She spun to face him. "I should think, since I am the one who slew that massive beast over a year ago while you lay stricken upon the earth, you'd have no room to question what good *I* will do."

The king became visibly smaller as his face grew nearly as green as it had when he'd been poisoned by enchanted roses. His gaze lowered to the table.

Fredrick looked to her in astonishment. "In that case... I accept your aid with gratefulness, Lady Hazel."

She and Fredrick left together, a number of his advising soldiers following behind.

He leaned in with all the smile she felt he could spare under the circumstances. "You never told me *you* slew the big one."

"I never told anyone."

"But why does everyone think Armond was the dragon-slayer? He's a legend for it."

"By the time it was slain, everyone had fled. It was assumed Armond had done it. When he showed such cowardice afterward, I needed the kingdom to believe he was capable of leading them."

"Well, they're certainly going to have their doubts now..."

"No, they won't. He'll claim I lied. It's the only way he'll keep the throne."

"And you won't correct him?"

"I won't be here to correct him."

A glimmer shone in his eyes. "You won't remain here then? After all, your name will have been cleared as a conspirator..."

"Of course I'm not staying. If we survive this day, I'm with Bashtii." She'd only realized her increasing attachment to it once she'd hit Kierelian shores. Being away from Bashtii felt utterly inappropriate now. She felt like a mother who'd abandoned her young to the mercies of the world while she'd gone off galivanting after an estranged lover. Though it was a captivating kingdom, she was certain this shift had everything to do with the spiritual bond she'd formed in the Cave of Nielsas. That connection had evidently intensified as she'd spent time there.

Fredrick appeared too pleased considering all they were about to face. "So, we have pinched the Lady Fortune."

"What you have now is the *Great Entity*," she scolded

"The Kierelian god?"

"The Bashtiian and Kierelian God are one and the same, Fredrick. He created *all* that is. Kierelia has no right to claim him as its own. Nor could they pin him to such an assertion. He's undomesticated, he's all-powerful and he's my friend. Moreover, he is the God I met through the Bashtiian rubies. We do not go forward without him."

She only hoped she was right.

31

It was all Hazel could do to keep Fredrick from sending her to the back of the ranks when they caught sight of the opposing army. It was twice what Kierelia had to defend with. She felt fear fiercer than experienced when facing the giant beast. The sight set her to shaking.

"Really, Hazel," Fredrick urged, "you've never faced anything like this."

She raised a brow at him.

"One dragon, no matter its size, compared to hundreds of men, is very different," he explained. "There are too many factors to account for. Not to mention, killing men is very different from killing a beast."

She stomped her foot and worked to steady her shaking body. "Fredrick, I worked too hard to save this kingdom. Though I no longer call it my own, I cannot sit back and watch it be taken away.

I'd rather die defending it than live to see it stolen."

He swallowed. "And *I'd* rather not see you die, so we are at an impasse."

She shook her head. "There is no impasse. I decide where I stand and I will not move from this spot until I am good and ready."

The sound of trumpets ripped their attention from one another. The roar of their enemy followed as they raced down the hill and across the expanse. In a few breaths, the armies collided and Hazel was suddenly more than grateful that she and Fredrick were not at the forefront. She needed time to think, to get her bearings. She reached for her sword before realizing she had no idea how to use it. Fredrick did not know this, of course. He was not aware of the sheer luck it had taken to slay her dragon.

What *was* she doing here? Armond was right. She had no right to stand in the middle of a battlefield. Her mind was her strength and she ought to be in the conferencing room devising a winning stratagem.

She shook herself, wringing her hands. She'd come to aid them and she would not be shaken from her purpose. It was imperative she did what she had known she would the moment she'd volunteered to join Fredrick. And why should she care what anyone thought? They already knew. They already detested her for it.

Gulping a large breath of air, she released a long, trilling note until it caught hold of the nearest enemy soldier. Instantly, he plunged backward through a number of other men. Fredrick turned to her for a moment's admiration before being drawn into the melee himself. She chose another victim and then another. But it soon became clear she had their enemy's attention.

One by one, then two by two, they came for her. With her voice, she held them off until it was all she could do to send them flying as they reached her. Fredrick shouted for his best men to surround her. But she was not doing enough to warrant stealing his guard. Therefore, she sang louder and found she reached more troops at once. Before long, the area around her was nearly cleared. That was when she realized how vulnerable Fredrick was. Instinctively, she dashed to aid him.

It was hours that this went on until the sun summoned the afternoon. Hazel was desperately weary and, despite their best efforts, the Bashtiian and Kierelian armies had done little more than defend the gates. They could not keep on at this rate and the less momentum they fought with, the swifter their enemy's victory would come. She stepped back for a moment, considering the scene, then reconsidered her gift. She kicked herself for not having further explored what she was capable of. Recalling the rain she'd summoned, she knew precipitation would do little for them.

Her eyes went to the sky. Rain was not the only thing that fell from it. Hail might do… but she could not control who it pelted. What of…? She raised a brow and roared out a new song. Lightning struck the ground. She sang again and three more strikes took out at least twenty of their enemy's numbers.

At last, she saw what she ought to have seen from the beginning: fear in their eyes. They looked to her as if she was a malevolent sorceress as she slew whole groups at once.

Without warning, her knees buckled. Calling on lightning had been taxing. She'd not known different uses could drain her in varying ways. In an effort to keep from distracting Fredrick with her wellbeing, she lifted herself off the ground and raced into the castle, then up the nearest staircase to gain a better view of the battle.

Her stomach dropped. There were *so many* Deep Southerners. She would never reach them all with her lightning before growing utterly spent. "Oh, what'll we do?" she murmured. "Armond was right. We are going to *lose*."

That was when she saw him: King Rakutan of the Deep South. He strode out silently. Wind tousled his long black hair as his eyes roved the ranks of his enemy. He searched for something, someone. *Her,* she felt certain. She raised a brow and made ready to sing at him when he paused. He'd located his target. It was not her after all. Leaning out the window, she could not tell who it was. He withdrew a small dagger from his boot.

"Fredrick!" Hazel screamed. Rakutan had struck him square in the chest. With a shriek, she flew to him, thrusting a song at Rakutan that propelled him from the vicinity like a limp ragdoll. She and a small number of troops dropped beside Fredrick. Her heart sank as one of the men pulled the weapon from his flesh.

"W-will…" she murmured, "will he…?"

The man cast her a warning glance, then tore a piece of cloth from his garment and pressed it into the oozing wound. Hazel's attention was torn from his actions when a hand touched her cheek. She turned to find Fredrick scrutinizing her face. He tried to communicate something, but she could not grasp it.

Desperately, her heart reached out for the Entity. What was she to do? Bashtii could not lose him! Moreover, as she gazed into his face… she found her heart clenching. She bemoaned having held herself back from him, for having always made herself out of reach. He *was* a good man. He'd deserved her honesty, at least.

Abruptly, his breathing shallowed and his lids dropped. Blood poured from his wound and the man working to save him went white. In frantic woe, Hazel sang. It was scarcely audible. She hardly had any voice left. It was a song of what *could be*. In her mind, she reached into his wound, demanding it to restore, for the fibers of his skin to rejoin. At last, she was cut off by a sob as she realized what he'd come to mean to her, what he might have been to her one day. What she should have been to him.

The soldier gasped as he watered a piece of garment and wiped at Fredrick's chest. "It is... *closed*," he whispered incredulously, continuing to wash the blood away.

Hazel shoved her fingers into the place the wound had been. She met fresh skin. Reaching for Fredrick's face, she patted at his cheeks. *"Fredrick,"* she urged. "Wake up."

His lids fluttered open. Looking at those around him, he seemed to recall what the trouble had been and felt at his chest. "What in the..." He searched the healer's eyes, but the man only shook his head in wonder.

Fredrick glanced at Hazel then, reading her face. She tried shaking her head, uncertain whether she'd really done what she believed. Taking her face into his hands, he kissed her forehead, then reached for his sword and started back into the melee. Hazel blinked after him. Had she really done it—healed his wound with a song? Healed him sufficiently enough to send him back into battle?

She stood and fell back a step. If she wasn't careful, her knees would give way again. Batting at the men who offered her assistance, she strode back into the castle and to her window. Fredrick was saved. But Kierelia was not. Their enemy's numbers had scarcely dwindled. Wars were supposed to last days, weeks, years. But the Deep Southerners had not come to start a war. They'd come to overwhelm them in a day. At this rate, Kierelia would have to surrender by sunset. They could not continue to ask Bashtii to sacrifice its troops like this. Her heart broke for those lost on the field—from both Bashtii and Kierelia. These were her friends and neighbors.

She wasn't certain if it was the result of pent up emotion over all that had happened in the last weeks, leading to this day. Perhaps it was merely the fact she had never seen battle before. Bloodshed was horrific and wrong. She'd avoided seeing what happened to most of those she tossed about with her voice. Her main goal had been merely to injure them beyond the ability to continue in battle. But she knew some may have died. It was, *oh*, so much worse than a game of Affrontery.

In the end, she fell to her knees and sobbed.

"*Oh, Great Entity,* what do we *do*?" she whimpered. "Oh, help us, help us…"

The floor shook.

But it was more than the floor. It was the castle itself. She heard yips and squeals throughout as the shaking persisted. It was clear the earth was betraying them. They were enduring a blasted earthquake in the middle of their darkest hour. Did they have to go down like this? Could it be the work of Maera?

She took hold of the windowsill, hoping the castle would not merely fall to pieces around her. But she fell back as one of the castle towers flew out to crash upon the enemy.

The singer leaned out her window to find the tower was still attached… and it was rising. In another moment, it came hurtling down again, smashing over the field where the enemy ranks were thickest. The breath was stolen from her as she realized multiple towers were performing the same feat. It was as if… the castle was actually defending itself. Like long arms, the towers extended in length to reach their victims.

Hazel flew from the castle. Impossible as it was, it was as she'd surmised. Fredrick and his men had ceased fighting and stood back with mouths agape. Even the soldiers of the Deep South seemed only able to stare. That was when King Rakutan reappeared, screaming to his men to not be swayed by a pile of rocks.

Hazel smirked. This was no pile of rocks. This was a castle proving itself to be ever so slightly alive… and fully capable of defending itself and those within. Even so, their enemy threw themselves into battle with more gusto, determined to win the day… before those towers could take them out.

While the men around her re-entered the battle, Hazel could only watch the castle's movements with awe. It was like absolutely nothing she had ever seen, short of the Entity's throne room. She blinked several times, even pinching herself. It was *real*... and it was *her* castle, the one *she'd* built and brought to life.

Of a sudden, she began to piece together what had been taking place as she'd laid those precious bricks. With every one of the old stones she'd touched, a spark had entered her. She'd been soaking up the remainder of the old castle's life. From there, it had entered the lodestone: the coal H.S. had asked her to swallow. Somehow, that coal had transformed into a diamond. When ready, it had birthed itself from her mouth, where she'd then placed it onto its hearthstone, thusly bringing the new castle to life... so that it could do *this*.

But the demonstration was not yet over.

Abruptly, the towers returned to the castle. Then, methodically, they repositioned themselves until there was an arm stationed at every corner. At last, they stretched, first up and then over until each had struck ground with a teeth-chattering blow. That was when Hazel began to fear for those within. With great effort, the tower-arms pressed against the earth, lifting the stronghold until it was free of the foundation. The castle rose to a stand and then... it drew one turret forward, and then another... crawling forward like the live thing it was.

"Fredrick!" Hazel screamed with what voice she yet possessed. "Tell the men to run!"

But there was no need. They were already racing from the massive castle-monster that was faithfully pursuing its prey: The Deep South. Namely, Rakutan. Hazel's brow flew up in amusement as he fell to the ground in terror. The fortress' shadow rose over him and he would have been smashed beneath one of its tower-legs had not his men thought to drag him away.

"*Look* at *that!*" Guardsman Gunther shouted with glee, throwing his helmet into the air.

Hazel did look. She watched as the army of the Deep South, the ones who'd thought to take the stronghold in a day, fled in sheer horror from the sight of it. Over the hill, they went and back into the mountain pass.

"Come on, men!" Fredrick shouted. "Let's get after them! Make them think twice before they ever march upon Kierelia again!"

It was clear the battlefield was what Fredrick was made for. He reveled in it—easy to believe in a moment like this. With a roar, he flew forward, sword raised to the sky. The men of the allied kingdoms raced after him.

Hazel stayed behind until she was quite alone, surveying her dear castle chase their enemy into the mountains. At the mouth of the pass, it froze. She wondered if it would drop then and there and the location of Castlehaven would be altered forevermore. But then it turned and, for a moment, she felt certain it looked to her. Repositioning itself, it came scampering back until it had re-planted itself atop the original foundation.

Hazel's hands rested proudly on her hips as she gazed up at Castlehaven. True, it had destroyed the gates and released every one of its prisoners from those dungeons... but it had *triumphed*. With a sigh, she sauntered up and placed a hand to its wall.

"You did *very well* this day," she said in a whisper. "...I *really* hate to leave you."

She was knocked back as the castle shuddered. Perhaps it was only settling into place, but she could not help smiling up at it.

"Don't worry," she soothed, once again standing to place a hand to it. "I will see you find a queen capable of caring for you as you deserve. And there will be a new ruler every lifetime, you know. You must promise you will care for each of them as you have cared… for me."

She recalled how it had gifted her that beloved tower and then had saved it for her. Somehow—though it was but stone—it had understood what a lost, forlorn, needy girl she was… and it *had* cared. It was ridiculous to think and she would never confess it to a living soul. Even so, she mourned that she must abandon it as she had been abandoned. But there was no taking it with her… not that she couldn't. She laughed aloud at the notion.

32

Hazel had just finished dressing when a knock sounded upon her door. She raced to it, hoping to find... well, she wouldn't admit who.

"Dorian!" she said happily. Not the one for whom she'd hoped but equally as welcome.

He hugged her. "You were *incredible* yesterday. Looked like an avenging angel out there, throwing your lightning about."

"But where were you? Did Armond make you remain with him to concoct a 'broader plan.'"

He nodded. "Until it was clear it was not but a losing fight. Every time we checked on the progress, hopelessness grew. At last, I could take no more of it and raced out to join you all. That was when I saw *you.*"

"So... you were not inside the castle when it, er, took its stroll through the sunset evening?"

He grinned largely. "I was not, but *what* a sight! What a fortress!"

"But you have to tell me..." She pulled him through her suite to sit on the balcony. "Was anyone injured in all that movement?"

He nodded. "Numerous bumps and bruises, but only one broken bone, so I'd say it was worth the cost."

She nodded. "It was either that or become Deep Southerners."

"Exactly. But, *my*, how I wish I could've seen the faces of those inside when it waltzed off like that."

"Oh, me *too*," she replied laughingly. But then a new thought sobered. "Dorian..."

"You're wondering what the people thought of your gift."

Nodding meekly, she knew she should not care, and didn't really. She was only curious...

"I'd say they're pretty divided. Seeing as how you did not act as an enemy of the kingdom after all, but rather in its defense, some think you're rather magnificent. Others... wanted Armond to burn you at the stake."

"And?"

"Hm?"

"What will Armond do?"

He rolled his eyes, releasing a sigh. "I don't think he knows what to do, so he does nothing."

"I see..."

"Hazel, I cannot believe he banished you. I was just going to visit you on the very day you arrived here. I would've gone sooner, but... I don't know. I just had the feeling you'd want me to make certain Armond wasn't in over his head before going."

She smiled warmly. "You know me well."

"I had the pleasure of meeting your friend, King Fredrick, last night."

"Oh?"

"He is a likable fellow. *Raves* about you."

She groaned. "I know."

"That a problem?"

"No," she said sheepishly.

"As I conjectured," he said with a grin.

Another knock sounded at the door.

"Who is it?" Hazel called.

"It is me, my lady," called her former lady's maid.

"Oh, come in, Anna!" Hazel cried, leaping to her feet to meet the woman at the door. But seeing the maid's face, she fell back a step. Perhaps Anna was among those who feared her. "What can I help you with?"

Anna entered and closed the door, turning to her with, "My lady, perhaps it isn't my place, but I thought you might like to be made aware of the latest event."

"Event?"

"Bashtii is under attack. I just overheard that courageous King Fredrick demand you not be told before he left. But I always thought you seemed the sort who wouldn't like such things kept from her."

"*Bashtii* under attack?" Hazel gasped. "From *who*?"

"The Deep South. I heard the messenger claim Bashtii must have been in their plans all along. Supposed to be why they didn't attack Kierelia when we were at our weakest. They required militia enough to take both kingdoms at once. As Bashtii would come to our defense, they knew it would be vulnerable."

Hazel's mind raced. It all made sense now. She had been concerned she'd not seen the dragons appear the day before. They weren't meant for Kierelia. They were intended for Bashtii. Her parents had managed to keep something from her after all. She spared a moment to wonder if the Bashtiian guards had located them, but it mattered little. Bashtii—*her* Bashtii—was under siege and almost utterly undefended.

It was very likely that that kingdom was the real pursuit. It was a far greater prize than Kierelia. And it would do them credit to attain both. Even so, in the end and after all this time, Kierelia was only the bate to divide Bashtii's troops… And, *oh*, how they had been divided. Fredrick had spared almost nothing to aid her.

"But I thought we chased their army into the mountains," Dorian said as he came up beside her. "How can they have got to Bashtii so quickly?"

"Seems they possessed another army," the maid explained. "It's said to be fiercer even than the one we faced and Bashtii only has what is left of their royal guard and the people themselves to defend against it."

"What does Fredrick mean to do?" Hazel questioned hurriedly, already strapping on her blade.

"He and as many men as a ship can carry are now headed for the harbor. The rest of King Fredrick's troops are to race across the peninsula in hopes of arriving to aid them before all is lost."

"Is Kierelian guard to go along with them?" Dorian asked.

Anna shook her head. "King Armond says he cannot spare what little is left of his own militia in case the army of yesterday should decide to return."

"But he's got this *whole castle* for defense!" Hazel shouted angrily, throwing her cloak over her shoulders. It was imperative she make it onto Fredrick's ship. He was not going to defend Bashtii without her. After all, she was the one who possessed the Bashtiian bond, the one who could call upon the Entity for favor. Could she do so when she was not on its soil? Wishing she knew how it worked, she tried it anyway, closing her eyes and silently sending up a supplication that Bashtii would not be taken before they arrived.

"I'm sorry, my lady, but I must go," Anna said. "I am Lady

Rebecca's maid now and she will be expecting me."

"Yes, go, Anna. And… thank you *ever* so much for informing me of this. I will never forget your service and friendship. You have taken such good care of me."

The woman swept into a low curtsy. "I will never forget *you, my Lady Fortune.*"

Upon the maid's exit, Dorian gripped Hazel's arm. "I'm coming with you."

"You cannot! You are part of Armond's personal guard and council. He needs you."

He shook his head. "My loyalty lies with you."

"That means… *so* much to me. But without your council to Armond, I firmly believe Kierelia will be no more."

"I understand your love for this land, even your peculiar loyalty to Armond… but my devotion to you runs much deeper."

She froze. Was she about to have yet another man profess love for her?

"I love you, my little Hazel."

"Oh, *Dorian,*" she gasped. "You cannot!"

"I do… but not in the way that sounded. My love for you stems from the ties of blood."

"Wh-at are you talking about?"

"It is brotherly affection."

"Well, yes, I love you with the affection of a sister, but—"

"Hazel." He shook his head. "I'm trying to tell you I'm your brother."

"D-Dorian, I don't have a brother."

"You do, but none knew it. I was concealed."

She stepped back. "You were… hidden?" Her mind was spinning. For that matter, so was her vision. *"Why?"*

"They did not wish me to have emotional ties with any but them."

"Who? My... parents, you mean? Dorian, this is utterly mad." So mad, it frightened her. If it was so, he'd been lying to her all along and in so many ways. She had no idea who this was standing before her, but he was no friend.

"Well, it *was* rather mad," he replied. "They raised me to be little more than a weapon. It's why I am so gifted in combat. It's all I ever learned. I was originally meant to replace King Zephuel when I grew older. But they rushed the assassination attempt upon hearing of his ties to Maera. They were afraid she could actually help him."

The wheels of her mind whizzed. He'd already known more about Maera than she had before going to visit her. And hadn't the sorceress promised she would make him king as he was always meant...

"But what right would *you* have to the throne?" she questioned.

"Our line runs closer to the crown than most understand. Other than that, very little."

"But then our parents failed... and were banished."

"Yes, they took me with them, forsaking you."

"Because I was not of enough use to them. I was a bother?"

"Not necessarily. You were of the most use to them *here*."

"So, they took *you* and left *me*... And they didn't let you form connections." It was utterly, ridiculously awful.

"It wasn't until some years ago that they let slip I had a sister in Kierelia. I confess it was the reason I volunteered to aid the Kierelian underground in their rebellion. That was another, former plan to crumble the Kierelian empire. But destroying Kierelia meant nothing to me. I came to find *you*."

She was breathless, numb. But under it all, she was experiencing pain as she'd never felt it before. "So, when we met in the woods..."

"It wasn't because I was looking for someone to use as a mole. I was looking for my sister... I wanted to meet you, to see what you were like. It wasn't until the underground discovered I was friends with you that they convinced me to... use you. That... is my greatest transgression. I came here to meet you, remained to be a friend to you. Then, I wounded you far more than our parents."

"*Dorian,* why didn't you tell me all this long ago?!"

"If I'd told you when we scarcely knew one another, you'd have never believed me."

"*Yes,* I would have. Even if only out of desperation to feel I had someone, I would have embraced you."

"I know that now... but I didn't then. And then, when I decided to take the information you inadvertently gave me to the rebellion, I was too ashamed. I tried to keep my distance, to not get attached. But... you are a very precious lady. It was impossible. By the time I was imprisoned, and then everything was destroyed by the dragons, I was too terrified of losing you to confess all."

"And *now?*"

"Now, our parents have contacted you... and I felt I couldn't keep it from you any longer."

"You've not only shared the information I gave you to the underground. You sent it back to *them,* didn't you?!"

"No! Well, only in the very beginning. I stopped after a few years and then I dropped them entirely when the dragons attacked. In fact, I believe it is why they wished you to be queen of the new Kierelia. You were to replace me in their plans. Especially as they'd heard tales of how much influence you had with the people. I think you turned out to possess more potential as a weapon than I did in the end. They probably dearly regret abandoning you."

She laughed almost frantically. "Serves them *right* for dumping me because I served no better purpose for their senseless schemes... and for raising *you* as a mere weapon. We were but tools to them. And now they seek to destroy *both* the kingdoms I love."

"I am not certain even they understood Bashtii was Rakutan's true target. At least, they never informed me of it. But now you must see that all this is why I must go with you. They must be *stopped*."

She pressed her palms against her eyelids as her head throbbed. Why was this so much harder than discovering he was a traitor to the crown? Because it meant he'd still been lying to her even after she'd thought he'd confessed everything. It clarified his change in demeanor after the imprisonment, why he always looked so guilty, why he'd wished to be imprisoned again, and then why he'd been so stunned by the Entity's offer of forgiveness.

She lifted her head, letting her hands drop beside them. The Great Entity had known all and had chosen to impart his mercy. If he could, so could she. She opened her mouth, ready to welcome him on the voyage, but stopped short. "You cannot come. Armond needs you."

"Why do you care so much what *Armond* needs?"

"Because Kierelia will fall apart without him... and he's an idiot. But he trusts you, *listens* to you. You can help him prepare to defend Castlehaven should the need arise. In fact, I think that would go much further in making up for all our parents tried to make you do. Show them your loyalty is to the very thing they wished to destroy."

She knew she'd hit on something when fire burned in his eyes. "I'll do everything I can then, but more for you than to show them."

Despite herself, her eyes welled. Not long ago, she'd had no one to care for her. Now, she had two people who did their duty for her sake rather than obligation. Who cared about Armond and his betrayal? He was so tiny compared to these grand friends, though flawed they may be.

She stood, realizing she would have to work doubly hard now to make it to the harbor before Fredrick's ship departed. "I must go, Dorian. But listen... see if you can get Armond to wed Dianna."

"What? *Why?*" He raised a mirthful brow. "Revenge?"

"Because she's clever. And I *think*, after all she's been through, if she could just have something going for her, she could do much more for the kingdom than Armond. Not to mention, I believe she may truly love him. Just... see what can be done. I don't trust Armond to choose wisely on his own."

"All right..." he said, looking to her as if she was mad. "But your little-girl-self would kill me for listening to you now."

She actually found herself laughing. "Isn't it a fine thing we've grown up then?"

For a moment, she thought about embracing her brother. But it was too soon, so she merely nodded and vacated the room. It was a peculiar tale—one she would need to learn more about at a later date. For now, she must shove it to the back of her mind. Even so, she realized how *right* it felt that he should be a true blood brother. After all, did not siblings support *and* fail one another all the time? They had certainly seen their share of both.

She had just reached the gates when she felt a hand on her shoulder.

"Dorian," she murmured. "Is something the matter?"

"No," he said, throwing his arms about her. He pulled back with, "I just want you to know you were the first and only friend I ever had. You mean more to me than anything... and I'm really proud of all you've accomplished. Bashtii is lucky to have you."

* * *

It had not been in her plans to find herself locked into a ship cabin with orders not to be released until Fredrick could return for her. She'd been standing at the hull, hiding beneath her cloak, and hadn't counted on his recognizing her unconscious humming.

"Hazel, what on Kaern are you doing standing upon this voyager?" he'd said from behind her.

She turned to face him. "You didn't actually think I'd let you go without me, did you?"

"Actually, yes. Yes, I did. Who told you?"

"You wouldn't know her."

"Hazel, I found you passed out on the ground when I returned to the castle. And you did not awaken the whole evening. If it weren't for the Kierelian healer assuring me you would be all right, I'd have never left your side. As it was, I was unable to rest all the night long for worrying."

She blinked back at him. She *had* wondered how she'd ended up in bed. "Well, as you see, I am perfectly fine."

"I see you are more stubborn than I gave you credit for." Clasping hold of her wrist, he tugged her along behind him. Before long, he had her in a fine cabin. She'd not thought to fight him until she heard the door lock and his orders to the captain to be certain she was not released.

She slammed her fists upon the door. "Fredrick, don't you *dare* do this!"

No answer.

"I will *never* forgive you!"

Still nothing. She peered out the small window in the door. There was no one.

Falling into the nearest chair, she sat huffing. She'd not thought him capable of such... she couldn't think of a strong enough word. He had no *right*. How dare he think he could toss her into a prison, lavish as it was, and she would let him get away with it? Or did he simply not care? Or… did he simply care more that she did not join in the battle when she was so weary from the previous one?

She sighed.

It was sweet in a way.

Her hand gripped the pile of parchment on the desk and tossed it against the wall. Then, she stood and began to pace. This would not do. She'd not scrambled aboard to be trapped inside while the fate of Bashtii hung in the balance outside her window. The ship would arrive in the harbor soon and she would go mad with anxiety over the outcome.

At last, she dropped into the chair again, for the first time admitting how utterly weary she was. Fredrick was accustomed to warfare. He'd grown up a soldier. All she had was her inexperienced gift and she didn't even know what would happen if she attempted to use it again. Her voice was hoarse as it was. Did she have anything left for singing?

Her brow rose. She licked her lips. Her eyes went to the lock. Hoarsely, she sang at it, but it was no use. Singing was not in the cards for her. With a huff, she folded her arms and sat back. Fredrick was right. Still… she didn't like the idea of being imprisoned on this ship, unable to know anything of what occurred.

Her eyes fell to the pot of steaming tea on the desk. Eagerly, she drank it, hoping it was enough. Then, she focused once more on the lock and hummed.

Click.

Hazel grinned. She'd done it. But she didn't dare free herself until Fredrick had vacated the vessel.

33

Hazel watched Fredrick's shoulders droop as he gazed out an upper window of Illuminas Palace. That wasn't a good sign. After sneaking out of the ship cabin, she'd followed him and his men through an underground tunnel system and into the palace. A servant or two saw her as she tailed them, but none knew she was not meant to be there. Moreover, they were all rather more concerned with what was happening outside the palace. Leaving Fredrick and his men behind, she made her way into a vacant bedchamber and crept over to the window.

Her hand went to her throat. The scene was much like it had been at Castlehaven, though the enemy militia was not quite so large. They'd known it would be unnecessary. Not only were most of Bashtii's infantry missing... this half of King Rakutan's army had dragons.

The beasts had not been unleashed as yet, but she spotted them in chains within the city streets, held in check by their trainers. But even without their aid, the spectacle in the courtyard was disheartening. Bashtiian soldiers fought with every bit of heart, soul and ability they possessed, but numbered among them (and the only hope Bashtii had up to this point) were the people. These included the nobility who lived in Bashtii as well as visiting knights and dignitaries, but most of them were commoners. They fought just as hard if not fiercer than the soldiers… but they were far less equipped and it showed. Yet, by some miracle, the enemy soldiers had not taken the palace. But they had gotten within the gates. The people within the courtyard were the palace's final defense.

Hearing Fredrick shouting orders to his men in the corridor, Hazel peeked through the crack of the door to watch them start in various directions. She must decide what her move would be. As she could scarcely sing, what help could she offer?

"Your view pleasant in there, Lady Fortune?"

The door opened and she fell back a step.

"How did you *know*?"

"I always have a scout track from behind," Fredrick explained, "to be certain we are not attacked by surprise. He spotted you just before the tunnel system."

"Ah…" she replied with a sheepish smirk. "Well, I am at your service, your majesty."

He chuckled softly, shaking his head. "I have half a mind to have you locked into this room…" He folded his arms and searched her, as if genuinely considering it. Unhappily, he ended with, "Yet, I am fairly certain you would throw yourself from that window before being kept from something you feel strongly about."

She folded her own arms.

With a sigh, he rubbed at the back of his neck. "Then you are to remain with me and my circle. I want my best eyes on you. Can you even sing?"

She lifted her chin. "Of course." She simply could not do so above a whisper.

Following him and a few of his men through the castle, they emerged from a side entrance. Silently, they made their way around the palace wall until they were surprised by an enemy troupe clearly meaning to steal into the stronghold unawares.

Immediately, Fredrick and his soldiers entered into the frenzy. When they had taken out the group before them, another troupe arrived from around the corner. Hazel merely stood back. She tried to sing, but though the power was there, she could not give it enough volume to reach the soldiers.

She cried out in surprise as a Deep Southerner leaped before her, took hold of her hair and twisted her about. Wrapping an arm around her neck, he held his sword to her chin.

"*Oy!*" he roared.

The fighters turned to view the spectacle.

"Surrender now or she dies!" he cried.

Oh, *why* had she insisted on "fighting" beside Fredrick? For the first time in her life, she was useless. She stared back into Fredrick's eyes that burned with the decision before him. Her mind raced for how to save him from it. *Of course.* She had her sword beneath her cloak. Surely, she did not know how to use it, but these men didn't know that. Not to mention, if she could just draw it before he realized what she was about, she might just shove its blade into his foot.

Slowly, her hand slivered toward the hilt and yanked.

Bright light cut the atmosphere as she drew it, causing all in the vicinity to gasp and fall back, shielding their eyes. Hazel herself could not look directly into the blade's light as it sang in her hand. It felt alive and extremely communicative—urgent. It pulsated under her touch, urging her on.

"But I don't know how to *use* you!" she whispered.

The light only grew stronger until she was forced to shield her eyes beneath the hood of her cloak. It hummed at her with the persistence of a dog sniffing out a trail. It wanted something from her, but all she could do was—

Sing. Opening her mouth, she released a pitiful sound, but it was intensified by the blade, just as it had been when she'd faced Maera. Five bolts struck the ground around her, three meeting their targets. It was a miracle neither she nor the Bashtiians with her had been harmed. Without another thought, she raced forward, ignoring Fredrick's pleas to wait for him.

Diving into the crowd in the courtyard, she pressed her way through the fighting and raced up the stairs of the palace. Reaching the top, she pointed her sword to where the densest of the enemy soldiers were assembled as they worked to press their way further onto castle grounds. With her meager song, the sword glowed and lightning struck in several places at once.

With a mischievous smirk, she called to Fredrick as he rounded the corner, "Get your people back!"

With a confused grin, he did as told while the enemy looked to her with a blend of fear and malice. At last, she released a hideous note, deafening thanks to the sword. Her song proved to reach over the whole of the enemy throng as they flew back, piling onto one another. She sang out again and they flew further. Again, and she had the army wrestling to vacate the courtyard. At last, they went running. She only stopped singing when her legs gave out, but she leaped to her feet before Fredrick could see.

Glancing to where he was, she found him staring stricken into the horizon. Stomach toiling for what it could be, her presumption proved correct. The dragons were approaching. In moments, they reached the courtyard where those fighting for Bashtii remained.

Any moment now, they would release flame. She wasted no time in singing at them, but they merely swerved out of the way of her bolts. Somehow, the beasts could sense when and where the lightning would strike. Her mind raced for what to do when the flames descended. Bashtiians screamed and ran every which way, working to avoid the onslaught. She tried to sing at the dragons again, this time in an effort to push them about. But with their great strength, they only righted themselves and returned.

"Oh, *Entity*, what do I do?" she murmured.

A warm, salty gust gusted through the expanse. The leaves of the trees shuffled noisily. It would have been a beautiful sight if they were not all about to die by dragon fire. Even so, H.S., the very spirit of the Great Entity, was in that wind.

"What *is* it? What do I *do*?"

Another blast rushed through, this time swaying the trees back and forth so they looked as if they would topple over.

Hazel raised a brow, recalling the last day of training in her Kierelian forest. She had made her beloved trees grow. If she could make them grow… could she make them *fight*? She planted her feet and pointed her sword to the nearest crop, but her voice was spent. Shaking her head, she recalled how Blythe had choked her with a mere hum under his breath. With the sword to magnify her sound, would a hum do?

Her eerie drone flooded the courtyard, reaching the trees. She smiled with satisfaction as they sprouted new branches. She heard the gasps of those around her as they witnessed the phenomenon, but she could not worry about them. She concentrated on the trees, manipulating their branches until they were long snakes slinking after their prey. In a whipping motion, one of them caught the foot of a beast and slapped it down into the city, wrapping its way around the monster's muzzle to avoid further flame.

It was at that moment that King Rakutan appeared at the

palace gates, his large army racing in around him. Somehow, he had sneaked aboard a ship and arrived to bolster his army to complete the task at hand. He had lost Kierelia. But given the winning of Bashtii and a little time, he might just gain it eventually. Either way, Bashtii was the real prize with its caverns full of rubies and various other riches. By the way he grinned at her, he had no intention of losing this time.

Furthermore, he had every intention of capturing her and making her his bride as arranged.

Her skin crawled and she fell back a step, continuing her mission. Despite the remaining dragons, Bashtiian soldiers, dignitaries and commoners re-entered the battle. Swiftly, she sent several more branches whipping through the air until she'd caught two more beasts. When they smashed upon portions of the southern army out in the city, she actually heard cheers from some of the Bashtiians. With three of the dragons out of the way, Bashtii began to stand something of a chance again. She was just reaching for the final dragon when fearful gasps alerted her to the first, who had freed itself from its bonds. Charred bits of wood fell from its muzzle and she recalled how very hot the giant dragon's body had been. Somehow, the mere touch of its skin had burned it free.

Unexpectedly, a pair of arms were around her and she was drug into the castle. With a scream, she wrenched herself free, but it was needless.

"Fredrick, you frightened me!"

He ignored her, going to the window to survey the chaos. He looked on as his people were burned by dragon flames and slaughtered by enemy swords. The color drained from his face and she understood what had happened. He had lost his mettle. He no longer knew what to do. After all, he had no lively castle to defend them. And nothing Hazel had tried thus far helped for long. She wondered why H.S. had led her to use the trees if they had proved only a momentary remedy. Yet, she supposed it proved that Bashtii was not so defenseless as they'd formerly seemed.

"Hazel, I don't know what we're going to do," Fredrick said. "It won't be long before those dragons have desolated my people. Meanwhile, the rest of my military won't arrive until tomorrow. I think… we must surrender now and hope my men can come up with a way to save us when they arrive. Our fate is in the hands of my generals."

"Wait…" she said abruptly, holding a hand up as her mind raced. "I think… I have an idea."

He raised a curious brow.

"These dragons can sense lightning and burn through trees," she said thoughtfully, "but they'd be useless if turned to gold…"

He hesitated, then shook his head. "It is a fine notion, but I have to be touching them in order to do it and even if you could force them to the ground, I'd likely be killed before I reached them. Not to mention, my people are not aware of my curse."

"They would merely love you all the more as their *golden* king if they knew, Fredrick. And it'll be rather a moot point if they're taken by Rakutan, anyway. As for getting near the beasts, I'm not sure that's necessary... How do we get to the roof?"

34

From the rooftop, it was much clearer that the scene below was a losing fight for Bashtii. But Hazel believed, if they could actually manage to pull off what she had in mind, they would be in a far greater position.

She held her sword outward. "Take hold of this hilt with me," she directed Fredrick.

"It is like Bashtiian ruby..." he said with astonishment, only seeing it up close for the first time. "No *wonder* it is so irregular. Its abilities must be similar to the rubies in the Cave of Nielsas."

"Wonderful. Now, place your hand on it."

He shook his head. "I cannot. I will transform it and then where will we be?"

"You don't have to transform it. I learned how simple it was to control and utilize my gift. I believe you can do the same."

"And what if I cannot?"

"Have you ever tried?"

"No. It's a curse—not something I wanted to cultivate."

"Turning things to *gold* is not a curse, Fredrick. It is wonderful—as wonderful as *my* gift. Just look at what I can accomplish! Now, you've seen how this sword amplifies my voice? I think, or I rather hope, my song can carry your gift to the beasts."

He chewed at his lower lip as he stared back at her, considering. Finally, he tore off his glove. "I'll try it, but I'm not touching your hand."

"Very well, just take hold of the hilt already."

Apprehensively, his fingers stretched out.

The sword sparked, striking his hand He swiftly tore it away. "It is too like the rubies of King Nielsas. It rejects me."

Hazel rolled her eyes at the weapon as if it was a misbehaving child. She was not giving up so easily. "Try again," she directed.

He did so but was burned once more.

"Ach!" she growled. "Place your hand over top mine then."

"Hazel, I'm not taking that chance…"

"I'll channel it forward before it can change me." It sounded simple enough, but she really had no idea what she was talking about.

He eyed her, then held out his hand, gently laying it atop hers. For a moment, she felt his gift attempting to work its way into her skin. With her unsteady hum, the sword glowed and she felt the gift flow into and then out of the weapon. Now, she had only to focus it.

Her breath was stolen by how promptly the procedure took effect. Almost instantly, the dragon writhed. It sickened her. She felt cruel. After all, she'd met dragons who had not been cursed by a sorceress. They were astounding. But it was this or the destruction of Bashtii.

As the transformation persisted, the dragon's flight faltered. With skin so hot, molten drops of gold sprayed upon those below and cries sounded.

"Pull back!" Fredrick roared to his people.

Many recognized the voice of their king and searched for him upon the roof, likely working to understand his part in what occurred. Hazel knew they would never guess and, as the hot drops descended, they swiftly obeyed his command.

At last, the metal solidified and the beast plunged, landing with an earth-shattering crash as the Deep Southerners scrambled for safety.

Hazel and Fredrick released the sword and drooped to catch their breath. Everyone in the streets and courtyard seemed to follow suit as silence overwhelmed the district. All were in shock of what had just occurred. It was not an occasion witnessed in every lifetime, that was certain... even if it wasn't a moving castle.

At the sound of a horn, Hazel crawled to peek over the wall. Rakutan had pulled the remaining dragons from the battle. Apparently, they were more valuable to him alive than as statues. She breathed hard as she watched him speaking with his generals. Was it enough to make him turn tail and run, as he had in Kierelia?

Seeming to read her mind, he peered straight up into her eyes. Then, he pointed behind him. Maera emerged from the shadows. So, she would keep her word to aid the Deep Southerners. Infuriatingly, Hazel shook with fear. As before, there was something about the sorceress that got under her skin. This woman considered herself Hazel's personal enemy, but Hazel could not imagine why. Maera had called her a prophet... Was it that she hated prophets?

"It is me *she loathes,"* the wind whispered.

Hazel looked about her as if she could see the Entity's spirit. Why should Maera hate the Entity? What could she have against *him*? He was wonderful.

"I chased after her the whole of her life, but she, knowing all, made her choice. She has gone after my people again and again. I have been driven to scorn her. Yet, if she turned to me even now, I would rescue her. But she will not."

Hazel nodded. It made sense. Still, she had to wonder what *precisely* Maera had done to cause this wonderful spirit to scorn her.

More to the point, Maera hated H.S. It was Hazel's understanding that prophets heard from the Entity. That had to be why Hazel was her inevitable adversary.

Instantaneously, Maera appeared over Hazel's shoulder. The singer yelped and scrambled to her feet, causing Fredrick to leap to her defense. Standing between the ladies, he pointed his sword to the newcomer.

"Who is this, Hazel?" he asked.

"This is the Sorceress Maera from the vicinity of the southern tribes," Hazel replied darkly.

"My *beautiful* fellow," Maera cooed, "I would like to offer my friendship to your flourishing kingdom. I can protect your people from all that mayhem below."

The scent of roses overwhelmed the rooftop. Maera looked at him the way she had Dorian and Armond. Hazel's stomach turned as she feared the worst. Would he be drawn in as they had been?

"We don't need you," he spat. "We've got Hazel."

Hazel's brows shot up.

"But she has saved you from nothing, my boy," Maera countered. "There is still a whole army below, ready to storm Illuminas Palace as soon as I have completed my business here."

"And what business is that?" he questioned.

"Hazel will come with me. She has much to learn if she is to become *all* she might."

Hazel stepped forward. "There is nothing I wish to learn from you, *witch!*"

"My dear girl, you have got this all wrong. You think these people will ever love you for the gift you possess? Indeed, I believe you have experienced otherwise. If you come with me, I will introduce you to powerful people like you. You will finally be accepted, even admired, for *all* you are."

Fredrick shook his head. "You don't know her at all if you think she'll fall for that."

Maera stepped back as Fredrick approached. Hazel looked between them. Was the sorceress afraid of him?

"She fears anyone she cannot control," H.S. whispered into her ear.

Hazel made ready to urge Fredrick onward when Maera lunged for her. But in another moment, the sorceress cried out. Instantly, she disappeared from them. Hazel looked about for Fredrick and discovered he lay sprawled against a far wall.

She fell to her knees beside him. *"Fredrick!"* she shouted, experiencing flashbacks of the horrible scene when he'd been so near death. "Are you all right? What has she done to you?"

Chuckling, he sat up and accepted the hand that pulled him to his feet. "I'm all right, Lady Fortune. She merely pushed me when I attempted to transform her into a golden effigy."

"Aaah!" That was why she'd retreated so suddenly. Hazel had to admit she'd flee as well if it came to it. As it was, Fredrick was holding her hand and she remained flesh.

"Fredrick."

"What is it?"

She pointed to his hand in hers.

"There's no law against wooing a woman in the midst of a war, is there?" he asked with a grin.

She shook her head. "I'm not gold."

His brows shot up and he attempted to pull his hand away, but she held him there. "You're gaining control over it. Probably been developing it your whole life."

Cheers sounded from below and the two scrambled to the edge.

"I can't believe it," Fredrick whispered.

"They're pulling out," Hazel croaked with relief.

"I really had nothing left. That whole turning a dragon to gold thing was taxing. I don't know how you do what you do."

"Do we go after them?"

He waved a weary hand. "Let them leave. I just want my people safe."

A roaring chant rang out below. Hazel couldn't make out what they said and looked to Fredrick questioningly.

"They are shouting your name," he said with light in his eyes.

She shook her head. "That sounds nothing like my name."

He laughed. "My people call you Fortune. That is what they're cheering.

Feeling self-conscious, she ducked behind the wall.

With a chuckle, he crouched beside her and stroked the hair from her face. "You are an exceptional human being, Lady Fortune."

Hazel swallowed and knew not what to say as she searched his face. She recalled how she'd felt when he'd been so near death. She'd known then she would let him in, yet when he was before her being all… *him*, it was much more difficult. In the end, she realized it was not her guardedness that kept him out so much as her discomfort in the fact that, well, she really *quite* liked him.

Suddenly, she took in what he'd meant, what the people were thinking, and swatted his hand away. "Oh, for pity's sake! Without the profound favor of the *Great Entity* these last few days, we'd *all* be Deep Southerners by now."

"So, your part counts for nothing then?" he asked with a raised brow.

She considered. Then, with a wink, she answered, "I was his gift to you people."

* * *

Hazel raced to the door of her chambers. Throwing it open, she threw her arms about Dorian. "It certainly took you long enough to get here!"

"Well, it took some doing to get this lady out of her suite, let alone the castle."

He stepped aside to reveal Dianna, heavily veiled and cloaked. In fact, Hazel would never have known the woman had she not summoned her to Bashtii herself.

Silently, Dianna stepped into Hazel's chambers. "This had better be *worth* it," she said quietly, as if at any moment someone might discover who she was and rip off her concealments.

Hazel merely smiled at Dorian.

Turning back to Dianna, she said, "Remove the head covers, please."

Dianna's gaze dropped to the floor. "Hazel, I don't understand what you think you can do for me, but I'd really rather not."

Hazel looked to Dorian again. "You saw her just after the dragon attack, correct?" she asked of him. "She was as bald then as she is now?"

He stepped up to the ladies and nodded, looking to Dianna reassuringly.

Dianna huffed. "Very well. I hope you two get some enjoyment out of this." Dropping the cloak and veils away, a shiny head was revealed. Just as Hazel had conjectured, she was a beautiful woman even without hair. Even so, she believed she had the means to reconcile Dianna's insecurity.

"Do you think you can bear to hear me sing?" Hazel asked with a smirk.

Dianna's eyes grew wide and she sank into the nearest chair. "By all means, if that is all you summoned me here for, I suppose I may as well endure it. I don't suppose you plan to strike me down with your lightning bolts, do you?"

Hazel laughed perhaps too jovially. "Not today." Taking a breath, she sang out. No lyrics, just a melody. She focused on what she wanted. When her song was complete, she directed Dianna to gaze into the mirror on the wall behind her.

With the narrowing of Dianna's eyes, the slightest glimmer of hope betrayed her as she stood. Turning as directed, stillness followed. With a sob, she crumbled to the floor, giving way to unconsciousness.

Hazel chuckled. "Did that girl just *faint?*"

Smilingly, Dorian went to the lady on the floor. He did not seem to relish the joke. "To her, this means freedom. We all began our new lives the day the castle was completed. But she's been trapped in the realm of those dragon attacks as long as she's been confined to her rooms."

Hazel drew near to where he held Dianna's head in his lap, eyeing him curiously. "Yes, but she imprisoned herself."

He shrugged. "A prison is still a prison."

She raised a brow. "So, did you fall for her before or after I asked you to set her up with Armond?"

His eyes darted to her. "How did you find out?"

"Find out what?"

"W-well, she made me promise not to tell anyone." Though, he dearly looked as if he would like to speak.

She folded her arms. "You had better not then."

He pressed his lips together, then patted Dianna's cheek as if to make certain she was yet unconscious. "We're…"

"Oh, for heavens," Hazel interrupted, "don't you dare tell me you've gone and engaged yourself to *Dianna* of all people!"

He grinned up at her like a small boy.

"Dorian, this is *Dianna* we're talking about. Couldn't you at least fall for Stacia?"

"There's more to Dianna than you'd think."

Hazel merely laughed. "I certainly hope so. In any event, I cannot blame her for loving you. And I hope the two of you will be happy."

"It's your fault, you know. I tried to do as you requested. I dropped the hints to Armond, but she refused to see him. So... I had to visit her in an attempt to follow through on my mission. After a while, things... shifted."

"I told you..." Dianna grumbled quietly from the floor, "not to tell anyone."

Dorian patted her shoulder. "It's all right. Now your hair's back we can be openly married instead of living in that dark cabin in the woods we talked about."

Dianna actually smiled docilely and let him help her to her feet before peering into the mirror again.

Drawing up behind her, Dorian said, "I don't suppose you'll want Armond after all, now you've got it back?"

Her eyes grew wide and she spun to throw her arms about his neck. "You'd *better* be joking, my darling criminal."

Hazel snorted but neither seemed to notice. And as the two remained fixated on one another, she went to the door to call for the nearest servant to have them shown about the palace.

Not long after, another knock sounded at her door. As she was engaged in a riveting tale about the birth of the Bashtiian empire, she huffed and shouted, "Who is it?"

"Is my lady busy, then?" Fredrick called in mock offense.

With an unconscious grin, she raced for the door and invited him in. "Where have you been?"

"None of your business," he said, leading her to sit with him before the windows.

"Oh, so we're keeping secrets now, are we? What about breaking our walls down and getting to know one another?"

He merely smiled. "I heard you restored a woman's hair today."

"I did."

"Is there anything you *can't* do with that voice?"

"That is a good question."

He took her hand and began fidgeting with her fingers. "Well, this gift makes you rather formidable, doesn't it?"

"Oh, *indeed.*"

"That could certainly come in handy for a queen."

She raised a brow. "…Too bad I'm no queen."

"But you could be…" He held up her left hand to reveal the ruby circlet he'd slipped onto her finger. "Would you?"

She looked up to find his eyes on hers. "Would I…?"

"Technically, you would become my wife."

She bit her lip to suppress a grin. "Your people really got to you, didn't they?" Hopeful rumors of their engagement had been circling since the day of the battle.

He shook his head. "I had this ring made the day after the Bashtiian ball."

"You… what? You've wanted to marry me since—"

"Clearly, the notion hadn't occurred to you," he said with a laugh. "But I can overlook that if you will claim affection for me and agree to marry me."

35

It was Fredrick's fault. He had insisted she sing for the ceremony. She'd tried every which way to excuse herself from the request, but in the face of those pleading, golden eyes and deep dimples, she'd acquiesced. Had he suspected what might happen?

She was overcome with emotion as Dorian walked her down the aisle. After all, Fredrick awaited her at the other end and he was... genuinely lovely. Never upon meeting him that initial evening had she suspected how deeply fortunate his future wife would be. After all, she'd thought him a pig looking to purchase a Kierelian bride. Now, she had willingly become that bride. His toothy, irrepressible smile upon seeing her in her gold gown made her gasp with pleasure. He was a rather beautiful man. Moreover, he knew everything about her and loved her more for it.

When it came time for her to sing her love ballad to him—one she'd written herself—she ought to have known it would be too much for her. Reaching into the rafters with her efficient soprano, Fredrick—along with everyone in attendance—raced to the rafters with it. She nearly dropped them in her dismay. With a humiliated smirk, she gently returned them to solid ground.

Astonishingly, the room erupted with applause as she swiftly concluded the song. Fredrick was bent over with hands on his knees—actually laughing. When he finally looked up at her admonishing eyes, his own were full of tears. Somehow, they were not merely of laughter but of wonderful emotion: bliss. He strode toward her with intent, took her hands into his own bare ones and urged the priest to complete the ceremony.

Afterward, he turned to the attendees with, "Well, we've done it, everyone! We've filched the Lady Fortune from the Kierelians! Long live Queen Hazel of Bashtii!"

AFTERWORD

Hazel awoke to the song of rubies. Looking to her sword in its sheath on the table beside her, she listened on. Her gaze turned to the starry scene outside her windows. This was the song of the Cave of Nielsas. Tossing off her coverlet, she swiftly changed and ended by strapping the crimson blade about her waist.

To her surprise, she had no trouble getting up a horse from the stable lad. She was queen of Bashtii—had been for many months. Even so, she'd not realized she could spirit off in the middle of the night without question. Then again, she supposed it was not the lad's place to do so.

"Can you keep a secret?" she asked.

He nodded eagerly, if timidly.

"I'm off to meet with the *Great Entity*. Do you know him?"

He shook his head.

"Try *The Book of Ancient Law and the Entity's Remedy*. You'll find it in the library. I am certain he would wish to meet you if you seek him with your whole heart." With that, she leaped upon the horse and started onward.

Entering the cavern, she found her torch was unnecessary. The ruby walls glowed in welcome as their song resounded. Drawing before the hand-stones, she stared down at them a moment, stealing her breath for where they would send her.

With a sigh of pure ecstasy, her teary eyes gazed once again upon the scene of that glorious Entity upon his astounding throne, surrounded by the immaculate creatures and beasts of his world. But rather than feeling herself unworthy, a peculiar confidence drew her forward. It had to be the blood of the Anointed One that made the change and she was glad of it. She wanted nothing between herself and the Entity. But just as she reached him, she was stopped short.

A new being appeared before her, much like the giant angels who had gone to guard over her journey to Maera's mansion. This one was well-armored and gazed down at her with blazing eyes, then bowed.

"Hazel of the Many Kingdoms," he said. "Thank you for answering the call."

She nodded, still questioning the name by which they called her there. Perhaps, one day, she would come to know from where it derived. "Who would ignore his summons?" she asked with a smile.

"Many more than one would suspect," he replied almost sadly.

"Why have I been summoned here?"

"I must request that blade of yours."

Her hand flew to its hilt. "My blade... you want it?"

He nodded. "In truth, it is mine."

She nearly choked.

"But I must now deliver it to another."

"Who?" Who else would love the blade as she did?

"Iviana the Glory-bringer."

Hazel folded her arms. "But this is such a special blade, and clearly so with its crystalline construct. How do I know it will be safe in the world with this *Iviana*?"

He paused a moment, actually smiling over her, then held out his hand. "May I see it, please?"

Her eyes flew to the Entity, who nodded. Almost begrudgingly, she withdrew it and did as bid.

Holding it in each of his hands, the figure turned to face the Great Entity. "Shall we?" he asked, looking into the Entity's face as if they shared thoughts on another field.

The Entity's eyes sparkled. "Indeed, High Warrior Viijelyk."

The high warrior turned back to Hazel, holding a completely different blade—quite unattractive in comparison to the shining crimson one. "He has transformed it. It will not be so easily identified as exceptional. Are you satisfied?"

"No..." she admitted. "But I am resigned."

With a nod, the being's wings began to flutter and soon he had vanished from her sight. Once again, she made ready to approach the enthroned one when the seven torches surrounding began to spin and draw together as one. In a billow of fragrant smoke, H.S. stood before her.

"Hello, my dear friend," he said ardently.

Stealing a sigh as she gazed into his face, she replied, "Hello again, you wonderful voice of the wind."

He pointed to the crystal floor then. "Now, watch."

Hazel crouched, resting hands on her knees as the scene played out on the sea of glass. Viijelyk appeared before the doorstep to a cottage. An older woman answered and led him through the dwelling until he had come to stand over an infant. Then, he lay her dear, well-sheathed sword beside the child and vanished.

"My sword has been given to a baby?" she asked in bewilderment.

"Not as yet—in *your* time," H.S. explained. "But one day, it will be. And she will grow to become the Glory-bringer, altering Realm Leader Latos' world forever. So, you see, it will not go to waste. Moreover, you have met the Glory-bringer. She is Ivi, friend of the prophet, Wynn."

"Oh..." she gasped in wonder. She had liked the lady and was glad the weapon would be cared for by her. "Thank you for showing me," she said, knowing full-well it was going beyond any kind of duty for him to have done so.

"You are most welcome," he answered with a wry grin.

"But what if I should need it again?"

"You will not, else it would not have moved on. It prefers to be useful, you see. And you have got your bond with us—both that of the Bashtiian strain and of the Anointed One's blood. Not to mention, you've your stunning voice. You are well equipped for everything you will face in future."

She nodded, her eyes going to the Entity beyond him. My, how beautiful he was—so much *more* than beautiful. Suddenly, her hand flew to her head. Somehow, her Bashtiian crown was upon it.

H.S. smiled and stood aside, waving her on. The Entity's eyes burned into hers. With a lovesick sob, she stole the crown from her head. Coming to stand beside those who cast their crowns at his feet, she heartily joined them.

PROPHET'S APPRENTICE
CHRONICLES OF THE CHOSEN

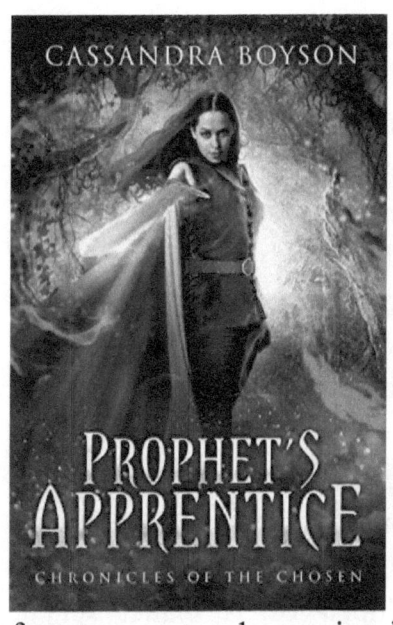

Fantastic creatures.
Supernatural adversaries.
A vast new realm of possibilities.

Hardened and friendless, Wynn is approached by Phillip, a tall, dark and clumsy stranger who claims she is destined to become apprentice to an ancient prophet who dwells in a forest filled with extraordinary creatures. If she accepts this proposition, she is to be trained to follow in the prophet's footsteps, not only moving in supernatural power but seeing into the time that has been and is to come.

Yet, not all is as it seems when she arrives at the cabin that is "ever so slightly alive," where the fireplace lights itself and a vanishing door leads to other worlds. But it is Maera of the Wood Beguiling and her Secret Circle of Southern Sorcerers that has Wynn anxious for the safety of those she is coming to love. As danger arises, she must discover a means to step into the fullness of her abilities or see her new life destroyed by a sinister, age-old enemy who's been preparing for decades.

Available in eBook and paperback.

SEEKER'S CALL

BOOK ONE OF THE SEEKER'S TRILOGY

Alone and searching for a place to call home, Iviana stumbles upon Tragor, the Great Dragon of the Ages, and Flynn, a strange young man determined to slay the dragon and steal its heart. Captivated by its beauty, Iviana intervenes on behalf of the beast.

After having earned his friendship, Tragor flies Iviana to his home-world, the Greater Archipelagos, a planet set in another universe. Populated by a people who are born with what they call the Great Gifts, the islanders prove to possess supernatural powers bestowed by their god, the Great One. It is there she must press beyond the rejection of the people to make discoveries not only about her own lineage but of her destiny: a call that could save the Greater Archipelagos from its demise.

Available in eBook and paperback.

Sequels *Seeker's Quest* and *Seeker's Revolution* also available

ABOUT THE AUTHOR

Based out of the Houston, Texas area, Cassandra Boyson is author of Amazon bestselling Christian Fiction series, *The Seeker's Trilogy*. She plans to release several more books in the Christian Fiction genre, revisiting the worlds previously introduced: Kaern and the Greater Archipelagos. Her books focus not only on inspiring the supernatural walk every Christian is destined to live out as Jesus did but on salvation and the matchless, intimate love of the Great One.

CassandraBoyson.com